To Emily
Nage

Nancy E. Dunne

Tempest:
Fall of the Nature Walker

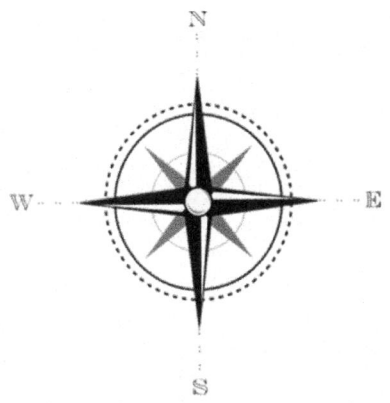

Nancy E. Dunne

Nancy E. Dunne

Copyright © 2018 Nancy E. Dunne
Cover design by Nancy E. Dunne and Brian Collins
All rights reserved.
ISBN-10: 198495380X
ISBN-13: 978-1984953803

DEDICATION

For *Teeand*, *Numtin*, and most importantly John, and the rest of *Fabled* that took me back and took me in when I definitely did not deserve it.

Nancy E. Dunne

ACKNOWLEDGEMENTS

Once again, thanks to Sean for your encouragement; to Brian and Mel for guidance, epic amounts of proofreading and outstanding treasure hunting skill; thanks to Mike as always for *Sathlir*; and to my Simon, ta very much for daring me to be brave.

Nancy E. Dunne

TABLE OF CONTENTS

Dedication	5
Acknowledgements	7
Table of Contents	9
Prologue	11
One	39
Two	67
Three	75
Four	83
Five	93
Six	105
Seven	119
Eight	129
Nine	133
Ten	143
Eleven	159
Twelve	165
Thirteen	171
Fourteen	175
Fifteen	193
Sixteen	201
Seventeen	209
Eighteen	217
One Month Later	229
Nineteen	231
Twenty	237
Twenty-One	243

Twenty-Two	247
Twenty-Three	259
Twenty-Four	273
Twenty-Five	285
Twenty-Six	295
Twenty-Seven	309
Twenty-Eight	329
Twenty-Nine	333
Thirty	351
ABOUT THE AUTHOR	355
Books in the Nature Walker series	355

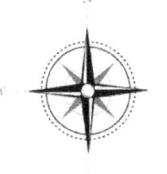

PROLOGUE

Qatu'anari – Many Seasons Ago

The island of Qatu'anari separated from the continent at the time of the emergence of the dragons from under the surface. The great felines such as lions and tigers were trapped on the island, and within them was created a sentient race that evolved over time to walk upright rather than on all fours, to create a language and culture, and to be able to understand and use the magic that took hold within them and changed them. They worshiped no deity, instead choosing to revere their ancestors and seeking to contact them through the veil between the worlds at certain times of the year.

On one of those festival nights, several Qatu females gathered at the fire pits in front of the city of Qatu'anari, the home of the Qatu race, as the moon hovered above, high in the sky. "Dhavra," said Kiara, one of the other dancers, "stop daydreaming and find your mark. We need to get started soon. The Rajah will be in attendance tonight!" The other dancers giggled and set about getting their fire pits ready and costumes in place. "Seriously, where is Savdhi?"

Dhavra winced. Her younger sister was not turning out to be the dancer that her parents had hoped she would be, and her lack of prowess was causing trouble for Dhavra. Savdhi was very intelligent and had far outpaced her sister in their academic pursuits, but she was as clumsy as she was clever. She had begged Nikka, the leader, to allow her younger sister to join, and it would be her fault if Savdhi did not do well. As if on cue, Savdhi came dashing up to the tent, her costume on inside out and backward.

"I'm here!" she said, toppling over her feet and missing the fire by a few inches. Dhavra snatched her sister up off the ground.

"Go fix your costume and hurry up!" she snarled at the younger Qatu. Savdhi sniffed and dashed into one of the huts nearby, emerging in a few minutes with her costume on properly. She took her place next to Dhavra, and the ceremony began.

The rhythmic sound of the drums was enough to lull onlookers into the same trance that the dancers entered, so it was no surprise that no one noticed the Rajah of Qatu'anari, Qa Kahzlir slip into the crowd. While the Qatu were, on the whole, an atheist civilization with no real affinity for the many deities of Orana, they were still deeply spiritual and knew with all certainty that their race had been created by the very magic that flowed just under Orana's surface. They were the children of that magic, the consequence of its eruption onto the surface that gave birth to the dragons to the east in the Volcanic Mountains. Qatu fire pits paid homage to that magic that had erupted from Orana herself in the form of magical sound, calling all of her favorite creatures to evolve and grow.

As a result, the Qatu and the dragons had a shaky alliance because neither would acknowledge the divinity of the other. Instead of seeking to implore or honor a deity with the fire dance ritual, the dancers sought instead to enter the trancelike state to communicate with those of their kind already passed beyond the bond of this world and into the heart of Orana. In this way, they could ensure a good harvest and prosperity.

The Rajah looked around at those of his subjects that had gathered for the ritual. His gaze moved from dancer to dancer, and he locked eyes for a moment with Dhavra. She recognized his teal eyes immediately and almost lost her place in the dance. His gaze shifted to her sister, and she breathed a sigh of relief.

Savdhi did not notice that the Rajah was watching her. All of her concentration was focused on getting the steps right, performing the chant correctly, and honestly not falling into the fire. She caught sight of her parents a few times, and saw her father smiling proudly at her and her sister. Beaming, she turned her attention back to the dance.

Finally, one of the priests clapped his massive hands together to signal that the ritual was at an end. "Brothers and Sisters, we have pleased our Rajah with our efforts. May we see a prosperous season ahead!" The crowd let out a mighty cheer. Dhavra looked around for her sister, and soon spotted her surrounded by what looked like members of the royal guards. She scampered over but was diverted by a *Sahi Kalah* high officer.

"Excuse me, sir," she said, "but my sister is over there with Hilan and…"

"And that is none of your concern," the officer replied. His eyes were kind, but concerned. "She is safe with my men, run along now."

Dhavra didn't know what to do. She returned slowly to her parents who were overjoyed at their performances during the ritual. "Where is Savdhi?" her mother asked, scanning the crowd.

"She is with the *Sahi Kalah*, mother," Dhavra said sheepishly.

"What did she do this time?" her mother snapped, concern and anger filling her features.

"Nothing, at least I don't think she did," Dhavra replied. "When I inquired after her, the high officer told me she was safe with them and to run along." She shrugged. "Maybe she knows one of them from school?"

"Maybe," her mother said, exchanging worried glances with their father. "But I fear that is not the case."

"I don't understand, where are you taking me?" Savdhi demanded, her voice high and pinched. She was trying not to let her fear overtake her. After all, these were the **personal** guards of the Rajah…her stomach jumped up into her throat as they headed into the palace.

"Your presence has been requested," one of the Sahi answered.

"My what?" She struggled slightly against the officers that held her arms. "By whom?"

"His Majesty," another said, smirking.

Savdhi's eyes widened. What was happening? She had little time to ponder as the *Sahi Kalah* that had answered her was now rapping on the large wooden door that lead to the Rajah's private chambers. "Enter," called a rumbling voice from behind the door that sent shivers up Savdhi's spine. The soldiers opened the door and the room that greeted her eyes was more lavish than she could have imagined.

A large poster bed sat in one corner of the room, covered in silk pillows and luxuriously fluffy duvets. Large velvet cushions were scattered about the room on the floor, and opposite the bed was an intimate dining table and chairs, all of which stood on solid brass carved Qatu feet. Savdhi's knees weakened at the extravagance and wealth before her and she hesitated, only to be shoved forward by the soldier to her left.

"Now, now," came a voice from the bed. "There is no need for roughness." A few sparse candles lighted the room, and Savdhi had to squint a bit to see who was talking from among the multitude of pillows. Her eyes widened as she recognized the Rajah. The soldiers released her, and she fell to her knees, face pressed into the lush carpet. For a brief moment she was thankful for the soft fabric beneath her forehead, and that she had not crashed headlong into the marble floors of the palace as she had on so many occasions with her fire dancer sisters. "Leave us," he said, and she heard him get up from the bed.

Not daring to move, she only looked up when she saw the soles of the Rajah's sandals come close to her nose. "Majesty?" she asked quietly, not daring to look up at him.

"Give me your hand, Little One, and let me help you to your feet," he said. Savdhi took a deep breath and raised her head until she could see a substantial hand extended in her direction. She took it, and rose to her feet but kept her eyes downcast. He did not release her hand. "You were lovely tonight, my girl," he said, his voice like a purr in her ear.

"You honor me, Majesty," she said, her own voice quavering a bit.

"Are you afraid, Savdhi?" he said. At the sound of her name, she raised her eyes to meet his briefly, and let them linger, studying the concern she saw there. "Are you afraid…of me?"

"Yes…I mean no…I mean…I only wish to please you, Majesty," she stammered, immediately wishing she hadn't as the look in his eyes changed dramatically. She had no idea what to say to him or if she was even supposed to be speaking at all…though it seemed rude to not answer when he asked her a question.

The Rajah sighed sadly as he released her hand. "I thought I'd seen something in your eyes, my girl, something… different," he said. "You may go." He turned away from her and strolled back over to the large floor cushions.

Images of her father hearing that she had not pleased the Rajah flashed before her eyes, leaving her desperate. "Majesty, no, please, what can I do to…what would you like me to be?"

He snorted. "I'd like someone with a keen mind, someone who can do more than just 'please the Rajah'," he said. Her mind raced. "If all I wanted was a female body, I would have visited one of the females that frequent the back of the palace, Savdhi." His tone was gruff, and it suddenly occurred to her to which women he was referring.

"Are you calling me a..." She clapped her hands over her mouth, unable to say the word. The females that gave themselves to males for payment were among the lowest in Qatu society, yet most of the nobles did nothing to curb their business practices. If they had, they would have to stay home with their own mates. "I am not a...one of those women," she said, eyes blazing a moment. "What an awful thing to say!", immediately regretting her outburst.

The Rajah spun around to face her. "Be careful, girl, about how you address me," he said. "Remember where you are." His teal eyes blazed, and when Savdhi met his gaze she immediately went to her knees, forehead again pressed into the carpet. Indignation quickly faded to amusement as he studied the young female. Not many in her position would be able to speak at all in the presence of the Rajah, let alone to contradict him to his face. She was clearly intelligent, if a little over-confident for her station.

"Apologies, Majesty!" she wailed her voice muffled by the ornate carpet. "I only meant to say that I am not one of ...those females."

"My mother was one of THOSE females," the Rajah said as he crossed back over to where she remained face down in the carpet. Savdhi was relieved that her face was turned away from the Rajah's so that he wouldn't see her shocked expression. To her surprise, he chuckled a bit. "But no, I can see that you are no *m'vehsha*, my girl. Seems there's a bit of fire in there though." He remained near her, his toes almost touching the back of her head. "Please, do recover yourself. There's no need for such displays now. We are alone, you and I, and to be honest I don't care for all the bowing and scraping."

Slowly Savdhi got to her feet, and then raised her eyes to meet his. He truly was handsome, she thought, and his eyes were such an interesting shade of blue, reminiscent of the Forbidden Sea off the Qatu'anari coast. "Forgive me, Majesty, but you're the Rajah, so the bowing and scraping comes with the job I think." He let out a hearty chuckle and she grinned at him. "We haven't been formally introduced," Savdhi offered, "My name is Savdhi."

"You have an enchanting smile, little one," he said, moving a bit closer to her. "You should smile more often. Your entire face lights up." Savdhi blushed to the roots of her fur. "How old are you, Savdhi, if you don't mind my asking?"

Savdhi nearly lost her balance at his compliment. "You can ask me anything, Majesty," she said in a rush. "I'm in my twentieth season."

He smiled at her. "I would have you do one thing for me, Savdhi," he said, taking her hand in his massive one. "Stop calling me Majesty. When we are alone, as we are now, you may call me Kahzlir, for that is my given name and think I should very much like to hear you say it."

"Yes, Kahzlir," she said, smiling up at him.

He closed his eyes and leaned his head back, still grinning. "Yes, that is much better," he said. "Again?"

"Only if you say **my** name again, Kahzlir."

"What shall we do next, Savdhi?" She grew wide-eyed at his question. "I mean, I know a thing or two that might be entertaining…"

"Like dice? A card game?"

"No." Kahzlir studied her. Time for a change of tactic with this one. "Tell me about yourself, Savdhi. I want to know all about you, and we have all night to talk. If you have questions I will promise to answer as truthfully as I can. How does that sound?" She nodded, smiling widely at him. Kahzlir found himself grinning in response.

Savdhi came to the Rajah's quarters almost every night for the next few months at his insistence, but he never made any sort of advance on her. Instead, they spent hours and hours at intellectual pursuits, and Kahzlir was impressed repeatedly by Savdhi's mind. She had clearly excelled in her studies more than she had at her fire dancing.

They talked about books, music, and art. They listened to poems and epic works by the kingdom's finest bards. He discussed politics with her, and often sought her opinion on matters awaiting his decision. After a few months, the Rajah sent word that she was to meet with Jaimla in the priest guild. When Savdhi arrived, Jaimla sat her down on one of the velvet sofas and took her hand.

"Savdhi, this is a very important and happy day for you. His Majesty wants you to become one of his wives," she said, her cool hazel eyes looking over Savdhi's common attire. "We need to do something about your clothes, and you'll have to learn how to behave as a member of the royal court, but..."

"Wait, what?" Savdhi's eyes were wide like saucers. "His what?"

Jaimla rolled her eyes. "One of his wives, you silly girl. What, did you think you were going to be best friends and have sleepovers forever?"

Savdhi blanched. "No, but...?" She was mortified, both at the suggestion and at her own clear lack of understanding of palace life.

"It is very important that His Majesty has a male heir, Savdhi; otherwise the royal house of Clawsharp will fall and the kingdom of Qatu'anari will be in jeopardy."

"A male heir...what are you saying?" Savdhi was shocked at what she was hearing. Was Kahzlir only courting her so that she could...meaning they would have to... Well, of course, he needed a mate and an heir, but her? She did not dare ask more questions when she saw Jamila's annoyed expression.

"He has commanded that you become one of his wives," said the older Qatu female. She touched Savdhi's arm, her expression softening at the abject fear that was clearly apparent in the younger female's expression. "This is a high honor, my girl. He wants you nearby and wants you to give him children! You could be the mother of the next Rajah! Are you all right, Savvy?" she said, using the nickname the Rajah had come up with for Savdhi.

"*Commanded!?*" Savdhi thought, infuriated. She swallowed hard before she spoke. "No, no I'm not. Would it be possible for me to see the Rajah now?" Savdhi said. She was seething and afraid in equal measure. She would not be a part of his stable of breeding females. She had more self-esteem than that. But Jamila had a point; Savdhi had honestly not given much thought to where their nightly discussions were leading, and even if she had, "*royal concubine*" would never have crossed her mind. But more than the anger and fear, Savdhi felt disappointed and sad.

For the first time, she had found someone whose company that she truly enjoyed – someone who understood her and shared her passions, who just *happened* to be the Rajah, she chided herself. And now she was just going to be cloistered away until she produced appropriate offspring for Kahzlir? This could not be happening. How could she have been so naive?

"Possibly," Jaimla said. "I will go and ask the *Sahi Kalah* if his Majesty is available. But Savvy, are you sure?" the older female asked. "Remember your place when you speak to his Majesty, Savvy. Be careful." All the palace staff had come to care a great deal for Savdhi and Jaimla was no exception. Her laugh and her bright demeanor had brought a joy to the palace that hadn't been present in years.

"I won't go and get myself exiled," Savdhi said. "Don't worry, Jaimla. I just need...I need to make sure that I have been clear with His Majesty, is all."

"Fair enough, Little One," said Jaimla. She stood and hurried off to speak to Kaynja, a *Sahi* who also happened to be very interested in Jaimla. In a few minutes the two of them returned, a smile spreading across Jaimla's face. "Come, Savvy, Kaynja will take you to see His Majesty." Savdhi followed Kaynja back to the Rajah's chambers.

"Stay here, Savvy. His Highness likes surprises," Kaynja said, winking at her. Savdhi was unsure of his meaning, but took a seat on one of the cushions on the floor. She had never known Kahzlir to dislike a surprise, but she was fairly certain that once he heard her out he would not be so happy that she was there.

"So, Kaynja, where is this surprise..." Kahzlir entered the room, slowing to a stop when he noticed Savdhi. "Savvy, what are you doing here?" he asked.

"Majesty," she said, bending forward until her forehead was touching the carpet. "I...there was a matter that I needed to discuss with you, if you would be so gracious?"

Kahzlir chuckled. "Majesty? Why the formality, Savvy?" he said, sinking into one of the cushions next to her. "Recover yourself, female, we are past that are we not?" Savdhi sat up but remained sullen. Chuckling, he took one of her hands in his and stroked the back of it. She fought the urge to relax into his touch. "You have only to ask, Savvy, and if it is within my power you know I will make it so." Savdhi closed her eyes, giving in and smiling, as Kahzlir carefully drew one of his clawed fingers down the side of her face and neck. It was a more intimate gesture than he had ever extended to her and she couldn't help but revel in the new sensations that she felt.

"I went to see Jaimla as you asked," she said, finally opening her eyes again. Her breath caught in her throat as their eyes met. "Did you really want to make me your...one of your wives?"

His eyes softened. "Savvy, it's not what you think," he said softly. "I just want...I feel...I need to make sure that you're taken care of, is all." He leaned very close to her, and she could smell the perfumed oils his servants had used on his fur after his bath. The heady scent made her lightheaded for a moment. "I need to know you're safe." He nuzzled against her neck and she let her head fall back, moving closer to him. "You are well educated and wise beyond your years, Savvy, but you're not..." She nipped at his fur just above his collarbone, interrupting his train of thought. He moaned happily and raised a hand to cradle the back of her head. "You're just not old enough or experienced enough to be First Wife."

Savvy pulled her head back suddenly, "So you want to put me in the harem with the rest of your cast offs?" she said, surprising even herself with her abruptly acerbic tone. "You don't want to lose me, but you don't want me as your true mate either. I am no better than the women at the back of the palace after all."

"You will not speak to me this way," Kahzlir growled. He took her face in one of his mighty hands and drew it close to his own, baring his fangs at her. She merely remained still, and he was aware that he could smell no fear on her. "You are truly not afraid of me any more, are you?" he said.

"Is that a requirement of First Wives?" she said sarcastically. He drew her face even closer to his as she winced, his claws digging into her face. "Either kill me or let me go, Kahzlir...Rajah," she said, "but you're hurting my face with this position." Kahzlir studied her, his eyes blazing, and then roughly pulled her to him in a kiss.

Savdhi didn't know what to do. Kahzlir had never passed the invisible boundary between them that made such intimate contact out of the question. He had touched her face before, held her hands, even embraced her on occasion, but the propriety had remained, always...until now. He pulled his face back from hers and looked at her, his gaze questioning. Savdhi made up her mind right then and there and pulled him back to her in another rough kiss. She would prove that she could be a good First Wife. Kahzlir growled - a low rumbling sound - and wrapped his arms around her, pulling her into him so tightly they seemed to merge into one being. His hands seemed to be everywhere at once, but Savdhi didn't know what to do with hers, so she clung to him tightly. After a few moments, he pushed back from her, studying her with a puzzled look on his face. "Did I do something wrong, Raj... Kahzlir?" she said. He smiled at her.

"I do want to ask you a question, and I want you to answer me honestly. Fair?" She nodded in response. "Have you ever...done this before? With a male?" Kahzlir rolled his eyes. "I mean of course with a male...unless you haven't...I mean, if you have with a female, that's...I mean..." Savdhi stopped his verbal torrent with a finger against his lips, shaking her head as she smiled at him.

"I know what you are asking, Kahzlir." She cast her eyes downward, blushing under her honey colored fur. "The answer is no, not with a male...or a female," she added, grinning slightly. "Not with anyone."

Kahzlir bit his bottom lip. "Ah," he said. He considered her a moment, tracing the outline of the spots on her fur with a delicate touch. She purred loudly in response. "Again, I must ask you to tell me the truth, Savvy. Do you... want to continue... this, with me, now?"

Savvy looked up at her Rajah, eyes shining. "More than anything," she whispered, hoping that he would not detect the fear that had settled in her stomach. Kahzlir smiled and stood before her, extending his hand to her.

"Come then. It should not be on the floor," he said, helping her to her feet when she took his hand. "Never on the floor for one such as you, Savvy." He led her to his massive bed, pulled back the velvet duvet, and stood back. She carefully climbed up and into the softest bed she had ever experienced. "What is it?" he said, watching her. "Your face just lit up like sparks from the fire pits."

Savvy blushed again. "It's just the most amazing bed," she said in a small voice, ashamed of herself. "So soft! It's like sleeping on a cloud, I imagine?"

"Aye Little One," Kahzlir said, sliding in on the other side of the bed and again wrapping his body around hers. "A cloud in the sky." He kissed her forehead, then the tip of her nose, then gently kissed her lips. Pulling her closer to him made her gasp. "The night sky, full of stars."

The next morning when Savdhi woke, she was alone in the enormous bed. She rolled over to see one of Kahzlir's servants standing across the room, eyes averted. The female looked up as Savdhi stretched and pushed back the duvet to sit up.

"Mistress," the female said, "His Majesty has left you some new clothes here, and asks that you attend him this evening for supper in the palace." Savdhi pulled a robe off one of the posters of the bed, slipped it on and padded over to where the maid was holding a bundle of clothing.

"Thank you! You can leave it here on the bed," she said to the maid. "Is there anything to eat?"

The female cleared her throat. "Mistress, you will be leaving soon, yes? May I pack you some food to take with you, if you are hungry?"

Savdhi turned around and looked the female in the eye. "Leaving soon? What do you mean?" she asked. "This morning? Now?"

Again, the female Qatu cleared her throat as though embarrassed by Savdhi's questions. "Aye, Mistress. It is, ahem, customary, is it not, for His Majesty's companions to leave in the morning?"

Companion. Something about the word stung as it floated in the room, like the horrible sand creatures on the beach that would latch on and keep biting and stinging when disturbed. Was that all she was to him? Savdhi bit back the tears pricking the corners of her eyes. Had the previous night meant nothing? Had what she gave to Kahzlir the night before meant nothing? Perhaps to the Rajah it hadn't, but that was not who she was. Savdhi reproached herself inwardly for letting him fool her so easily.

"Yes, apparently it is. If you will, carry a message to His Majesty for me? It will not be possible for me to attend him at his supper tonight, I have another engagement." She was amazed that all the words made it out of her mouth without a sob escaping alongside them.

The maid gasped, and then nodded as she cast a sideways glance at the bundle of clothes. Savdhi followed her gaze and bit her lip. "You may return those to His Majesty with my unfortunate message," she said, taking a last look at the jewels that encrusted the hem of the clothing. The maid nodded again as she picked up the bundle with quivering hands and left.

Once the door shut behind the maid, Savdhi sank to her knees onto one of the large floor cushions. "*Companion* indeed," she hissed, incredibly finding herself more angry than hurt. "I wonder what the penalty is for a WIFE that disobeys the Rajah?" she wondered aloud. Moving quickly, she gathered her things up and slipped out the door. The penalty was most likely quite stiff, and she decided that she'd rather not stick around to experience it firsthand.

The maid approached the throne room and whispered to the *Sahi Kalah* at the door that she had a message for the Rajah. Once the doors were closed behind her, she flung the bundle of clothes on the floor and went to her knees, her forehead touching the red carpet that ran from the door to the desk in front of the throne.

"Recover yourself," Kahzlir called out. "Has Savvy not gotten out of bed yet?" He continued to pour over the paperwork on his desk as this was the day that the petitioners came.

"Aye, Your Majesty," the maid said, her voice trembling a bit.

Kahzlir looked up, puzzled. "If she is awake, then why are you here and why are the clothes I sent for her here on the floor?" he asked, a low growl of annoyance behind his words.

"Your Majesty, she sent the clothing back to you, and asked that I tell you that she would not be available to attend you tonight at your supper." The maid pressed her face into the carpet, fearing the explosion that was bound to come. Kahzlir was a fair ruler, but he was not known for his patience when it came to females.

"She WHAT?" he thundered, slamming his fist down onto his desk. After a few deep breaths, he remembered the maid now prone and trembling on the floor in front of him. "Stand up," he ordered, and she jumped to her feet like a marionette on a string. "You are the same size as Savdhi, are you not?" The maid nodded, her head bobbing up and down as her fearful eyes stayed trained on the floor. "Keep the clothes and leave me," he said, trying to keep a rein on the anger rising in him. The maid snatched the bundle off the floor and fled.

"She's not available? NOT AVAILABLE? It was not a request!" he shouted at no one. "I am the Rajah!" He stomped up onto the dais where the throne stood and plopped down on the seat in a most undignified huff. After a few minutes of silence, images of Savdhi's smiling face swam about in front of his eyes. He remembered their long nights reading to each other, and the spirited debates in his chambers. He had destroyed all of that in one slip of judgement. "What have I done?" he said, his head resting in his mighty hands. "She was too young. She is too young." The reality of the situation landed heavy on him, and he sagged in his seat as though under a physical burden. He had fallen in love with her, and he had thought she had loved him, too. Had last night meant nothing? How could he have been so naive? No. No, this was unacceptable.. He would have her back...but how?

Many months passed and Savdhi did not return to see Kahzlir, nor was she seen anywhere in the palace. He sent quad after quad to find her in the beginning, but as they continually returned to him without her, he began to lose hope. The Rajah grew despondent and angry, quick to temper with his citizens and with his wives. His daughter, the Princess Royal, was sent with her mother on diplomatic missions so that he would not have to see either one of them.

He had refrained from bringing in her family members for questioning, fearing that she would hear of it and never return. But as the time since he had last seen her grew longer, he began to lose patience as well as hope. How dare she treat him, the Rajah, this way, when he had offered her a lavish life where she would want for nothing? But deep in his bones he feared he knew why, and he knew whose fault her disappearance was.

Savdhi, hiding in plain sight in the tenement buildings behind the castle, took up potion making as a trade, and spent a lot of her time away from Qatu'anari on the hunt for new ingredients. She met many interesting new friends on her travels, and eventually took on a second residence with the priest's guild in the human settlement just north of the forest.

Kahzlir spent his evenings watching the fire dancers, hoping to see her there or to at least gain news of her from her sister, Dhavra. After searching for the better part of a year, he managed to ascertain that she had taken on training to be a priest, and that she was due to return to Qatu'anari within the month. He left word with Dhavra that when her sister returned, she was ordered to report to his chambers. Dhavra passed that message on to her sister upon Savdhi's return as she set herself up in one of the small grass huts on the beach near the embassy buildings.

"I cannot attend His Majesty yet," Savdhi said, her tone exasperated and heavy with fatigue. As she removed her traveling cloak, she moved her hand protectively over her distended midsection. "You must tell him that you haven't seen me, Davi, please?"

"What difference does it make when you see him?" Dhavra said. "He has been at ritual every night this season, Savvy, standing on the edge and watching us. He's watching for you. What did you do to him?"

"What did I do to him?" Savdhi sneered. "Quite the other way around, Davi, thank you very much."

"But I don't..." Dhavra's eyes flew to her sister's abdomen. "You mean...did you...that cub is..." Her eyes were as wide as saucers. "Are you sure it is his?"

"Aye," Savdhi said, rubbing her pregnant belly affectionately. "This cub is the Rajah's child, and I fear what he will do to me and to the child when he finds out. We can only pray that this little one is a girl so that he will leave me and my cub alone."

"Is that why you left him, Savvy?" Dhavra looked at her sister with something akin to jealousy. "You ran away because you knew you were with the Rajah's child."

"No," Savdhi said, her eyes filling with anger. "It was because...I was an absolute fool who loved him, and he did not see me as any different than all of his other wives... And then, when I found out I was carrying his child..." Her voice trailed off as she bit back the torrent of tears that threatened. "I will not be added to a stable like a mare kept only to breed warhorses for His Majesty, thank you very much, and my child will never..." A sharp knock at the door interrupted them.

"Savdhi!" rang a deep male voice. She recognized it as one of the Sahi that guarded the throne room and the Rajah's private quarters. "Dhavra! Open the door!"

Dhavra's eyes widened in fear. "What do we do?" she whispered. "They know you're here!"

"No, they know YOU are here because I imagine they followed you from the palace, Davi. Hopefully they haven't seen me yet," Savdhi said, scanning the room for a hiding place. She dashed into the cupboard in the kitchen and pulled the door behind her, but it would not shut all the way. She was too greatly pregnant to fit. Cursing under her breath, she ran to the back bedroom. "Just tell them you're alone here," she called back softly to her sister. "They won't press the matter."

Dhavra opened the door to find two large Qatu males standing there, expectant looks on their faces. "Where is your sister, Dhavra?" one of them asked.

"I'm alone here," Dhavra stammered, knowing that they would clearly see that she was lying. She stood staring at them, rooted to the spot.

The guard that spoke turned to the other one. "Search the place," he said. Dhavra did not respond, but continued to stare as one of the guards pushed past her and began searching the house.

Soon, the other guard cried out from the back of the house. There was the sound of a scuffle, then some curses in Qatunari, and finally the guard returned, holding Savdhi by the elbow. As he led her across the kitchen, she doubled over in pain. Dhavra hurried to her sister's side.

"What is it, Savvy? What did he do to you?" she cried, wrapping an arm around Savdhi's waist and shaking off the guard's hand. He took a step away from them.

"It's the cub," Savdhi grunted. "My daughter seems to want to be born NOW." She sank to her knees and Dhavra helped her lie down on the floor.

"You!" she yelled at the *Sahi Kalah* standing by the doorway. "Go fetch the midwife down the row! NOW!" The male stood his ground, ignoring her. "Whose cub do you think this is? How would the Rajah like hearing how his offspring was born alone in the dirt?"

The *Sahi* scoffed, "You expect us to believe that this cub is…"

"Yes!" Dhavra cut him off with a shout. "Why do you think he's been searching so hard for her?" He considered her words and with a nod from the other *Sahi* he left through the front door. He returned in a few moments with a female Qatu whose fur was midnight black with gray spots on her legs and tail. Gray fur highlighted her eyes, nose, and made her look wise beyond her years. She pushed back the hood on her cloak before unbuttoning it, and then surveyed the room as she hung it on a hook by the door.

The other *Sahi Kalah* watched the elder Qatu enter and, despite his bearing as a member of the royal household, bowed his head reverently to her. She looked at him for a moment and then dismissed them both with a nod. "Dhavra, get me some water and blankets," the midwife said as she crossed the room. "Savdhi, we need to move you to a bed, my darling girl. This will not happen on the floor, never on the floor." Savdhi frowned at the familiar phrase, but her frown exploded into a screech as another wave of contractions slammed into her. "You," the midwife said, pointing at the guard that had brought Savdhi from her hiding place, "can you please carry her into the next room and be sure she's comfortable on the bed? And you," she indicated the other male by the door that had gone to fetch her, "need to go back to the palace with your friend and tell His Majesty that Savdhi will not be joining him there tonight."

Savdhi struggled in the arms of the guard who had scooped her off the floor and was walking slowly with her toward the bedchamber. "Do not tell Kahzlir…" She cursed loudly at her mistake and then sank into the bed just as another contraction hit her, causing her to try to double over and wail.

"Off you go boys," the midwife said. "The Rajah will understand. Shoo! Now, Dhavra, let's bring this new cub into the world, shall we?" Dhavra nodded and moved to the other side of the bed. She took her sister's hand, and squeezed it.

The cub was born, but it was not a daughter as Savdhi had hoped. Those that lived near the palace knew her to be pregnant, the palace guard knew that Savdhi had given birth and that the Rajah now had a son and an heir, even though the cub's mother was not one of his wives.

Savdhi looked down at the face of her son as he wiggled in her arms early one morning. "It's been two weeks now, what shall we name you, then, my son?" she said, tracing a claw gently down the side of his tiny face. He fussed, sticking out his tiny pink tongue to be fed. She smiled at him. "We could name you after your father, but that would be too obvious. Perhaps a combination of his name and mine? Would you like that Little One?" He purred his tiny kitten purr and nuzzled against her. "Anything, just feed me, huh?" she said, laughing. "Right. Um…Sathlir! Sathlir it is. Sathlir…Clawsharp." She turned him around in preparation for feeding him, but looked up as the door to her bedchamber opened. The two *Sahi Kalah* who had been guarding her since her son was born stood there, staring at her and little Sathlir.

"How dare you barge in here?" she said, trying to be brave as she covered her son's head with the duvet. He immediately started fussing and wiggling.

"We need to take the Prince," they said.

"I don't know what you're talking about. Get out of my house, you have no right to be here," Savdhi demanded.

"We've come for the Prince," the guard repeated. "His Majesty wishes that his son be raised in the Palace."

"We can't possibly move to the Palace," Savdhi said, her voice showing a bit of her fear. "This is not the Rajah's son anyway. Like I said, I have no idea..."

"We know who the child is, Savvy," one of the guards said. She recognized him as Kaynja, Jaimla's friend. He looked at her sternly as she climbed out of the bed and put Sathlir in his crib. "This doesn't have to be difficult. Jaimla will take good care of the Prince."

"Jaimla?" Savdhi felt faint. Gripping the side of the crib for support, she glared at Kaynja. "No one will take care of my son but ME," she hissed, her eyes narrowing.

"I am sorry, Savvy, but our directions were only to bring the Prince, not you." Kaynja stared down at her..

"NO!" she screamed, grabbing a now mewling Sathlir from his crib and holding him to her. "NO!" She backed into the corner of the room, still screaming and clutching her son. "I will come, I will stay there, I will do whatever His Majesty asks, I swear, please..." She sank to her knees, holding Sathlir to her chest. He screamed and flailed, tiny furry arms escaping from his swaddling, knowing something was wrong but not what. Kaynja took a step closer and Savdhi hissed and spat at him.

Kaynja looked at his fellow *Sahi Kalah*. "We can't take the chance that she might hurt the cub," he said in a low voice. "Let's take both of them."

"But the Rajah said..."

"We will deal with that. Savvy understands, she will do whatever needs to be done to protect the cub," Kaynja said. He turned back around and looked at Savdhi, still crouched down in the corner clutching her son. "Savvy," he said, moving slowly toward her and crouching down. "Savvy, no one is going to take the cub from you. We simply want to make sure you're both taken care of and safe. How about you and the Prince…I mean you **and** your son come to the palace with us?" She looked up at him, her eyes wide and red rimmed from tears.

"He is MY son," she whispered."

"Of course he is," Kaynja said, standing and helping her up from the floor. "We will step out of the room and let you pack your things and then we will escort you to the palace. Yes?" She nodded slowly, putting the cub back in his crib. He backed out of the room, pulling the other guard along behind him, and shut the door.

"The Rajah will not like this," the other guard said under his breath.

"When the cub is weaned, he will go into the nursery with the Rajah's other children. Until then, what can it hurt to let her care for him? We will deal with her when the time comes."

Once settled at the palace, Savvy found life to be as close to normal as it could be in such close proximity to the Rajah. He had not greeted them on arrival and while she had not had audience with him, she knew that he had taken to visiting Sathlir during the play times he took with the other young in the Royal Nursery. As Sathlir grew and was eventually weaned, Savvy feared Kahzlir would have her removed from the palace. But that day never came and her fear slowly turned into curiosity. Savvy and Sathlir lived in a room on the top level of the palace with the oldest daughter of the Rajah, the Princess Royal, Maesha. Her bodyguards, all female Sahi, took turns watching over the young cub while his mother slept. By the time Sathlir was two, and old enough to take his first upright steps, he would toddle from bodyguard to bodyguard, making them giggle as he held his tiny arms out to them. He always knew who his mother was, though, and would run to her on his stubby little legs, his tail waving wildly behind him.

Several years passed and Sathlir grew into a fine young cub. He played in the nursery more and more with the other children of the palace servants and nobles of Qatu'anari. When he was five years old, the Rajah's oldest daughter approached her father during one of his visits to the nursery and said that she felt that it was time for Sathlir's mother to either take up a position within the royal household or return to her duties as a potion maker.

"I will not have my son raised elsewhere," said Kahzlir sternly to his daughter on one of his visits to the nursery. Sathlir ran to his father, holding his arms up to be picked up. He ruffled the cub's fur on the top of his head but didn't pick him up. "Why do you think it so important that your brother be without his mother?"

"He is my HALF brother," Maesha snapped. "My mother is gone now and I have no siblings. To me, you are my only family, and I liked it when it was just you and me, Papa," she said, her voice growing soft and quiet, "like when Mama went on her missions alone, and I could stay here, with you."

"I will think on it," Kahzlir said, pulling her into a hug. "Now, off to your studies, my daughter." Maesha purred loudly and grinned at her father before dashing off to her quarters to finish her homework. The Rajah looked back at Sathlir, who was the spitting image of his mother. "What will I do with your mother, my son?" he whispered. As if on cue, Savdhi came into the nursery calling for Sathlir.

"Oh, your Majesty," she said, kneeling immediately and blushing to the tips of her fur. She and Kahzlir had only seen each other in passing over the past five years that she and Sathlir had been living in the palace and she still found herself on guard when around him, for fear that he would take Sathlir from her. "My apologies, your Majesty, I did not know that you were here to visit your young ones. Shall I come back later?" Sathlir wrapped himself around his mother's arm. "Or I shall go on and take Sathlir with me now, out of your way?"

"Recover yourself, please. Savdhi, I should like it if you would attend me for a meal this evening and bring my…bring the cub with you," he said. He stared at her, momentarily mesmerized by her eyes and the curve of her neck. Her fur had been like satin under his touch…he wondered if it was still as soft. "Or perhaps it will be too late for our son to be out. He could stay in the nursery tonight, perhaps?"

"Of course, Majesty, whatever you desire," she said, smiling at him.

"You have forgotten, Savvy." He moved closer and extended a hand to help her up. "You had stopped bowing and scraping, and I believe you called me…" Sathlir stepped in between his parents and grabbed his father's hand, making growling noises like he was protecting his mother.

"Kahzlir," she said, her eyes sparkling. "You let me call you Kahzlir." As she rose from the floor, she moved a step closer to him. She always smelled like sunflowers, and he breathed in deeply as she stood just in front of him. "I think that Sath can stay in the nursery tonight, Kahzlir."

"Much better," he said, gently touching the side of her face. She purred under his touch, then remembered herself and stepped away. He looked down at her, confused.

"Tonight. Your chambers?" she asked, smiling up at him. He nodded, and she swung Sathlir up into her arms before dashing out of the nursery toward her quarters.

"Yes, I think that tonight things will change for our Savvy," he murmured, watching her go. "I think it's time Qatu'anari had a new First Wife, a new Queen."

Qatu'anari, many seasons later...

The young Qatu females huddled in groups in the nursery, giggling and whispering. They were in their tenth year now, and were preparing to leave to begin training in their various disciplines. Here and there, the early signs of those talents were already coalescing in the furry young faces: a willowy young one with downy grayish fur covered in black spots sat with two others, playing a lute softly and only stopping when their eyes would start to droop sleepily.

Clearly destined for the bard's life, Annilanshi had been in the royal nursery as a child because her grandfather was a *Sahi Kalah*, killed protecting the Rajah from a spy during the Forest Wars and her parents were a high-ranking *Sahi Kalah* and one of the *Sahi Pahl* or First Wife's guard. Sejah, her mother, had just left Annilanshi in the nursery one morning and left Qatu'anari. Kissing her daughter on the head and walking out of the nursery, across the city to the bridge, and off into the thicket that surrounded the city walls. She was never heard from again.

Annilanshi, or Anni as she was known, was a precocious young cub, and she and her best friend Kazhmere dreamed of adventuring outside of the city's thick stone walls. When the moon loomed large in the sky, they would sneak out onto the rooftop of the building where the nursery was and study their maps from school, planning their invasion of the continent that lay to the south of Qatu'anari.

"That's Calder's Port," Kazhmere said, pointing at a large section on the lower right corner of the map one sweltering evening as the two young cubs studied by the light of the full moon. They were crashed out on reed mats, lying shoulder to shoulder and propped up on their elbows. "We can't go there first, that's where the humans are and everyone knows they outnumber us greatly.

We need to go…there." She pointed to the north, which was easily the biggest region on Orana. "It's too cold for most of the puny races of Orana over there, that's Volcanic Mountains. Nothing but ice and snow and good hunting and exploring."

Anni wrinkled her nose. "Ice and snow? There are dragonkind there too, you know. No thanks. What about…" She chewed on one claw as she tried to remember the names of the continents they'd been taught by the royal tutors. "The Grasslands! Which one is that?"

"Here, but go too far south, and you're up against the humans. I don't think we can see on this map," Kazhmere said. "But that's partially a jungle, like Qatu'anari, hot and green and crawling with lizard men and other beasts. Sounds a bit too much like home," she said, giggling.

"Like you'd ever get to go there anyway," Anni said. "The Princess Royal can't…"

"Shut it Anni!" Kazhmere roared at her friend.

"What? There's no one up here to hear us, Kazhi," Anni snapped. "Besides, I don't know what the big deal is, everyone knows that females can't hold the throne of Qatu'anari so it's not like you're in danger or anything."

Kazhmere rolled over and glared down at her friend. "Anni, you are the ONLY one that knows who I really am. I'm not even supposed to know, not after my brother took off like he did. If Maesha knew…" Maesha was the current Princess Royal, daughter of M'Neesha Clawsharp, Rajah Kahzlir's most senior wife after Savdhi, Kazhmere's own mother and First Wife. Maesha kept the ceremonial title even after M'Neesha went mad and ended her own life after Kahzlir brought Savdhi into the Royal Palace, and displaced her in his heart and bed.

"She won't know, Kazhi, I swear," Anni said, taking Kazhmere's hand in her own. "I know what that...*m'aakindi* is like and what she's capable of, and I know how much she hates your brother because Savdhi became First Wife instead of M'Neesha." Anni's use of the very unflattering word in Qatunari made Kazhmere grin. Anni rolled her eyes. "Can you imagine if that horrible female had become First Wife? She was twice as mean as Maesha and many times over as spoiled. I never revel in the deaths of others but I do not miss her. I feel sorry for Maesha not having a mother but First Wife is kind and would probably take care of her if Maesha would let her."

Kazhmere scowled. "Sure she would. Sath was her treasured cub. Maesha needs a mother. Well, what about Kazhmere? I am her daughter! I am HIS daughter, though he has never acknowledged it. I was born AFTER Momma became First Wife and..." She paused and wiped tears from her teal eyes.

"I know. They said that the cub had died because you were born female." Anni smiled sadly at her best friend. "But that is in the past, and we are the only ones that will make our future, Kazhi. So, it's to be ice and snow then, is it?" She smiled and squeezed Kazhmere's hand. The true Princess Royal threw her arms around her friend in a most unceremonious fashion and squeezed her, purring madly.

"Ice and snow," she whispered. "To the Volcanic Mountains, never looking back to Qatu'anari."

Nancy E. Dunne

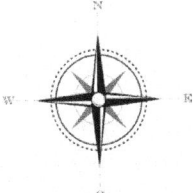

ONE

It had been three years since Sath and Anni had left the Outpost for the last time for Qatu'anari. At first, they would visit and hunt with some of the members, but in recent days none of the Fabled Ones had heard from him. Occasionally, Teeand would send a message to Qatu'anari in the hopes that it would make it through to his old friend, but the responses stopped coming back so he eventually gave up.

A new cadre was growing, but slowly, among the remaining members of the former "Fabled Five" and Taeben. He had been accepted into the Fabled Ones at the request and recommendation of Gin, who was serving as their leader in Sath's absence, but he was still given a wide berth by Teeand, Hackort, a gnome with extensive warrior training, and Elysiam, Gin's sister druid and fellow wood elf. She took requests from those in need and the group would take on the tasks, but for the most part, it was a tenuous partnership at best among the five of them. Occasionally Elysiam would agree to hunt with a group that included the wizard, but for the most part, she kept to herself when Taeben was there. Where Elysiam went, so went Hackort, so in the end most missions included Teeand, Gin, and Taeben only. Now and then, a new guild member would join the hunt with them, but it was not the same.

While on a particularly mundane mission, the three of them found themselves back sleeping rough in the foothills of the Volcanic Mountains. Taeben, to his credit, kept his displeasure at such accommodation to himself, but it was clear that he would have preferred an inn. When it was his watch, however, he was free to grumble under his breath as the others slept.

A loud pop from the fire startled Gin awake. She rubbed her eyes, wondering for a moment where she was. Staring up at the night sky, it all came back to her…she was in her bedroll on the all too hard ground in the foothills of the Volcanic Mountains. She rolled her head over and nearly jumped when she saw a red shock of hair and blue robes sitting wrapped up in the bedroll, huddled in a cross-legged position near the fire.

She had been dreaming of similar missions in the past, and expecting Sath's furry smile to be looking down at her or at the very least his magical tiger to be inches away, purring in its sleep. However, Sath was gone now…well, not *gone* she admitted, still a part of the Fabled Ones, but he never hunted with them anymore.

"Go back to sleep, Little One, and stop staring at the back of my head," Ben murmured, without turning to face her, as he pulled the blankets from his bedroll that he draped around his shoulders, further up around his neck. Gin smiled, amazed as always at the connection the two of them had, even here and now. She rolled over on her side and pulled the fur-lined blankets up around her chin. Once the sun set out here, the temperature plummeted.

Her mind, determined to deprive her of sleep, wandered for a moment to times when Sath had crawled into her bedroll next to her to warm her because she had again forgotten to pack appropriate gear for the often frozen north. Gin shook her head to clear it and closed her eyes. Sath was warming someone else now, she reminded herself, her heart sinking at the memory of him wound around Anni in the grand hall.

Truthfully, she was glad that the Qatu couple had stopped hunting with the Fabled Ones, not because Gin no longer wished them to be present, but because Sath had only seemed interested in Anni, who similarly needed reminding to target her musical magic at anyone **but** Sath. They acted like a couple of lovesick teenagers most of the time, and it had cost the group injury and near death on more than one occasion. At the least, Gin and Elysiam had become more than proficient in healing magic as well as casting spells that would transport the group to safety.

Healing magic. Gin thought about that for a moment as she stared up at the stars that formed intricate patterns as they surrounded the moon. Admittedly, she had not much experience with bardic magic, but she knew enough to know that, when reminded, Anni could play a song that would wrap around all of them, healing them and strengthening them in ways that Gin's own druidic magic simply could not. Why she had not simply done that, rather than only healing Sath, was beyond her.

However, Gin had to admit that Sath could be charming enough to throw anyone off their game. It certainly had happened to her. Gin pinched her nose just in between her eyes for a moment, as though that simple act could force the Qatu from her mind…and heart. It did not.

"Okay, what's troubling you?" Ben asked as he turned around to face her, leaning back until he was propped up on one elbow. His slender fingers spread out across the blanket as Gin watched, distracted. She closed her eyes a moment and felt her clarity return. "It is quiet tonight, Ginny, and the stars are lovely, don't you think?"

Gin nodded, not even cross with him for calling her Ginny, though she couldn't remember for the moment why…and then it came to her. "Stop it," she hissed. "No magic, Ben, you promised." Druids and wizards both possessed magic that would allow them to lull another into a state of utter calm. It was often used by both types of spell casters to keep a dangerous enemy from attacking, thus allowing the druid or wizard to escape. He shrugged and looked back at the fire.

Gin held her head in her hands a moment, feeling her energy draining, the sensation leaving her nauseated. She looked up at Taeben, who seemed suddenly well rested and alert for someone that had been on watch for several hours. "Ben, really?" This sort of magic was an ability solely given to the wizards, and allowed them to surreptitiously take the life force that granted magical ability from those nearby should the wizard find him or herself in trouble and drained of energy. She closed her eyes and focused on resisting him, but only felt the pull more strongly than before. When she opened her eyes, she gasped to find that he had moved only inches from her face, one willowy finger over his lips.

"Something is out there, Ginny," he said, his voice barely audible. "Something over there, by that group of trees…do you sense it? Familiar, yet most certainly not friendly." Gin's eyes widened. "I said do you sense it?" he demanded, shaking her slightly by her shoulders. "Has your tracking ability left you suddenly or are you just completely incapable of keeping us safe?"

"Neither," Gin hissed, annoyed. "Maybe if you stopped stealing my damned energy." She tried to get to her feet to have a better look but Ben yanked her back down to her bedroll. "Hey!"

"Shush, you'll wake Teeand," Ben whispered to her. She was not sure if it was malice or fear that she sensed in him, but either way she didn't like it. He pulled her closer to him and she felt her fear subside a bit as his willowy yet strong arm wrapped around her. His heartbeat was strong and steady, and Gin found her own heart slowing to match his. "It's right over there," he continued, one slender hand pointing in the direction he had turned them to face. Gin scanned the trees but still came away empty…until she noticed a rustling in the tree branches just to the right of where Ben was pointing.

"That?" she whispered, pointing at the trees. Ben was silent a moment and then she felt his body relax a bit into a smile.

"Aye, my Little One," he said. Gin felt his pride pour over her like the warmth from the fire. "Very well done! You did as I have been teaching you just now, didn't you? Clearing your mind? Projecting your senses forward?"

"Um, no, I just sat still and then there it was," she replied, immediately wishing she hadn't been so cheeky when she felt Ben's arm constrict around her, making it harder for her to take a breath. "Ben…too tight…"

"Cast invisibility and go determine what it is," Ben snarled in her ear.

"Go over there...alone?" He had loosened his grip somewhat, but she was still gasping for air.

"Aye, and before I lose my patience with you would be even better, Ginny."

"But it might be..."

"GO." He shoved her forward and Gin barely managed to recite the spell that would render her invisible before she was running toward the rustling in the trees. She reached the edge of the woods in no time at all. Her forehead wrinkled in annoyance as she realized that Ben must have cast magic on her as well to make her run faster. What if the whatever-it-is in the woods could see through her magic? He just didn't think sometimes. Her inherent ability to track was already telling her that it was a large something and that it was potentially very dangerous.

The trees came up on her quickly and she skidded to a stop, trying to do what he had taught her. Gin closed her eyes and cleared her mind, thinking only of a white expanse, just as Ben had encouraged her. She slowed her breathing, and then her heart followed suit until it was uncharacteristically quiet within her. That would allow her to focus on the quiet outside of her.

"Well done," Taeben's voice said from somewhere... behind her? Gin whirled around, almost crashing into a nearby sapling. She lost her focus and cancelled the effect of the magic that kept her out of sight. She steadied herself and then looked around for him.

"Where are you? How are you close enough for me to hear you but I can't see you?"

"You can't see me, Little One, because I'm still over here by the campfire. But you have done well in opening your mind to me, and you will allow me to see through you now," his voice continued. Gin's brows knotted.

"I will what?" she whispered. "Ben, what are you talking about..." Suddenly Gin could not see anything at all, as though someone had blindfolded her. She tried to reach up to her eyes, but instead felt her legs move. She started toward the trees again, though it felt like someone was controlling her, like she was a puppet on strings. "Stop it!" she hissed. Her body stopped moving, and a blinding pain shot through her head, forcing her to her knees in the bracken.

"You will not speak to me that way," said Taeben's voice in the back of her mind. She continued on, blind, unable to control her body, for a few minutes until she finally found the strength to resist him and push him back out of her mind.

She stood there for a moment, not able to process everything that had just happened. Gin felt violated and in a bit of shock as her eyesight returned. What kind of dark magic was that, and where had Taeben learned how to control it? Was he working on THIS spell for Lord Taanyth? The harder she tried to work out what was going on…the more muddy her memories became. She looked up toward the tree she was standing under and took an involuntary step backward as a familiar pair of teal blue eyes met her own.

"Well, hey there *darlin*," said a familiar Qatu voice. Sath dropped out of his perch, on the largest branch of the tree, and landed soundlessly on the ground in front of her. "You're not out here alone, are you?" His eyes twinkled in a way that Gin had never seen before, and something about it made the hairs on the back of her neck stand on end.

"No," she replied, trying to sound more brave than she felt. "Are you? Is your mate not with you?"

Sath chuckled. "No, Anni's over at our campsite on the other side of that ridge asleep. I don't know how she can manage that, with the moon high in the sky and so many stars to see. Remember how we…" his voice trailed off as he studied her for a moment, then frowned. "You out here with Tee? I'd love to see him."

"He is asleep at our campsite. It was Ben's watch but I woke up when we heard you rummaging around over here," Gin replied. Their shared memory of lying under the stars had hit her as hard as it seemed to have done for Sath, and she bit her lip to hold back long buried emotions that surprised her with their intensity. "I'd let that alone, Sath. Tee is none too pleased at how you just abandoned us."

"Abandoned...I did not...what?" Sath scratched his head and Gin thought for a moment that he genuinely looked surprised. He ran one of his massive hands over the top of his head and then smiled down at her. "You're right, I wouldn't dare wake that dwarf just to say hello." He considered her for another long moment. "So, your Taeben is hunting with the Fabled Ones full time now?" he asked, grimacing. "Never would have thought that Tee would have allowed that."

"Yes he is, and Ben is amazing at what he does," Gin said, pointedly ignoring the pained look that now spread across the Qatu's face. "He is the most accomplished and talented wizard I have ever known and has saved **all** of us on more than one occasion." She twirled a lock of hair that had come loose from her ponytail around her finger. "Ben may be a bit rough around the edges, but he has a good heart and he only wants to protect me...and the rest of us, of course." She swallowed hard as Sath studied his feet. "So what are you doing here, anyway? Did you kill all of the game on Qatu'anari?"

Sath had moved a bit closer to her and she was trying to resist the urge to run. The way he was looking at her was both drawing her in and frightening her at the same time. "Of course not. I just love hunting out here and I love the stars and how clear it is," Sath replied. "But I'm not sure why she...why my..." He made another swipe over over the top of his head with his hand. "What was I saying?"

"Are you all right?" Gin asked, her concern overtaking her hurt.

"I don't know," Sath replied. "I feel dizzy, like I'm coming out of a fog or something." He shook his head to clear it and then beamed a toothy grin down at her. "Now, tell me *darlin*, why are you running around on your own? You said that Taeben is on watch so I guess he knows you are over here, right?" He took a step closer to her and Gin noticed that his gaze seemed to sharpen the closer he was. In fact, he seemed to come into focus as he took another step closer. She felt her face flush. "Does he know who you are with now?"

"Aye, he does," she managed to say, unable to take her eyes off of his. A small, steady voice in the back of her mind was urging her to step back but she ignored it. The voice grew more and more angry. "May I ask you a question?" she asked. Sath chuckled.

"Have I ever been able to stop you?" he said, grinning. "What is it, *darlin*?"

"Okay, well two questions, but we will get to the second one later," she said, scowling at him. "Why did you really leave us, Sath? I know that you love Anni and all but both of you could have come hunting with us." The change in his expression intrigued her, and she reached out tentatively to touch his arm. "Tee misses you, but you know how he is, he won't even say your name. Stubborn dwarf. Calls you Cat."

"Anni didn't feel comfortable with all of you after what happened in the Tower with that dragonkind sorceress, Gin," Sath replied. Gin thought his words sounded rehearsed but she let that idea go. "She didn't think you would trust her."

"Aye, she is right about that," Gin replied grimly. "Especially considering her ability to forget all of us save you in a fight. But the question is, Sath, why do you trust her at all? She nearly got Kazhmere killed. Killed! Your only sister! Doesn't that mean anything to you?"

"Of course it does, Gin," Sath said, his voice gruff. "But she is my kind, Gin, and I have known her since we were children. Anni is young and inexperienced. She didn't know what she was getting into. What if I had run off and left you every time you singed my fur with misplaced spells?" Gin frowned. "She and I...we make sense, Gin. I...love her."

Gin nodded her head as Sath's words passed slowly through her heart like a white hot blade. He loved Anni. The blade twisted and Gin felt short of breath. But why? She may have had some misguided feelings for him in the past but now she had...Taeben. It was crystal clear to her in that moment. "It's like me and Ben," she said, suddenly more sure of herself. "We were childhood friends. We are both elves. I get it."

"You mean...you love...Taeben?" Sath asked, his words forming slowly. The fog lifted with sudden alacrity and Gin saw anger and...jealousy in his teal gaze. That was new. "Have you let him...has he..." The Qatu snatched her up from the ground and buried his face in her hair, holding her wriggling form tightly as he inhaled, his face moving down her neck and onto her shoulders. "His scent is on you, all over you," he hissed, disgusted, as he dropped her.

"I am not sure how that's any of your business anymore, Sath," Gin replied as she stood and dusted herself off. She turned to head back to the campsite but looked back over her shoulder at Sath to find him with his face in his hands, inhaling deeply.

"Sunflowers...Gin...I'd forgotten...," he said softly, then closed the space between them and again grabbed Gin up in his powerful arms and crushed her to his chest. Gin did not fight him this time but instead wound her fingers into the fur around his face and on his neck, snuggling into his warmth. There was almost an audible clap as the defenses in her mind that kept Taeben out slammed shut and Gin came back to herself. She loved him, Sath, not Taeben, that was all she knew, but he did not love her back; and this feeling of safety and...something else? Whatever it was, it would have to end soon and he would go back to Anni and their life. Gin pushed back from him until she was looking him in the eye.

"Sath?"

"Yes, *darlin*?" he replied, his eyes hooded and his gaze warm.

"Do you really love Anni?" At her question, he squeezed her back against his chest, inhaling deeply before he carefully set her back on the ground. "Do you?" she asked again. Still he remained silent as he looked at her, hooking one of his clawed fingers under her chin and lifting her face to meet his gaze as he knelt in front of her.

"Aye," he said, sounding unsure. "At least I think I do. Do you love Taeben?"

"No," she whispered. The confusion in the back of her mind started up a dull roar that soon built to a painful wail, but it was merely noise. She stepped away from him and turned on her heel. It was a few moments before she heard the groaning of the tree as he leaped back up to the branch. "I love **you**, *darlin*," she whispered as she walked swiftly back toward her campsite and what was sure to be a furious Taeben. She knew the extent of Sath's preternatural hearing abilities meant he could hear her still. "Always you." Up in the tree, hidden by the leaves, Sath smiled.

Gin took her time returning to the campsite. She was angry and afraid, and she did not understand anything that had just happened. By the time she got back, she was seething. How dare he do something like that, whatever it was? Taeben was sitting, cross-legged, and meditating. He did not look up as she drew close to him. "It was Sath, but I suppose you already know that, don't you?" she spat at him, not wanting to wake Teeand but too angry to remain silent. Taeben did not respond. "Ben, did you hear me? What were you playing at just then? What were you thinking?" He remained silent. "Answer me!" Teeand shifted in his sleep and Taeben looked in the dwarf's direction for a moment before quietly getting to his feet and moving away from the fire and toward Gin. She took a step backward but his long legs closed the gap between them and kept moving, grabbing her arm and dragging her along with him. "Let go of me! You're hurting me!" she protested as she tried to fight him off. "

"I could not possibly care less. Is there a good reason why you reek of wild animal right now?" he responded curtly. He released her arm with a shove, frowning angrily as Gin kept her balance and glared back at him.

"You know very well, why, don't you? You somehow saw the whole thing, didn't you?" She fisted her hands at her sides and took a few deep breaths in an attempt to calm herself, but the attempt was futile. She was livid and wary in equal measure. This was a new side of Ben.

"Are you quite finished? Taeben stared down at her. His high elf features, normally hawkish, only intensified Gin's wariness as she struggled to hold his gaze. Her heart begged her to run, to port away from him; her mind raged at the violation and sought to understand it so she could make sure it never happened again.

"For now," she said no longer caring if she woke Teeand. He would rip Taeben apart for what he had done. Gin longed to look over her shoulder toward the fire but she dared not take her eyes off Taeben. "In fact, I think we are quite finished, Ben. When I tell Teeand what you have just done…"

"Wrong answer, pet," Taeben said, and before Gin even saw him move, he was on her, crushing her to him as he wrenched her head upward with one hand and looked into her eyes as the other covered her mouth. She struggled against him for a moment, until darkness started creeping in around the edges of her vision. He was speaking a strange language and she felt light, floaty, and very glad that he was holding her up.

Ginny?
Yes?
You need to go to sleep, my sweet girl. You are very close to making me angry.
Oh, no, I'm sorry Ben. I will go to sleep.

Taeben carried Gin in his arms back to the fire and tucked her into her bedroll. She opened her eyes and smiled up at him, and for the briefest of moments he felt a twinge of revulsion at having to shut her down like that - but it was for her own good as well as his. Who would protect her if that stupid dwarf had hurt him or worse? He brushed the side of her face with his fingers, avoiding the scar, and she closed her eyes and rolled over.,

"I think you will dream of the Qatu tonight, Ginny," he whispered as he tucked the blanket up around her chin. Soon she dozed off, and her dreams were filled with memories of meeting Sath in that tunnel so long ago followed by images of him in the guild hall with Anni. She tossed and turned and finally gave up on sleep.

"Would you like to start your watch early?" Taeben asked her. His back was to her and she couldn't see his grin.

"Yes. Fine," she snapped as she got up and took his place facing away from the fire.. Taeben crawled into his bedroll and snuggled in, grinning as he drifted off to sleep. His success with influencing her dreams was promising.

The next morning, they were up at first light. The object they were sent to retrieve, a piece of a statue long thought to be destroyed in the Forest Wars, was now believed to be in an underground burrow, used by bandits to surprise unwary travelers. The request for the piece's retrieval had come from a high-ranking Alynatalos general who had been willing to pay quite a bit for its return, and the Fabled Ones jumped at the chance – but the work involved with finding the exact location of the burrow was starting to wear on them, Gin especially. She was exhausted, having not given up watch to anyone else for fear of the dreams returning.

As they sat around the map that Teeand had unrolled next to the smoldering remains of the previous night's fire, Taeben scooted close to Gin, handing her a mug of hot tea and half of his chunk of bread. She took the tea gratefully, but shook her head as he offered the bread, keeping her attention on Teeand. Taeben frowned.

"What's wrong, Ginny?" he whispered.

"Not now, I'm paying attention to Tee," she hissed back. On the one hand, his dream walking had worked, clearly. Gin looked as though she hadn't slept in a week, with dark circles under her eyes that were bloodshot with exhaustion. On the other, though, it would do him no good to make an enemy of her, or any of the others, truth be told, and she didn't seem to remember the previous night's row..

"Sorry." Taeben continued to nibble on the bread as he pretended to listen to the dwarf order them around like children.

"And you, firebug," Teeand said, pointing a stubby finger at Taeben, "let's not test our Gin's healing abilities too soon should we run into trouble."

"Fine," Taeben said under his breath. "I'll just freeze them instead."

"What was that?" Teeand leaned across the map toward Taeben, who put his hands up in submission, spilling crumbs all over the map. Gin giggled as she brushed the map clean.

"I won't burn anything until you say so, Teeand," Taeben said, his tenuous grasp on his anger apparent in the pinched tone of his voice.

"Thank you," Teeand replied. "This is a simple one, in and out quickly once the target is acquired, no need for any burning. Nevertheless, just in case, the plan is that I engage, Gin heals, and Taeben gets ready to transport us out of there. Agreed?"

"You know she can do more than just heal," Taeben growled.

"You know that you are not in charge of the mission," Teeand barked back.

"You both know that I am RIGHT HERE, right?" Gin snapped, scowling at both of them. "Honestly!" Her outburst took the wind out of the sails of the dwarf, and he patted her hand, smiling at her.

"Of course you are," he said, "of course. This will be an easy one, our girl, shouldn't tax you too much." Turning his glance to Taeben, the smile fell away from Teeand's eyes. "And there is no one on Orana that I would trust with my life more than you, my girl. No one."

Gin blushed. "You are kind, Tee. Now let's get this done so we can move on to targets that the wizard CAN burn, yes?" They laughed and Taeben smiled at them, all the time imagining how long it would take the dwarf to roast in his green armor. Not long at all.

Taeben was still contemplating charred dwarf when Teeand gave the call to engage. The leader of a small band of thieves was holding the piece of the statue; in the time they had spent camping just out of sight of the burrow, they had learned the patterns of the humans within. First thing in the morning, they would all emerge, bedraggled and a bit hungover, leave for most of the day, and then one by one they would return. One morning, Gin had undertaken a scouting mission and cast an invisibility spell on herself before entering the burrow on the heels of the returning thieves. Taeben had tried to stop her, but she had cast another spell that allowed her to increase her speed prior to the invisibility, and she had quite literally ducked out of his reach and run toward danger.

She brought back the news that bandits were discussing their "daily hit list" and that they would be leaving soon. Sure enough, after about an hour all of them filed out of the burrow. The Fabled Ones watched to see how long they were gone, and after a second day to watch and record, decided that this was a pattern. On the third day they would enter the burrow and retrieve the piece of the statue with no trouble at all.

"Well? Come on then, wizzy," Teeand called out. Gin punched him in the arm when she noted the grin on his face. Taeben hated being called 'wizzy' and Teeand knew it. "You are our ride out of here." Taeben mumbled something about a 'one seat only rule' in his own dialect, and Gin made a mental note to be ready to call up her own transportation magic just in case.

"*I wish the two of you could get along,*" she whispered to Teeand in his language. The dwarf shot a glance at her from the side but said nothing. Gin knew that he did not trust Taeben, but she also knew that Teeand was not the same without Sath around. The old, familiar squeeze on her heart at the thought of the Qatu spurred her on as she led the way into the burrow with Teeand right by her side. The visual range of dwarves was not quite as extensive as that of the elves, and Teeand was bumping into things left and right. She pushed out in front of him and he opened his mouth to object but shut it immediately and simply took her elbow in his meaty hand. She could just imagine Taeben's scowl as he brought up the rear.

After a long walk through increasingly shorter tunnels, they walked out into an open space that meant Taeben could stand up straight again. Again, Gin heard him uttering some unpleasant things in his dialect, and she ignored them. "Look, Tee, is that it over there on that…altar?" she asked, pointing in the direction of what seemed to be a shrine. Two crates served as the legs for a wide piece of wood draped with a ragged piece of blue cloth. On the cloth, random glass vases and small wooden boxes were arranged, and there were medium sized rocks here and there. The marble hand from the statue of Tsarra, First Caeth of Alynatalos during the Forest War - believed by many to contain the magic of her mate, the First Cleric - rested in the center of the cloth.

"Yep, well spotted, our Gin!" Teeand responded. "Taeben, get ready to get us out of here. Gin, if you would, a light to guide my way?" He grinned at her as she snapped her fingers, pouring just a bit of her magic into the air and causing a circle of flickering lights to appear above his head. They were tiny fireballs, and provided him with just enough light to move across the room, grab the hand, and start back toward them.

"STOP." Gin's voice was barely a whisper but Teeand froze in place as she closed her eyes and turned her head back toward the tunnels. "Several, moving fast." She furrowed her brow as she concentrated.

"Humans?" Taeben whispered and Gin nodded. "What are they saying, Ginny?" he asked and her face screwed up even tighter. Teeand was still a few feet from them and Gin beckoned him closer with the flip of one of her hands. Taeben moved in behind her and started speaking the words of magical transport under his breath as he wrapped an arm around her.

"Four. Ambush. Now, Taeben, quick as you can. Tee, hold on to me," she said before mumbling something under her breath. There was a pause, and then she and Taeben said "Great Hall" simultaneously and the trio disappeared just as the humans came bounding down the tunnel and into the room. They landed in a heap on the floor in the middle of the great hall.

"What were you saying?" Taeben hissed in her ear as Gin scrambled to her feet. She held up a finger to him, not making eye contact because she knew that made him furious.

"I'm off to deliver this," Teeand said as he headed for the door. "Well done on the tracking, Gin, we would have been sitting ducks in there without you." She smiled at him as he left the great hall, and once the door closed behind him she turned to face Taeben.

"I was casting my own transportation spell," she replied coolly. "I wish you and Tee could get along, but I am not foolish enough to think that you will just for me. So, I needed to make sure that there was more than one seat on the ride out of there." Taeben scowled at her.

"I'm sorry, Ginny, but I just don't like how they underestimate you," he said sourly, hanging his head. "I'm going to go do a bit of research, but I will come back later...if you will be here, that is?"

"Where else would I be?" she asked as she smiled sadly. "I will see you later, Ben."

Once that mission had ended and the piece of the statue returned to Alynatalos, Teeand, Taeben and Gin went their separate ways, as they often did upon returning to the great hall. Many nights Gin found herself sitting in the Great Hall, up on the balcony at the old walnut desk, gazing up at the stained glass window behind it that depicted a nighttime scene on the grassy plains to the south. Her memories of the past with the Fabled Ones often seemed more real to her than current missions. The star in the stained glass reminded her of the twinkling stars she saw during long shifts watching over her group members while out on missions or hunts, and with that memory came thoughts of Sath. She could still hear his rumbly laughter in her ears; when she closed her eyes, his teal gaze and toothy grin burned into her mind's eye.

One night, as she sat pouring over the mountains of paperwork required to keep a guild running, she paused just before she tallied up the invoices for the craftspeople that practiced their trades within the guild hall. Her mind, set free for the moment from credit and debit columns in the ledger, sped across the length and breadth of Orana, recalling stolen moments here and there with Sath and the others until landing on the moment when she last saw him. He and Anni were walking through the Outpost, and Sath had one arm around the Qatu female. They fit together, their height and build the same...they fit in a way he would never have done with her. He never even looked back at her...or the others, for that matter, as he left. An all too familiar pain settled in Gin's chest as she went back to the paperwork.

"It's late, shouldn't you have gone home by now?" Taeben said from behind her, startling her a bit. Gin sighed and put down the quill she had been using as the corners of her mouth tugged slightly upward into a smile. He had a habit of sneaking up on her like that, and was the only one that seemed able to evade her innate tracking ability that would alert her to anyone approaching. "I'm sure the Fabled Ones' leader gets time to rest like everyone else, doesn't she?"

"Why am I the leader again?" Gin muttered as she stood and turned to face him, the rest of the tired smile spreading across her face as she did. "Someone has to do this, Ben, and it's not like I'm out hunting all the time anymore. I'm not sure I'd know what to do…not sure I ever did."

Taeben scowled. "Of course you would know what to do, don't be ridiculous. Finest druid in Fabled's ranks, you are."

"Don't let Elys hear you say that," Gin replied, chuckling. "What brings you here so late?"

He fidgeted for a moment before speaking. "Ginny, can we talk about something before you go home for the night?" Taeben asked, his eyes searching hers. She nodded, and as always, when her icy gaze took hold of his Ben felt weak in the knees but managed to keep himself upright. He moved a step closer, toward her.

"Of course, just one second. It will do me no good to have to sort this mess out AGAIN in the morning." She stacked the papers on the desk and then turned back to face him. "Now then. Downstairs?" She thought for a moment about how different her time with Taeben had been, and continued to be, from her time traveling with Sath and the others. She remembered with a frown hunting once near a ruin that was deep under the warm waters off the coast at Calder's Port, magically kept intact by the very founder of the Port herself. She recalled trying to hang on to Sath's tail as it became slippery from the water, or trying to make sure that Hack could keep up when his tiny legs and arms couldn't swim as fast as the rest of them. With Taeben, hunting anywhere was almost effortless. Almost.

"No," he said, taking a step toward her and holding out his hand. "Somewhere else, this conversation needs to be in private, if you don't mind?" Gin nodded, smiling at him, and took his hand. He pulled her in close, her back to his front with his arm wrapped protectively around her. "Seclusion," he whispered.

Gin cocked her head to one side, puzzled. That was not part of any transportation spell she knew, nor was it a place in the world that she had visited in the past. The magic commenced and she felt herself slammed into Taeben's chest as the inside-out feeling of magical transport overtook her. This time, though, it seemed to last too long; Gin clung to his arm, her fingernails digging into his skin.

The black nothingness of the void that transport magic used to travel between places in the world did not lighten when Gin felt ground come up under her feet and Taeben's grip on her loosen. She held fast to him, closing her eyes as her stomach turned flips while her inner equilibrium sought to right itself. It was as though wherever they had landed, they were upside down. Goosebumps raised on all of her exposed skin, and she found that her clothes were wet, as though they had been dragged through an icy ocean.

"That wakes you up every time, doesn't it? I can't believe that worked..." Taeben said, chuckling amid gulps of air. Gin nodded, frantically rubbing her arms with her hands to bring her body temperature back up. She scanned the area and found that they were nowhere that she could recognize. The landscape was dull and brown, and the sky was an inky black, scored with millions of tiny pinpricks of light. She shivered and increased the intensity of her hands rubbing her arms. "Oh, Ginny, here, I'm sorry," Taeben said, gathering her up into his arms and wrapping his thick cloak around both of them. She was too grateful for his body warmth and still too stunned by where they were to be surprised, so she snuggled in next to him, closing her eyes tightly.

As quickly as he had taken her into his arms, Taeben pushed her away, ashamed of himself for the lapse of judgement. She had not fought him off, that was true - quite the opposite really - but it was too soon to show his hand. He quickly called up a fire bolt and set some driftwood alight that he had found piled near them. Gin moved over close to the fire, a puzzled look on her face as she focused on the flames. "I'm sorry," she said quietly. "That was... It was too familiar. I wasn't thinking; I was just cold."

"No, no, it is I who should apologize, Ginny. I was the one that was out of line. I just wanted to make sure you were warm." Taeben looked at her. "It was nice, though, for a moment." She smiled at him as she continued to rub her hands together. "I think it would be best if we go ahead and talk while we warm up. Is that okay?" Gin nodded at him. "Excellent." He sat down near her and reached into his robe for a magical pack he had acquired just before setting off. It was waterproof and he soon produced food and drink for them as well as a warm blanket that he handed to her.

"Don't you need it, Ben?" she said as she tentatively took the blanket from him.

"Not as badly as you do, from the look of you," he said. "Here." He took the blanket back and wrapped it around her shoulders. She sighed in relief as the warmth spread over her, making him smile.

"Where are we, anyway?"

"It's a surprise, Ginny," Taeben responded, an almost silly grin across his face making her grin back at him. "I will get to that in a moment, but first I feel that I need to talk to you about Bellesea..." Taeben's words trailed off as Gin scooted away from him suddenly, wrapping her arms around her knees and hugging them tightly as she glared at him. "No, no, I don't mean to scare you, Ginny," he said as she stared at him, eyes wide with a mix of fury and terror. "I didn't think you'd have that reaction, I promise. I thought enough time had passed..."

"Enough time that I would forget what you did to me there?" she hissed. Taeben tried to suppress the tide of rage that was building inside of him. What **he** had done? Had she forgotten about Lord Taanyth, and how everything had been by the dragon's orders, not Taeben's own? Why had he given her an opening to talk? He should really know better by now. "You didn't help me when Dor held me prisoner, even though you knew who I was…you stood there and watched while that dragon…while he…you let him torture me…" Her ice blue eyes blazed with fury as she spoke. "I have forgiven you, Taeben, because you went through enough with that sorceress and I cannot let myself believe that you would do something like that unless forced, but I will not forget." She swallowed hard as she scrutinized him, and her eyes narrowed as realization settled. "Wait… Are you bringing me here…to take me back there? Did you think that you could…"

"ENOUGH!" the wizard roared at her, rising to his feet and towering over her head. "You stupid, ungrateful wood elf! Of course I'm not taking you back there. I WAS A PRISONER TOO!" As she looked up at him, Gin's stare turned hollow, and Taeben recognized the look in her eyes from when she was held in the ruined keep. It was not fear, but her defense mechanism, her way of protecting herself from whatever onslaught ensued, and he found, to his genuine surprise, that it hurt his heart to see. "Oh, Ginny, I'm so sorry," he said, making his voice as soft as he could as he took a knee in front of her. She did not flinch nor pull away from him as he smiled and took her hands in his; she kept up the hollow stare and said nothing. He rubbed the back of them and watched her relax slightly.

Eventually, the light sparked in her eyes again and she spoke. "It's… It's all right. I think that I just stuffed all that away after it happened, and I worked so hard to help Sath forgive me…" Sath. Gin's train of thought came completely off the rails as a vision of the Qatu male floated into her memory and she pulled her hands back and out of Taeben's grasp. "Anyway, I'm sorry I snapped at you, Ben. Can we start over?" She patted the ground next to where she was sitting. "I will even share the blanket while you tell me where we are and why we are here… And just exactly where 'here' is."

Taeben smiled, his heart in his throat as he settled down on the cave floor next to her. He waved off the blanket. "You need to get warm and dry," he said. "Now, I wanted to talk to you about

Bellesea because I know that you can't forget what happened. I can't either, and I know that you don't completely trust me when we hunt together because what happened there…and in the tower." Gin opened her mouth to protest and Taeben put a slender finger to her lips, causing her to flinch. "See? You have just proved my point. I want you to trust me, Ginny, as you did when we were children. But more than that, I want to keep hunting with you because I feel like we could make a good team."

"We have a good team," Gin said, confused. "Tee and you and me? Good team."

"I mean just the two of us." Taeben looked at the fire because he was afraid of drowning in her eyes and revealing his true opinion of the dwarf. "I think that because we have similar magic, similar fighting styles, you and I. We could do very well exploring, and we would be safe because of your expertise in healing."

Gin scowled. "Again, Gin to the rescue with healing magic."

"No, not at all," Taeben said, reaching out impulsively and taking her hands again. "Gin to the rescue because your healing skills are second to none. Thing is, I want to help you learn the other parts of being a druid because some of it is similar to being a wizard. You can do so much more than just heal, Gin. I saw you kill Dorlagar." He paused a moment, expecting her to become emotional at the memory, but she merely watched him talk. "You have it in you, Ginny, to be an amazing hunter. You just need someone who doesn't think you need protecting all the time, someone who treats you like a partner and an equal." He moved a bit closer, wanting to grab her up in a kiss but biding his time. "Leave the Fabled Ones to Teeand and come with me. You need someone like me, who believes in you rather than dominates you, like the Qatu did."

"Sath didn't try to…what are you talking about?" she replied, trying to even out her tone as her face betrayed the attempt at indignation in her words. "He believed in me."

"As a healer, of course he did. We all do. However, he also thought of you as someone he needed to protect and shield. How many times did he stand by and watch while Elys charged after an enemy but said nothing? It did not seem to bother him to see her take risks, learn, and grow; but you he kept safely out of harm's way. Ginny, I saw him hurt you in the tower rather than try to fight my mistress's hold on him because he didn't think you could fight her and...well, the truth is that I know you had it in you then, and you do now."

Gin looked away but Taeben hooked a finger under her chin and pulled her gaze back up to meet his. He tried again to push into her mind, and almost made a toe hold before she pushed him back out. Wondering if she realized she was doing it, he released his hold on her.

"There is so much more to you that he doesn't want to evolve and grow because then you won't need him anymore," he said softly. "I believe that you don't need him now. You don't need me now, really, but I think we could make each other even better if we stay together...to hunt, of course. This is why I brought you here, to this place between the worlds, so that we could make a new start, together."

"Between the...what? Ben, *where* are we?"

"This is the void, Ginny. You travel through it every time you cast a transportation spell, but I have found a way to stop here and stay here. Don't you see what this means for us? We travel our world, we fight, we learn, we grow, and then we come back here where no one can find us, not even the Qatu. You will be a goddess, Ginny, my Queen, and no one will ever look down on you again."

Gin chewed on her fingernail as she thought about what Taeben had said, trying to keep down the fear at his words. Were they really in-between now, in the cracks in the world? Taeben had faith in what she could become, and his belief that Sath was holding her back...what did all of it mean?

Sath had told her outright that he would always come looking for her to rescue her if she needed it. He would come looking for her to **rescue** her... Why had he put it that way? Was Taeben right about Sath? Did Sath only need her – want her - in order to have someone that he could rescue? She thought that she had seen the beginnings of a genuine connection between herself and Sath, but now she was not sure at all. If he had truly loved her why did he take up with Anni so fast…unless Anni was charming him…like in the Tower…realization dawned a second time and Gin nearly jumped out of her skin. "Ben, what do you know about charm spells?" she asked suddenly.

"Why?" His response was curt and took her off guard. Not being privy to the train of thought leading to her question, he clearly had no idea what she was suddenly on about.

"Sorry for the abrupt change in topic," she said. "I wonder sometimes if Anni has charmed Sath, and that's why he left me…and the others to go be with her." A tear escaped from one of her eyes and Taeben reached out to wipe it away. His fingers grazed the scar on her cheek and she pulled away as he glared at her.

"How did that happen, by the way, that scar on your face? Why didn't you heal it?" he demanded.

Gin blushed as she touched the side of her face. "I can't believe you've never asked me that before," she said despondently. "Sath did that, the first time we met. He was still… well, he was not Sath, really, he was still the Bane of the Forest. I met him in the tunnels between the forest and the grasslands and he tried to steal my food and water and…well…" she indicated the scar with her hand, "this happened. It was an accident, I'm sure, and he probably still feels horrible about it. I let it heal too much naturally before I tried to heal it with magic, and at that time I hadn't learned enough to make it completely disappear anyway."

Taeben's expression grew grim. "He has been hurting you since the day you met him. He is a monster, Ginny, a beast, and you are well to be rid of him." He frowned as her face clouded over. "Apologies, I've said too much."

"No. It's just that Sath is not a monster or a beast, Ben. Truly. But maybe he is better off with his own kind."

"About that…" Taeben paused a moment, flexing his slender fingers and gathering his thoughts before turning his attention back to Gin. "I need to tell you something else, Ginny, and I fear that it will make you hate me rather than trust me, but I want us to start out on equal footing, always honest with each other," Taeben said after a long moment of silence. He was taking an enormous chance here, but it was a means to an end and he was running out of options. The Qatu was still at the forefront of her mind, and that might be what was keeping him from being able to enter. "I fear that you are right about the bard, about Annilanshi." He took a deep breath, feigning distress over the revelation. "I overheard them in the grand hall, and I heard her song. I knew what she was doing, but I didn't tell you because I knew it would hurt you," he said. Gin did not respond so he continued. "Little did I know this was just one instance in a long line of them, as far as that Qatu hurting you is concerned anyway. Annilanshi holds him in her thrall, or at least she did at first. I do not know if she continues to charm him or if he has actually fallen in love with her."

Gin's eyes bugged out of her head as she balled up her fists at her sides. "What did you just say to me? Why have you not...we could have...Ben, we could have saved him from her!" she exclaimed, leaping to her feet. "That night in the grand hall, we could have saved Sath and you just let me leave him there with her!" Taeben, on his feet in an instant as well, pulled her to him and held her fast, his slender fingers curled around the back of her head as his thumb gently stroked the scar on her cheek. She struggled against him but his height gave him an advantage over her.

"Saved him so that he could do THIS to you again?" he hissed at her. Staring her down, Taeben pushed again into her mind. His gamble had paid off, and the barrier she had put up against him in the past shattered at her emotional reaction to his news about the Qatu bard. Her eyes closed first and his followed, and then he eased into her mind like a serpent, first winding itself around a tree branch and then coiling about the length of the trunk. When he opened his eyes and looked at her, Gin's face upturned to his, her blue eyes were wide and unseeing. "Ginny? Can you hear me?"

"Yes, Master," she whispered.

"No, not Master. Never call me Master. You will continue to call me Ben, yes?"

"Of course, as you wish, Ben," she said.

"Ginny, do you love me?"

"Do you want me to love you, Ben?" she asked, her forehead wrinkling in confusion.

"Aye, Ginny, I do," he said, tentatively.

"Then I do, of course I do," she said, smiling brightly. Taeben pulled her face to his roughly and kissed her, delighted as she returned his kiss. He realized that she was on her tiptoes to try to match his height, so he released her.

"You are a very good girl, Ginny," he said. "Now, I'm going to withdraw from your mind just a bit, so that you can be on your own, but you will still do as I say, will you not?"

"Of course I will, Ben," she said, her voice dreamy.

"Good girl. Here is what I want you to do. You will never see the Qatu again, and you will permanently forget what you saw me do in the forest that day when we escaped from the Keep," he ordered, his voice stern. "The only memory of the Qatu Sathlir Clawsharp that you will have is that he is the Bane of the Forest and he means you harm, **dire** harm. Only I can protect you. Do you understand?"

"As you wish it, Ben," she said, nodding her head.

"Good." Taeben placed one of his hands over her eyes for a moment as he spoke the words that his horrible Mistress Salynth had taught him, and then felt the withdrawal from Gin's mind. She blinked a few times behind his hand and he released her. "Are you sure you're all right, Ginny?" he asked, taking her arms just before her knees gave way. "I think you're too weak to go back tonight. We can make camp here and carry on in the morning."

"I...don't know what happened," Gin said. "I was talking to you and then I just must have gotten dizzy. Where are we, anyway?"

"In the Void, Ginny, remember? Somewhere that you do not have to worry about the Fabled Ones anymore. That Qatu will never find you here," he said, watching her reaction carefully. "You will finally be safe."

"Oh, thank you!" she said as she burrowed into his arms. Startled yet pleased, Taeben slowly wrapped his arms around her and held her close. "I knew that you would save me from him before he hurts me again." Taeben swallowed hard, choking down the last bits of revulsion at what he had done, and then smiled as he stroked her hair. "I love you, Ben, I've always loved you."

"And I love you, Ginny," he replied. The time with Salynth had been worth it after all.

After a few hours of sleep, Taeben stirred and smiled down at the female in his arms. Far better a prize than the others would be this druid, his Ginny. The wizard closed his eyes and imagined her seated on the floor at his feet in the throne room of Qatu'anari, and the disgraced Prince Sathlir on a chain at his other side. His entire body hummed with excitement as he opened his eyes and gently rubbed Gin's arm to wake her. "Ginny?"

"Mm-hm?" she murmured as her eyes fluttered open. "Ben? Where are we? What happened?" She sat up quickly and looked around, blushing to the roots of her hair when she found his arms still around her. Gin quickly hopped to her feet. "How long have we been here? Lairky will be sick with worry!"

Lairceach. Taeben scowled. He had forgotten about that annoying little female, Gin's younger sister. Often, since Sath had left the Fabled Ones, the sister had hunted with them, and Taeben had found Lairceach to be hot headed and bloodthirsty like Elysiam, but not nearly as careful. She was of no use to him, really, other than a means to near-death...or a distraction so he could escape.

Gin was right, though, her sister would be out of her mind with worry if they did not go back to the Forest. One more impediment to deal with before his plan could progress. Gin was busy stuffing things into her packs as Taeben stood to help her. "How long will it take us to get back?" she asked.

"You genuinely don't remember where we are, do you Ginny?"

"Ben, please, stop calling me that. If Hack overhears you…"

"Because a two-foot tall blowhard with an axe scares me," Taeben chuckled under his breath. "I'm sorry, Gin. You genuinely do not remember our talk last night, do you? We are far away from all that. None of the Fabled Ones are here, especially not Hackort. We can just use magical transport back to check in with Lairky, no worries."

"I don't think you should go, Ben," she said carefully. As she clearly had expected, he turned on her, his face contorting angrily. "Wait," she said, placing one of her tiny hands on his chest. "Lairky is a bit…careful about with whom she associates these days, and she doesn't really trust you, after all she has heard from Elys." Taeben placed his hand over Gin's hand, and found it to be trembling. The pressure he applied to her hand served to help him hold his own anger at bay. "I trust you, Ben…I mean, you kept me safe and warm last night." She smiled at him and he felt like his brain would explode. Had she always smelled like sunflowers? He took a deep breath, allowing her nearness to wash over him.

"I can just send you, Gin," he said, "if you're sure that you want to go without me." He looked deeply into her eyes, hoping to rekindle the bond he had placed into her mind the night before.

"Why don't you go on to the Outpost and wait for me? I have some business there after I see my sister," Gin said as she looked up at him. His gaze locked onto hers and he could swear he heard the thud as the bond solidified, like a bolt on a locked door falling into place. "Or perhaps we should both just go there…you're right, I really don't want to go without you." She giggled, and Taeben found the sound to be like bells tinkling in his ears. "How weird. My head is suddenly somewhat foggy. I mean, not that I don't trust you or anything, Ben, but it's almost like you charmed me, just like that horrible…in the tower charmed…oh…dear…" He could almost see the thoughts of Sath creeping into her consciousness, and Taeben decided to act quickly.

"Sssh, no thoughts of the past now, Gin. To the Outpost it is, my lady!" he said with an exaggerated bow that brought Gin's attention back from thoughts of the Qatu and made her giggle all over again. Using the old familiar phrase she hadn't thought of in a long time, he said, "Hug the…wizard?" She grinned and wrapped her arms around his midsection, making him blush and smile wickedly as he recited the magical words for transportation.

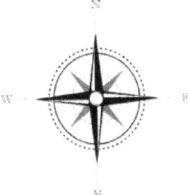

TWO

Lairceach, or Lairky, as she was called by most who knew her, paced about in the training hall after practicing her forms. She was too distracted to continue, so she put the weapons away safely before allowing her mind full access to the matter at hand. It had to be the case that the clockwork eye that she had hidden in her sister's bag had malfunctioned. The tiny contraption, filled with magic that allowed Lairky to see through it, regardless of where it was, had come in handy more than once. Lairky made sure that she always kept a supply of them in her bag for finding a path to get out of dangerous spots. But this one must have been damaged.

Surely, what had appeared before her eyes had not been the truth? The eye must have been playing up. Taeben had done something awful to Gin, something involving the darkest of magic. She was not sure what he was up to, but Gin did not love him, Lairky was sure of that. Gin loved that Qatu, *Sathlir*, whether she knew it or not...or if it was wise or not, Lairky thought with a grimace. Maybe her lip-reading skills were not as keen as she had thought. Maybe she had gotten it wrong…

Moreover, where had they been when she saw them through the eye? She had thought that the wizard had said something about the Void, but that was not a real place, was it? That was the space between, the undersides of the world, not somewhere that you could visit. Could that have tampered with the magic of the clockwork? Lairky frowned. The Void was not a place. While she was not a magic user like Gin, not by any stretch, surely she would have learned something about that from her sister if it were the case. More lies from the wizard, more likely.

She packed up her poisons and extra clockwork eyes, and then slung the pack over her shoulder as she left the training hall. Because her mind was awash with the images from the eye and she was not looking where she was going, suddenly she felt the wooden platform come out from under her feet coupled with the whoosh of air and the lurch of her stomach that indicated she had fallen off of one of the levels of her treetop home…again. Lairky quickly righted herself in midair and landed as she'd been taught, right in front of the spot where Gin and Taeben materialized.

"YOU!" she shouted as she pointed her tiny finger at Taeben. Gin quickly stepped between them. "Where have you two been? What did you do to my sister last night?"

"Now, Lairky, wait," Gin began, moving toward her younger sister with her hands out in front of her, "nothing happened last night. We left the Outpost to go exploring and we…took a wrong turn, but we were absolutely safe where we ended up. Taeben suggested we camp with a warm fire rather than travel all night to get home, and that seemed a reasonable idea to me." She looked over her shoulder at Taeben who was glaring back at Lairky and then rolled her eyes before looking back at her sister. "He was just looking after me, Lairky, but I'm fine. See? I'm here now."

"But I thought…" Keen not to reveal the existence of the clockwork eye that she had stowed in Gin's bags, Lairky shut her mouth before she revealed what she had seen. "I thought you would be out looking for the Qatu," she said, reveling in the thinly veiled rage that crept into the wizard's eyes at the mere mention of Sath. He was threatened, so he must know that Gin loved Sath and not him. Interesting and worrying. Lairky leaned around Gin and glowered at him.

"Why? He has made his choice," Gin said bitterly. "Anni may have charmed him in the beginning, but he is still with her, so it is of his own choice now. Ben has helped me see how dangerous that relationship was." Taeben had moved up to her side and wrapped an arm around her shoulders, and she smiled up at him.

Lairky's eyes narrowed. "Seems you've made yours as well?"

Gin blushed. "Well, Ben has been kind enough to help me hone some of my skills, and I am thinking about going on an extended hunting trip with him. I just need to clear up some things here in Aynamaede and then I will head to our place at the Outpost and pack up my things and take my leave of the Fabled Ones. Teeand can manage the guild until I return." She didn't seem to notice that her younger sister's eyes were bulging out of her head in surprise. "Would you like to keep our place there for yourself? I can pay the rent ahead of time so that you don't have to worry about it."

"Um, sure." Lairky didn't know what to do or say. Malice and evil intent seemed to surround the wizard like a cloud that had tendrils coiled around Gin. The way he looked down at Gin was more like he was looking at a pet rather than a lover. How was her sister not seeing any of this? "Gin, are you sure?"

"Listen," Taeben said, clearly only addressing Gin, "why don't I go take care of what I need to do in Alynatalos while you tie up your loose ends, love? You spend some extra time with your sister, and then we can meet back here and head out on our journey? First light, tomorrow?"

"Aye, sounds like a good plan." Gin smiled up at Taeben in a way that Lairky had only ever seen her smile about Sath, and the younger wood elf felt her stomach churning. "Lairky, shall we?"

"I'll walk, thanks," Lairky replied. "Your port magic turns my stomach inside out." She stalked off toward the path that would eventually lead out of the forest and to the Outpost, where she supposed Gin would be waiting. Perhaps away from the wizard she could make her sister see reason. As she walked, she popped the cork on one of her potions that would increase her speed, and after swallowing the contents and feeling the magic flow to her legs and feet, Lairky ran.

"Don't worry about her," Taeben said, taking both of Gin's shoulders in his hands and turning her to face him. His eyes bored into hers, strengthening the magical hold he had on her. "She will come around. I will meet you back here before you know it." He kissed her forehead lightly and she smiled, her eyes closed happily.

Several hours later, Gin was sitting in the middle of the floor in the tiny apartment she shared with Lairky when her sister arrived. "Magic is much faster," she taunted, grinning at the younger wood elf who scowled in return. Gin frowned as her sister's expression faded into one of concern and sadness. "What's really wrong, Lairky?" she asked, rising and walking over to her baby sister. Lairky shook her head and turned her attention to her backpack. Gin nodded and stood patiently, watching Lairky stow potion bottles and remove her sharpening stone and dagger. Once her things had been put away, Gin led Lairky back over to the cushions on the floor by the fireplace and they both sat down.

The younger sister stared into the fire for a few moments, keeping her hands busy with the stone and dagger, before speaking. "Gin, you can't be serious about going anywhere with that wizard," Lairky said as she focused on the blade. "I don't trust him. He wants something from you, I can feel it, and it isn't anything good!" The older wood elf sighed, clearly exasperated.

"This again? Lairky, you just don't know him like I do," Gin said. "Ben and I were friends when we were kids, while you were still with Mama."

"Yes, yes, I know, but this time I think you're just giving him the benefit of the doubt as you do everyone and it will get you hurt!" Lairky replied. "He has changed, Gin, and he isn't the Ben you knew, not any more. Everyone sees it. Why can't you? Just ask Elys, or...well, Sath didn't trust him, did he?"

Gin's eyes blazed with a mixture of anger and fear. "I'll thank you not to mention him." She stood up from her place by the fire and walked over to start packing her things for the journey with Taeben.

"See? This is what I mean, Ginny. Something is very wide of the mark here. You love Sath and he loves you. You don't know it, he doesn't know it but I can see it, and you know I wouldn't suggest that otherwise because I am no fan of his. But saying you have feelings for Taeben? This wizard has done something to you; I can just taste it!" Lairky thundered. Gin turned her back to her sister and ignored her as she pulled her haversack around in front of her on the table. She reached down inside and frowned as her hand hit something metal.

"What is this?" she said, wrinkling her eyebrows and then smiling broadly. "Oh, maybe Ben left me a..." She pulled the clockwork eye out and stared at it, then at Lairky as realization settled. The smile faded to an angry glower. "Lairky. Tell me you had **nothing** to do with this."

Lairky held her hands up in the air as the color drained from her face. "Ginny, before you get mad, let me explain."

"Explain spying on me? Really, Lairky?" Gin wasn't sure why she was so upset, but she was positively teetering on the edge of furious as she stared at her sister. "Invading my privacy? You were watching me and Ben! There is no explanation for..."

"I DON'T TRUST THE WIZARD!" Lairky shouted. "I'm sorry, Ginny, but I don't and...you're all I have." The fire seemed to go out in her older sister's eyes. "Now, if what you say is true about Sath being charmed then it will be an easy fix to get him back. Just kill the bard."

"LAIRKY." Gin's voice, so reminiscent of their mother's voice when she was angry, stopped the younger elf cold. "You will not be killing any bards, not even ones who probably deserve it. Even if I wanted Sath back, even if I ever had him to start with, there is no way I'm going to let you do this," Gin said as her sister stood and glared at her. "You can just go back to your training, Lairky. One meeting with Sath was enough for you." Once she finished with her packing, Gin returned to her spot on the floor with her spell book, to try and calm her mind by focusing on the faded pages.

Lairky studied her sister for a moment, and then plopped down on the floor next to Gin, making her sigh with annoyance.

"Nothing will happen to me, you know that," she said, picking up her battered whetstone and returning to sharpening her dagger. The *ssshink-ssshink* sound made Gin's skin crawl as she'd heard it many times before when Sath sharpened his clawed weapon. She held her breath as long as she had, but the sound was turning her stomach.

"Lairky!" Gin exclaimed as she grabbed her sister's hands to silence them. "Please. Stop." Lairky dropped the stone away but held the dagger, her eyes blazing. "Put that away. I forbid you from going anywhere near Sathlir Clawsharp, or his...or Anni, is that understood?" She looked deeply into her sister's dark brown eyes. "Answer me."

Lairky yanked her hands back from Gin, careful not to cut her sister's hands with the dagger. "Yes, it is very clear that you don't want me around him." Gin breathed out in an agitated manner, fanning the fringe that framed her face up in the air as she did. "But I know that you love Sath..." Gin grabbed her sister by the wrist and pulled her close.

"You will never mention his name again; are we clear?" Gin hissed. This was uncharacteristic anger from Gin, and Lairky feared that the wizard had been watching the conversation all along. Was she certain that this was really her sister, and not the wizard under an illusion? That was not possible, was it? Lairky trembled in her hand and Gin released her, but did not break eye contact. "Never again. There is nothing between me and the Bane of the Forest but peril. Nothing. End of."

Moving backward quickly, Lairky put as much distance between herself and her older sister as she could. Gin's focus returned to her meditation. "We are clear," Lairky whispered, her voice almost inaudible. "Gin, can I borrow your cloak? I need to check in with my guild master and I've left mine somewhere again," she said, already removing Gin's cloak from the nail by the door. Gin nodded without opening her eyes and Lairky dashed out the door, jumping as it swung shut with a bang in her wake.

For a long time, Gin was still and quiet, trying to rid herself of the anger that she felt toward her sister. This was new. Lairky had been challenging to raise after their parents died, but the way that she admired Gin had made her easy to be around. Cursik had been a help for a time, but he had disappeared again about the time that Gin had left Aynamaede for the Outpost.

She thought about the things Lairky had said about Sath, but found that just letting his image fill her mind brought along intense fear and anxiety. How could Lairky have missed how dangerous Sath was? Gin shuddered from head to toe as she recalled her sister's account of her one meeting with Sath, and how close Lairky had come to dire harm. That would never happen again.

Gin stood and crossed the room, swearing under her breath when she noticed that Lairky had in fact taken her cloak when she left. She picked up her pack and decided that magical transport was indeed faster. Ben had been teaching her a spell that would bring her to him if ever she was in trouble or needed him, so she closed her eyes and focused on his image, smiling down at her, opening his arms to her. She spoke ancient words of magical transport followed by "Taeben," and winked out of sight.

Nancy E. Dunne

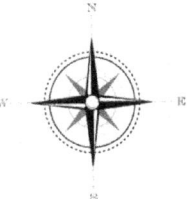

THREE

"And then what? Ben, finish the story!" Gin begged as Taeben slowly chewed the hunk of bread he had placed in his mouth after dipping it in the stew she had made. He had to admit that her cooking was improving, but not by a lot. They had been living in accommodations just south of the Elven Outpost for only a few weeks. He forbade her from using magic to conjure their meals and insisted that she actually cook what they hunted and gathered, because he thought that it would be an efficient means to keep her busy so that he could continue the spell research that Lord Taanyth had started without her noticing. He would cast the spell on her while she was chopping vegetables or kneading bread dough and then watch to see her reaction. Could it be that the reaction was that he was removing her cooking skill rather than her resistance to him? Total control of her had not yet been possible, but he was making strides in that direction. It did not hurt, he mused, that she was completely in love with him.

"And then, I had the druid hanging onto the back of my robes with her eyes closed because she did not like caverns and would not follow me into them in any other way. Sadly, there was a cliff…" he paused as he put another bite of food into his mouth. Gin glared at him but when their eyes met, he was pleased to see her expression soften. She bit her lip, clearly to keep from asking him to continue, but it drove him to distraction and he reached over and pulled down on her chin, popping her mouth open only slightly. "There was a cliff," he said as he swallowed the bread, "and she went right off the edge of it."

The color drained out of Gin's face. "Did she...was she..."

"She was a wood elf like you," Taeben said, trying to stifle the grin that threatened to spread across his face. "How many times have you fallen out of the treehouse your kind calls home?" He chuckled, pleased that Gin mirrored his smile. "She was shouting something as she went down and after a few minutes I saw her head come levitating up over the edge."

"Mental note: Never close my eyes when you're leading me somewhere," Gin said giggling.

"You don't trust me?"

"Of course I do, Ben," she said, her face flushing. "I was just...I mean you get so focused...I just meant that..." Gin stilled a moment, and Taeben actually felt some pushback in her mind. He allowed it and she narrowed her eyes at him. "I just need to remember that when you have something on your mind I'm an afterthought, and am responsible for making sure I don't plunge over a cliff."

Taeben felt a sharp pain in his chest. He put the bowl and the loaf of bread down on the table and scooted closer to Gin, taking her food from her hands and placing it next to his own. "You," he said as he turned back to her, "are never an afterthought." He heard her sharp intake of breath and smiled at her, his eyes hooded. "Never." She leaned in toward him and he ran his lean fingers down the side of her face, enjoying the renewed flush in her cheeks and goosebumps on her skin at his touch. "I love you, Ginny, never forget that."

"Never," she whispered, her eyes closed as a smile tugged the corners of her mouth upward. The pushback in her mind dissolved and he once again filled her consciousness. Her eyes popped open and she looked up at him, ice blue turning dull as he recognized his own presence in her stare. "What can I do for you, Ben?" she asked. The pain shot through him again, lesser this time but still present, but he pushed it away.

"Continue to love me," he said softly as he brushed a stray lock of her hair back behind one of her delicately pointed ears as she nodded. "Continue to obey me, in all things." She nodded again, never taking her eyes off his. "You are a good girl, my Ginny."

Her eyes brightened and he felt the blow to his soul. This was not her…but it could be, given time. He withdrew from her mind and was ready to support her weight when she fell forward onto the table. Her eyes fluttered and then opened wide, and he could see no trace of himself there. Deciding that he couldn't leave anything to chance, Taeben pulled her to him, his fingers palming the back of her head as he kissed her. She returned his kiss for a moment, but he felt her body stiffen and quickly pulled away from her. "I'm…sorry…" she stammered as she put space between them. Taeben sighed and handed her back her bowl of stew.

"It's all right, Ginny," he replied. "I should be the one apologizing. I shouldn't have pushed you that far."

"It isn't that," she said as she fiddled with a loose string on her tunic. "I've just never, I mean I don't…I mean I haven't…" She paused, pulling her mouth into a tight line. "I haven't any experience with…"

Taeben nearly fainted from relief. The Qatu had not touched her, other than to leave that horrible scar on her cheek. "Oh, Ginny," he said in an uncharacteristic moment of emotion, "please don't worry for a moment about that. I wasn't trying to…take advantage of you." He watched her silently for a moment as she processed that thought, waiting for her to reply or react somehow, but she remained focused on her bowl of stew. "Ginny, I would never…not without your permission…you know that, right?" She nodded without looking up and he fought the urge to make her look at him.

They had remained at the edge of the forest, not far from Gin's treetop home of Aynamaede, as they prepared for the long journey to the Volcanic Mountains. Initially Gin was not interested at all in returning to the snowy landscape that covered the very top of Orana, but after the awful farewell with Lairky, she was more and more open to venturing that far north. Taeben hoped that this would be their last temporary journey, and the next one would lead them to the home he had secured for them. From there he would perfect the spell he had started researching for Lord Taanyth and then it was on to... "Ben, are you listening to me?" Gin was waving a hand in front of his face.

"Of course I am, sorry love, I thought that I'd heard something is all," he replied. "Do go on."

"I was asking you a question," she said, her forehead wrinkled in consternation. Taeben motioned for her to get on with it as he pushed into her mind and smoothed out the frustration therein. "I just wanted to ask if we could bring Lairky with us on our next journey."

It took every bit of willpower that Taeben possessed not to scream. "Lairky?" he managed, his voice halting and clearly angry. "Your sister, Lairky?" Gin shrank back from him but he did not soften his tone. "Is it not enough that I pay for her lodging and make sure she has the best tutors in her guild? Am I not doing enough for your precious baby sister, who, by the way, **hates** me, in case you'd forgotten, Gin..."

Again, he wanted to sweep into her mind, ignoring the safeguards and the risks, and make her understand what he was doing for her, who he would help her become, and how he would use her in his grand plans, but he resisted. If she realized and fought him, he might accidentally obliterate all that made her who she was. She would be his in every sense of the word, but she would not be Gin anymore. He glared down at her as tears broke over her eyelashes and traced paths down her face.

"You're right," she said, sniffling. "She would not come with you anyway, and never needs to know that it is you that keeps her safe, though I wish that we could tell her because it might change her mind. She is so young, Ben, and she never recovered from the loss of our parents." Taeben fought to keep his eyes from rolling.

"Of course." He studied her for a moment, and then wiped a tear from her cheek, making her smile softly at him. "Now, Ginny, we need to make a plan for our next trip to the Forest," he said, hoping to draw her away from the subject of her sister. She nodded and leaned toward him on one arm, making him smile. Every time she moved, the scent of sunflowers filled his nose and set him off balance. "I think our next trip north should be longer, because it seems that we just settle into a rhythm hunting and making camp and it is again time to go home."

"That's a fair point."

"I was hoping you'd feel that way," he said, smiling. "Perhaps we need to change where our...home is, and only visit the Forest now and then."

Gin's eyes narrowed. "What do you mean, Ben?"

"I mean that I have a place where we could live just along the southern coast of Qatu'anari," he replied, looking down into her eyes and pushing slightly into her mind just in case she resisted.

"Qatu'anari? Where...close to...Ben, that's where Sath and his kind are from," she said, and he was pleased to see the fear in her eyes that he had placed in her mind.

"Yes, I know, love, but where we will be living is on the coast, closer to the Volcanic Mountains, but far enough away that the dragonkind in the tower will not sense our presence. I don't think that either of us is ready for them, and I certainly do not wish to be close to them after my time in the tower with Salynth." He shuddered, hearing the sorceress's laugh in his mind as he did so often. He startled as Gin placed her hand on his and rubbed his wrist up under the sleeve of his robe. She had tried to heal the scars left just above his hands by Salynth's chains, but the wounds were too old.

"I'm so sorry that happened to you," she said softly.

"Bah," he replied, pulling his arm away, "it is what it is." He rubbed his hands together a moment and then looked back down at her. "So, will you come with me? We will not have to travel the entire way on foot. I have worked up a spell that will take us directly there from the Forest, but I do not have a way to take us back yet without going on foot." Gin chewed on her lip a moment and then looked up at him, her ice blue eyes dancing as a smile spread across her face. "So if we go, it will be to stay for a while before we return. Will you come with me?"

"Of course I will, my love," she said. Taeben held his breath a moment. He had withdrawn from her mind and yet she had agreed.

"Really?" he whispered, and then chided himself inwardly for sounding so weak. "Are you quite certain?"

"Of course I am," she replied. "Where else would I be but with you? I have no home in the trees any longer and Lairky is taken care of…the Fabled Ones will be fine on their own, as long as we can check in with them in the grand hall from time to time?"

Taeben frowned. He only hoped that she would be worth every complication that he had to burn to the ground to have her attention all his own. "Of course we can, love, of course. I think that we should visit them from time to time, just to maintain relations." He bowed and made a flourishing gesture with his hand, making Gin giggle. "As you wish, my fearless leader," he said, looking up at her and smiling before he stood back up. They might possibly need the strength of the Fabled Ones to overtake Qatu'anari, so why not let her keep up her relationships there? "Is there anything else?"

Gin smiled. "No, Ben, let's just get back to the Forest and set all of this in motion as soon as we can. I think I'm quite ready for a new adventure, and if it has to be on Qatu'anari then so be it, as long as I'm with you." She leaned toward him and snuggled up under his arm, sighing happily as he wrapped that arm around her and held her tightly.

"You will be my queen, Ginny," he murmured into her hair, "and I will be your king and we will rule Orana, you'll see." He moved around behind her and gathered her into his lap as they watched the flames in the hearth die one by one, replaced with smoldering embers. Taeben pushed her forward and began kneading the tight muscles in her back, smiling as she moaned happily. His lithe fingers moved slowly up to her neck and under her hair, wrapping nimbly around her neck. Her skin was so soft under his fingers and he fought the urge to tighten his grip and pull her head back into another kiss. Instead, he leaned his head down close to her ear. "You're mine," he whispered hoarsely.

"Yes." Her voice was husky.

"All mine. All of you," he said as his hand slid around onto her collarbone. She nodded and then he felt her body tense again as his fingers circled her neck, but he did not ease off. He pushed into her mind again but encountered resistance.

"Ben, what are you doing?" she asked, her voice barely a whisper. She tried to pull away from him, but he did not release her.

"Rubbing your back, love," he replied, whispering into her ear as he pulled her back close to him, his hands still resting on her collarbone and neck.

"That's not what I meant…are you…I mean, of course you aren't, how could you…" He tightened the hold on her, and her eyes popped open wide. "Ben, you're hurting me," she said, her voice hoarse as she fought for breath.

"All mine," he repeated, and again made a desperate push into her mind. This time the resistance gave way, and he went in as far as he could. "You will not do that again, Ginny, do you understand me?" She nodded, eyes wide and lips parted. "You cannot resist me because I do not wish to hurt you. I am the only one that can keep you safe." Gin nodded, still wide eyed. "Do you love me?"

"Of course, even if you didn't tell me I had to," she replied.

"What?"

"You asked me if I loved you…and I do and I have loved you since we were children," she said. "I remember every moment of that time." Her voice and tone were childlike and she seemed quite proud of her memory. Taeben's heart jumped in his chest.

"Of course you do," he said, turning her face toward his and covering her lips in a kiss. "I only wish you could tell me that on your own."

"I will, if you wish it, Ben," she said, her voice mechanical.

"I do, Ginny, I do," he replied. "Now, will you share my bedroll with me?" She stood like a puppet being pulled up by strings, and then climbed into his bedroll and then held an arm out to him. He slid in behind her and wound around her with his arms and legs, holding her to him as she sighed happily. "Sleep, Ginny," he commanded and soon her breathing fell into the rhythm of sleep.

Taeben withdrew from her mind and held her tightly, smiling as he fell asleep.

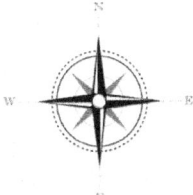

FOUR

After leaving the Outpost, Sath and Anni had taken their time on their journey home to Qatu'anari. They had hunted alongside their ancestors in the Grasslands, explored the tunnels that lead through the mountains toward the Volcanic Mountains, and had to hide out a few times when they took the wrong tunnel and almost stumbled into the Forest. Anni was playing the tune that she used to charm him less and less, and Sath was becoming quite smitten by the female at his side. She could match his speed running, she was a ferocious hunter, and she would often bound out ahead of him after prey, able to take care of herself in a fight just as he could. His memories of Gin were fading, though he would wonder from time to time if she was with the Fabled Ones and keeping safe.

By the time they had reached the Outlands, she had almost completely stopped playing the song at all. They were walking along, reminiscing about long lost Qatu friends, when Sath stopped in his tracks and sniffed the air. They had long since only spoken Qatunari with each other, and even though the name that sprang to his mind was human, he still called out in his language. *"Raedea... Raedea..."*

"*Who?*" Anni asked, relieved that he had not said Ginny. At the thought of the wood elf, Anni felt Taeben nudge the back of her mind.

What is wrong? His voice was sharp.

Nothing, she thought. *All is well, sir.*

Why is Gin in your mind, then? Has the Qatu remembered her?

Anni rubbed her temples. *No, sir,* she thought frantically. *He no longer mentions any of you.*

Good girl. Anni felt Taeben withdraw from her mind and the pain in her head eased. She looked back toward Sath and he had stumbled ahead a few feet and was kneeling before what looked like a mound of dirt. "Sath? Who is Raedea?"

"She is...she was an old friend," Sath said. "I did not keep a promise I made to her a long time ago...and then that wood elf stole my kill and dispatched Rae's good-for-nothing brother, Dorlagar." Anni stared at him in wonder. She knew that he had lived an entirely different life before he had helped her rescue his sister from the dragonkind sorceress, but she found herself a bit jealous of these other relationships with other females.

"Was she...dear to you?" Anni asked, fearing the answer.

"Yes, very dear...oh, you mean was she my mate?" Sath asked as a slight grin spread across his furry face. "No, no, nothing like that. Raedea was...like family to me, like a best friend, like..." He scratched his head a moment, his eyebrows furrowed. "Strange that I can't remember that name."

Anni hummed the charming tune low in her throat for a moment before she spoke. "Whose name?" she asked, readying herself for an onslaught of angry wizard in her mind if he said the wood elf's name.

"That dwarf," Sath said, and Anni nearly collapsed with relief.

"Teeand?" she asked carefully. "The one that knew our language?"

"Aye, that's the sod, Teeand," Sath replied, grinning. "Rae was like that to me, my best friend and my first non-Qatu friend." His smile lingered for a moment or two before fading. "Rae didn't deserve anything that she got, from being born as a twin to that horrible..." Sath rubbed his chin for a moment. "Well, her twin brother, whatever his name was, he was a piece of work and if I could have spared her the act of killing him I would have."

"Wait, I'm confused...Raedea killed her brother?"

"No, um...wood elf...the druid...um..." Anni felt the wizard gathering strength in the back of her mind like an oncoming tornado.

"*Elysiam?*" she offered, knowing the right answer was **Gin**, based on the reaction of the wizard.

"*Maybe.*" Sath rubbed his hand up over the top of his head. "*Not important,*" he said, placing an arm around Anni's shoulders and pulling her close to him. "Rae didn't deserve him and she didn't deserve to die as she did, at the hands of those humans from Calder's Port." After giving Anni a squeeze, he released her and walked toward the tiny gravesite, kneeling next to it. "Rae, I hope wherever you are you can forgive me," he whispered. "So much has happened, but I hope that you would be proud of my life now. I've worked so hard and I have a beautiful mate and one day, maybe, I will be able to live up to who you thought I could become."

Sing. The voice resounded in her mind, startling Anni because it had come without the usual feeling that he was watching and listening. She started to hum as she walked closer to Sath, placing a hand on his shoulder. Her song grew louder but was hidden within a purr, as she had learned to do when he started to notice.

"She didn't even know who I really was," Sath said as he looked up at Anni and covered her hand with his. "*I think she was starting to work it out, that I came from better than I was, but she didn't know who my father was, and yet still she was so certain that I could be a leader.*" He released her hand and looked back down at the ground. "*She was wrong.*"

"What?" Anni's song stopped abruptly but luckily she did not sense that the wizard had noticed. "*Of course she wasn't, Sath. When I called you by your title, I meant it. You have every bit the bearing and temperament of your father, coupled with the compassion of your mother. You would make an unparalleled leader for the Qatu.*"

"*Doesn't matter,*" Sath said as he drew her into his arms and looked down at her, teal eyes burning into her. "*I am Sathlir Clawsharp, no more and no less. I am no Rajah. I just…hope that is enough for you?*" Anni answered him with a loud purr as she rubbed her face against his. He ran his claws lightly down her back and she arched her body against his, their purrs each increasing in volume as they became replaced with low growls. "*We need to keep moving,*" Sath whispered in her ear, his breath making her fur stand on end. "*For now anyway.*" She nodded and he took her hand, and then after a long moment of silence he left Raedea's gravesite and kept moving, headed north toward the coast that would lead them home to Qatu.

By nightfall they had reached the point where the foothills of the Volcanic Mountains began to flatten out to coastland. Sath trudged onward but Anni was starting to stumble from fatigue. "*Sath, can we make camp?*" she said wearily as he tugged on her hand to keep her moving. "*How are you not tired?*"

Sath slowed his pace and finally stopped. He turned to face her and she frowned up at him, the scowl on his face so much like that of his father. "*Of course, but we need to be careful.*" He scanned the beach and then smiled, having located what he was looking for not far ahead of them. "*Look, Anni, see the fishing hut over there?*" She nodded, following his arm with her gaze. "*We can sleep there, I used to do that before with…*" He paused for a moment, frustration evident on his face as the memories would not come as bidden. "*Oh, it's been so long, must have been when I was hunting with the Fabled Ones.*" Anni released the breath she had been holding and they started moving toward the small grass hut.

Once inside, Sath propped all of their bags against the door after using his staff to secure the handle, and then turned to face Anni. "*Who am I to you?*" he asked.

"*What kind of a question is that?*"

"*Answer me!*" he roared. Anni immediately fell to her knees with her forehead pressed into the dirt floor of the hut. Sath sighed loudly. "*That's what I was afraid of,*" he said sadly. As she raised her head up to look at him, she saw him unrolling his bed on the other side of the hut, his shoulders sagging.

"*I'm sorry, I didn't know...what did you...*" Anni scrambled to her feet but kept a bit of space between herself and Sath. "*What is happening?*"

Sath paused but did not look at her. "*You didn't ask me to stop for the night until you were falling down with exhaustion. Why? Because you don't make requests like that of your Prince. You never stopped thinking of me as above you and I am most certainly not that, Anni.*" He sighed loudly. "*I don't want to be with someone who only wants me because of my family,*" he said sadly as he sat down on the bedroll. "*There is no hope that you will be First Wife, Anni, I need you to know that.*"

"*Are you saying that you want me...that you want to...are you talking about taking me as a mate, Sath?*" Anni asked breathlessly.

"*It had crossed my mind.*"

Before he could blink she was across the room and crawling into his lap. "*I don't care about being First Wife or any of that,*" she said as she rubbed her face on his and then showered kisses down his throat. Growling, Sath wrapped his arms around her and pulled her to him. "*I don't want the Rajah. I want you.*"

He pushed her back for a moment, looking at her with one eyebrow raised. "*Are you certain?*" he asked. Anni nodded, eyes shining with happiness. "*Then you shall have me,*" he said just before nipping at the back of her neck and drawing her down into his bedding. Anni's last thought before surrendering to Sath was of the wizard, pleased with her performance and smiling at her.

The next morning as they left the hut, Anni was positively vibrating. Sath was subdued, but he was not sure why. This was not his first time to be with a female. Nevertheless, something was eating at him and he couldn't put a finger on it. Maybe he was still not convinced that Anni was with him just for him. Who wouldn't jump at the chance to bed the Crown Prince of Qatu'anari if given the opportunity? They walked along the beach in silence until they reached the small dock where a few rowboats were tied up. He paid the gnome that was sitting on the edge, his tiny feet dangling as he stuffed Sath's money into his pocket.

"You're on your own to row," he said.

"Of course," Sath replied. "Many thanks." He helped Anni into the boat before boarding it himself, being careful to avoid any motion that might send him plunging into the water. As they rowed, he thought about his father and the life that had been taken from him. His mother had always cared for him but his father was distant. Why? Maybe being the *Rajah* just took too much time. *"Anni, do you have any brothers or sisters?"* he asked.

"No, that's why Kazhi and I are so close I suppose," she replied. *"Why do you ask?"*

"Just thinking about families...my family, specifically," he said. *"Beyond Kazhi, I have a half-sister that I don't know very well. Papa...the Rajah was always careful to keep us apart from her, but I don't really know why."*

Anni frowned. *"Sath, I think I know why."* Her stomach lurched in time with her oar sliding into the water and she winced. He slowed his pace and reached out to her, clearly worried. *"I'm fine, just a bit of a headache,"* she said, smiling at him. *"I think that the Rajah kept you separate from Maesha because he wanted her to be married to a high born and then she would be able to succeed him, in a way."* Sath frowned and, as he guessed she would, Anni fell silent.

"Go on, you seem to know more of my older sister than I do," he encouraged her as he resumed his rowing speed, happy that she was able to match it. He had been on a boat before with...well, someone...probably the dwarf who couldn't match Sath's rowing speed because his arms weren't as long. In fact, the dwarf's arms were even shorter than... *"Anni, what was the name of that wood elf druid?"*

Anni's face screwed up again. *"Elysiam,"* she said, and then as quickly as the expression had hijacked her features it was gone.

"Right."

"Why?"

"*I was just thinking about a trip on a boat in the past and a wood elf druid. It must have been Elys,*" he replied. "*So please, tell me about my older sister. I want to know, and my Papa...the Rajah never told me.*"

"*It must have hurt you a lot when he exiled you,*" she said, stopping her rowing for a moment to rub his arm sympathetically. When he did not respond, she resumed. "*Her Highness is not as kind as you and your Mama and Kazhi,*" Anni said, her voice low and conspiratorial. "*She was often left in charge of us in the nursery, do you remember?*"

"*Yes,*" Sath said, rolling his eyes and stifling a low growl.

"*I don't know if she knew Kazhi's true identity, but she was awfully mean to us females. She used to tell us time and time again that it was time for Qatu'anari to have a female ruler and that once she had married...*" Anni scratched her head, trying to remember. "*What was his name? OH! Hulan,*" she said, smiling sadly. "*Once she married him, then he would behigh born enough that your Papa would make him Rajah and then she would be able to rule through him. Poor Hulan.*"

Sath gripped the oar almost to the point of snapping it in half. Hulan was a childhood friend of his, and as far as Sath knew had only ever had eyes for his sister, Kazhmere. He would have a horrible life with Maesha. "*Go on, please,*" he said between gritted teeth.

"*That's really most of what I know. We thought for a while that the Rajah might be in danger from Maesha's plotting, but to be honest, after the way he treated you and Kazhi...*" Anni bit her lip. "*I would never dream of speaking against the Rajah or anything, Sath, please believe me, but if something were to happen to him I don't think I would shed a tear.*" He glanced over at her to see her face screwed up again.

"*Are you all right, Anni?*"

"*Bit seasick is all,*" she said, rowing with only one hand as the other massaged her temple. "*No worries, Sath...I'm sorry to have said that about your Papa. It wasn't fair of me.*"

Sath growled. "*Stop calling him that. I have no Papa,*" he said as he again nearly reduced the oar to splinters. Soon enough, they were on the beach, and as they tied up the boat to the dock run by another gnome, Sath looked around, his teal eyes filling with unexpected tears.

"*How long since you've been back home?*" Anni asked as she watched him intently.

"*Too long.*" His voice choked and Sath fell to his knees in the wet sand, which he scooped up and pressed to his face. There it was: the smell of home, of palm trees, salt and ocean air. The tide skated up behind him and lapped at his feet and he sprang up and away from it. "*I hate water,*" he exclaimed. Anni stifled a laugh. "*What?*"

"*Oh, the almighty Crown Prince of Qatu'anari, His Highness Sathlir Clawsharp, is undone by a wave,*" Anni said, giggling.

"*Undone? Undone am I?*" he said, laughing as he got to his feet. Sath sprinted toward her, throwing her up onto his shoulder without changing his speed and thundering down the beach. Anni laughed wildly and clung to him, digging her claws into his back as she bounced up and down on his shoulder. He reached a patch of mossy grass under a tree and tossed her onto it, inwardly pleased that he hadn't hurt her. He didn't have to be as careful with her because she was like him. She understood him. Sath flopped down onto the moss next to her and rolled up onto one elbow as he smoothed the fur on her face. Anni purred into his hand, and he could almost make out a tune behind the soothing sound. "*I love it when you purr like that,*" he said, feeling delighted as her face lit up. "*It's like music, your purr.*"

"*You bring it out of me,*" she said, before she took his face in her hands and drew him down into a kiss.

Where are you? Why do I sense that you are on Qatu'anari?

Sath has brought us here, Sir, I thought that's what you wanted? I thought here he would be far away, like you wanted?

No, you idiot, I am coming there with Ginny, I have to meet with that horrible hag of a Princess Royal. You were to keep Sath far away from us.

I am sorry, Sir. I will keep him here on the coast, but it was his idea to come here. I thought you would stay with your Gin near the Forest. I am sorry, Sir.

Anni's knees buckled under the pain that coursed through her entire body. She had sensed the wizard's power before but had never felt anything like this. Sath had been visually scouting the beach for an empty building that they could stay in temporarily, but at her gasp he turned to her and was immediately at her side.

"Anni, are you all right?" he asked as he helped her back to her feet.

"Of course I am," she replied as she shook off the wizard's presence. "Just tired." Sath looked at her worriedly. "Sath! I'm fine." He grinned in response. "What?"

"I think that might be the first time you've called me Sath without first hesitating and almost calling me Highness or Majesty," he replied, beaming a toothy grin at her that made her giggle. "I like that laugh." He wrapped an arm around her and pulled her to him, making her gasp. "I like that sound too." He nuzzled her shoulder and Anni felt as though she might explode as he pulled her even closer.

That's right, keep him occupied. You are doing really well, Anni.
With respect, Sir, GO AWAY.

Anni felt the wizard chuckling as he withdrew, and for the first time she did not sense him at all. Usually he would fall silent, but she would still be able to feel him lurking in the dark corners of her mind, always listening and ready to correct her when she made a mistake. She hoped that he had found his own happiness with that Ginny wood elf and that maybe he would leave her alone with Sath.

Nancy E. Dunne

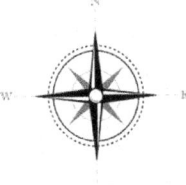

FIVE

Taeben rubbed his forehead and temples. The closer that Qatu female was, the easier his communication with her was, so being on the opposite edge of the Great Forest while she was apparently on Qatu'anari was stretching his abilities to the breaking point. He blamed himself for her deciding to go there with the Prince. He had been thinking about how it would be a safe place to take Gin while Sath wasn't there, and apparently some of that had bled over into the female's mind. No matter. She would not risk letting that filthy cat see Gin anyway. Never again.

Now that he had a plan, he had decided that they would take one short trip to Alynatalos before making their way to Qatu'anari. After collecting the things he needed from his family's home, Taeben hurried through the streets of the citadel, heading for the main gates that would lead to the lush green of the Great Forest. Normally he was hesitant to leave, taking long moments to memorize his home before departing again, because he never really knew for certain that he would return. This time, though, it didn't matter. Return or not, he did not care. He was going toward Gin and she was his home now. In fact, he was paying so little attention that he nearly ran over a messenger that was approaching him, hand outstretched, holding a parchment roll.

"Taeben?"

"What?" he barked in response.

"Message for you, sir," the male figure replied. Taeben snatched the scroll and the messenger scurried away. Taeben unrolled the parchment and began reading.

Taeben,

You will make your way to the palace at once. The time grows nigh for us to put our plan in motion. The Rajah is close to figuring me out, and I will not have him discover our plan until it is set in motion. I will expect you in two days' time at the tavern just to the north of the palace in Qatu'anari.

Maesha

Taeben swore under his breath as he crumpled up the scroll before stuffing it into his pack. "Stupid, filthy cat," he spat as he increased his speed heading for the city gates. "Her petty intrigues will not interfere with my plan, she has her place and needs to stay to it!" He stormed past the messenger and did not slow his pace until he was out of the city gate.

"Ben?"

"WHAT?" he bellowed, turning on his heel to glare at… Gin. When they arrived at Alynatalos, he had pushed into her mind and told her to wait for him; so she had been sitting outside the gate waiting and he had blown right past without even seeing her. "Ginny. Gods above, I am so sorry." She was frozen to the spot, icy blue eyes wide as she stared at him. He extended a hand to her and she took it hesitantly as she rose from her seated position on the ground.

"You told me to…"

"Yes, yes, love, I'm sorry," he said, slight annoyance in his voice. "It's just been a rough day. Did you get to see your sister?" Before he released her hand, Taeben drew her fingers to his lips and placed a kiss on her knuckles, smiling as she blushed.

"Aye, she seems to be in a bit of a strop but I don't know why," Gin replied. "But I am packed and this time I have packed an extra cloak in case we end up somewhere cold," she said, grinning and patting her rucksack as she swung it up on to her shoulder. Taeben smiled at her and gestured for her to go ahead of him.

They began walking away from the Alynatalos on the path that led north, out of the Forest and toward the tunnels leading to the mountains. It would be a day's journey, with an overnight just on the other side of the tunnels. Taeben had a journal that he kept with him at all times to record the locations of pubs and taverns and inns so that he could avoid sleeping rough if at all possible. "How far can you go before we retire for the night, love?" he said, thumbing through his journal as they walked. "I have made note of two taverns prior to the tunnels and a third just the other side, so it all depends upon…" He stopped talking as he heard Gin start to laugh. "What is so funny?"

"Taverns? Inns? Oh come on, Ben, don't be so much of a high elf!" she said in between giggles. "We are on an adventure, yes? What better bed is there than the open ground, next to a campfire, with the stars above to count until you fall asleep?"

"There are lots of better options," he said, scowling. "Ginny, forgive me, but you are not running wild with the Fabled Ones anymore. We gave your way a try, but now you and I are civilized, and we will find lodging like civilized people."

Gin stopped walking and doubled over, laughing. "I'm sorry," she said as she wiped tears from her cheeks. "Civilized?" Another giggle fit overtook her, and through his annoyance Taeben found that he so enjoyed the sound of her laughter that his mouth was starting to move upwards at the corners to form a grin. Gin looked up at him and then bent over into a comically exaggerated bow. "Your Majesty!" she said, giggling.

"Ah, now you're talking," he said as he grabbed up one of her hands and pulled her upwards, again bringing her knuckles to his lips. "My Queen," he said, his eyes hooded as he looked down at her. His breath on the back of her hand as he spoke had caused goose bumps to rise. Taeben was finding that he so loved the flush that entered her oaken-tinged skin that he held her hand fast for a moment before releasing it. "Now, as I said…"

"Seriously," Gin said, rubbing the back of her hand with her other fingers, "Ben, we need to conserve our money. Sleeping rough is amazing, you'll see. I have magic to hold off the clouds and the rain, and it will be glorious." Taeben scowled. "Please?" He looked down at her and then immediately away. The sparkle in her eyes threatened to undo him.

"Fine, if you want to be Queen of the Dirt, who am I to stop you?" he scoffed as he continued walking and stuffed the journal back into his bag. She would be the First Wife of Qatu'anari soon enough, sitting at his feet as he took the throne as *Rajah*. He kept his eyes on the ground just in front of his feet as he walked. Gin scurried along behind him, almost reaching up a few times to take his elbow but seemingly not quite fast nor tall enough.

"Ben, you are walking too fast," she said. He ignored her and kept up his pace, only slowing to try to listen when he heard her mumbling behind him. He felt the familiar rush of a spell being cast, and suddenly she was not only keeping pace with him, she was a bit ahead of him and hovering just above the ground. He chuckled.

"Now who's showing off?" he asked as he closed the gap between them and fell in alongside her. "I like this trick," he said, "because now you are at my eye level. I don't have to worry about tripping over you, oh Tiny Highness." Gin laughed, but suddenly her face became a mask of concentration. "What is it?"

"Sssh," she said, holding up a finger. Ben knew that the wood elves had amazing tracking abilities; an innate ability born out of their need to protect themselves after their kind left the Alynatalos for the trees of Aynamaede. It was just one of the many reasons he needed Gin with him. "To the south," she said, cocking her head in that direction for a moment and closing her eyes to concentrate. "Moving fast." Gin's brow furrowed. "Two, I think." Taeben tried not to smile proudly.

"Following us?" he whispered.

"Not certain," she replied. "But we can ask them ourselves soon, they will be upon us momentarily." Taeben's entire body tensed, but Gin laid a tiny hand on his arm and he relaxed a bit. Strange how she had that effect on him, being no sort of real protection for him whatsoever. "Let me make us harder to find," she whispered, and then he heard her speaking ancient words in their shared language that would cover them in a magical cloak of camouflage.

"Still coming?" Taeben asked, frustrated, after a long few minutes of silence from Gin.

"Sssh!" she said, placing a hand on his chest while still looking southward. Taeben frowned but kept quiet. There would be time later to remind her about appropriate ways to speak to him. He watched her expression change and was surprised to see a smile break across her face.

"What is it?" he whispered. His eyes widened as Gin threw off the magical cloak that dissipated to the winds as it hit the ground and turned to face southward. He did not remove his cover just yet.

"It's fine, Ben, we know them. It's Elys and Hack, I'm almost certain," she said. Taeben looked at her incredulously and then down the road in the direction she was facing. The figures moving toward them did seem to be that of a wood elf and a gnome, but he was just not certain that she was right. As they drew close, he reached out to Gin and pulled her close, a hand over her mouth, and turned his back to the road. She struggled against him but with his back to the road she could not be seen. Thankful that he was larger than she and strong enough to hold her still, he waited many long minutes until he could look over his shoulder to the north and see the figures disappearing off into the distance, none the wiser to their position on the side of the road.

Gin stopped struggling and Taeben released her, fearing that he had been cutting off her breathing in the way he was holding her. "What was THAT, Ben?" she demanded, spinning around to face him, hands on her hips. "I told you it was safe!" He stepped closer to her, taking her shoulders in his strong hands and pushing into her mind. "OH stop that," she said, catching him off guard. He released her shoulders and stared at her.

"What do you mean, love, stop what?" he asked.

"You know exactly what I mean. You look at me with those beautiful eyes of yours and I forget why I'm angry at you," she replied. Taeben nearly laughed aloud in relief.

"I'm sorry, love, I just wasn't willing to take any chances that it wasn't actually your friends that were approaching us," he said, forcing himself not to sound as gleeful as he felt. "I know your tracking abilities are beyond reproach but I could not have protected you if it had been something more nefarious." Gin still scowled at him, but he could feel her anger fading. "We should find a place to make camp soon, I guess, if you're still dead set on sleeping rough tonight."

"Well…" Gin chewed on her fingernail for a moment. "I suppose we could make it to that inn just outside of the tunnels. I hadn't realized how unsettling it can be for someone that isn't used to it." She tugged her rucksack back up onto her shoulders and continued down the path ahead of him. "I would have thought that all the time you ran with the Fabled Ones would have made a difference but I suppose you are who you are," she said, chuckling.

"And just who am I then?" Taeben asked as he followed along behind her, grinning.

"The King of All He Surveys!" she said, sarcasm dripping from her voice. "And it looks like he should be surveying an inn very soon." Taeben laughed and closed the gap between them, taking her hand in his and enjoying the flush that rose up the back of her neck. They followed the path for many hours, occasionally stopping for a snack or some water, and finally the encampment just outside of the tunnel came into view.

"Wait, Ben," Gin said, squeezing his hand. He looked over his shoulder at her, puzzled. She released his hand and pulled her traveling cloak out of her rucksack and then put it on, being careful to pull the hood up until it obscured her features.

"What are you doing?" Taeben asked, knocking the hood back so that he could see her worried face.

"Ben, you've not been around my kind for a long time," she hissed. "After I stopped running with Naevys and returned home, I was not exactly welcomed back."

"Yes, I know."

"Well, when one of our kind is exiled, the news is sent to the four corners of our world. See that leaf on the corner of the sign there?" She pointed at the sign that hung over the door to the inn. Taeben followed her arm up to the corner of the sign, noticed the small green leaf in the corner and nodded. "That means it is a friendly place for my kind. Those were placed there after the Forest War when our dark elf cousins learned how to conceal themselves by wearing illusions that made them appear as wood elves; true wood elves knew this is a haven for our kind."

"Yes, I took history from my tutors," Taeben snapped. "Look, if this is dangerous for you, we can just keep moving, Gin." His patience was becoming very thin.

"Or we could have just camped somewhere within the tunnels, but here we are," she snapped back. Her bravado was wearing on his nerves. "Now, if you would go on inside and get us a room, I will duck in the back and meet you upstairs." She pulled her hood back up and then put her hands on her hips as he stood still, grinning down at her. "What?"

"Just one room?"

"Oh, stop being such a teenager and just go!" she exclaimed, shoving him ahead of her as she dashed around the back of the inn. Still grinning, Taeben walked through the front door and strode over to the bar.

"Can I help you, love?" said the barmaid that was wiping off the counter in front of him. "Food, ale, or a room for the night?"

Taeben flashed a winning smile her way and she looked close to fainting. "All of the above, my lady," he said, pushing his way right into her mind. He shuddered at what he found, and what she was willing to do for just a bit of coin. His plan had been to obtain their food and lodging for free, but he found himself unable. He withdrew from her mind and dropped a bag of coins on the bar. "Enough for two, plus traveling provisions waiting for me tomorrow morning. And a room, back in a corner if possible?"

"Yes…of course…" The girl gaped at the bag a moment and then snatched it up and put it into one of the many pockets in her apron. "Thank you sir, thank you so much." She nearly threw the key to the room at him as she fumbled about, flustered. "I can bring the meal up to you, sir, if you like?"

"Certainly," he said, winking at her and enjoying the fact that she seemed to go weak-kneed in response. "Room four is it then?" He held up the key and looked at the crude fob attached to it with the number four burned into the wood on one side. The girl nodded and he bowed his head in response before crossing the room to the stairs. As he stepped onto the first one, he sensed eyes on him and he looked up toward the top of the stairs. Gin was waiting, hood still up but ice blue eyes twinkling at him from the darkness. Taeben quickened his pace, taking the steps two at a time until he was right in front of her.

"I think you have an admirer," she whispered.

"Jealous are you?" he replied, grinning at her. "Were you eavesdropping?"

"Irrelevant," she said as she turned on her heel and headed down the hall. Taeben chuckled as he followed her. He handed her the key and she unlocked the door, charging into the room and dropping her rucksack on the floor. As he locked the door and looked back over at her, he saw that she was unrolling her bedding.

"What are you doing?"

"Making up my bed, it won't take me long to eat and I'm exhausted, Ben, aren't you?" She smoothed out the bedroll and then sat down on it to take off the mail tunic she wore when traveling. "Is your new friend bringing up our food?"

Taeben walked around to the window in the room, behind where Gin was sitting, and looked out onto the street for the moment before answering her. "Yes, she is," he replied. "What's wrong, Ginny?" he asked, closing the gap between them and kneeling down in front of her so that they were at eye level.

"Nothing, why would anything be wrong?" she responded without looking up at him. Taeben resisted the urge to force her to look at him.

"Then what are you doing?"

"There is only one bed in this room, Ben, don't be ridiculous. You know what I'm doing." She stacked her armor, and then placed the dagger she had removed from her boot under the pillow she had made with her cloak. "Now, where's your girl with our food?"

"You're jealous."

"Don't be stupid."

Last straw. Ben took her chin in his hand and forced her gaze upward to meet his. "You may call me any number of things but I am not stupid, Ginny," he snapped. Locking his gaze on hers, he forced his way into her mind before she had time to put up the barriers that he had encountered recently. Her eyes glazed over and became vacant as she smiled up at him.

"Of course you aren't, Ben," she said. He gripped her chin harder and she made no response to the pain it had to be causing her. "Would you like me to go see why the girl hasn't brought our food yet?"

"No. Stay here on your bedroll and do not move an inch until I return," he growled. Gin nodded and settled, cross-legged with her hands resting on her knees, on the bedroll. Taeben stood but kept an eye on her for a moment. "Do not forget to breathe, my love," he said, noticing that her chest was very still and her face was beginning to turn a bit pink. She took a deep breath and then smiled again.

"Thank you, Ben," she said, her voice hollow. "Though I have magic that allows me to breathe underwater, I don't know that it would have worked in here." Taeben sighed loudly and turned on his heel but did not release his hold on her mind. This sort of thing was a good reminder for him about the dangers of going too far. Not breathing without his permission? He left the room, closing the door behind him with a bang, and nearly ran into the girl bringing a steaming tray of food.

"I am so sorry, sir!" she exclaimed as she skillfully righted the tray without spilling a drop of stew or ale. The only casualty was one bread roll that fell to the floor and rolled right up to Taeben's boot. He bent and picked it up, then opened the door to their room and filled the space, extending a hand to the barmaid.

"I will trade you, my dear," he said, and she handed over the tray of food in exchange for the roll. With a curtsy, she scampered back down the hall but not before Taeben saw her tuck the roll into one of her pockets. Hungry as well. He shook his head as he entered the room, shutting the door with his boot before placing the tray on the floor in front of Gin. "There is no table here," he said, "so we must eat on the floor."

"I will be careful with my food, Ben, I promise," Gin said. The sing-song quality of her voice was starting to grate and he contemplated withdrawing from her mind, but thought that he should make sure he knew what was going on therein first.

"I know you will, Ginny, you're a good girl," he said. "I have a question for you before we eat." She looked up at him, face full of adoration. Taeben swallowed hard before he continued. "You were upset with me when we first arrived here, what has made you angry?"

Gin's face fell. "I would never be angry with you, Ben."

"Don't lie to me, Ginny, that will make ME angry."

"I was jealous before, not angry. I want you to notice me like you did the barmaid but you never do. But I do not want to disappoint you either." She hung her head. "The truth is that I am an outcast and a wood elf, and the barmaid is human and beautiful, and I cannot compete with that."

"Ginny…" Taeben fought back a smile. She loved him when she was not being controlled. She **was** jealous before. "Eat your stew," he said, and then just before she picked up the bowl he withdrew quickly from her mind. Her head slumped forward a moment, and then she lifted it and looked around, slightly panicked.

"Dear spirits, did I doze off? I didn't even know the food was here," she said, her voice barely a whisper.

"Aye, you did, love," Ben said. "But now you are awake and can enjoy this stew." He frowned as she picked up the bread roll and nibbled on it, staring at the stew. "What's wrong?"

"Nothing." Gin picked up a spoon and plunged it into the bowl, taking only vegetables and leaving the huge, steaming hunks of meat. Taeben could have slapped himself. She didn't eat meat, none of the druids did if there was anything else to be had. He watched her over his own bowl as she carefully picked around the meat and occasionally tore off a corner of the bread to dunk it into the bowl.

"Take the bread, Ginny," he said, smiling at her. "I don't need any of it because I can eat the meat in the stew." She smiled up at him as she tore off a larger piece and chewed on it thoughtfully. "We need to talk about the next stage of our journey."

"Yes, Ben...are you sure it will be safe there?"

"Aye. Don't you trust me?"

"Of course I do," she snapped. "It's the Qatu I don't trust."

"They can't get to you as long as you're with me," he said, trying to soothe her without taking control. "I have a place ready for us. It's an embassy of sorts, where the dignitaries that come to visit the Qatu are housed."

"But won't the ambassador need it?" Gin asked, frowning.

"Hmm, let me see, will I need it?" Ben said, grinning. "Yep, I will, I will need it so we will be fine."

"You are the ambassador from the Citadel?" Gin asked, her eyebrows raised with surprise. Ben nodded. "Is that why we had to go back to the Forest, and why that messenger was looking for you?"

"Messenger?" Ben's eyes narrowed.

"Aye, he asked after you as he entered the Citadel and I overheard him because I was waiting by the front gate," she replied. "Oh, Ben, I'm so proud of you!" His frown softened as he could feel the sincerity of her words.

"Thank you," he said. "But Ginny, what that means is that I have to go to the Qatu Palace...alone." Her eyes widened. "Do not worry, you will be in the embassy on your own and you will be very safe there. I have magical protections I can put in place so that no one can enter without my permission."

"No need for that," she replied. "I will be fine on my own. I trust that you wouldn't leave me anywhere dangerous, Ben." She finished the rest of her meal in silence and placed her dishes next to his on the tray, which he set just outside the door before shutting and locking it. "Good night," she said as she crawled into her bedroll.

"Ginny, don't be silly, come up here with me," Ben said, patting the bed as he sat down on it. "I promise I will behave myself." She looked at him, eyes narrowed, but then sighed and crawled back out of her bedroll. Slowly she crossed the room and climbed into the bed, maintaining a wide chasm between them. As he watched, she snuggled down into the bedding and soon relaxed, her breathing slowing to the rhythm of sleep.

Ben smiled. He longed to reach out and smooth the hair back off her face or run a finger down her cheek. His arms ached to pull her close to him, to feel her tiny body snuggle up next to his. He could have her closer if he wanted. He could have HER if he wanted. However, tonight, the fact that she had come to him on her own was enough.

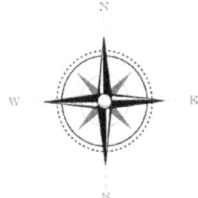

SIX

Anni stepped into the building that Sath had indicated and turned up her nose. Life with the Crown Prince of Qatu'anari…in a place like this? Clearly this had not been occupied by an ambassador in a long time from the look of it. There was a great room which was where she stood, and opposite the front door was another door that only closed with a curtain. Anni crossed the room, taking care to avoid the piles of garbage and broken furniture, and pulled back the curtain slowly. More of the same destruction greeted her. A dark hallway led to another door at the very end, but there was an archway about halfway down that had no door. Anni carefully made her way to the archway, and upon turning left found a kitchen.

It was crude and small but this was something she was hoping to find. Anni was a very good cook, having been trained in the palace kitchens when she was a cub. She was sought after for adventuring groups because of her ability to turn whatever could be caught into a delicious meal. There was a fireplace in one corner with a spit that almost disappeared up into the chimney; and lots of rusty cast iron pots and pans lying around. This could be fixed. She carefully crossed the room, righting overturned chairs and pushing them under the small table directly across from the fire as she imagined long nights during the cold season, sitting at the table with Sath and discussing...anything and everything. Anni wrapped her arms around her midsection and hugged herself.

"Cold?" Sath said from the doorway, startling her.

"*How long have you been there?*" she asked, turning to smile at him as she hummed and purred.

"*Long enough,*" he said, his eyes twinkling. "*What do you think? Can we make a life here? Raise a family?*"

Anni stopped in her tracks and stared at him. "Raise...a family?"

"Well of course," Sath said as he closed the gap between them and took her in his arms. "*You want little ones, don't you?*"

"*With me? You want a family with me?*" she stammered, unable to keep up the purring and humming as she spoke.

"*Of course I do, don't be daft,*" he said as he rubbed the side of his face against hers. "*Anni,*" he said as he held her at arm's length a moment, "*don't you want young?*"

The voice in her mind was curiously absent, so she did not know what the right answer was this time. She had never wanted cubs, having not enjoyed the time that she was left in charge of the younger cubs in the royal nursery. She had only just found Sath and their life together hadn't even started, and already he was asking her to share him with a cub...or, even worse, several. Anni furrowed her brow.

"I guess I hadn't thought about it before."

"Well," Sath said, wiggling his eyebrows at her, "*I'm thinking about it.*" He pulled her close again, running his nails up and down her back which caused her to arch her body into his.

"Here?" she gasped. "Now? Sath, this place needs to be fixed up before we...before..." Sath nibbled on the edges of her ear and she completely lost her train of thought. "*I suppose...if we are quick...*" His growl in her ear told her he agreed.

Taeben sat straight up in the bed, and then held his breath as he made sure that he had not awakened Gin. Her breathing was still the easy rhythm of sleep, and he sighed in relief. What was that stupid Qatu up to now? In his dreams, he would project into her mind as he found it easiest to take total control when she was also asleep.

Anni!

Sir? Now is…not a good…

What are you playing at? Why are there thoughts of cubs in your mind?

It is what Sath wants, Sir.

Is it what you want? Answer me, and do not lie because I will know if you are lying.

No, Sir, I do not.

Taeben felt a wave of emotion from her that made him a bit dizzy. Anger, sadness, jealousy…and fear, of him and fear of losing Sath. He clenched his fists to clear his mind. This was not part of the plan.

Can you change his mind? I thought that you were more advanced in your charming skills than this. Did I make a mistake?

NO! No Sir, you did not. I can take care of this.

No cubs, Anni, do you understand me? That is NOT part of the plan. I don't care what you have to do, but make sure that does not happen.

Yes, Sir.

Taeben scowled. There did not need to be **another** potential heir to the throne, and if they were planning a family then she clearly did not understand her mission. When he had approached her all that time ago in the grand hall, he had not shared his entire plan with her but had made sure she understood that she was to keep Sath Clawsharp out of the way until Taeben could kill him. That was how this was supposed to end, not with a cub and a happy family snug in front of a fire…or worse, in front of the Qatu Assembly as the cub is presented as the heir to the throne of Qatu'anari.

He rose from the bed and stalked about the room for a few minutes. How could Gin sleep so deeply? Finally, he pulled on his robes and left the room in the hopes of finding a pot of tea downstairs that would calm his nerves. This was why he never trusted others, not even Gin, to get things done. If you want something done, do it yourself. He crept down the stairs, trying to avoid the creaking, and soon found himself at the bar.

"Can't sleep?" a female voice said from behind him.

"No," he said, turning to find the barmaid seated by the fire on the other side of the tavern.

"Cold? Come join me if you like, this fire's nice and toasty." Taeben wandered over in her direction after a quick check on Gin upstairs. Still soundly asleep and dreaming of him, interestingly enough. He grinned.

"Thank you...um...I'm sorry, I don't believe I know your name," he said as he settled into a chair by the fire.

"Keiley," she said, holding out her hand. "And you are?"

"Taeben. Pleased to meet you, Keiley," he said as he took her hand and raised it to his lips. She did not break eye contact with him as his lips brushed the backs of her knuckles. He found that he liked that; Gin always looked away, blushed, or pulled her hand back. "I don't suppose there is a kettle in which I could make some tea about, is there?"

"Stay here," she replied, smiling through hooded eyes as she pulled her hand back from his and rose from her seat. "I can bring us both a cup of tea." She swished away toward the kitchen and Taeben watched her go, thinking of how long it had been since he had been with a female of any race. He had never been with a human, that sort of thing was normally utterly beneath him. But Keiley's chestnut hair, pulled into a tight braid at the back of her head, might be easily wrapped around her neck and her vibrant green eyes could plead for him to...

Taeben shook his head. What was happening to him? Never in his life had he touched a woman in that way that did not deserve it. His time with that hag from the tower had clearly awakened something in him that he wasn't sure he liked. He stood up and walked into the kitchen where Keiley was bent over the fire, attaching the kettle to the bar on the spit so that it would boil water for their tea. He moved quickly over to her and wrapped his long arms around her, pulling her to him as he covered her mouth with one slender hand. Instead of fighting him as he had expected, she pressed herself against him and his mind was flooded with images of times that she had been in just this situation before with different males…and some females. Taeben released her and pushed her away from him, smoothing the front of his robes in an effort to remove all of the past moments from him as though they were actually clinging to his clothing.

"What's wrong?" Keiley asked as she sidled up to him like a snake winding around the trunk of a tree. "Do you not like me?" As soon as she touched him, the bond with her mind came sharply back into focus and Taeben again pushed her away.

"You don't have to do that for my benefit," he said. "Don't pretend just so that I will give you more food or money. It makes you a liar when you do that and I don't like liars."

"Do what?" Again she advanced and this time he stood his ground, easily looking her in the eye. Human women were taller than he had remembered.

"My dear, I know what you think I want from you and what you will get in return and…I do not intend for any of that to happen." Her face fell and she stepped back to the kettle, stoking the fire with a poker that she picked up from the side of the fireplace. The images of what would happen to her at home threatened to break his heart, a feeling to which he was utterly unaccustomed. She was just as lonely as he was.

"You are lovely, but…you do not have to make advances on me," he said softly, taking the poker from her hand and replacing it before taking both of her shoulders and turning her to face him. "So lovely. How is it that you are here? How do you find yourself in this situation?"

"What do you mean?"

"Here in this tavern, tending the bar and tending to… the male patrons?" he asked. She frowned at him. "I'm sorry," he said as she turned back to the fire. "That's not what I meant, but you did just…I mean we…"

"Where else would I be?" she asked. "Papa only sent the boys to school. I'm not pretty enough for a husband and I can't cook or clean well enough for that either, but I can pull a pint with the best of them and...I keep customers coming back for more." Taeben looked into her mind once more and found not much there to contradict what she had said. She truly believed her words. He met her gaze and wondered how he had not noticed the hollowness in her eyes. It was like Gin when he...

Gin. He could not find her with his mind. Taeben sprang to his feet. "I thank you for your trouble, my lovely," he stammered, "but I must really try to get some sleep. Pushing off early in the morning." Keiley tried to block his path but he easily pushed her aside. As he left the kitchen, he dropped a small bag of coins on the table by the door. "Get out of here," he said, glancing over his shoulder. "Make something of yourself." He dashed through the dining room and up the stairs, not caring how much they creaked under his weight.

Flinging open the door, Taeben entered the room to find Gin still curled up as he had left her. Her consciousness came back into focus in his mind as he watched her sleep. She was dreaming again, but this time it was not of him and he had to put a stop to it.

After softly closing and bolting the door, he entered her mind but did not take control right away, instead settling onto the bed in a seated position to observe where her mind was taking her under the guise of sleep. He saw her walking through the tunnels that they would be entering later that same day, trying to find her own way and relying on her memory rather than her book of maps. Taeben was proud of her. She continued past a turn she should have made and it was then that he, because he had a different vantage point, saw the Qatu Sath lying in wait for her.

He bit his fist, trying not to cry out to her to wait. This must be when she got that horrible scar on her face! He was seeing through her eyes now and she had no idea that the giant feline was there. He sensed confusion from her that brought him back from his repressed anger and then allowed him to see through her eyes source of the confusion. A rucksack, hers, from the recognition he felt in her mind, stolen from her, now lay in the middle of the path. He knew that just beyond that rucksack waited that filthy cat, but he found that without taking control he could do nothing to warn the dream-Gin before she got too close.

Taeben watched in horror as she crept toward the rucksack and snatched it from its spot on the ground before turning and running back the way she had come, this time making the turn that would take her closer to her home in the Great Forest. She stopped and leaned against a wall, finally giving into sobs as she sank down to sit on the roots that made up the tunnel's floor. Had she changed the memory? Had he not attacked her? Had she lied to him?

Taeben felt the control he was holding on his anger toward the Qatu weakening. He took control of her mind and stepped out of the shadows into her dream. "Ginny, what happened?" he asked, and dream-Gin nearly came out of her skin.

"Ben! What are you doing here?" she exclaimed, tears still streaming down her face. He held open his arms and as he had expected, she ran into them, clinging to him as though to avoid falling into an abyss.

"Now, now," he said, smoothing her hair with one hand as the other one held her tightly against him. "What's happened to you, Ginny?" he asked softly. She looked up at him and he saw the fresh wound on her face, still new but already starting to heal, so magic could not remove it. "Who did that to you?"

His question launched a new round of choking sobs and he fell silent, holding her until she managed to compose herself. "It was…him, the Bane of the Forest, Ben! He was here, here in this tunnel and he took my things and…" her hand moved to her face and then to the piece of leather that held her hair in a ponytail and pulled it free. Her hair covered the wound. "He took my bag," she said, speaking slowly, "and I've just found it here in the tunnel, everything save the food is still…" She pushed away from Ben and rummaged about in the bag. "Almost everything is here," she said.

"What is missing, love?" he asked. She looked up at him curiously and then smiled shyly at him. Taeben cursed himself inwardly. This was a younger version of his Ginny, no wonder she reacted that way to the pet name.

"Nothing important," she replied. She was lying to him. It must be because she was still in a dream state. Taeben hadn't thought her capable of lying to him after the last time he entered her mind. "Where are you headed?"

Taeben gritted his teeth. "I will tell you, love, but you have to wake up first." He withdrew from her mind sharply, as he had done to Kazhmere the first time in that awful tower, but not before he reinforced the fear that he had placed in her mind as far as the Qatu were concerned. Gin's body convulsed on the bed and then stilled, as her eyelids fluttered. As she came awake she sprang into a seated position on the bed and scooted back into the pillows, breathing heavily. Taeben scurried across the bed toward her. "Ginny, what's wrong? Were you having a bad dream?"

"I...am not sure," she said haltingly as she rubbed her eyes with balled fists. "Probably, I can't remember." She looked down at herself in only her tunic and the rumpled bed sheets and then looked up at him, questioning.

"I was a perfect gentleman, I'll have you know," he said, smirking. She smiled shyly up at him, just as dream-Gin had moments ago. Taeben reached out and tucked a lock of hair behind her ear, enjoying the flush on her face that followed his hand. He kissed her on the forehead and then stood up from the bed. "How long until you are ready to keep moving?" he asked. She yawned as she got out of bed herself, and then made a beeline for her armor.

"Just a few minutes. Do we still have any bread rolls for breakfast?"

Taeben almost offered to get some from the kitchen but remembered his encounter with Keiley and thought better of it. "You get dressed and I will see what I can find in my pack," he said. She nodded, yawning again as she crossed the room and started picking up her armor. Taeben looked out the window and then turned his attention to her. "Ginny," he said, handing her a piece of fruit that he had produced from his pack, "we need to make it to Qatu'anari today if possible. I cannot be too long taking my office as ambassador, and I fear that will have to be done, as I told you, alone." Gin nodded as she took another bite of the fruit. "Are you ready to go?"

"Aye," she said, her mouth half full of fruit. "Let's go." He noticed that she was trembling slightly and smiled. The terror that she felt at any mention of the Qatu would surely keep her safely inside the embassy building while he met with that wretched Princess Royal. Taeben longed for the day when all of these irritations were behind him, and let that longing motivate him forward. They put on their packs and soon were out of the inn and back on the path that led into the tunnels.

It took the better part of a few days, but Anni soon had the bedroom and the kitchen clean and habitable. Sath made daily hunting trips out to the beach and the forest to bring back as much food as she could cook or prepare to store for the cold season, and each day he ventured a bit closer to the palace. His curiosity would bring him almost to the gate, but once he recognized the *Sahi Kalah* outside to be males he had grown up with, he decided better of getting too close. He longed to see his sister, but knew that he would one day…once he and Anni had a cub they could approach his father about returning to the palace, not as heir but as another family in the royal household. There his Anni and his young would be safe, and he could relax.

But for now, it was living rough…or semi-rough anyway, as rough as one could in the embassy huts outside the palace on the beach. He had watched Anni tidy and straighten and add her own touch to the residence, and it was becoming homey in its own way. It was theirs. Sath paused as he slipped behind one of the broad based palm trees that formed the barrier between the jungle of Qatu'anari and the beach. He had been tracking something by smell this time, and he would have given up the scent hours ago but it was triggering something in his mind that he couldn't place. He would have to ask Anni later if he didn't find it and identify it. When he had holes in his memory she was able to fill them. He smiled as an image of her from that morning crossed his mind, sleeping peacefully in their bed with a blanket tucked under her chin. He had taken great care to tiptoe out of the embassy building to avoid waking her.

He hadn't intended to hunt down that strange scent, so faint initially but that now filled his nose and made him think of…someone in his past. His mother? It was sunflowers, of that he was certain, and they did not grow in the shady jungle environment. His nose led him to one of the other embassy buildings along the coast, externally like the one he lived in with Anni but internally, he imagined, more clean and possibly occupied. The embassies had been used in the days leading up to the Forest Wars, and had housed representatives of most of the races of Orana. After the wars came to their bloody conclusion, the peace-loving Qatu had decided that contact with outsiders wasn't a top priority, and the embassies were left abandoned. Occasionally, Sath remembered, his father would house important dignitaries there and Sath would be allowed to play with the children of the ambassadors, but those chances were rare.

He was about to move out from behind the tree when he heard the sound of one of the doors opening. He quickly scaled the tree to a higher vantage point to find out who their neighbor was, since he had no information from the palace to go on. He squinted into the morning sun. The figure leaving the embassy wore robes with a hood so Sath was unable to ascertain the race from this distance, but he would guess high elf from the bearing and the gait of the stranger. High elves, in Sath's estimation, walked as though they thought that they were better than everyone else, looking down those sharp, pointed noses at the other races like dirt under their feet. He also guessed male, but again had no way to be sure. All of the high elves, male and female, were tall and willowy and with the hood up, nothing was left to help him distinguish between the sexes.

Happy to put the sunflower mystery to rest, Sath waited until the stranger was out of sight and then emerged from behind the tree. Again using his preternatural sense of smell, he scanned the area for more prey. A few more wild boars would serve his little family well into the cold season. Creeping ever closer to the embassy buildings, Sath thought he heard a rustle in the low brush back at the tree line. He flattened himself against the wall and waited. More rustling brought him up off the wall and charging at the tree line, his staff high above his head as he channeled the magic all of the Qatu had within them to slow down the beast ahead of him. He had almost reached the trees when his quarry stepped out on to the sand in front of him.

It wasn't a boar at all, but a female wood elf. Sath skidded to a stop in a flurry of sand and salt spray as he made eye contact with her. She froze in place and stared at him, her ice blue eyes burning into his memory. He knew her, but how? He took a few steps closer but she did not move, likely frozen to the spot by the fear that he could now smell rolling off her in waves. The fear…mixed with the scent of sunflowers, filled his nose and his head and set off recognition deep in his soul. A name tried to coalesce in his mind but faded in and out just as he thought he was sure of it.

"*Leave me alone!*" the female shouted in her own language. Sath was momentarily amazed that he understood her. How would he have learned the language of those tree dwellers? Elysiam, had to be, she must have taught him while he was with… Sath shook his head to clear it. He had known Elysiam when he was with the Fabled Ones and… "*I said leave me alone!*" He took a step closer and the female fell to her knees. Her eyes filled with tears, those eyes that he knew…

"Gin?"

"How do you know my name?" she said in the common tongue, her voice trembling along with the rest of her. Sath moved a step closer as he dropped his staff in the sand and put his hands up, indicating that he was unarmed. Clearly, she could see him now and her eyes widened. "I know who you are…"

"Gin, how are you…are you real?" He inhaled deeply. She was very real. "It's me, Sath…are you all right?" Memories began coming faster now, of hunting with her, of being in a grand hall with her, of fighting alongside her…Sath shook his head but it wouldn't completely clear. How long had it been since their paths crossed while he was hunting with Anni? "Gin, how are you here? Are you injured?"

"You just stay back," she said, scrambling to her feet and holding her own staff out in front of her. "You won't get another chance to hurt me." Sath inhaled sharply as memories of Gin and that human...Dorlagar...entered her mind. Bellesea... He had hurt her that day but they had made peace, hadn't they?

"Gin, please," he said, falling to his own knees in order to be closer to her height. "I won't hurt you, *darlin*, I promise." He used the Qatu word on purpose, remembering how it had made her smile up at him - that smile that she reserved only for him. Why was she acting so afraid of him now?

"Don't call me that," she said, waving her staff back and forth at him. "Save that for your Qatu... your... *Annilanshi*!" She scowled. "I can't remember the Qatu word for...what she is..." Sath roared in frustration, immediately regretting the sound as he watched the color drain out of her face, that face that was just starting to trust him, that face he had marked accidentally so long ago...how long had it been since he'd seen her face?

He took a step back from her and rubbed a hand over his face. Fuzzy memories were becoming clear, while what he thought he knew became fuzzy. *Annilanshi*... Anni... That was clear. She was his mate...wait, what? Sath shook his head again and looked back down at Gin who was starting to creep away from him. "Wait!" he said, knowing with a sudden clarity that if she got too far away from him he would forget everything that was currently a haze in his mind. "Gin, wait, please..." She darted past him and his hand shot out and caught her by the arm, lifting her into the air and swinging her back around until she crashed into his chest with a thud. He covered her screams with his other hand while leaning in close to her and purring loudly as he spoke. "Gin. Please, it's me, Sath, I would never hurt you and you know that." She stilled and he released her mouth - a move that turned out to be a mistake.

"LIES," she screamed as she struggled against him. "You have hurt me; you have killed my friends and family. I knew it was a mistake to come this close to you and your savage kind, but Ben had to come!" At the mention of the wizard, Sath's entire body tensed and he was sure that Gin could feel it.

"The wizard is here with you?"

"Of course he is, he is the ambassador to Qatu'anari from the Forest," she whimpered. "He loves me and he takes care of me, and when he finds out that you are here and that you tried to hurt me again... put me down." Sath released her quickly and moved away.

"There is no need for that," Sath said quietly. "I am sorry; I should have left you alone." His mind was reeling. What was wrong with her? Was she still upset over what happened in the tower? "Will you just tell me how the others are?" The names were flooding back and he almost couldn't say them fast enough. "Tee? Elys? Hack? Are they well?"

"I don't know," Gin replied as she again brandished her staff in his direction. "Ben and I are on our own now."

"Figures, he never could share you with anyone," Sath muttered.

"Don't you DARE talk about Ben like that!" Gin swatted at him with the staff and Sath had the grace to jump out of the way as though afraid. "Ben loves me and wants me to be the best I can, unlike you."

"Wait, what do you mean by that?" Sath asked, catching the end of her staff as it again whistled past his nose. He pulled her close to him with it before she could drop the staff.

"I mean that he is teaching me how to fight and survive. You never taught me anything because you only wanted me around so that you'd have someone to save," she replied. Sath frowned, a low growl forming in his chest. "You're just like Dorlagar, rushing to save poor, helpless Gin."

"That is enough!" Sath roared, flinging the staff and her backward into the wet sand. "Do not EVER compare me to that human again. You win, Taeben!" he shouted, arms outstretched and head flung back to address the wizard, wherever he was hiding. "She clearly has chosen you! I wish you luck with her!" He stalked on down the beach, unaware of his surroundings for a moment until he caught Anni's scent on the wind. He did not look back to see Gin sitting up in the sand watching him walk away, her tiny hands gripping her staff until she nearly broke it. Soon he reached the clearing that led away from the beach and ran headlong into his mate.

"*Sath, where have you been?*" Anni said, throwing her arms around him and purring loudly to mask her humming the tune used to charm him. After a moment his body relaxed and he wrapped his arms around her. "*I was so worried, I woke up and you were gone. I thought the Rajah had found you and killed you!*"

"*Never happen,*" he murmured into her fur. "*He can't hurt us now.*" He nuzzled her neck, breathing against her ear and making her fur stand on end. "*Come on, I've hunted enough.*" Before she could respond he grabbed her up in his arms and broke into a run toward their home, Anni clinging onto him and smiling as they went.

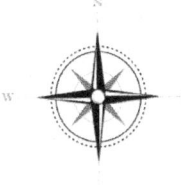

SEVEN

Maesha was waiting for him in the designated place, and it was clear to anyone nearby that she was of noble birth, despite the ragged disguise she wore. "Taeben!" she called out as she saw him enter the tavern. "You keep me waiting. I do not like to be kept waiting."

"Of course not, Highness," he said, summoning up all the charm he could muster as he took her offered hand and kissed the back of it. "Did you have a difficult journey here?"

"No, I am quite accustomed to traveling. Shall we sit?" Taeben nodded and pulled out one of the seats at a table for her. Once she was seated, he took a seat opposite her. A tavern girl, young Qatu female by the look of her, drew near to take their drink order. Taeben waved her away.

"Now, Highness, what can I do for you? I understand that there is some...discord in the royal house of Qatu'anari?" Taeben asked, barely able to keep himself from trying to push into the Princess Royal's mind. It had worked with Kazhmere, who surely had a more complex mind than the female across the table from him.

"You can call it discord I suppose," she said flatly. "However, a more accurate way to describe the situation is that the *Rajah* needs to be removed." She licked her lips and then looked down at her clawed fingers as she spoke. "There is no reason why a daughter of the *Rajah* cannot become the ruler in her own right. There are legends that tell of such things, among our ancestors, the first generations of Qatu. Female rulers. Queens. I am next in line for the throne and I intend to claim my birthright."

"Of course, Highness," Taeben said as calmly as he could. "But what of the son of the *Rajah*? Sathlir Clawsharp, your half-brother? Or his sister, Kazhmere?"

"It depends upon whom you ask, wizard, to know which happened first, my father disowning his bastard son or Sath renouncing his name and exiling himself. Either way, he and his sister are of no concern in this matter," Maesha replied. "I am not sure what possessed my father and convinced him that making that *m'vehsha* his First Wife was a good idea, but he has brought nothing but shame on our kingdom and the house of Clawsharp since he met her." She hissed as she spoke. "I tried my best to have the female Kazhmere taken and killed, but her pesky brother showed up and saved the day…as you well know, Taeben. I am told that you were also in the Tower when I made the deal with Salynth to execute Kazhmere and Sath, were you not?"

Taeben nearly fell off the chair in shock. So there had been a plan! He knew that it had to have been more than a coincidence that the captive dragonkind female in the tower who had the ear of the leaders of the Dragon Empire just happened to have both the heir to the throne of Qatu'anari and his sister captive at the same time. He just could not work out the last piece of the puzzle, how they had ended up there. *Ah, Annilanshi, you were more cunning that even I knew,* he thought. *Shame that you had to be collateral damage in this quest.* "Yes, I was, Highness. I had taken up study under Lady Salynth that went…wrong. However, I owe my freedom not to that filthy Sath, but to the kindness of a wood elf that I had hoped to bring to meet you today. I feel that she has unlimited potential that will be of great help to…"

"Bah, I have no use for those tree dwellers," Maesha said. "In fact, I can barely tolerate the sight of you, but I am led to believe that you are the missing piece that will complete my plan to take the throne. Otherwise I would never have seen to it that you were made ambassador." She looked him up and down as she drummed her razor sharp claws on the table. The black stripes that zigzagged across her bright orange fur seemed to dance on the backs of her hands.

"I hope that I am that, Highness," Taeben said, trying to hide the rising anger that he felt at her words and keep focused on the images of her chained at his feet with her half-brother Sath. "What would you have me do?"

"It is my understanding that not only do you possess the skills of a wizard, but ancient magic, not seen since the time of my ancestors, as well. Is that true?"

"Aye."

"So you can enchant or charm as well as bring down destructive magic?"

"Aye." Taeben cocked an eyebrow as he looked at the Qatu female. "Why do you ask me these questions? You would have me remove the *Rajah* myself, Highness?" This was beginning to spin a bit out of his control, and Taeben was growing anxious.

"Of course not. An elf taking down the *Rajah* of Qatu'anari?" Maesha laughed, and Taeben was not sure if the sound behind the laugh was a purr or a growl. He was using all of the control he possessed not to call down every destructive magical force he could on the haughty female across the table. "I merely need you to control some of the more…easily persuaded members of the *Sahi Kalah*. Then charm my darling father so that he does not fight back, and help them to execute him with your magic."

Taeben stared at Maesha. "You do not need me, Highness. A simple sorcerer could do what you ask," he said. "Forgive me but I do not understand what my wizard magic could add to the equation."

"Your transportation magic for one, Taeben," she said, leaning closer to him. She spread out her hand and carefully hooked the edge of his sleeve with one terrifying talon, as she looked him in the eye. "For this to work, the first thing that must be done is that ridiculous First Wife must be dispatched. The center of one of the volcanos would be most unpleasant from my understanding, no?"

Taeben's face melted into a wicked grin. "Indeed. Perhaps we can avoid any bloodshed within the walls of Qatu'anari by merely transporting both the *Rajah* and his First Wife together to their doom?"

"No." Maesha flexed her hand and Taeben yanked back the arm of his robe, making her beam a toothy grin at him. "No, my father will suffer for what he has done. He forgot all about his true First Wife, my mother, when he saw that whore at the Fire Circle. He forgot about ME, his first born, and he will pay for that," she hissed. Taeben swallowed hard. An angry Qatu female was a fearsome sight indeed. He would have been drawn to her, in truth, had she not been a filthy Qatu. "I do, however, think that letting him watch as his precious Savvy is sent screaming into the embrace of the Mother Dragon's lair would be most amusing to watch." Her golden eyes glittered with hatred as she imagined the scene. "Can we do that, wizard?"

"As you wish, your Highness," he said. Maesha was a female of worth indeed, just as cunning and vengeful as Taeben himself. Pity she was a Qatu. When he took the throne, all of her kind would serve him. Taeben smiled as he imagined Maesha next to her brother Sath in chains. Fine pets they would make indeed.

Gin sat in the sand for a long time, wondering, worrying, and trying desperately to remember something that seemed just a blank space in her mind. Nothing made any sense to her, regardless of how she tried to focus on this image or that, this memory, that smell, this sound…there was just nothing there.

That was certainly the Bane of the Forest earlier on the beach, he had introduced himself to her and she was certain that she would recognize that growl anywhere. She wrapped her arms around her knees and hugged them up close to her chest. Taeben had told her that he would keep her safe and that Sath only wanted to hurt her. Gin considered that notion and horrifying images of Sath snarling at her or swiping at her with his awful claws filled her mind and made her tremble. However, he didn't seem threatening just then... The growl was scary but all Qatu were scary for that reason. It was simply a part of their language, the growling, wasn't it?

She thought of Kazhmere unexpectedly, and tried frantically to remember how she knew the female Qatu who had never been anything but kind; and Anni, Sath's mate - Gin paused a moment, a pain shooting through her chest. His mate? Yes, Taeben had confirmed that after they saw them together in the Fabled Grand Hall. And then Sath had just left the Outpost with her and never looked back...hadn't he? He had all but abandoned the Fabled Ones and her.

Gin rubbed her eyes with her fists and then replaced her arms around her knees. Why would Taeben have brought her somewhere that close to the Qatu? Because Taeben was the ambassador, that's why. But so close to Sath and Anni when he knew Sath was a danger to Gin? How was he to protect her from the Qatu if he was seeking diplomatic relations with them? Something rang untrue, and Gin forced her mind to follow that thought. A fog seemed to lift in her mind and she tried even harder to remember anything, her eyes closed and her breath even and slow.

Darlin. That word had remained. She could still hear Sath's voice saying it. *Darlin.* That rumbly wonderful Qatunari word. That word that meant...her. She was his *darlin*. She closed her eyes and was inundated with images of Sath looking down at her and smiling, calling her *darlin*...Gin's eyes popped open. She had to find Sath. Something had happened, surely, to make her so afraid of him - but what? An image formed in her mind...that had to be it! The dragonkind sorceress in the tower! Salynth!

She got to her feet quickly and picked up her staff. She had to apologize to Sath. He had been trying to make amends for hurting her when he was charmed, he was trying to be kind, and she had turned into a banshee, screaming and threatening him. Gin's eyes widened as the hand not gripping her staff covered her mouth. She had compared him to Dorlagar. Dear spirits, what had gotten into her? Moreover, why, even with all of these memories and understandings, why did she still feel slightly afraid at the thought of catching up to Sath? Was she afraid that she would find him…with Anni? Perhaps how it would hurt him to know she was with Ben, or if he even cared? Gin shuddered at the thought, and then wondered why she was reacting that way. Should she just let it go? *Darlin.* No, she could not let it go. Something was wrong here, and she had to find Sath in order to find out what it was.

Luckily, he had left big footprints in the wet sand that she could follow, but she was looking at her feet as she ran instead of up ahead of her, and ran headlong into someone approaching from the opposite way. She fell backward, and when Gin sat up in the sand, she saw Taeben standing only a short distance away. He did not look happy.

"I hope that the embassy is on **fire**," he snapped as he stalked toward her, holding out a hand to help her up from the sand. "Otherwise I'm not entirely sure why you are this far away from it when I distinctly remember telling you to stay inside." She placed her hand in his and he yanked her roughly to her feet.

"I'm sorry, Ben, but I wanted to make you something to eat so I came outside to hunt and I…well, I ran into…"

"Spit it out," he barked.

"I ran into Sath, Ben." She watched his reaction carefully, knowing that he was no fan of the Qatu that had formerly been the Bane of the Forest.

"And?" He appeared relatively calm, but Gin could feel the anger pouring off him toward her.

"And he tried to talk to me, but I wouldn't listen to him," she replied and could almost see Taeben relax.

"He didn't hurt you?" Taeben said, slowly moving closer to her as he spoke. She tried to read the expression on his face but could not. "You are all right?"

"No, he didn't even **try** to hurt me, Ben," Gin said, utterly confused by his reaction to what she was telling him. "I was certain that he was going to try to kill me but he didn't. He asked after Tee and Elys and Hack like he and I were friends."

Taeben was now inches from her, and Gin gasped as he grabbed her up in his arms and held her to him. "You are not leaving me to go find him, then?"

"Ben!" Gin pushed him back but could not completely get free of his hold one her. "I am not leaving you, no, but I was going to look for him because something… Something is wrong. I fear that maybe he still suffers some effects from the magic of that hag in the tower."

Ben's eyebrows furrowed as he let her go, again balling up his fists. "You…were going…to look for the Qatu?" he asked, his voice barely audible. "You were going to do the very thing I warned you not to do, weren't you Ginny?"

"Ben, I said I'm not…" Taeben cut her off with a hand over her mouth as he drew her right up to his face and glared down his nose at her, his other arm holding her fast against him.

"Look at me," he said and she did as he ordered. His gaze burned into her and she tried to look away but found that she could not. She struggled against him but felt suddenly as though her entire body was made of stone and she could not move.

"LOOK AT ME!" Taeben forced his way into her mind, toppling the barriers that she wasn't even aware that she was putting up against him and planting the suggestion that she would not be able to move to fight him. "You have disappointed me, Ginny," he said and noted the sadness in her otherwise hollow eyes. "You have disobeyed me. I thought that I could leave you and you would be waiting when I came back, safe in our home, but that is not what I found."

Tears rolled down her cheeks and for a moment Taeben lost his resolve, fearing that he had pushed too far and her consciousness had been destroyed. However, he soon regained his fury as he watched her memory of the encounter with Sath play out in her mind. "I can see what happened and I can see," he whispered menacingly as he threw her to the ground, "that you let that Qatu touch you. After how he has hurt you, and what he has done to try and control you, YOU LET HIM TOUCH YOU!" Gin remained still on the ground where she had landed but shook from head to toe. "How am I to ever want to touch you again after that?"

Her voice was distant when she finally was able to speak. "Please forgive me," she begged. "I didn't mean to disappoint you. I told the Qatu he was no better than Dorlagar and he left me where he had found me, calling out to the heavens that you were welcome to have me. Please, Ben, don't leave me, please…I'm yours, Ben, I'm still yours."

Taeben swallowed hard before turning back to her. "Get up," he barked. She did so, on marionette-like legs. "Come with me." Every muscle in his body was tense including those in his jaw, which he had clenched so tightly he could barely speak. He stalked into the embassy with Gin right behind him, her vacant stare locked onto him as she stumbled through the door. "Sit," he said, indicating a spot by the large hearth in the corner of the room. She headed for a plush chair but he grabbed her arm to stop her. "On the floor, Ginny," he snarled, and she did as she was told. He sat down in the chair and gripped the arms, trying to calm his anger before he ripped them from the chair itself.

"I'm sorry, Ben," she whimpered after a long period of silence. He did not respond nor did he look at her, and after a few minutes, he heard her crying.

"Ginny…" He withdrew from her mind, slowly this time, leaving a trail of images in his wake to renew her fear of all the Qatu - especially Sath. Once he was completely free of her, he expected her to fly into a rage but all she did was continue to cry. With his elbows resting on his knees, Taeben held his head in his hands. This just did not have to be so difficult. If only he could jump ahead to the part where he had the throne and Gin was truly his and Sath was dead. He opened his eyes and looked down at her, still staring up at him, still crying, but she was herself again, and he held out his arms to her. She leaped into them and held him tightly as he wrapped himself around her and pulled her up onto his lap. "You must not do things that scare me like that, my love," he whispered into her hair.

"I know," she murmured. He felt her heart, first beating like the wings of a bird against a cage now slow and ease as he held her. "The next time you go to the palace, even though it is filled with Qatu, will you take me with you?" Taeben pulled away from her and held her at arm's length. "I fear that Sath knows where we are and it will only be a matter of time until he tries to find me again, and the next time he may take me."

Taeben smiled at her. "Of course I will take you with me, love. I will never leave you behind and if that awful mangy cat should try to take you from me I will always find you." He stroked her cheek and she closed her eyes in contentment. "You are mine, Ginny, and there is nowhere on Orana that you can go that I will not find you." Soon she was asleep, and Taeben lifted her carefully and took her to the bed. He tucked her in and watched her sleep for several hours, resisting the urge to enter her mind when he was sure she was dreaming.

Gin's consciousness was always present in the back of his mind, as was that of the Qatu who was keeping Sath at bay. Gin was a constant hum, a pleasant feeling of safety and security, while Annilanshi was a buzz or a low growl that he had only recently been able to understand. Gin was easy: constant hum was good, lack of hum was bad. He noted as she slept that the hum was growing more faint, and wondered if she was building up defenses against him while unconscious. That could be remedied later. The Qatu buzz had grown louder, and he focused his mind there for a moment, pushing through just enough that she would not notice that he was there.

Nancy E. Dunne

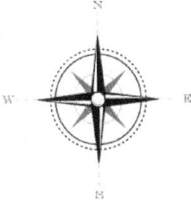

EIGHT

Sath rolled over onto his side on the bed, propped up on one elbow. *"You said that you were looking for me because you were worried that the Rajah had taken me, Anni? Why would you think that he would care where I am?"* he asked as he stroked the fur on her back. She was facing away from him, curled into a ball in the thick covers of the bed, and as his fingers moved, he traced the path from one dark spot in her gray fur to another, as though he was connecting the dots.

"The Rajah would care, Sath, because I have news that I fear has gotten to his ears," she said. Sath took her shoulder and as gently as he could, rolled her over to face him.

"What do you mean **news**?"

"Sath, I am…we are…you're going to be a father." Sath was not sure he had heard her right and stared at her, jaw hanging slack. *"Well, say something?"*

"You mean you…I mean we are…I mean we did…Dear spirits, Anni!" he exclaimed, pulling her in tightly to him in a hug.

"This is why I have grown so fat," she said, frowning. Sath could not think of anything more lovely right in that moment than her pouty lips. *"Why are you looking at me like that, Sath?"* Anni asked, though he was sure that she recognized the look in his eyes by now.

"How far along are you?" he asked, suddenly chastising himself that he hadn't even noticed she was with young. "You look amazing to me, Anni, you always do. You are the most gorgeous and perfect female in the world."

"Well, that is why I fear that the Rajah may know, Sath. Today while you were hunting, I went to the palace to see a friend of mine that is working as a midwife. She…thinks that it will be mere weeks now before the cub is here," Anni replied. Sath searched her eyes for the cause of the sadness in her voice.

"Your friend is trustworthy?"

"Oh, aye, of course she is," Anni said hastily. "But Sath…I saw your mother on my way out of the palace. She was in disguise and was with some of the females that…work in the back alleys in the City." Sath growled low in his throat. His mother was not one of those women, called *m'vehsha* in Qatunari. "She was giving them food and medicine, Sath, and because I was also concealing my features she tried to give some to me. As soon as I spoke, she recognized me." Anni lowered her eyes. "She worries for you, Sath, so much. I wanted to make her happy so…"

"So you told her you were carrying my cub," Sath said, his voice low and angry. "Anni, what have you done? If the Rajah knows that there is another Clawsharp on its way and even suspects that it might be a boy, do you understand that he will have all of us imprisoned at best and killed at worst?" He leapt out of the bed and pulled a sheet with him, wrapping it around his midsection as he paced. The floor shook with his steps. "Do you not understand the danger that…" As he spoke, Sath turned to face his mate and found her on the floor next to their bed, forehead pressed into the stone floor.

"I'm sorry, Sir…I mean Sath," she said through choking sobs. "I did not think…I was so happy, we were so happy, I did not think about becoming with young and then our poor First Wife, she seemed to be so happy with the news…"

Taeben stood on shaky legs, balling his hands into fists as he backed away from the bed where Gin still slept. Why did everyone disobey him?

I SAID NO CUBS!

There was no response from her, so he sent a shock of pain to her that he felt as it rocketed from her head to her toes.

I am sorry, Sir, I am so sorry.

She was weeping now and he got the feeling that she really did not want the little Clawsharp that was now growing inside of her.

I could rid you of that problem if you like, Annilanshi.

No sir, please, it would kill Sath, please...I will be more careful sir. This will be the only cub; I swear to you.

Taeben wasn't sure that he could trust her, but she didn't think that she was lying to him so he decided to leave her be for now. Besides, the cub might be female, in which case would be no threat, and if it was a male then it could be leverage. He withdrew until she was merely a low buzz in the back of his mind and turned his attention to Gin. She was still asleep, but whimpering so he crawled into the bed and wrapped himself around her, holding her until she stilled.

"*Get up, Anni,*" Sath said, rubbing a hand over the top of his head as he did when frustrated. "*I thought you promised me you would never assume that position in front of me again.*" He reached down and she took his hand, standing on unsteady legs. "*Of course my Mama was pleased to see you and pleased that you are with young. When it is born, we will deal with keeping our little family safe. Just pray that it is female, so that the Rajah will not care, just like with my sister, yes?*" Anni threw her arms around him and he held her close, his eyes still troubled. *Please,* he thought, *please be female.*

The days came fast for Sath, now that he was under a self-imposed deadline to make sure that he and Anni were safe and the embassy building was ready for a cub. Qatu females were only pregnant for about twelve weeks before they gave birth, and because he was too concerned that she might lose their cub or cubs he made her stay in the building most of the time and in bed if he could enforce it. She fought him on that last point, and often could be found in the kitchen making food or, in Sath's estimation, far too close to the cook fire. He would shoo her back to the chair in the far corner of the kitchen and pull up something to prop her feet on, and then try to finish whatever she had started making. Sath was not skilled in cooking.

She purred a lot, he noticed, and he wondered if she was communicating not only with him but also with the cub as she did. It still sounded musical to him, like a sweet tune that he heard in his mind even when she was not nearby. He hoped that she was as happy as he was, but he could not be sure.

NINE

Princess Qa Maesha Clawsharp had seen many things in her life at court in Qatu'anari. Her mother had been a prominent potion merchants in the Quarter before the *Rajah* had spotted her one day and fallen in love with her. He was merely the Crown Prince at that time, but as the only son of the *Rajah*, he was heir to the throne. M'Neesha, Maesha's mother, did not become First Wife when her husband became *Rajah*, but instead was added to the royal harem and soon after, Maesha was born. Citizens of Qatu'anari whispered that it was because she had only managed to give him a daughter and not a son and heir that she would never be First Wife.

However, the *Rajah* had not ignored his first born and only child by any means. As Princess Royal, Maesha had a quad of female personal bodyguards and was educated by the finest tutors from Qatu'anari as well as those imported from the world outside of their island. She spoke most of the known languages and traveled extensively as she grew up. She and her mother took on many diplomatic missions, and it was because of their work that the Qatu enjoyed almost unlimited access to other parts of Orana. Neutral to their very core, the Qatu were the epitome of rich culture, religious tolerance and progressive thought…with one startling exception.

There had not been a female ruler of Qatu'anari since the time of their ancestors. Even then, there were only legends of *Rajahanis* but no written proof that the practice had ever been allowed by their race. All over Orana, civilizations had both Kings and Queens who ruled equally, but the Qatu did not. There was a *Rajah* and a First Wife, but the First Wife had only diplomatic duties. She had no say in how her husband ruled their people.

Maesha first became fully aware of the situation in which she found herself when her father decided to make his latest and youngest wife, Savdhi, First Wife. Maesha was furious. She had always thought that as the Rajah's only heir, the rules would have to change and she would be Rajah after he was gone. After all, even if his other, lesser wives bore him children, she was the eldest. However, she was not the child of the First Wife, which was a complication. Maesha's mother had died the spring prior, and it was rumored she had taken her own life in response to the *Rajah*'s refusal to make her First Wife – Maesha's title was purely ceremonial because she was female and the oldest of the Rajah's offspring.

She had just entered her thirteenth season in her studies, and was starting to receive gifts and tokens from the nobility with a view to marriage alliances. Maesha was going to confront her father and tell him that she had no interest in such things as diplomatically advantageous marriage when she overheard a conversation between Kazhmere, who would turn out to be the *Rajah*'s daughter with Savdhi, and Kazhmere's best friend Annilanshi. It was life changing for Maesha. The two of them were sitting on mats up on the palace roof, and Maesha slipped behind a column to listen in on their conversation. Palace gossip was always a useful thing to have in one's possession.

Kazhmere, who was tall and fair of fur like her father, glared at her friend. "Anni, you are the ONLY one that knows who I really am. I am not even supposed to know, not after my brother took off as he did. If Maesha knew…"

"I know what that…*m'aakindi* is like and what she's capable of, and I know how much she hates your brother because Savdhi became First Wife instead of M'Neesha." Anni's use of the very unflattering word in Qatunari made Kazhmere grin. Anni rolled her eyes. "Can you imagine if that horrible female had become First

Wife? She was twice as mean as Maesha and many times over as spoiled. I never revel in the deaths of others but I do not miss her. I feel sorry for Maesha not having a mother, but First Wife is kind and would probably take care of her if Maesha would let her."

Kazhmere scowled. "Sure she would. Sath was her treasured cub. Maesha needs a mother. Well, what about Kazhmere, Savdhi? I'm your daughter! I'm HIS daughter, though he has never acknowledged it. I was born AFTER Momma became First Wife and..." She paused and wiped tears from her teal eyes.

Maesha had stared at the marble column in horror, her eyes wide. She knew that Sath was her half-brother and now that Savdhi was First Wife, he was heir to the throne. But another daughter? Kazhmere was her half-sister? The Qatu had been told that cub was born dead! Had the *Rajah* lied?

One thing, though, had been very certain. Kazhmere had to go. If there was no heir and anything happened to the *Rajah*, there might be enough support for the full-blooded offspring of the *Rajah* and the First Wife to take the throne. Maesha decided then and there that she would not let that cub take away her birthright. Instead of going to argue matters of marriage and state with her father, she set out for one of the remote locations she and her mother had visited on diplomatic missions. She went to the dragonkind sorceress, Salynth, to beg her to help Orana be rid of the two Clawsharps in exchange for power and prestige with the royal house of Qatu'anari.

That plan had failed, however, thanks to the Prince coming to his sister's rescue with a group of adventurers rather than on his own. Sitting in her chambers now and recalling the setback, Maesha scowled at the memory. "That wizard Taeben is lucky that I don't take that defeat out of his naked hide," she hissed. Patience and waiting had never been a strong suit of hers, and even now, as close as she was to having the throne, she was still so nervous that she picked at the threads woven in great detail on the cushions on the floor of her sumptuous bedchamber.

"Did you say something, Highness?" said Paruh, one of her bodyguards who was seated at her right hand side, working on a tapestry with Jihli, another bodyguard. The females had grown up together, but even though her quad would do anything to protect the Princess, they knew her too well and none of them really cared for her as a friend.

"Nothing that is your concern, Paruh," Maesha spat. She stood up and stretched. "I am bored out of my mind here. Go and find me something to amuse me for the afternoon." The quad shared glances, giggled, and stood as a unit to leave the chamber. In a few minutes, they returned with one of her father's *Sahi Kalah*, an orange and black striped male named Koby. "Ah, yes, that will do. Leave us." Jihli shut the door behind her as they left Maesha and Koby alone.

In another part of the city, Taeben and Gin had just arrived at the front gates and were being questioned by one of the *Sahi Kalah*. "State your business!" the guard said for the third time. Taeben stared at him.

"I don't speak Qatunari," he said. His haughty tone plainly irritated the guard.

"*We are here to see your city, nothing more,*" Gin said in halting Qatunari. Taeben turned to stare at her, amazed. "*May we pass?*"

"*Yes, little one. All are welcome to marvel at the wondrous kingdom of Qatu'anari,*" the guard said, smiling down at her. He stopped smiling and looked at her closely. "*Your Qatunari is very good for a wood elf. I am Kinjab. Do I know you?*"

"*No, I don't think so,*" she replied, pulling her cloak up around her ears. "*I'm sure all wood elves look alike to you.*" She beamed a smile up at the guard who chuckled and waved them on through the gate. Once they were through, Taeben pulled her to one side, shoving her roughly up against one of the cold stone walls of the outer city.

"What was that?" he demanded, his face very close to hers. "When did you learn to speak that filthy, barbaric language that well? What did he say to you?" He cocked an eyebrow as he leered at her. "Was he coming on to you? Did he remind you of Sath?"

"Ben!" Gin glared at him, exasperated. "I told him what you told me to say if we were stopped, that we were just tourists here to see Qatu'anari." She put her hands on his chest but could not shift him. "Did you really think that...I mean, after what Sath did, I can barely stand to look at another of his kind! Seriously, Ben!" He met her gaze and pushed into her mind. He quickly scanned the conversation she had just had and saw that she was telling the truth.

"I'm sorry, love," he said begrudgingly. "I just worry so much that one of these filthy felines will be loyal to Sath and something will happen to you. It's only because I love you so." He blushed, the emotion genuine this time, then immediately returned to his normal chilly demeanor. That might have been a mistake, telling her how he felt, but if so he could always erase the memory later.

"You...love me?" Gin said, awe and wonder in her gaze as she stared up at him. Her ice blue eyes twinkled with a light spray of tears and her smile threatened to stop his heart.

"Aye." Taeben glanced around them and then kissed her quickly. As they made contact he pushed back into her mind to remind her that she loved him too, and then pulled back from her. The look on her face was that of a lovesick child. Taeben smiled at her for a moment, but then his countenance darkened. "We must get to the meeting place with our contact. I will find you a safe place to wait, and then I will meet with her, just like last time, yes?" Gin nodded, clearly lost in Taeben's magic and his physical closeness.

He followed the map to her chambers he had been given by the Princess when they'd met in the tavern, but was stopped by four armored female Qatu who stood protectively at the door. "*State your business, wizard,*" one of them said in angry sounding Qatunari.

"Gin? A little help?" Taeben sputtered, angry that he was being spoken to in Qatunari. Surely Maesha had told them he was on the way?

"*Ben is here to meet his contact,*" Gin said, her Qatunari stronger in her current state. The light trance seemed to free up her mind to access this, her third language, while her inhibitions were down. "*He says that he is expected and that I am to remain somewhere safe.*" The females smiled at her.

"*My name is Paruh,*" one of them said. "*Your Master is here to see our Mistress. You may wait here with us; tell him we will keep you safe.*" She turned to the female next to her. "*Jihli, will you let her Highness know that the wizard has arrived?*"

Gin stared at the two Qatu females and then turned to Ben. "She says that they will take care of me while you, my 'Master' speaks to 'Her Highness' inside. Ben, who is it you are here to see?" she asked, her blue eyes blazing.

Ben smiled down at her. "Jealous are you?" Gin looked away from him, folding her arms over her chest and stomping her foot. He grabbed her face and forced her gaze back up to his, causing the Qatu to all snap to attention. "It is none of your concern," he said, forcing his way as far as he could back into her mind until she went limp with compliance. "Tell them that I agree and then go with them, love." Gin nodded and then relayed his message to the females who were still eyeing him warily.

The doors to the Princess's bedchamber opened and a young male *Sahi Kalah* emerged, looking ruffled and a bit frightened. "Taeben?" Maesha called from inside. He released Gin's mind and strode into the chamber, pushing his way past the females. "Koby, you will wait with my quad, you and the wizard will have work to do," she said as the door swung shut. The male, looking a bit sheepish, stood just past the doorway. The females turned on Gin, speaking in fast and excited Qatunari.

"*Does your mate always tell you what to do like that?*" one of them asked.

"*He must be excellent in the mated bed for her to put up with that much disrespect,*" another giggled.

"*He is not my mate, not exactly,*" Gin protested. "*And don't talk so fast, Sath didn't teach me that much Qatunari before he…left…*" She stared off into space, trying to make the memories in her head make sense. As the thoughts became more crisp they brought with them the barriers that pushed away Taeben's influence over her.

"*Sath? Sathlir Clawsharp?*" Paruh asked, bending over so that she could look Gin in the eye. "*The Rajah's son? You have been with Sathlir? Does the Rajah know?*"

"I'm sorry," Gin said, coming back from her fog sharply, "I don't think I know that word, **Rajah**? What does it mean?"

"I am still not sure what you think I can do to help you, Maesha," Taeben said as he reclined on one of the extravagant cushions opposite her. She was barely dressed, but he did not find her distracting in the least.

"The *Sahi Kalah* that was just here, Koby? You will take him and charm him and make him kill my father," she said matter-of-factly. Taeben stared at her.

"That was not the plan," he said, rising from the cushion. "If I am implicated then there is no way that I will be able to...I mean, it will make it obvious that you had something to do with it, Highness."

"There is no way you will be able to do what, Taeben?" Maesha said as she traced one of the patterns on her duvet with a razor-sharp claw. "Oh dear, you didn't think that this plan would lead to you sitting on the throne of Qatu'anari, did you?" She laughed heartily. Taeben glared at her, wondering how fast she could call her guards if he just happened to let loose a little magical lightning. Not fast enough, he wagered with a smirk. Maesha studied him a moment, then continued. "I have only heard this morning that First Wife is taken ill having heard of the death of her son, Sathlir, in a fire in one of the embassy buildings. She will not stand in our way. You will go with Koby and dispatch my father in the most unpleasant way your tiny little brain can think of, and then when I am queen you will be first wizard in the court. You can bring your little tree-dweller with you if you wish."

"Maesha, forgive me, Highness, but I do not believe your half-brother is dead." Taeben almost hit his knees, forehead to the floor as he had while prisoner of Salynth so many seasons prior, when he saw the angry look rocket across the Princess Royal's features. "My apologies, Highness, I thought you knew. His mate, Annilanshi, is with his young and to keep that knowledge from you, Sath must have the building alight. He lives, my mate Ginny has seen him with her own eyes only weeks ago." He hoped that she would accept the story, since it was the first he had heard of a fire in one of the embassies so he was making it up as he went along. The part about Annilanshi being pregnant was at least true.

"Sath lives? His whore is pregnant?" Maesha roared. "You are dismissed, wizard. I will finish this. Get out of my sight. *Koby! Attend me!*" She sprinted about her chambers in a rage, and Taeben barely made it back out the door as the *Sahi Kalah* entered. Gin was sitting off to the side with the quad of bodyguards, her arms again folded across her chest and her brow furrowed. Her angry look made Taeben sigh loudly. What else would go wrong?

"Ginny. Come," he barked. She stared back at him, and the tentative hold on his temper that had kept him in check so far shattered beyond repair. "NOW."

"No." Taeben stood stock still, unable to believe what he had just heard. "I know what you are up to, Ben, and it makes me so sad. I thought...that you really loved me," Gin said, her voice choked with emotion. The four bodyguards stood two on each side of the wood elf, as though they were her personal quad now.

Taeben swallowed hard, pushing down every bit of rage and the need to volley magical lightning about the room, and then spoke. "Love, I have no idea what you are on about, but it is time for us to leave. It is no longer safe for you to be in Qatu'anari." He held out one slender hand to her, willing with all of his might for it to remain steady. The four females made an almost imperceptible shift forward into what was definitely a protective stance against him. "Ginny, please."

"My name is Gin, thank you," she said. "I'm not going anywhere until you admit that you are having an affair with the Princess Royal...and that you know who Sath really is..." Her face lit up with understanding as Taeben felt the last brick fall into place in the wall she had put up against him in her mind. "Why didn't you tell me that he was…a Prince? Is that why you tried to make me fear him? What have you done to me? If Sath is the Prince that means…And *Kazhi*, dear spirits, she is…" Paruh turned her attention toward Gin, puzzled.

"Kazhi? Kazhmere? You know her?" Paruh's eyes narrowed. "How is she involved in all of this? I thought Sathlir's mate was Annilanshi…though I never understood that, so far beneath him, really."

"Gin, there is no need to become involved in the intrigues of the court of Qatu'anari. We **really** must be going," Taeben pressed, his hold on his temper disintegrating rapidly. He began silently reciting words of transportation magic, finishing the spell just as he was close enough to grab Gin's hand. The two of them disappeared in a flash of fire, leaving the Qatu guards scrambling.

"That wood elf knows more of our Prince than she was able to tell," Jihli snarled. *"Should we ask Her Highness to have her and that horrible mate of hers brought back to us?"*

"No," Paruh said, a sad smile on her face. *"I think that actually the wizard was right. My senses tell me that something is horribly wrong, and Qatu'anari will not be a safe place for very long. We must attend our Princess."*

Nancy E. Dunne

TEN

Lairky dashed across the Outpost to the Market, where vendors from all of Orana came to trade their wares. She had been coming to the settlement on the edge of the forest ever since she was old enough to come with Gin, and as a result she could find her way around with her eyes closed. When her older sister had come back from traveling with Sath and the Fabled Ones, Gin had taken up residence in the Outpost. Lairky worshipped the ground her sister Gin walked on so she followed her and lived in the tiny apartment above the bank with Gin. Others that hunted with them - like Kazhmere, a Qatu female that was not very friendly to anyone but Gin - visited occasionally. When Kazhmere came around, Lairky tended to make herself scarce. Qatu frightened her, as she was raised with the tales of Sath's time as the Bane of the Forest. It didn't help that the giant cat reminded her a bit too much of Sath himself.

Lairky knew that deep down, Gin felt that Anni had taken Sath away from her, but up until that point the two had never really been honest about their feelings for each other. And why would they be? How could that ever work?

Gin was with Taeben now, not much of a better choice really. Lairky tried to push those kinds of thoughts out of her mind, but found it difficult. Even if Taeben had never violated the trust of the wood elves, even if he hadn't been the very bane of her kinswoman

Elysiam, how could Gin expect to have a life with one so different than she? At least he was an elf, but still… Lairky bit the inside of her cheek. She knew all too well that the heart did not always consult with the mind when it settled upon a prize to be won.

Growing up, she had been taught that wood elves do not stray from their own tree city when it comes to finding suitable mates. However, Lairky knew whom she wanted, and it wasn't a fellow wood elf or even a high elf or human, but one of the dark elf cousins of Lairky's kind. All it had taken was a glance in a crowded tavern one night to start a conversation with him, and half a day later they were still talking. She would sneak out of the space she shared with Gin at night and find him, and they would go hunting together.

Once Gin had taken up with the wizard, Lairky and Kamendar would spend long nights in the tavern room that was all hers, talking and planning battle strategies…and falling deeply in love. He was the sweetest, kindest male she had ever met, but he had a ferocious side too that set her heart racing. They could talk about weapons and fighting as they fell into each other's arms, carefully keeping to the shadows of the tavern in the wee hours of the morning. They burned almost a bit too brightly, with their mutual fascination for each other keeping them entwined as often as he could sneak away.

Back to the task at hand, she chided herself inwardly. Lairky sat down next to the stone steps that lead to the Fabled Ones grand hall, not wanting to go inside for fear that Gin might have stopped in before heading off with that wizard. "Taeben," Lairky hissed under her breath. As much as she loathed the wizard, the larger threat was the Qatu, she knew what had to be done for her sister. Smiling as she packed up her potions, she stood and headed for the one person that would know.

Kamendar was sitting cross-legged and meditating outside of his own guild's grand hall as she approached. Before she got too close, Lairky popped the cork out of one of her potion bottles and drank it, grimacing. The illusion took hold just as a dark elf couple walked past her. Lairky walked up to Kamendar and was about to say something, but Kamendar held up a finger. "Nice try, Lairky," he said without looking up.

"How did you know that it was me?" she said, exasperated. She plopped down on the ground next to him and inched closer to him. He took her hands in his, smiling as he gave them a light squeeze.

"Your eyes, pet," he said, running one of his dark-skinned hands over hers, admiring the quality of her illusion. "This does suit you, though, I think." He lifted one of her hands to his lips and she noticed that her hands were the same near blue tint as his. His eyes were as dark with centers as red as blood, which resembled two little crosses staring out at her. He smiled at her and placed a kiss on her knuckles, then held her hand there. "They are still wood elf eyes, love. The illusion didn't change that, a fact of which I am very glad." He leaned over to kiss her on the cheek but she pulled back from him. "What?"

"Nothing, I just want my illusions to be authentic, otherwise what's the point?" she snapped. "How can I do my job if I can't get into places?" Kamendar smoothed a hair behind her ear but she hopped to her feet, shaking the illusion away.

"Now, there's my girl," he said as she sat back down. "You don't have to pretend here, Lairky, not to be with me. This is why we meet in the Outpost, yes? Now, to what do I owe the pleasure?" He cocked his head to one side and the set of his cobalt jaw distracted her for a moment. She shook her head to clear it and then smiled sweetly at him.

"I need a reason to see you?" she said, trying to be coy.

"You're the worst liar ever, love," he said, chuckling. "Out with it. I know when you're up to something and this sweet and innocent little girl routine doesn't suit you at all."

Lairky laughed. "Fine. I need to find someone," she said. "But it needs to be just between you and me, okay?"

"Of course, pet," Kamendar said. "Who is it?"

"Sathlir Clawsharp," she whispered.

"Are you mad?" Kamendar demanded, his eyes wide. "What do you need with the Bane of the Forest?" He wrapped his hand around his own blade. "Has he done something to hurt you? Or was it that female he is with, the one that communicates with that filthy high elf wizard?"

"Any of the above," Lairky said, nearly spitting her words. "I honestly don't know which one to start with, Kam, but I have to do something. Gin is so sad and it breaks my heart to see."

"Your sister is a kind soul," Kamendar said. "The few times I have met Gin she has been nothing but polite to me."

"That's because she doesn't know about us, Kam," Lairky said sadly. "My older brother Cursik had a relationship with one of your kind, and that nearly killed Gin. Put her off your kin for a long, long time." Her eyes narrowed. "Could also be because that inker nearly got Cursik killed," she said under her breath.

"Inker. Interesting." Lairky looked up at Kamendar, horrified that he had heard the slur. Her eyes met his as the red cross in the center of them began to spin and deepen in color, indicating anger.

"I didn't mean…I'm sorry, it's just that…" One of Kamendar's dark fingers against her lips silenced her. He took a few deep breaths before he spoke.

"I must tell you something, Lairceach. I know of your brother Cursik. I have not wanted to tell you, for I fear that you will not forgive me for the omission, but it was my sister Maelfie to whom he was mated." Lairky stared at him in total disbelief. "Once their union was discovered, she was disowned by my family. I thought at the time that it was irrelevant," he said, his eyes returning to normal as he removed the finger from her mouth and gently stroked the side of her cheek. "Maelfie's twin, my other sister Elspethe, found out the name of our Mae's wood elf mate and when I learned that was your brother…I could not bear to tell you for fear you would leave me. I still fear it, but I wish to be honest with you, my little love.

"I can see in your face now how much you loved your brother, and I wish that we all could have known each other. Mae was very much like you, fiery and bold and never one to keep in her place as a female." Lairky remained silent, her eyes wide with shock. He took hold of her chin and his eyes searched hers. "I would give all that I have to be a wood elf, like you," he murmured, pulling her face close to his. She hesitated and he sighed, releasing her. "Not in public, of course," he said with an annoyed sigh. "I almost forgot. Can you ever forgive me for what I have kept from you?"

"Can you help me find the Qatu?" Lairky whispered, trying to keep herself focused on her goal rather than allow herself to become lost in anger with Kamendar and mourning for her brother all over again. "All I have to do is kill him, and his hold over my sister will be broken." There would be time to sort out how this would affect their relationship, such as it was. Perhaps he knew more about Cursik's death? But that would have to wait.

"Don't you mean kill the bard?" he asked, concern etched into his cerulean features.

"Yes, isn't that what I said?" Lairky immediately began studying a blade of grass near her boot. "Kill the bard and her hold over Sath will be broken. Yes."

"That is **not** what you said," Kamendar said sadly. "But yes, I have heard that the Qatu and his mate are living in one of the embassy buildings just outside the Qatu'anari City gates. It is most unusual but there seems to be quite the rift between the Prince and his father."

"The who?" Lairky's eyes bugged out of her head as she stared at Kamendar, who immediately realized his mistake. "No, no, you have to tell me what you know, Kam, right now," she demanded. "No secrets between us – total honesty, remember? Sath…Sathlir Clawsharp…is a Prince?" Kamendar sighed.

"I do not know all the details, my little love," he said quietly, "but it seems that your Bane of the Forest is also a member of the Qatu'anari royal family. Our northern contacts let my kind know that the Rajah, at about the same time that the killings began in the forest, exiled the Crown Prince of Qatu'anari from the city. It has to be the same male that became the Bane of the Forest." Lairky stared at him in disbelief. "I have not wanted to tell you for I knew of your sister's… connection with the male and I feared that he kept that knowledge secret for a reason... and as close as you are to your sister, my Lairceach, I couldn't risk anything happening to you. There are many in our world that would see the *Rajah* removed and the Qatu reduced to slaves under the command of another of the races of Orana and I just..." Lairky put her fingers to his lips to stop his rambling, as it grew louder with every word.

"Sssh, Kam, I'm fine, just...tell me what else you know of this Crown Prince? Does Anni know who he is?" She paused and rubbed her forehead as the knowledge settled on her in a painful wave. Were there any more revelations forthcoming? Lairky could barely concentrate as it was. "Of course she did, that's why the wizard chose her, isn't it? Kam, this is bigger than just my sister. That wizard aims to use Anni to take over Qatu'anari!"

"I would not worry about that, my pet," Kamendar replied as he took her trembling hands in his. "The throne of Qatu'anari is safe and the Prince is nearby in an embassy outside of the City gate. The Prince and his mate have a young one who is..."

"What?" Lairky's jaw fell slack. "They have a cub?"

Kamendar's face fell. He could not seem to keep anything from her anymore, even if it was for her own good. Once the floodgates of truth opened, there was no turning back. "Aye. I have heard that once they discovered that the bard was pregnant, the Prince tried to burn down the embassy where they lived in order to convince all in the palace that he was dead, but it did not work. I do not know its name, or if it is male or female; but I would imagine it is a male and an heir to the throne. It seems that the First Wife came and took her grandchild to the royal nursery shortly after its birth, at the behest of its mother. The Prince tried to take the baby back, but was met with some...resistance at the city gates."

"Oh, it just gets better and better," Lairky hissed. "I am going to make that Qatu AND the wizard pay." She got to her feet with Kamendar right behind her and turned to head for the path out of the Outpost to the north. She was stopped by Kamendar's strong hands on her shoulders.

"Do not do this, my Lairky, please," he said, his voice soft but rumbling with that same ferocity that burned at her core. His touch on her arm now was light, but firm, and he turned her to face him without releasing her. "I cannot see a way that this will end well and…" his hands tightened on her arm, nearly causing her knees to buckle, "and I will not lose you over a vendetta belonging to your sister. I have lost so much already, I will not lose you."

"Let me go, Kam," Lairky said quietly. She resisted the urge to tell him he was hurting her. "I will be fine; you know how I can fight." He shook his head, his grip tightening on her arm.

"Let me go with you. We can sneak in, dispatch both the Prince and his mate, and be back out before anyone knows we have been there, if that is your wish," he said, his voice tight with concern. "Just please do not do this alone. I will go with you whenever you are ready."

"No. It will be easier with just me." He released her and she turned to face him. After quickly looking around to make sure they were alone, Lairky threw herself at him and took his lips in a deep kiss, pressing herself close to him. It was a long time before she pulled back from him. "When I am done, we will go away, Kam," she whispered. "We will find a place to go where no one cares what we are, and I will be yours. Just be patient."

Kamendar's eyes blazed blood red for a moment, the crosses seeming to spin around as he frowned down at her. The stare faded, replaced by a sad smile. "You are already mine, and I am yours. I love you, Lairceach," he said. "More than my own life, to forever and back."

"And I you, Kam." Lairky released him and stepped back from him. "And if I don't go now, I will never go." He nodded and sat back down to his studies. Lairky turned on her heel and ran toward the other side of the Outpost on the path leading north. Just before leaving the gates, she looked briefly over her shoulder, and then opened another potion from her pouch and downed it in one gulp. "See you soon, Cat," she whispered as the illusion took hold. With magical enhancement, it would only be a few hours trek to the coast of Qatu'anari, and with her second potion, Lairky felt her feet gain the speed of the wolves of the forest and she ran. Before long, she was paying the gnome at the port for a seat on the boat across the narrow strip of the Forbidden Sea with money she had lifted from his own cloak.

After thanking the gnome for safe passage across to Qatu'anari, Lairky hopped out of the boat. She snuck from the cover of one large palm tree to another as she crossed the beach toward the huddle of embassies. Lairky almost stopped at the first embassy she had passed because she had the strangest feeling that Gin was nearby. Slowing to a walk, she approached the building only to be thrown backward by a magical ward. As she rose from the damp sand, Lairky rubbed her elbow, trying to alleviate the stinging trace of magic on her skin, and then set out to explore the other embassy buildings.

It was not hard to see which one was the home of the Prince and his concubine, as half of it was in ruins. Kam had told her about the rumors that he tried to destroy the embassy in order to hide himself, Anni, and the cub from the *Rajah* but the plan had failed. "Idiot," she hissed under her breath as she headed for the crumbling marble building. "This ends now." She downed the last potion in her belt and ran toward the massive front door ahead of her.

"*Sath?*" Anni roused herself and propped up on one elbow. Sath was not in the bed, and it looked as though he had not been there all night. "*Are you all right, my mate?*" She sat up in the bed, gathering the thick blanket that they slept under around her shoulders as she got to her feet. She knew very well where he was, and what he was doing.

Sath and Anni were still living in the back part of the ruined embassy building, since the birth of their son, Khujann. Upon hearing of her grandson's impending arrival, First Wife Savdhi had come not only for his birth but also regularly afterward, to see the child. When Khujann was only a few weeks old, in Sath's absence, Anni had begged her mother in law to take the infant back to the royal nursery. She had told Savdhi that she feared for the child's safety at the hands of the group that Sath had formerly called friends, the Fabled Ones, and that they hated Sath for leaving them and would take any chance to exact revenge on Khujann. Savdhi had wanted to wait and speak to Sath, but he would not see her; he made himself scarce any time he knew she was going to visit.

The truth was that Anni did not want the cub at all. She had all that she needed in Sath, and could not stand the way that he looked at the young one with more love than he seemed to have for her. The cub would grow up with others of his kind and Anni would have Sath all to herself. It seemed a mutually beneficial arrangement.

The only hitch in the plan that Anni had not foreseen was how angry Sath would become when she told him that Savdhi had taken Khujann. She tried to reason with him, reminding him how he had told her that the wood elf was with the wizard now, and that they posed a great threat to the cub. All the while she had that same wizard speaking into her mind, telling her what to say and do, but Sath would have none of it. He tried to take Khujann back from the nursery but his father doubled the guard on Anni's tip that someone was coming to do the infant harm.

As a result, Anni played her lute and hummed the tune under her purr night and day to keep Sath with her. Until the birth of their son she had all but stopped playing and only had to hum now and then, as he seemed to have forgotten about the Gin druid and his life outside of Qatu'anari. But after the cub arrived, she had her lute in hand almost constantly, at Taeben's insistence, to make sure that Sath remained with her.

In truth, it did not take much reminding from "Sir" as she still called him. Anni knew that to keep Sath with her she had to keep him charmed, and so she played as much as she could. This morning she found him sitting in the large room just outside of their bedchamber, a steaming mug in his hand as he stared absently at the door. *"How are you, my mate?"* she asked.

"How long has it been since she took him, Anni?" Sath asked in the common tongue. Anni's eyes widened. They only spoke Qatunari to each other. She could barely remember how to answer him.

"I am not sure, my mate, but why do you ask?"

"*Stop humming that tune and come over here,*" Sath said gruffly. "*It grows tedious. You are growing tiresome with the constant humming and strumming. Can we not just sit in silence for once?*"

No, tell him NO!

Taeben's voice ricocheted through her head, bouncing about off the inside of her skull. Anni rubbed her temples. "*As you wish, my mate, but what has caused this mood?*"

"*Do you even know any other languages besides Qatunari?*" Sath asked. He reached out and pulled her roughly to him, wrapping his arms around her midsection and looking up at her. "*Do you think if we had another cub she would come and take it too, like she did my son? Maybe if the next one is female, she would leave us alone.*"

Anni's face fell. "*You wish for another young one, Sath?*" she said in disbelief. She had only just gotten rid of the male!

"*Don't you?*"

"*I want whatever you desire, Sath, you know that,*" Anni said, reaching down to run her claws down the sides of his face. He shivered at her touch and she started humming again, trying to once again conceal the tune in a loud purr. Sath suddenly pulled her close, burying his face in her fur.

"*I miss him,*" Sath said, his voice muffled. "*So much. I never thought I could love another being as I do our son. I am not brave and strong like you, my mate.*" Anni's eyes widened in surprise as she felt his giant body quake with one sob and then another. She stroked the back of his head, unsure of what to do.

NO MORE CUBS.

"Sir" was very clear. "*I miss him too, my mate, but can we afford to bring another one into the world? Would that not give them another target?*" she asked. "*Can we afford to let the wood elf and her consort have another chance to hurt us?*"

Good, good Annilanshi.

Sath looked up at her, his teal eyes reddened around the edges from his tears. *"Aye. I never would have thought that Gin would hurt a cub, especially not one of mine, but with that wizard in her ear who knows what she is capable of doing."* Anni nodded down at him, forcing the grin that threatened to burst across her face back down where it belonged. She continued stroking his head and ears, and smiled as he purred. The wizard glowered in the back of her mind, angered at Sath's statement about his control over the wood elf no doubt, but he did not retaliate against Anni. *"Now, you go get ready and we'll go out for a hunt,"* he said. *"Would you like that?"*

"Aye!" Anni nearly clapped her hands with glee. Even though this trip would only likely be for food, in her mind Sath was at his most magnificent when he was on the hunt, even without his magical tiger. He was glorious to behold in battle, and she could almost feel a tingle start within her as she imagined him standing over fallen prey, staff in his hand, blood staining his armor. She dashed back to their bedchamber and began pulling on her own armor. She was packing her lute and drum in her haversack when she thought she caught the scent of an elf nearby.

Inside the building, Anni felt her panic rising. That was definitely the scent of an elf, a wood elf to be exact. She felt the wizard awaken in her mind. *"Sath!"* she cried out but he was already in the doorway.

"Stay back here, I will deal with this," he barked, clearly having caught the same scent. The strong aroma of flowers nearly masked the scent of wood elf, but it was still there.

"Gin," Anni hissed. Confusion wracked her mind as Taeben became aware of what she was sensing. *"Sath, let me handle..."*

"I said stay BACK, female!" Sath shoved her back into the bedchamber and stormed out into the great room to find the intruder standing there, hands on her hips, surveying the scene around her.

"Posh, except for the burned bits," the female wood elf said, as she looked around the great room. She pushed a lock of chestnut

hair over her ear, the other hand firmly placed on her hip. "I'm impressed, Cat. I guess being the son of the *Rajah* has its perks."

Sath took a deep breath, and then rubbed his eyes. The fog that seemed to permanently linger in his mind cleared just a bit and he recognized the scent. "Gin," he said, his voice low and menacing. "What are you doing here? I thought we settled everything between us."

"I've come to put something right, Qatu," the elf replied. "Where is your Anni, by the way?" Sath took another deep breath. No fear on this female... It must be Gin. She was never afraid of him when she was out from under Taeben's control, though he had given her plenty of reason to be wary.

"*Who is out there, Sath?*" Anni called out from the back room. She hoped that Gin's proficiency in their language had not gotten any better.

It cannot be her!

Taeben's voice was like a wail in the back of her mind. She tried to soothe the wizard just to keep him from driving her mad with the screaming.

"*Stay back there, Anni, I mean it!*" Sath called back as he moved closer to the elf. She made no move, which made him smile. This was not the simpering female he had encountered on the beach. Maybe he could reason with her. "Gin, what are you doing here? Are you hurt? You should not be here. Where is the wizard?"

"Why shouldn't I be here? Because I should be afraid of you?" she replied. "I will never fear you again, Sathlir." Her jaw tightened as she stared up at him. Sath met her gaze, trying to assuage a tiny, niggling feeling in the back of his mind that something was wrong. The sound of Anni's lute started up, distracting the elf and giving him a chance to reach out for her. "Oh, no you don't, you monster, not this time." She easily ducked under him and headed for the bedchamber. "Time to change the tune at this dance, I think."

Sath spun around and almost lost his balance as he lunged for her. The tiny female was quick, so quick, and he heard Anni's lute stop abruptly. A sharp and blinding pain shot through his head as Anni screamed and he struggled to keep his feet, still trudging toward the bedchamber. The screaming stopped and Sath fell to his knees, unable to keep walking.

"*Sath? Where are you? I'm...cold...?*" Anni whimpered. The elf that Sath was still fairly certain was Gin appeared in the doorway, covered in blood and scratches as Anni continued her mewling cries for Sath from the bedchamber. Suddenly Sath was awake, and realized that Anni was dying and the enemy was in the doorway, staring him down.

He lunged faster than the elf could have seen him move and was on her, pinning her to the ground. She gasped and fought him off, her tiny fingers tearing at his fur and trying desperately to shove him off of her. Fear poured off of her now, intensifying his bloodlust as he picked her up off the ground and held her aloft, far enough from him that she could do nothing but struggle in vain.

Sath beamed a toothy grin at her and then closed his clawed hand around her neck, his eyes closed in bliss at the sound of her neck snapping under his grip. He threw the body of the now dead wood elf to the floor and charged back into the bedroom doorway. Anni lay in a heap on the bed, still, cold, and covered in blood. A dagger was sunk to the hilt in her neck, and there were smears of blood all over the bedclothes, all the size of tiny wood elf hands.

"*Annilanshi,*" he said as he ran to her, but he stopped just shy of the bed. His head was clear, clearer than it had been since...he didn't know how long. Sath rubbed his eyes and blinked a few times, and saw the scene with new eyes. His eyes, which were now free and clear of the fog of the bard's charm.

"*Oh...Gin...*" he whispered as he turned to see her body on the floor. "*No, no, NO!*" His cries became a deafening howl as he scooped her petite body up from the floor and held her close. Sath sank to the floor while he continued to hold her, rocking back and forth in time with his keening. Finally, after a few long minutes, he garnered the strength to look at her. Her hair, chestnut with fiery auburn flecks, had dulled to black. Her ice blue eyes, still staring yet unseeing in death, were practically black as well.

Sath nearly dropped the body he was holding. He pulled her up close to his face and took a deep breath. No sunflowers. After looking at her for a few moments, he recognized her finally, and his heart sank. "Lairceach..." he murmured. "Oh, little Lairky, what have you done...what have I done?" He carefully placed her body on the floor and stood up, pacing about the room. "I am so glad," he said, his voice raspy from sobbing, "that it was not you, Gin. I could not live with that. But Lairky... Gin will never forgive me for this." Sath crossed the room and pulled one of the sheets from the bed, knocking Anni's body off onto the floor as he did. He looked back at her corpse for a moment and frowned, and then returned to the great room. With the care that a mother would wrap a newborn, he wound the sheet around Lairky's broken body, avoiding covering her face until the very last. Once he was finished, he returned to Anni's body and knelt down, taking her in his arms just as gently as he had Lairky's body and placing it back in the bed.

His fingers lingered on her lute, and another level of fog lifted from his mind. She had been charming him. *"Why all this, Anni, just to make me love you? You didn't need any of that evil magic. Who was behind this?"* He stroked the fur on her face, a face he had looked into a thousand times but now barely recognized. *"I do not believe that you did this on your own...and it was never needed. You were a good and worthy female, and I did love you, despite that blasted tune you were always humming."* He covered her up, closing her eyes with his hand before pulling the bedsheets up over her face.

Returning to Lairky's corpse, Sath placed the body outside of the house and then went back inside for a moment, returning with his blood-blackened armor in place and a haversack, already packed for the hunting trip with Anni slung over his shoulder. In one hand he held a bottle of wine, and in the other a blazing torch. Sath threw the bottle into the center of the great room and then sent the torch the same way, not even recoiling as the very flammable wine caught with a boom that shook the rafters of the building. He scooped up Lairky's body and then headed toward the beach to catch a boat to the mainland. The least he could do was return Lairky's body home to the Forest. He would deal with the consequences for her death as well as all those dealt by the Bane of Forest, and his son would be free.

Nancy E. Dunne

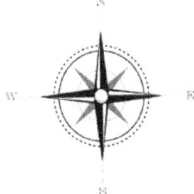

ELEVEN

Gin waited at the dock for Taeben to return, fiddling with her staff and tracing images into the wet sand. She scanned the tree line for his red hair and blue robes but didn't see him. A movement by one of the embassy buildings caught her eye and she quickly picked up her things and ran toward it, grinning. "I was starting to think you'd...changed...your mind..." She skidded to a stop, recognizing Sath's gait and his black armor. "Sath?" she whispered. "What are you...?" Her head began to pound and she could feel Taeben's presence even though he wasn't anywhere to be found.

Taeben rummaged around in their quarters in the Forest Embassy like a madman. The bard was dead! He had felt her death as though it had happened to him directly and now he had no hold over the Qatu Prince. He threw things into his haversack and ran for the front door, pausing only for a moment to reach out with his mind for Gin. He had to get to the docks and get Gin out of there, or just use magic to transport both of them away. She wasn't letting him in completely but he knew that something was very wrong.

"Sath? Answer me. What are you doing here? What is...that?" she asked, indicating the linen-wrapped bundle in Sath's massive arms. Sath stared down at her, his teal eyes rimmed in red. He couldn't bring himself to speak to her, so he carefully laid

Lairky's body down and took a knee in front of her. Gin's icy stare bore into his soul. "Answer me, Sath, what has happened? Where is your mate?"

"*Annilanshi* is dead," Sath said, marveling for a moment at how that statement evoked no feeling whatsoever.

"What happened?" Gin said, her gaze softening a bit.

"She was killed…by your sister Lairky."

Gin stared at Sath in disbelief. "Lairky…killed…"

"She was in disguise, Gin, if I had known it was Lairky…you have to believe me," Sath begged her. "I was charmed, that wretched bard charmed me and took me away from…all of you. I never would have left had she not…"

All of the color had drained from Gin's face. She knew what Sath would say, but she had to ask the question anyway. "Wait, Sath… What disguise?"

"What?"

"What did she look like, Sath? How did she appear?" Gin demanded.

"Don't, Gin, it will only make it harder," Sath said, his voice barely a whisper.

Suddenly everything clicked together as Gin looked down at the bundle Sath had been carrying. "No…" she whispered as she took a step closer, and then another, and then she was sprinting over and falling into the wet sand by the dock. "No, please, Mother Sephine, please…" Her hand shook as she reached for the edge of the linen sheet at one end of the bundle and pulled it back.

Taeben skidded to a halt. The scream that cut through the normally peaceful early morning chilled the blood in his veins. "Gin…" All of her defenses dropped and he was able to see exactly what she was seeing without having to take control of her mind. It was just too good to be true. He picked up his pace, nearly flying along the sandy beach.

Tempest

"Gin, you have to understand...I didn't know..." Sath reached out for her as Gin looked up at him, and the wild look in her eyes stopped him.

"Don't." She pulled Lairky's corpse into her arms, smoothing the dark hair away from her younger sister's pale face. "Lairky...what did you do?" she whispered. "What did you do?"

"She was disguised as you," Sath managed to say, and then realized that was a mistake. Gin fell silent as she again looked up into Sath's teal eyes. She put her sister's body carefully down on the ground and got to her feet. "I was still charmed, Gin, I didn't know what I was doing."

"Go away, Sath. **Now**," she said quietly yet firmly.

"Gin, you have to understand..."

"*I don't have to understand ANYTHING, Sathlir*," she hissed at him. "Now, get out of my sight." Taeben rushed up behind Gin, staring in disbelief at the scene. He had no idea what she had just shouted at the Qatu in his language but he didn't care. This was so much better than he could have hoped when he realized that the bard was dead. Gin would NEVER forgive Sath for this and the number one obstacle between them, her younger sister, was eliminated. Taeben could barely contain his glee.

"If we can just talk," Sath said, "alone?" Taeben stepped in between them and pushed Gin behind him. "That means without you, wizard."

"You do not deserve to look at her, Qatu, let alone speak to her..." Taeben barked at Sath, but her hand on his back silenced him.

"No." Gin's voice was soft, but firm. "No, I have nothing left to say to you, Sath." Gin looped her arm through Taeben's and he pulled her into his arms. She looked up at him, her blue eyes filled with tears, and he pushed into her mind, relieved at how easy it was compared to the first time.

Ginny, it's all right.
He killed Lairky! I do not think that is all right.

Ginny, you must not be sad. You must be happy to be with me and I will protect you from the Qatu. You must forget Lairky for now. Can you do that for me?

I would do anything for you Ben.

Once he was sure that she was out of the way, he looked up at Sathlir who was standing still, staring at them in shock.

"I don't know what you did to my little puppet, Anni, but it means that you are going to be all alone now, Your Highness," he said to Sath. Gin kept her arms around Ben, looking up at him, glassy-eyed and smiling.

"Shut your mouth," Sath said, a warning growl rumbling in his throat.

"OH, that's right, your half-sister did mention that you wouldn't be a contender to her throne because you don't want it anyway," Taeben said, grinning. "Such a lovely feline is Maesha. A Qatu after my own heart, that one."

"Say what you like, wizard. Take my half-sister, take Qatu'anari, I don't care. But if you hurt Gin..."

"You mean like you did? Here?" Taeben spun her around and she laughed like a child in a game. He indicated the scar on her cheek and Sath grimaced. "Yes, well, I think I can do a damn sight better with our Ginny than that." He wrapped his arms around Gin who snuggled into them. "Seems she's less ours and all MINE now, don't you think? Now do something with that dead wood elf, will you? I don't think you should take her to Aynamaede, though. They tend to throw people off the edge for much less." Taeben whispered something in Elder Elvish and a ring of fire surrounded the two of them. They disappeared, leaving Sath standing by Lairky's body.

The Crown Prince of Qatu'anari fell to his knees in the sand and scooped the body up into his arms. He held her to him and finally let some tears go that had been building up since Anni sent his son went to the royal nursery. Finally, after a long time, Sath found the strength to stand and shake off his grief. He didn't know how long he had been curled up around Lairky's body, but he knew it was time to move on. Gin had made her choice, even though it was influenced by that wizard, and Sath knew that there was no future for them now.

The future…his mind flew back to Qatu'anari, to the palace, to the tiny cub that was waiting there for him. With Anni gone, it stood to reason that her magical influence was also gone. His half-sister would never take the throne any more than his sister Kazhmere would, because they were female, his father would see to that. Sath cracked his knuckles in frustration. It seemed to be time for a change for the Qatu. He picked up Lairky's body and made his way to a boat that would take him to the mainland, toward the Fabled Ones, and his oldest friend Teeand. The dwarf would know what to do.

Nancy E. Dunne

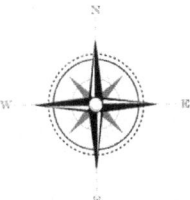

TWELVE

Sath placed his hand against the wooden door of the Great Hall. He carefully pressed each of the secret locks in turn, and was pleased to hear the locking mechanism click inside the door. He pushed it open with the same hand as he held the body of the dead wood elf to his chest with the other.

Elysiam was seated in the middle of the great hall, meditating, and she opened her eyes as Sath entered. "Well, I'd say look what the cat dragged in, but seeing as you ARE the Cat..." She paused as she noticed the bundle that Sath carried. "What is that, Sath? What has...where is that bard of yours?" She got to her feet and took an instinctive step back from him. "Sath? What has happened?"

"Anni is dead, Elys." Sath knelt down and reverently placed Lairky's body on the floor. "I have wronged your race, Gin's family, and our guild and I no longer deserve to be called a brother of the Fabled Ones. I have come to give up my charge and accept whatever punishment is fit."

Elysiam stared at the body on the floor, and Sath could see in her face the pieces fitting together. "Oh, dear Spirits, Sath you didn't...that isn't...tell me that's not Gin..."

"No!" Sath took a deep breath. "No, this is not Gin. This is the body of her sister, Lairceach." Involuntarily Elysiam sank to her knees, and a great keening sound erupted from her. Hack appeared at the door to the healing pool and quickly made his way to Elysiam's side.

"What did you do, Sath?" the diminutive warrior said as he glared up at the Qatu. "Elys, sssh, it's all right..." Hack pulled her close to him, which was much easier with her on her knees, and held her close. She wailed and sobbed for a few long moments, but then suddenly got herself together and pushed Hack away.

"He's killed our Lairky, that's what he did," she said, pointing an accusing finger at Sath. Hack looked at her, puzzled and Elysiam exhaled loudly. "Gin's baby sister, the bravest of us all!" she said. Hack nodded, realizing whom she was talking about, and then shot a puzzled glance up at Sath.

"Is that true, Sath?" he asked, his voice strained as he clearly struggled to comprehend what Elysiam meant. "Did you...kill Ginny's sister? Do I have to take you off my list?"

"Here now, what's all this yelling?" Teeand called out as he came out of the room with the healing pool. His smile faded as he made eye contact with Sath, who quickly averted his eyes. "What are you doing here?" the dwarf snarled, his hand already on the hilt of his battle-axe.

"He's brought us his latest kill," Elysiam hissed. "See? There on the floor? The Bane of the Forest has struck again."

"No. Elys, no, if you would just let me explain..." Sath began, but Teeand stopped him with a look.

"Out. Everyone out but Sath," Teeand ordered. "Hack, can you and Elys please...can you take...never mind, I will deal with it, just get OUT." He waited, not moving a muscle, with eyes trained on Sath, until Hack managed to drag Elysiam away from Lairceach's body. Hack whispered something to her as they lingered a moment in the doorway, and then Elysiam spoke the words of magical transport and they disappeared in a column of light.

"Right, Tee, if you'll just..."

"Shut your mouth, Cat." Teeand marched over to Sath, who was still kneeling, and looked the Qatu Crown Prince in the eye just as he would anyone else. "Just yes or no answers for now will do, thank you. Is *Annilanshi* with you?"

"No."

"Is she likely to follow you here?"

"No."

Teeand considered his oldest friend for a moment. "Are you here of your own accord?"

"Aye."

"Was *Annilanshi* charming you? Is that why you left us?"

"It's why all of this happened, Tee, I…"

"I said yes or no!" Teeand barked. His stranglehold on his own chaotic emotions was growing weak. The dwarf was overjoyed that his best friend was standing here before him without that awful bard wound around him like a serpent, but he was still furious that Sath had left them in the first place as well as unsure about what to do with the wood elf sized bundle on the floor. "Were you charmed, yes or no?"

Sath hung his head. "Yes."

"Did she force you to kill Lairceach?" Teeand asked hesitantly. He could feel the tide turning, and hoped against hope that Sath's answer would be yes.

"It's complicated."

Teeand roared in frustration as he moved closer to Sath, making sure that he had the Qatu's attention. "It isn't complicated! Were you charmed when you killed Lairky or not? YES OR NO?"

"Aye."

"See? I knew it!" In an uncharacteristic show of affection, Teeand ran at his friend and threw his arms around Sath's neck, hugging him tightly. "I knew we'd get you back from that snake of a female, Sath! I knew it!" Sath did not return the hug, and soon Teeand released him and looked Sath dead in the eye. "What else is there?"

"I thought she was Gin, Tee." Sath's voice was low and filled with anguish. "Lairky had disguised herself as Gin, down to the color of her eyes this time. The potion was…convincing." He paused, expecting an outburst from Teeand, but nothing came. "She killed Anni, right there in front of me. Stabbed Anni in the neck."

Teeand allowed a sad smile to cross his lips. "Our Lairky... She was so brave and talented for one so young," he said softly.

"Only Anni didn't die right away and she kept humming this tune...I suppose that was what kept me charmed. I hated that tune. She didn't play it all the time, not like in the beginning when she..." Sath paused a moment. "I hadn't realized till just now that there is a lot that I can't remember."

Teeand balled up his fists to keep from screaming at Sath to continue the story. His patience was long since gone. "Lairky stabbed Anni, and then what happened?"

"All I know is that Anni was hurt, dying...I could smell the blood...and I was angry. I saw her there, Lairky, but she looked so much like Gin...and she was taunting me and I picked her up and...well, their necks are so tiny and..." Sath couldn't continue his sentence and just balled up his clawed hand, cracking his knuckles as he did. Teeand stared at him in horror.

"You thought you were killing our Gin, Sath?" the dwarf whispered, unable to believe what he was hearing and nearly unable to speak the words aloud.

"Anni was still humming, but just after I dropped the body she must have died because I...I came back to myself. I looked into our bedchamber, she was dead, there was so much blood, and...I didn't care. I should have cared, Tee, but I didn't. I came back out to see Gin curled up on the floor and right then I knew, Tee, I knew what I'd done and..." Sath stopped, choking down a sob. He was silent for a moment before he could continue the story. "I picked her up and held her and...and her illusion fell away. And it wasn't Gin, it wasn't her, it wasn't my little dru...but it was almost worse because it was Lairky, an innocent, so young..."

Teeand ran a stumpy-fingered hand over the top of his head. "Blimey, Sath," he said as he tugged on his beard. "This is bad, this is very bad. Have you...does Gin know?"

Sath closed his eyes and nodded his head. "The wizard is the high elf ambassador to Qatu'anari so he and Gin have been living in one of the embassy buildings. I was bringing Lairky's body back to her home, and I ran into Gin and that wizard at the docks waiting for a boat to the mainland. She will never forgive me, Tee. She's run off with Taeben and I think we've seen the last of her."

Tee stood quietly a moment and then put one of his hands on Sath's arm. The two friends locked gazes. "She will come around, Sath."

"I don't think so, he's charmed her or something, Tee. She's gone, and it's all because..." He paused a moment, cracking his knuckles to fill the silence that hung between him and his oldest friend. "Do you forgive me? Will Elys ever forgive me?"

"I do, Sath, but really there is nothing for me to forgive. You were not yourself when this happened. But you are now. *You are our Sathlir again now,*" he said, the last and most important sentence spoken in carefully crafted Qatunari.

"Your accent hasn't gotten any better," Sath said with a forced grin. Teeand smiled back at him, but the smile was less than genuine. "So now what do we do, Tee?"

"We give Lairky a proper warrior's pyre, as she deserves, and then we resume our travels as normal. If our Gin comes back to us, we will worry about that then. But for now...we leave her with that wizard, I suppose," Teeand replied. "I don't know what else to do."

"I can't hunt with you," Sath said. "There is much more that I need to tell you, Tee. So much more." Teeand had bent to pick up Lairky's body, and Sath quickly moved to help him. "After we have done right by our Lairky, I will tell you a story about the newest Prince of Qatu'anari."

Nancy E. Dunne

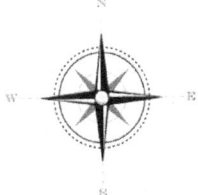

THIRTEEN

Over the next few days, Teeand managed to broker a fragile peace between Sath and Elys, and they arranged to all meet at the ruined druid stone circle in the forest to honor Lairceach. Sath bore her body into the middle of the circle but then stepped back outside out of respect for her and the others of her kin that had fallen at his hands. "Gin would not invite me here," he said to Teeand, who tried to convince the giant feline to rejoin them in the circle. "None of her kind would. You know that as well as I do."

"Well she isn't here now, is she?" the dwarf hissed back. Elysiam shot them dirty looks and Teeand shrugged his shoulders. "Fine, as you wish... *Highness*," he said, using the Qatu word for the title and giving Sath a mocking bow. Sath scowled and then sat down with his back against a tree where he would be able to see the ceremony. Elysiam spoke loudly in words that Sath only partially understood. He had never learned the elder version of the Elvish language as only the high elves and the priests used it and his tutors had never figured he would encounter either in his life at the palace. It struck him that not only would it have helped him understand Gin's spell work but also the ambassador to Qatu'anari was currently a high elf. Sath clenched his jaw as he thought about how very wrong his tutors had been.

Elysiam held her arms above her head, and Sath could almost see an aura of power coalescing around her hands. Still not understanding all the words, he was able to decipher that she was calling out to the All Mother, Sephine, and Her Consort, Kildir, to accept Lairky's sacrifice, because she kept saying the wood elf's full name, Lairceach. And Cursik, was that Gin's older brother? Ah, gone to the spirits along with her parents, or so Sath was piecing together.

Next, Elysiam spoke the word that reverberated through Sath's entire being. **Ginolwenye**. His *darlin*, his little dru. How could things have gone so wrong between them? He had thought he would have a lot of making up to do after Salynth charmed him but this was much, much worse. She would never accept him after this, nor would she accept his son.

Khujann. A low growl started in Sath's chest at the thought of the cub. Would he even recognize the young one? Did *Khujann* know that Sath was his father? Did he still bear the name that his parents had given him? His parents. The growl grew stronger at the thought of Anni. Sath was angry at her, so very angry, for taking him away from everything that he knew and loved, but at the same time he was sad for her because she clearly had not been alone in her treachery. She had been a willing pawn of the wizard's because of her feelings for him. "*Oh, Anni,*" he whispered.

Hack and Teeand had moved to the center of the circle and lifted Lairky's body to place it on the pyre. "Wait!" Elysiam held up both her hands and spoke in the common tongue. "Sath, will you enter the circle?" Sath's eyes widened but he did as she had asked, his head bowed respectfully as he approached the wood elf. She nodded at Teeand and Hack, who moved to either side of Lairky's body as Elysiam took hold of it at the shoulders. "We are all brothers and sisters in the Fabled Ones, Sathlir Clawsharp," she said. "Today we add to our ranks a new sister, Lairceach, and she should have all of us helping her on her way to meet the All Mother and her Consort." Sath's heart caught in his throat as he moved closer to take hold of the other shoulder. The four of them lifted the body onto the already smoldering pyre and then stepped away, each at one corner. Elysiam took aim and sent a magical fireball into the center of the wood and it burst into angry, lapping flames.

Sath looked down at his feet, but soon felt the tip of Elysiam's scimitar against his arm. "You will watch," she hissed. "Do not be the coward that lowers his gaze. Bear witness. You are the cause of this and you will see it through." He nodded and settled his gaze back on the tiny body at the center of the inferno. "She will forgive you, Sath, she always does. She loves you, you know that, and deep down she knows how much you love her. And... I forgive you." He looked down for a moment and saw Elysiam wipe a tear off of her cheek and then resume her stony gaze.

"I hope you're right, Elys. I really hope you're right."

Later, as they all sat around the hearth in the great hall, Teeand was laying out maps and planning their next journey. He had an idea about exploring the frozen wasteland at the northernmost point of Orana, and was plotting a course.

"I will travel with you as far as I can," Sath said, "but I must make a stop for something at Qatu'anari. I can catch up with you."

"We can just go with you," Hackort said. "I've always wanted to see where you come from, Sath."

"I will not be there that long," Sath replied. "I will be a day or two at most, and then I will catch up with you."

"*Royal business?*" Teeand asked in very deliberate Qatunari. Sath nodded at him, almost imperceptibly.

"Okay, fine, but while you're gone the dwarf has to teach us some of that growly grumbly language of yours, Sath. It isn't fair. You know all of ours," Hackort demanded, tiny hands folded across his chest. Sath chuckled.

"You are right as always, wee man," he agreed. "We set off at dawn then?" There was agreement all around, and they broke for the night, each moving to a different part of the grand hall to get some sleep. Teeand followed Sath into the room with the magical healing pool. "*Got something to say, Tee?*"

"*Is it that obvious?*"

"*Aye, spit it out. I'll have no secrets between us ever again,*" Sath replied.

"Fine. Why are you going to Qatu'anari, Sath? You're not really going to join us later, are you?"

"I've got a bad feeling, Tee," Sath replied, rubbing his hand over the top of his head as he tended to do when deep in thought. "My half-sister, the Princess Royal, has been in league with that wizard all along and I think they mean harm to my father."

"So? You've said yourself that he is more or less dead to you."

"True." Sath paused a moment before continuing to speak. "But my sister, Kazhi, is there, and my Mama, and Khuj..." He paused a moment, clenching his fist before he continued speaking. "I can't let that wizard end up in control of my homeland if I can help it."

"You think that's his plan?"

"He didn't say so outright, but yes," Sath said. "He has Gin with him and if he tries something she may get hurt and..."

"...and we can't let our girl be hurt by the likes of him." Tee replied, a genuine grin across his face. "Go do what you need to do, Sath. You know where to find us if you need us." They clapped arms, and Sath pulled the dwarf into an awkward hug. "Always my brother," Teeand said.

"Always."

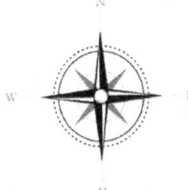

FOURTEEN

The embassy building where Sath had lived with Anni was nothing but rubble. This time, the explosion he had set off had been hot enough to burn it to the ground rather than just give it the appearance of ruin, as they'd done to hide from the Royal Family. Sath kicked at a charred brick as he walked through the remains, his face hidden by the hood of his cloak. A male Qatu dressed in the livery of the *Sahi Kalah* stood guard near what had been the bedchamber of the building, watching Sath closely.

"*You there!*" he called out. "*This is a crime scene. State your business and be on your way at once.*"

"*Those that lived here, what became of them?*" Sath asked, hoping that the other male would not recognize his voice. He was almost certain that the *Sahi Kalah* was Kinjab, a male that he had played with in the royal nursery when they were cubs, but he dared not reveal his identity just yet. Pulling on the hood of his cloak, he moved closer.

The *Sahi Kalah* swallowed hard before speaking. "*Those that lived here were His Highness, Sathlir Clawsharp, Crown Prince of Qatu'anari, and his mate Annilanshi. They perished in the fire. No remains were found that could be identified.*" He moved closer to Sath, sniffing the air as he did. "*Who are you that asks after His Highness?*"

"*Just a friend, a concerned citizen of Qatu'anari,*" Sath muttered. It was definitely Kinjab, because only a friend of Sath's would refer to him by his title after the *Rajah* had disowned him. He pulled the hood of the cloak down further over his face. *"Why do you guard it if there is nothing here, really, to guard?"*

"It seems that the Rajah had a change of heart," the *Sahi Kalah* said, again moving closer to Sath, who did not move away this time. "The death of his son caused him great pain, and he has named Khujann, his grandson, as the Crown Prince and his successor to the throne." He sniffed the air again and smiled. "It would do your father good to know that you were not in the building when it burned, Sath." Sath knocked back his hood and Kinjab beamed a toothy smile of relief at his old playmate.

"You cannot tell anyone that you have seen me, Kinny, do you understand me? I will reveal myself to my father in my own time. Until then, tell me, is my son safe in the royal nursery?" Sath asked, his teal gaze locking on his childhood friend, wiping the smile off Kinjab's face and making the *Sahi Kalah* tremble a bit.

"Aye, Highness, he is fine," Kinjab replied. *"You know from your own experience how many Sahi Kalah are guarding the nursery at any given time. Sath… Highness, if you will forgive me, you look so much like your father. It is…unsettling."* Sath growled low in his chest and Kinjab took a cautionary step backward.

"I am nothing like my father," Sath snarled. *"You will do well to remember that. But I must have my son, I must know that he is safe. If I go to the palace, I will be arrested on sight, that was my father's promise."*

"Go to the Rajah, Sath," Kinjab said. *"He is a changed man. I have heard rumors from his personal Sahi Kalah that he is thinking of acknowledging your sister, Kazhmere, and giving her the title that Maesha holds. He grows old and is starting to think of the kingdom more than just himself…or his First Wife."*

"He did love my mother, I will give him that," Sath replied. *"More than any of us, he loved my mother and still does, I imagine. Right. I will go to the palace. What have I to lose?"* Sath stepped closer to his old friend and extended his hand. Kinjab looked at it and then cautiously took it, and Sath pulled him into a tight hug. *"Thank you, Kinny."* He released the *Sahi Kalah* and turned on his heel and left.

"I'm just glad you're back," Kinjab replied to the space Sath had left. "Your Mama and Papa will be glad as well." He resumed his watch over the ruin, but this time couldn't help the broad smile that he wore.

Qa Kahzlir, *Rajah* of Qatu'anari, sat alone at the giant desk that occupied almost all of one end of the Throne Room. The business of running a kingdom such as Qatu'anari meant that there was endless paperwork to sort and approve and file, and he wished sometimes to be as carefree as he had been as a younger cub.

As if on cue, Kahzlir's grandson Khujann burst into the chamber, a nanny and a *Sahi Kalah* hot on his little heels. "AMPAH!" he squealed as he ran up to the desk. "*I don't wanna go back to the nursery, please Ampah!*" Kahzlir laughed and held out his arms to the cub who climbed him like one of the palm trees that grew in the city.

"What have you done this time, Little One? You've brought an entire army on your heels it seems," Kahzlir said, chuckling and bringing the cub up close to his own face. Khujann rubbed his tiny head against his grandfather's cheek and purred his tiny kitten-like purr.

"*Nothing, Ampah, I promise.*" The nanny scoffed loudly. "NOTHING!"

"Jala? You disagree?" Kahzlir said to the nanny, who immediately went to her knees, face pressed into the marble floor. She raised her face only enough to answer his question.

"Respectfully, yes, Rajah. Prince Khujann has been most naughty this morning. Not only did he leave the nursery but Maluki stopped His Highness as he was attempting to leave the city walls!" the nanny replied, her voice unsteady. Kahzlir's eyes narrowed as he looked at his grandson, and then bent and offered a hand to the nanny to help her up off the floor.

"Is this true, Khujann?" he said as she stood on shaky legs. The cub opened his mouth to protest and then shut it quickly, nodding his head as shame crept into his features. "Leave us," the *Rajah* said to the nanny and the *Sahi Kalah*. "I would have a word in *private with my grandson."* Immediately the two fled the throne room, and as soon as the stone door slammed behind them Kahzlir turned his attention fully on Khujann. The cub shivered in fear.

"*Khujann, you are so much like your father was,*" Kahzlir said sadly. "*So adventurous and fearless. But you must NOT put yourself in harm's way, do you understand me?*"

"*But I get so bored, Ampah!*" Khujann exclaimed. He crossed his little arms across his chest, growling low in his throat. "*Nothing will happen to me!*"

Kahzlir's teal gaze searched his grandson's matching one. It was amazing, so much like looking at his own son when Sath was just a cub. Kahzlir thought back to those days with a mixture of sadness and affection. How had things gone so wrong with his son? "*Listen to me, Khujann, I have something I need to tell you, and I fear it will make you very sad but you must be a brave little soldier, yes?*" The cub nodded his fuzzy head, his tiny teal eyes narrowing in anticipation of a great secret. "*Do you remember your Mama and Papa?*" The Prince's brow furrowed a moment and then he sadly shook his head. "*I was afraid of that. Your Papa was my son, Sathlir. He was a very brave and strong Qatu, skilled in battle and fiercely protective of those he loved.*"

"*Where is my Papa?*" Khujann asked. "*Why don't I live with him and my Mama?*"

"*That is the sad part of the tale, Little One,*" Kahzlir said. "*Your parents sent you here to live with me and your Ahma to keep you safe. There are many people outside of our city walls that would do you harm because you are my grandson.*"

"*But why? Everyone loves you, Ampah,*" Khujann replied, his brow still furrowed. "*I don't understand.*"

"*The only thing you need to understand, Little One, is that your Papa and Mama loved you very much, and would be so proud of you if they could see you now.*" Kahzlir paused a moment, lest his own emotion get the best of him. "*You are the light of your Ahma's life, I think, because you remind her so much of our Sath. But there is more you must hear. You have an Auntie that you don't know about.*"

"*Auntie Maesha? I don't like her, she is always cross.*"

Kahzlir chuckled at his grandson's expression. *"No, Khujann, another Auntie, and it is time that I acknowledge my entire family...it is time we are all made whole,"* he said.

*"Past time, **Papa**,"* Maesha hissed as she slipped out from behind one of the columns at the other end of the throne room and scowled at her father and the cub that now clung to the *Rajah*'s neck. She had snuck in as the nanny and the *Sahi Kalah* snuck out, and now stood with one hand gripping a staff and the other firmly on her hip. She was wearing her leather armor, stained black, which made the black stripes on her fur seem to leap out from their background like some sort of war paint. *"It is well past time."*

"Maesha, what is the meaning of this?" Kahzlir roared, and then immediately checked himself to avoid frightening his grandson. *"Khujann, you need to go find your nanny. Koby!"* The *Rajah* waved the *Sahi Kalah* who stood with his daughter to the desk, and the male immediately complied. Maesha scowled at his back as he approached the *Rajah* and took a knee. *"You will take the Prince back to the royal nursery."* Khujann hissed but stopped with a glance from the *Rajah*. *"No arguments, Little One."* He kissed the Prince on the top of his head and then handed the squirming cub over to Koby. *"Remember, Khujann, your Ampah loves you just like your Papa did."* Khujann struggled and spit as Koby removed him from the throne room, still wailing to return to his *Ampah*. *"Now, Maesha, you will tell me what you are doing here without my permission?"* the *Rajah* said, his rage simmering and threatening to boil over.

"Your days of ordering me around are over, Kahzlir," she hissed.

"YOU WILL NOT ADDRESS ME IN THAT MANNER!" Kahzlir roared. *"You are as troublesome as your mother was!"*

Something snapped in Maesha just then. Her eyes narrowed as she took a few steps closer to her father. *"Troublesome? You find me troublesome? I will show you troublesome, Kahzlir!"* she shouted. *Eldyr* words flew from her lips, and an angry swarm of magical insects surrounded the *Rajah*, stinging and biting at his flesh. Maesha turned and hooked her staff through the handles on the great stone door, effectively locking it from the inside and buying her some alone time with her father. *"I have a sister that I didn't know,* it seems. So many secrets you have kept from me. But it doesn't matter, does it? Because we are females and not suited for the throne." She punctuated that sentence with an icy magical bolt that seared into her father, pinning him to his spot. He roared again in pain just as the pounding of the *Sahi Kalah* personal guard assigned to the *Rajah* was heard on the Throne Room doors.

"*Maesha...you do not...want to do this...*" Kahzlir stuttered, unable to shake the frigid blanket of magic that surrounded him. "*You are my first born...I love...*"

"SHUT UP!" Maesha screamed at him. "*You do not love me! You love that grandson more than me! But what you do not know, father of mine, is that your son, your precious Sath, is not dead.*" She drew near to her father who was starting to warm up to the point that he could move about, and dodged a swipe of his claws.

"*You lie,*" Kahzlir hissed as he scanned his desk for a weapon, still shivering.

"No, **Papa**, it's true," Maesha said, her voice barely a whisper. She moved in behind Kahzlir, in one motion drew a dagger from her boot, and plunged it into his neck. Kahzlir howled with rage and pain as Maesha wrapped her arms around her father's neck, holding the dagger in place. "*Once I am finished with you, I will take care of that cub. Then no one but YOU will know that Sath lives, and I will be queen!*" she hissed in his ear. Kahzlir choked and gurgled as his lungs filled with the blood that poured from the wound in his neck. Maesha held him and the dagger fast until his knees buckled and he fell out from under her.

"*Maesha...my...daughter...*" Kahzlir sputtered. His teal eyes scanned hers as she bent over him. "*How did I wrong...you?*" He flailed about, trying to get to the dagger to remove it, but found that his arms were not cooperating.

"Let me count the ways, Father! Oh, no, you don't have that much time, do you?" She squatted down next to him. "*I could end this for you now but it is much more satisfying, watching you suffer.*"

The door to the throne room burst open as Savdhi, First Wife of Qatu'anari, and Kazhmere entered in a rush flanked by *Sahi Pahl*. The *Sahi Kalah* assigned to the throne room had alerted the First

Wife that something was wrong, and Kazhmere had been attending her mother at the time so she ran along behind. Luckily, the females that guarded the First Wife were strong enough to break the hold the staff kept on the door handles.

"KAHZLIR!" Savdhi shrieked as she flew to his side, knocking a surprised Maesha out of the way. The Princess Royal recovered quickly, though, and shoved Savdhi to the floor, her other dagger that she retrieved from her boot now glistening in her hand. She stared down the *Sahi Pahl* that had taken a protective stance around Kazhmere, who was spitting and fighting to get away from them to her parents.

"*You will not interfere, whore,*" Maesha said, rising to her full height, dagger poised to strike. "*And you,*" she said to the *Sahi Kalah* who seemed to be creeping toward her and the body of their *Rajah*, "*You will not interfere either or you will see your First Wife join her mate.*"

"*What are you doing, Maesha?*" Savdhi wailed. "*Why would you do this to your father, who loves you so?*" Kahzlir made a rumbly sound and then fell silent, his eyes on Savdhi. She stared at him in horror.

"*Let all know…Kazhmere…is my…daughter,*" he said, every word a struggle. "*Maesha…is… exiled.*" His eyes rolled back in his head as his body convulsed in the last throes of death. The *Sahi Pahl* stood in slack-jawed silence at his words, then stepped back toward Kazhmere at a nod from the First Wife.

Savdhi scrambled to her mate's side, giving Maesha just the opening she needed to strike again. She plunged the shining weapon into Savdhi's back, and pinned her to the body of the *Rajah*. Savdhi did not cry out, but held fast to Kahzlir as her life drained away onto the marble floor.

Kazhmere, still flanked by the two *Sahi Kalah*, sat in a corner, saucer-eyed and unable to move as the other *Sahi Kalah* streamed into the room. The one at the door had sounded the alarm as the First Wife and her entourage had broken down the door, and it seemed now that soldiers were coming from every corner of the city. They surrounded Maesha and took her from the room, hissing and spluttering that she was not finished, and that the Princess must die. As the crowd of armor and weapons began to thin, one male Qatu stood in the doorway to the throne room, his features obscured by a dark brown traveling cloak.

Taking deep, rattling breaths, Kazhmere slowly rose from her perch in the corner and as the *Sahi Pahl* parted, she walked stiffly toward the bodies of her parents. Kinjab, who had come when the alarm sounded, moved to her side, but she dismissed him with a sad look and he left the room, nodding to the cloaked figure in the doorway.

Unable to continue walking, she went to her knees and crawled up close to them, and then reached out a trembling hand toward the dagger in her mother's back. She wrapped her clawed fingers around it and gave a half-hearted pull, but then recoiled, retching, as the blade hung in her mother's back. Again, she reached out and took the hilt.

"*Stop, Kazhi,*" said the cloaked stranger in the doorway. Kazhmere's head shot upward as she inhaled deeply.

"*Sath?*" she asked, barely able to form the name on her lips.

"*Yes.*" In an instant, the new Princess Royal was on her feet and in her brother's arms.

"*I haven't seen you since the tower! They said... you... fire at the embassy....*" Kazhmere's attempts at speech faded into a long, keening wail. "*Mama... Kahzlir... Papa...Did you hear what he said?*"

"*No, what?*" Sath asked, barely able to keep his own emotions in check as he looked down at the body of his mother. He had not even been able to tell her goodbye, or that he loved her.

"*He acknowledged me, Sath! He called me his daughter.*"

Sath pulled away from Kazhmere's embrace, holding his sister at arm's length. "*Who else heard, Kazhi?*" he asked brusquely. "*Anyone?*"

"*The Sahi Pahl, his Sahi Kalah, and Kinjab heard, and Mama and Maesha,*" she said, her voice tight. "*Maesha. I will kill that...*"

"*She is already dead, Kazhi,*" Sath said, loosening his grip on her shoulders to wipe the tears from her cheeks. "*The Sahi Kalah that took her will see to that. But the important thing is that no one outside of the palace knows what Papa said."

"Why is that important? I am legitimate now! The Princess Royal!" Kazhmere pulled away from her brother. "You don't know what it was like, Sath, coming back here, unable to call him Papa, being kept in the shadows like when I was little." She sniffled and wiped her nose on the back of one of her hands. "Mama visited me when she could but we were never alone. I had gone to her tonight to beg her to intercede with Papa because I could no longer bear it, with you and Anni gone..." She stopped a moment, her mouth making a perfect O as something occurred to her. "If you are safe, then is Anni...?" Her brows furrowed as she watched Sath's face darken in response. "What has happened to Anni, Sath?"

"You will do well to never mention that name in my presence again, Kazhi," he snarled. "There is much I need to tell you but for now, you need to get somewhere safe. A member of the royal family has assassinated the Rajah. There will be those looking to take advantage of that fact."

"I can fight as well as you can and you know it, brother," Kazhmere hissed in return. "But I will take your counsel. I do think, however, that there is someone else that should hear of this from you above all others." Sath cocked his head to one side, puzzled. "Stay here, I will return in a moment," she said as she slipped out the door. Sath pulled his hood up onto his head and then stood looking at the mess on the floor until a sword point in his back interrupted his thoughts.

"You will put your arms out where I can see them," the *Sahi Kalah* said from behind him. Sath recognized the voice as that of Hulan, a Qatu male younger than he, who had followed Kazhmere around like a lovesick fool when they were cubs.

Sath did as requested and the guard quickly pulled his hands together behind him, holding them as he turned Sath around. "Hello, Hulan," Sath said, beaming a sad grin at his old friend. Hulan immediately released Sath and fell to the ground in front of him, forehead pressed to the marble floor.

"Your Highness, forgive me, I did not know...We heard rumors that...I do not understand, how are you alive?" Sath chuckled and stepped back from the genuflecting male at his feet.

"Get up, Hulan, I don't have time for this nonsense," he said, holding out a hand to help the stunned male up from the floor. "Where have they taken the Princess Maesha?" Hulan's face fell.

"We came in to rescue her, having heard shouts and arriving too late to save the Rajah and First Wife," Hulan said. "I am so sorry, Highness. You have to know we would have done whatever we could to save them."

"I know, and please, call me Sath. I'm no more Highness than you are, Hulan."

Hulan swallowed hard. "Right...Sath...we took the Princess to her chambers and...it was as if she had gone mad, screaming and fighting us, bragging about...killing the Rajah..." The *Sahi Kalah* hung his head, looking every bit the young cub that Sath remembered. "Some of my brothers at arms...well, they were angered by her words and...she is dead, Sath. The Princess Royal...I suppose she is no longer, is she, since His Majesty exiled her, so Maesha is dead. There is no Princess Royal now. As her intended consort, it is my duty to inform you." Again, the younger male looked down at the ground, expecting an outburst from Sath. None came.

"Hulan, I am going to tell you something that will stay between you and me until I make it public, do you understand me?" Hulan nodded, his eyes still reverently downcast. "*Do you remember Kazhmere, from the nursery?*"

"*Aye, Sath,*" Hulan said, finally raising his eyes to meet Sath's teal gaze. Sath was pleased to see he lovesick cub still present in those eyes. "*She witnessed the killing of the Rajah and the First Wife, did she not?*"

Sath nodded. "*Kazhmere is not an orphan, as you and the others were told. She is the daughter of the First Wife and the Rajah. She is the cub that was allegedly stillborn. She is my sister, and now, the Princess Royal.*" Sath couldn't contain his grin any longer. He did know how it had hurt his sister to be unknown and unclaimed. He had watched her grow up, noticed how upset she had been when parents came to claim the other cubs from the nursery and she was left behind. It had almost killed him to leave her there when he was exiled, but she was too young to hunt with him and he had thought it was for the best.

"But...I don't...oh, Sath, if I have said or done anything untoward...you must believe it is because I did not know her status...I..." Hulan searched Sath's eyes but all he saw was amusement.

"Hulan, you are the one I share this with because you are the **only** one that I trust to watch out for my sister. No one must know who she is until I...until there is a new Rajah on the throne and we are sure she is safe."

"But that new Rajah is you, Sath. You are the Crown Prince. Your mother was First Wife," Hulan said. "The only reason your father named Khujann as his successor was because he believed you to be dead. It is simple, we present you to your Sahi and then to the Qatu, and they swear loyalty. There is no need for formal coronation, considering the circumstances."

Sath nodded. "How many know that I am still alive?" he asked, lowering his voice.

"None know for sure I as far as I know, Sath," Hulan replied. "Rumors have gone round among Maesha's bodyguards and servants but they were merely that. And now I know why Kinny has worn a stupid grin for a few days." Sath chuckled, nodding. "Although... There was a foreign visitor at Maesha's chambers recently, high elf if I remember correctly. If Maesha knew, then she might have told..."

Sath's heart skipped. "Male or female?" he asked, not daring to hope.

"Well, the wizard was male but he had a wood elf female with him. My sister is one of Maesha's Sahi Pahl, and was full of stories of the fierce little wood elf whose mate treated her like a slave," Hulan said. Sath's breath caught in his throat along with a low growl. Slave? "I can fetch her if you like? My sister, I mean. I suppose I could also find the high elf because I understand that he is the ambassador to Qatu'anari from Alynatalos of the Elves in the Forest."

"No, the fewer that know I am alive the better for the moment." Sath felt as though his heart might explode up through the top of his head. It was too much of a coincidence that his father was murdered on the same day that his half-sister had a visit from a wizard and a wood elf. In addition, living in an embassy! A long-suppressed memory surfaced of Gin on the beach hovered in the back of his mind. That had been real, after all. *"Tell me, Hulan, was the wizard red haired by any chance?"*

"Aye, Sath, but I don't know his name."

"That's fine, Hulan, you've told me what I needed to know," Sath said, turning and crossing the room to his father's desk.

"One more thing, Sath. The wood elf was named Ginny apparently," Hulan said. *"I know this because my sister thought it was the ghastliest sounding name when the wizard called her that."* Sath froze, and then balled up his fists, causing his knuckles to crack.

"That will be all, Hulan, if you don't mind. I'd like...a moment alone with my parents. Can you hold off the guard that will be coming to take...their bodies?" He glanced over his shoulder and Hulan nodded, then inclined his head and left the room, closing the massive doors behind him.

Sath wandered over and sank down onto the floor next to his parent's bodies. *"Oh, Mama, you always did love him, didn't you? No matter what he did to you, Kahzi, or me? You saw the good in him."* He reached over and carefully pulled the dagger from her back, then tossed it aside. To his surprise, she stirred a little bit, groaning in pain. *"Mama?"*

"I must...be dead..." she whispered, her voice weak and small. *"I am with my Sathlir."* She turned her head to look at him and her eyes lit up. *"You are alive, my sweet boy... Take care...of your sister, my proud cub,"* she said. Sath drew close to her face so she could see him, and placed one of her cold hands on the side of his face, holding it there because he knew she did not have the strength. *"So handsome, just like your father,"* she whispered, and the light just winked out in her eyes. Sath roared and wrenched her body up off that of his father, holding her to his chest.

"No, no Mama, no..." he moaned. The sound of footsteps in the hallway outside the door brought him back to sharp focus. He carefully laid her body down on the floor next to Kahzlir's, and then

took a long look at his father. *"I heard what you said, Papa,"* he whispered just before the doors flew open. *"I loved you too."*

"Step away from the Rajah and First Wife at once!" barked one of the *Sahi*, his spear raised toward Sath. Sath could hear Hulan in the hallways pleading with them to wait.

"Gladly," Sath said, standing and turning to face them, his hands in the air. As soon as they recognized him, the lot of them took a knee in unison.

"Prince Sathlir, you must forgive us, but…how are you…we thought…" The captain of the personal guards of the *Rajah* had risen and approached Sath, his weapon in both hands extended toward Sath. *"We swear our loyalty to…"* Sath raised a hand to silence the oaths taken by the *Sahi* at his feet.

*"I know what you thought. It was better at the time for me to continue to be dead, in case there were plots against my family. Little did I know that the greatest threat of them all came from **within** my own family,"* he said sharply. *"I trust that my half-sister has been dealt with appropriately?"*

"Aye, Highness," the captain responded. *"Or, should we refer to you as Majesty now? You are taking the throne, are you not?"*

Sath remained silent for a moment, and then a sad smile crossed his face. This was his destiny; the fact that he knew now that he loved Gin with all that he was had nothing to do with this. A wood elf could not be First Wife of Qatu'anari, and clearly she had made her choice to be with that wizard. Or had she? Hulan's words rang in his ears, about the elf whose mate treated her like a slave. Fierce, he had said his sister called Gin. Yes. Fierce she was. *"Stay fierce and strong, my little dru,"* he whispered in Elvish.

"I'm sorry, Majesty, what did you say?" asked the captain.

"I said yes, yes I am claiming my right to the throne of Qatu'anari," Sath said, the words sounding hollow in his ears.

"Long live Rajah Qa Sathlir!" the assembled *Sahi Kalah* chanted in unison. *"Long live Rajah Qa Sathlir! Long live Rajah Qa Sathlir! Long live Rajah Qa Sathlir!"* Someone stirred at the back of the armored throng, and they parted to form a path from the door to Sath. Kazhmere stood in the doorway, holding Khujann tightly in her

arms. Sath's breath caught in his throat. How fast his son had grown from the wriggling, mewling infant that Anni had handed over to Sath's mother. He went to a knee, overcome at the sight of the young Prince, his arms open wide.

Khujann stilled in Kazhmere's arms, pointing right at Sath. *"Who is that, Kaz...Auntie Kazhi?"* he said in the loud whisper at which young ones are so proficient. It was apparent that the young one had not forgotten what his grandfather had told him earlier about his new Auntie.

"That's your Papa, Khuj," she whispered back as she smiled at her nephew. *"He is my brother, Sathlir. Why don't you go say..."* Her sentence was cut short as the tiny Qatu leaped from her arms and landed on the marble floor with a thud. Before anyone could help him, he was back on his feet and running as fast as he could to bound into Sath's arms, wrapping his tiny arms around his father's head. The *Sahi Kalah* in front quickly rearranged themselves so that they were blocking the young one's view of his dead grandparents as the soldiers in the back began the process of removing the bodies from the room.

Sath's eyes bulged from his head in surprise for a moment, and then he closed them and hugged his son tightly. A rumbling purr filled the room. *"Khujann, my son..."* he murmured into the Prince's tousled fur.

"I love you, Papa," the cub said. *"Thank you for coming to get me."* The *Sahi Kalah* filed out, having removed the bodies, and Kazhmere followed them.

"Kazhi, a moment?" Hulan said, breaking ranks and sidling up next to her.

"For you, anytime, Hulan," she replied, licking her lips and smiling at him. *"Majesty, with your leave?"* Sath waved her off, making a mental note to tell her that she didn't have to call him that. But for now, all he needed was right there in his arms.

"Khujann, I will always come to get you, anytime you need me," Sath said. *"But you should not need that ever again. Papa is here, and we are safe. Nothing can touch us now, my son. Nothing."* His thoughts wandered to oaken tinged skin, a freckled nose, a smile that was

only for him... Sath wondered if she had really chosen to be with that wizard, or if the *Sahi Pahl* that had served his sister was right in calling Gin a slave. He tried to tamp down on the growl that started deep in his chest whenever he thought of her with Taeben.

"*Where is Mama?*" Those three words brought Sath instantly slamming back into the present.

"*Do you remember your Mama?*" Sath asked Khujann, looking into those tiny teal eyes that mirrored his own. The cub thought for a moment, almost causing Sath to giggle at his tiny screwed up face, but then shook his head. "*That's all right, my son,*" he said, a bit relieved if he was honest. "*Your Mama was named Anni, and...*" Sath paused, unable to think of anything he could tell Khujann about Anni that didn't involve how angry he was at her deception and her place in everything that had happened to him and Gin...and the Fabled Ones. "*...and her best friend in the world was your Auntie Kazhi. You should ask her about your Mama. I'd like to hear what she has to say.*" Khujann nodded but wound his little fingers into his father's fur. "Is something wrong, Khujann?"

"*I don't want you to leave me, Papa, like you did before.*" Sath fought back a growl. "*Ahma told me that when Mama brought me to live here it was because Mama was afraid that you would not want me.*" The cub started to squirm. "*Papa, you're holding me too tight!*" Horrified, Sath loosened his grip on his son and almost dropped him, but Khujann was already hooked into his Papa's fur with tiny sharp talons on the end of each finger. "*Careful, Papa!*"

"*I've got you, son, I just need to sit down,*" Sath said sheepishly as he quickly crossed the room to the cushions next to the throne and sat down. "*There. Now I am sure not to drop you. I am just not used to holding...a young one like you.*"

"*That's okay, Papa. Ahma said that Ampah did the same thing with you when you were a cub,*" Khujann said, giggling. Sath found that the beautifully perfect sound of his son giggling had almost washed away the grief and anguish over his parents' deaths.

"*That explains a lot,*" Sath said, chuckling. "*Khujann, I did not send you to live with your grandparents because I did not want you. I need to know that you understand that. I was...your Mama and I were afraid that there might be people that would want to hurt you, just because you are my son."*

"Yeah, I know, the wizard and the...elf," the cub replied, rolling his eyes in an exaggerated fashion that nearly made Sath laugh out loud.

"About that..." Sath paused, unsure of how much he wanted to tell the young cub. *"Khujann, that wood elf was a friend of mine a long time ago. She would never, ever do anything to hurt you. Your Mama and I were wrong about her."* He paused a moment, watching until Khujann nodded in response. *"Her name is Gin, and if anything ever happens to your Papa and your Auntie Kazhi, and you need someone, look for her because she is good and kind and she will make sure that you are safe just like I would. Can you promise me that?"* Khujann nodded and Sath noticed that the lids of the cub's eyes were growing heavy. He stood slowly, cuddling his son in the crook of his arm, and carried the drowsy little Qatu out of the throne room. He was headed toward his old chambers when he ran into his sister in the hall.

"Where are you going?" she asked in the common tongue, taking him by surprise. "Don't look at me like that, Sath, we had the same tutors, I know more than one language," she snapped, making him chuckle.

"I was taking my son to his bed," Sath whispered, *"but I fear I don't know where that is. I barely remembered the way to the throne room."*

"You are headed for your old chambers, which will be his when he is a bit older, my dear brother," Kazhmere replied, smiling at him. "But for now he is still in the Royal Nursery. Would you like me to show you?" Sath nodded and she padded down the corridor in front of him. He looked at her and then looked down at the now-dozing cub in his arms. Could he be this lucky? Did he deserve this?

"Sath?" He looked up to see his sister standing in the corridor, her hands on her hips, waiting. There was no answer to his question; only a pang of regret that Raedea - his first real friend and former travel companion - had not lived to see this day because he knew she would say he deserved every second of it.

"You'd be so proud, Rae," he whispered and then continued down the hall after Kazhmere to the Royal Nursery.

Nancy E. Dunne

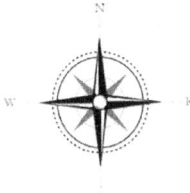

FIFTEEN

Gin tried to remember how she had come to be on the marble floor where she now found herself, but the events of the recent past were so blurry. Every time she tried to call up specific events, all she got was a pounding headache and the vaguest sensations of memories. She didn't know how long she had been there, only that periodically Taeben would enter the room and she would lose track of things for what she assumed was a few minutes. When she came back to herself, there would be food, water, and clean clothing where he had been.

"Ben!" she cried out. "Please!" Rubbing her eyes with the heels of her hands, she stood up, pleased to find that she had regained enough strength that she no longer wobbled, and looked around to get her bearings. The room was well appointed. There was a poster bed in one corner and green marble walls and floors. Luxurious rugs adorned the floor by the bed and under a polished dark wood desk opposite the bed. Her traveling kit was still propped up by the desk, but she had long since searched it and found it to be empty. There were no windows, but Gin could hear the sounds of the surf and the marine wildlife that told her she was most likely still in the embassy building on the shore of Qatu'anari…or at least that was her best guess.

The door to the room opened and shut with a whoosh and Ben was there, standing before her…at least she thought that's who it was. The face was right, the demeanor, even the arms folded flat against the chest of the sapphire wizard's robes. But the hair... His hair was solid white, like the landscape of the frozen lands to the north. His eyes were a similar icy white, and when his gaze met hers she shivered involuntarily as though he could freeze her to the spot with just a look.

"Are you feeling more yourself now, love?" he asked. Taeben's voice oozed compassion as though he would take her in his arms, but he remained where he was, standing just inside the marble door.

"What...am I doing here, Ben? Where are we?" She took a step toward him and he backed up into the door. "Why are you acting so strangely? Why can't I remember anything? All I know for certain is...oh...Lairky..." She sank to her knees, the memory of Sath holding her sister's body shooting through her mind like an angry hornet. Taeben came to her side but did not reach out to her. "And what has happened to you? Your hair? Your eyes?"

"You truly do not remember?" he said, a smirk present on his lips as he spoke. "I fear that it was shock, my love, that turned my hair white. Shock that you would think that I was carrying on in an inappropriate manner with that disgusting Qatu female. Shock that you knew as much of their barbaric, growly language as you did. Shock that you would believe those gossiping *Sahi Pahl* over me, whom you know you can trust."

"That is the most ridiculous thing I've ever heard," Gin said, brushing herself off as she got to her feet. "Qatu female? Gossiping felines? What are you talking about? The only Qatu I remember is Sath... Now, where are we?" Gin shook her head to try to clear it.

"We are at home, love. We need never leave again."

"But where is home? Is this Qatu'anari? The embassy?" Gin demanded. "Are we in Alynatalos? Why won't you tell me what is going on? Why don't I remember anything?" She rubbed her elbow absently with her hand, then paused as a sharp pain caught her attention and caused her to pull up the sleeve of her tunic. Cuts and bruises crisscrossed her skin, and she found welts further up on her arm as it joined her shoulder. "Ben?" she whispered, "What has happened to me?" She felt her face and winced as she found bruises and more cuts.

"Ginny. What am I going to do with you? Don't you remember when we met in Bellesea Keep, and Lord Taanyth was using you to test his spell, in order to find the resistance your race holds out against it?" Gin stared at him, wide-eyed and silent. "Well, I thought, why let that spell go to waste when I have all the research right here in my mind?" He tapped the side of his forehead as he grinned at her. "Think of how powerful we will be, love, once I have perfected it!"

"You've been testing that spell on me?" Gin was incredulous. "Is that why I can't remember? That nearly killed me before! You said you loved me, Ben."

"And I do...I've been testing it on myself as well, which is the real reason for the change in my hair and the eyes," he admitted. "I would never do anything to you that I haven't already done to myself, Ginny. I love you too much for that. The shock over your affinity for the Qatu was not really that surprising, in retrospect." Gin took a step away from him and toward the door but Taeben held out an arm in her way. "Oh, no, I don't think so my love, you will not be leaving just yet. Think of **us**, Ginny. We don't need to stop with just ruling that flea-bitten Qatu city. We will simply start there, and then we can rule all of Orana with this spell." He rubbed his slender fingers together in anticipation. "We will be gods, you and I."

"You're insane," Gin whispered, backing away from him and nearly tripping over the plate of food. She closed her eyes and began to recite a spell that would transport her away from wherever she was, but Taeben knew the words and snatched her up in his arms before she could finish. She struggled to get away from him, scratching and biting, until he finally backhanded her across her cheekbone to quiet her. She glared at him, holding the side of her face with one hand.

"I feed you, I clothe you, I love you, and look how you treat me!" he yelled at her. "I do all of this for you, for US, and it is NEVER ENOUGH! I should shove you out the door and let those loyal to me tear at you as they have been begging to do since I brought you here!"

"I'd rather be out there with THEM than with you," she spat back at him, and as he was coming at her again with his hand raised, there was a knock at the door. He dropped his arm and pointed at her menacingly.

"Move from that spot and I will kill you myself," he swore at Gin, then moved to the door and opened it a crack. A Qatu male, dressed in the livery of the *Sahi Kalah* of the Royal House of Qatu'anari, stood at the door, a fearsome and tall creature. Gin found herself shaking at the sight of him. "Yes?" he said, clearly irritated at the interruption. The *Sahi* said nothing but handed Taeben a piece of parchment that he had clutched in his clawed hand. Taeben yanked the paper from the male and slammed the door in his face before unrolling and attempting to read it. "This is written in Qatunari, Gin, if you would?" She stared at him, not moving, so he grabbed her by the neck with one hand and shoved the parchment into her hands with the other. "READ."

Gin's voice was halting as she worked to translate the document. She did very well with spoken Qatunari, but had little practice with the written form. "Lord Taeben, Ambassador from Alynatalos of the Elves, this…this is to inform you that…" She bit her lip for a moment, struggling with the next word, and Taeben tightened his grip on her neck. "Diplomatic relations are ended due to the death of… the death of the Rajah, Qa Kahzlir, at the suspected hands of Maesha, formerly the Princess Royal and your patron in the Qatu Council. You…will vacate the embassy and…" Taeben yanked the paper from her hands, releasing her as he ripped it to shreds.

"Oh dear spirits no… She had no right… Now I have NOTHING! Once again, a cursed Qatu has ruined all that I have prepared for! That stupid Maesha, she has gone and killed the *Rajah*! I have no contacts left in the palace!"

Gin felt a pang of sadness in her heart. Maesha's quad that had taken care of her while Taeben was meeting with the Princess Royal had told her of the fire that they thought had claimed Sath's life, and even though Gin had seen him on the beach with Lairky's body, she couldn't remember clearly when that had happened or if it had actually happened at all. For all she knew, the *Sahi* females were right and Sath really was dead. They had tried to explain to her that Sath was the next in line for the throne but it had not made much sense to Gin's magic addled mind at the time. If Sath was truly dead, then Kazhmere - the only Qatu Gin knew that she could trust - was also the only member of his family left, and she would be so alone. "Oh, *Kazhi*," she murmured.

"Ah yes! Kazhmere! The true Princess Royal!" Taeben's face lit up with a happiness that Gin had not seen from him in so very long. "Perhaps there is still a chance! Sath would not dare risk the life of his sister just to keep his throne."

"Sath...is alive?" Gin said, barely able to believe what she was hearing. Ben bit his lip, annoyed at himself for letting that information slip. "And the throne? Ben, what are you saying?"

"Oh, just that your little kitty-cat turned out to be very important to me, and the death of that horrible half-sister of his has left the throne wide open for me if I can just get to *Kazhi* first. She will trust me..." He mused briefly, eyes closed, and Gin saw her chance. She ran for the door, attempting to push it open and dart out before Taeben even opened his eyes again, but his arm shot out and grabbed her, holding her fast as he leaned on the door to shut it.

"You know that the Qatu will kill you if you leave, Gin," he said, filling the door as he stood between her and freedom. "You won't have my protection anymore. There are many out there in the wide world that would love a shot at the mate of the wizard that will be the *Rajah* of Qatu'anari. They would kill you as soon as look at you."

"What do you care, Taeben? One less thing to worry about. One less thorn in your side, one less annoyance...I would think that rather than blocking the door you would be shoving me through it and onto their blades." she said, striding over to retrieve her things and slinging her backpack over her shoulder.

"I need you, Ginny, you know I do. I love you. It's you that doesn't care." He stood his ground, crossing his arms over his chest. "It's you who runs around on me when you think I'm not looking, or sneaks out for a tryst with that Qatu the one time I leave you alone here. It's you that leads me around by my nose because I love you so much."

Gin looked at the floor, biting her lip. "Move, Taeben," she said. "You can't control me anymore, I won't let you."

"No." He stood still, arms unmoving and folded across his chest.

Gin looked up at him, and then placed her hands on his folded arms in an attempt to move him out of the way Gin looked up at him, and then placed her hands on his folded arms in an attempt to move him out of the way; he opened his arms and flung her backwards. She stumbled and lost her balance, catching her head on the edge of the dressing table. A tiny trail of blood appeared on her forehead, making her wince as she touched it.

The sight of that blood on her head seemed to flip a switch in Taeben, and as Gin felt clearer headed that she had in ages he was at her side, trying to help her up, but she fought him off. He clearly could not maintain his hold in her mind when he was that concerned for her wellbeing and she took advantage of the situation. "Ginny, love, I'm sorry," he said, "I didn't mean to hurt you." His eyes filled with tears that seemed to surprise both of them, and he wiped them with the back of his hand. "It was an accident, love, I swear."

"Right," she said, wiping the blood off her face and moving past him to the door. "This time it was. What about all the others? I don't ever want to see you again."

"I didn't mean it, Ginny, please..." His voice, so genuine and full of fear, threatened to break her heart but she didn't turn around. A tendril of his control had started moving through her mind but she blocked it as best she could. "I meant what I said about always finding you, love," he said, moving closer to her. A sneer spread across his face. "You belong to ME and I will hunt you and I will always find you, no matter where you run." He was right behind her, close enough to grab her and take her, but he remained only inches away. Gin focused her magical will in his direction, causing the very marble in the floor to liquefy for a moment before encapsulating his feet, holding him fast.

"Then you'd best be ready to start looking," she said, anger rising in her voice. Taeben stared at her in disbelief. Without him at the forefront of her mind, she was free to feel, free to think on her own and defend herself, and she took advantage of it. "You would be nothing without me. You cannot function without me. The slightest injury could kill you without me there to heal you, and that, my sweet Taeben, is why you want me here. No more, no less. I am stronger than you will ever be, and you know it, and it makes you furious. The spell work didn't turn MY hair white, now did it?" She laid a hand on the doorknob and paused. "You beg me to stay, but I think my answer is **no more**. Goodbye, Taeben. May the All Mother have mercy on you for I am certain I cannot."

Taeben screamed from behind the door that Gin slammed behind her. His voice rang in her ears, nearly drowning out the howling of the wind as it blew down the beach off the turbulent ocean. Once she was out the door of the embassy, Gin planted her feet in the sand and began moving her lips in silent recitation. Inside, Taeben finally freed his feet from her magic and ran out the door, lunging for Gin and dragging her back toward the door by her midsection. However, she had started her spell recitation early enough, and with the last word she vanished from his arms with a flash of white light. She had cast a spell to transport only herself, and he was left behind grasping at thin air.

"NO!" Taeben screamed as his arms closed around nothingness. "Oh, this will not do!" He paced about as electricity crackled and sparked from his fingertips. "The Qatu will pay for this! All of Qatu'anari will pay for this! There is nowhere you can hide, my Ginny! I will always find you. ALWAYS."

Nancy E. Dunne

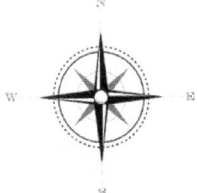

SIXTEEN

Sath leaned back against the plush velvet cushions and sighed, rubbing his forehead with one of his giant hands. In the months since he had assumed the throne, he had learned that the paperwork to keep Qatu'anari a bustling and prosperous city was endless. There were reports of shipping trade to be gone over, betrothal requests to formalize, and the seemingly never-ending stream of new citizens coming to swear allegiance... Sath smiled; they were swearing allegiance to him, in his proper place as the *Rajah* of the Qatu.

His brow furrowed as a memory crossed his mind. He could still smell the damp ocean air mixed with the stench of dried blood and death. He could still feel the tiny body of the wood elf cold in his arms. He could still hear Gin's screams when she realized what he had done. Sath closed his eyes as he balled up one mighty hand into a fist. The image of Lairky's body in his arms shifted and changed into that meeting on the beach when she had not known who he was, and he snarled. His tiger - a magical creature always present at his side though now allowed a velvet cushion of his own - sensed his master's distress and perked up his ears. Soon Sath felt the mighty head of his closest companion slide up under his other hand, drawing him out of his memories and bringing a sad smile to his face.

"Bah," he said as he stroked the mystic beast's fur. "*She's better off, I'm better off, we're all better off,*" he said, a growl slightly present behind his words. "*Go back to your place, my old friend, I'm fine.*" The tiger did as it was bidden, and soon settled back into the plush cushion, its eyes fixed on his master.

"*Papa, Papa...Papa!!!*" A tiny Qatu burst into Sath's private chambers, hurtling his tiny body up onto Sath and sending reports flying everywhere. Khujann stared up at his father in admiration which soon turned to fear at his father's expression.

"*Khujann!*" Sath roared. "*How many times have I told you about disturbing your Papa when he's at work? Where is your nanny?*" He held the squirming young one in one hand as he studied the tiny face.

"*I don't know,*" Khujann lied, his gaze quickly shifting to the desk and away from his father's penetrating stare.

"*Want to try that again?*" Sath said, tipping the boy's face up to meet his gaze with one finger. He was careful not to hurt his only child with his massive claws... This another lesson Gin had taught him so long ago when he'd accidentally cut her cheek.

"*No,*" Khujann said, tears brimming around his eyes. Sath's resolve melted and he grinned at his son.

"*How long has she been locked in the kitchen, Khujann?*" he asked, barely able to contain a giggle. Khujann's eyes flew up to his father's, betraying him.

"*How did you... I mean, she's not... I mean...*" Sath stared intently at his son in mock anger, one eyebrow raised. "*Just an hour,*" the tiny cat admitted.

Sath sighed. "*I know because the other cubs and I used to do the same thing to our nanny, m' boy,*" he said with a wistful smile. "*Now go and let her out, and leave me to clean up this mess you've made, eh?*"

"*Yes sir,*" Khujann said, hanging his tiny head. "*I'm sorry, sir.*"

"*Bah, save your sorries for L'lanna,*" Sath said, grinning. "*She's going to have you washing bed linens for a week this time.*" Khujann scowled at him and scampered off. **So much of his mother in his face**, Sath thought.

The image of *Annilanshi* brought a grimace to his face and a growl to his throat. He loved his son more than his own life; at the same time, he could not help the hatred that had grown in his heart for the boy's mother. Anni, under the direction of that wizard, had single-handedly ruined his life with Gin by bewitching him away from her and the rest of the Fabled Ones...and that same power she held over him had led to the death of Gin's only sister, Lairceach. Again Sath closed his eyes and rubbed at his forehead as the sound of Gin's screams echoed in his head. *"One day,"* Sath murmured, *"I'll make that right...if she will let me."*

Gin felt like she had been walking forever. When she had first left Taeben and the island of Qatu'anari, she had landed near the tunnels and had headed south toward the Outpost, seeking out any shelter granted to her. Unfortunately, what she had found was that the wizard had been careful to destroy most of the relationships she had from her past life. Inns that were marked as safe houses for elves from the time of the Forest Wars were already off limits to anyone not friendly with the denizens of Aynamaede, but Taeben had been careful to ruin her name with other establishments as well.

She had nothing when she left the embassy that morning save a bit of money she had been able to hide away in the moments she was lucid. As she walked, Gin tried to piece together all of the time that she had been with Taeben, but so many blank spaces remained in her memory. She wasn't even sure how long she had been with him - the best she could come up with was that it had been several months since that awful day when Sath brought her Lairky's body.

The image of him holding Lairky in his arms was like a knife in Gin's heart, not easily banished. He had taken her only family from her, save some cousins that still lived in Aynamaede and were not likely to give her shelter anyway. He had thought that he was killing her, not Lairky, proof that any chance of a life together for them was out of the question. And Lairky, poor, proud, strong

Lairky had not been given a proper burial. Gin whispered a quick prayer to the All Mother to keep Lairky's soul close until Gin could figure out a way to make that part right, as that was the only part of this she could control.

"Hey there, pretty," said a voice from somewhere off to Gin's left. She slowed her pace but continued moving, whispering words of magical protection as she went. "I said hey there!" the voice called out. Gin paused. Male, possibly human, speaking the common tongue so probably human. She opened her hand and her staff swung up into it, shooting sparks of defensive magic as it did. The humming sound it made vibrated into her arm, giving her courage.

"Who is there?" she said, trying to keep her voice calm. "Show yourself."

"Turn around." Gin turned slowly to see a human male standing in the path behind her. He looked so much like Dorlagar to her that it took her breath for a moment. "What's the matter?" he asked, cocking his head to one side. "Never seen a human before?"

I've killed a human before, she thought. "Sorry, sir, you looked like someone I used to know. How may I be of assistance?"

"I'm so glad you asked," he replied, and then let out a loud whistle. Several more men appeared on the path from behind the trees, closing in around Gin and leaving her little room for escape. "It's been a long time since we've seen anything as pretty and tiny as you in these parts, not since the Wars ended I reckon." The other men grunted their agreement and Gin felt her heart jump up into her throat. This would have been the point that she would have cast a magical snare to hold them and dashed out of the middle as they fumbled while Taeben started sending magical lightning bolts and fire raining from the sky down on them until they fled. But there was no backup coming this time. She was on her own.

"Probably not, we don't tend to venture this far south anymore unless we are trading or on diplomatic business," Gin responded, angered by the tremble in her own voice. She thought that she could still feel Taeben in the back of her mind, but decided that she was imagining that and shook her head to clear it. "And speaking of which, I'm on an assignment from the Ambassador to the Qatu from the Forest, so I must be on my way." She hoped that they would believe her.

"QATU!" the first man bellowed, laughing. "Hanging out with those oversized beasts, are you?" He bent over and slapped his knees, laughing. "All you need is a bucket of water to keep them at bay, little one, or didn't you know that?" He moved closer and his henchmen followed suit until Gin was looking up at him, her back toward another man and one on either side of her. She stood still, refusing to break eye contact with him but not saying a word. "Oh, look, it can't talk now," he jeered.

"No, but I can," Taeben said. Gin froze in place, unable to believe what she was hearing. Had she gone insane? Was this a hallucination? She had heard his voice in her mind so many times before, but not with this clarity and volume. "*Ginny, if you please,*" Taeben said in carefully crafted Elvish, "*come along now, and do as I say for once.*" She cut her eyes around toward the tree but saw nothing there. "*Hit the one in front of you with your staff while calling up that snare,*" he said. Gin swung her head around wildly, trying to spot Taeben but unable to see him anywhere. "*You know what to do, Ginny, just do it.*"

"Where are you?" she hissed.

"Right here, love, you want me first?' the man in front of her said to her. He reached down to grab her shoulders, smiling lewdly.

"*Now, Ginny!*" Taeben hissed.

Gin stared right at the man reaching for her and spoke the words that caused magical roots to rise up from the ground and hold him fast. He nearly fell over in surprise, giving her the chance to thrust her staff sharply up and then backwards. It connected with the throat of the man that was standing behind her with a sickening thud that was followed by gasping as he desperately tried to take in air. Spinning around to her left, Gin managed to sweep the legs out from under one of the two men left standing. His head hit the ground with a crack as she turned to face the last of the four. He started to grab for her and then thought better of it, turning instead to run away.

"*Yes! That's my good girl! Now, finish him, Ginny!*"

"*Ben, where are you?*" Gin clapped her hands together above her head and magical electricity flowed from the space between them into the back of the man that was running away. He screamed as the energy entered his body and sent him sprawling forward, unconscious but, Gin hoped, still breathing.

"You're a naughty girl," said the first man, now behind her as he had managed to get his feet free of the roots and lunge toward her. "You need some manners, elfy." Gin took a deep breath and again clapped her hands together, drawing down more electricity into the top of his head. He staggered backward and, after her staff swung up into her hand, she cracked it across his face, knocking him unconscious.

"Manners?" she bellowed at him. "How's that for manners?" Gin turned slowly in a circle, looking at the damage that she alone had done, and laughed. She found that she could not stop laughing, and that soon her laughing turned to hysterical sobbing. Gin lost her footing and fell to her knees, her staff clattering out of her hands just out in front of her, as she continued the heaving sobs.

Suddenly she felt hands on her shoulders, lifting her up off the ground and pulling her into a tight embrace. She couldn't open her eyes or mouth, and she almost couldn't breathe. Her arms were held tightly at her sides and she felt as though the ground had come out from under her feet. Her heart beat wildly as she gasped for air. "*Quiet down, love,*" Taeben's voice whispered into her ears - or into her mind? "*Sssh...You've done it, you're safe now.*" Gin couldn't work out how he was there, or how she could hear his voice, but she nearly melted with relief that it was just Taeben and not one of the men she thought she had dispatched. "*Just come home to me, now, you know the way,*" Taeben cooed. Gin thought about how lovely that would be, just to go back to the embassy with the cool marble floors and the soft bed and Ben...

"Wait." She forced her eyes open and found that she was standing alone in the clearing, the bodies of the men all around her. "No. NO!" She backed up involuntarily and nearly tripped over the charred remains of the first man, who had apparently caught fire from the magical lightning and then been knocked out by the blow from her staff. "I don't know how you're doing this, Ben," she shouted as she turned around, looking in all directions, "but you will not have me again! Never!" Gin snatched up her rucksack, threw it over her shoulder, and then held out a hand, smiling as her staff flew up into her grasp - the one **good** bit of magic he had taught her.

In the back of her mind she could hear him screaming as he had when she left him...how long ago was that? Not long enough. Gin wiped her hands off on her tunic and then continued walking, ever away from the Aynamaede as it was no longer home, but instead toward the Outpost. It was only a few hours walk away, give or take, but she needed to be a bit more presentable before she returned to beg the forgiveness of...Gin paused again, chewing on a fingernail as she often did when thinking. What if Teeand didn't forgive her this time? There was no one there to ask, no one there to take her in...and did she even need that after all? She had just dispatched four humans. She didn't need anyone anymore...and if Taeben could find her, as he claimed, then she didn't need to put anyone else in danger. She nodded her head and continued her walking. She would stop at the Outpost, finish her business with the Fabled Ones, and then move on...to where? Wherever the wind took her.

Taeben sat on the floor in the embassy, meditating. Charred bits of fabric and wood and food surrounded him, due to him taking out his anger on everything in his path. The Qatu wouldn't have an embassy left, he mused, if their ambassadors kept on burning them to the ground.

The Qatu. Taeben scowled. Mangy cats, certainly beneath him and not worth his time. Sath. That grinning, cocky face and those teal eyes stared out at him from his memories. That Qatu would pay with his life, as would they all. Sath's interference had driven away his Ginny and ruined his plans with Maesha. Taeben absently drew spells on the marble floor as he meditated, causing sparks and flames that were soon put out by cascades of water, all magic.

He did not need the druid anymore, but how magnificent she had been, taking care of those hideous humans that tried to put their hands on her! The wizard smiled for a moment. He did not **need** her, but he certainly did **want** her. With that sort of power on his side in battle and her ability to heal, the two of them would be unstoppable.

What were the barriers, then? What did he need to do in order to have her and have control, of not only Qatu'anari, but of the whole of Orana? Again came the face of that blasted Qatu, Sath. He was a challenge not just because he was the *Rajah* now, but also because he was the main barrier to Taeben having full access to Gin's mind. He had to die, there was no way around that. Taeben cleared his mind and then focused on sending out his consciousness into the immediate area, then further across the sea and into the highlands, looking for a mind that would be useful to him in his quest. To his surprise, he found one, in a very unlikely place.

Who are you? He was careful only to ask and not to invade, at least not yet.

Just let me die.

Female. High elf? Wood elf? Hard to say, but thinking in Elvish. *You are familiar to me. What is your name?*

I do not know. Just please let me die.

If I help you to escape, will you tell me your name?

Why do you care? The responses were growing stronger, only by a little, but stronger just the same. *How are you talking to me and yet I cannot see you? What is YOUR name?*

Will you tell me your name?

Help me.

Taeben smiled. There was work to do.

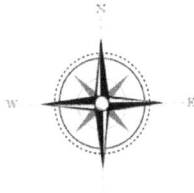

SEVENTEEN

A small hand traced the outline of the face on the great hall's door. Tiny fingers caressed the metal embellishments that adorned the heavy oak and iron door, and carefully tripped each lock before finally pushing it open. With silent footsteps, the wood elf entered the great hall and jumped with a yelp when the door closed behind her with a loud thud.

"Who's there?" called out a familiar voice. "Make yourself seen, we've no need for beggars in Fabled's halls."

"I'm not a beggar," she said, her heart in her throat.

Teeand rose from his usual seat by the fire, his eyes wide as he recognized the voice. Carefully resting his stein on the ground, he stood and took a deep breath. "Then show yourself that I may be seein' who you are, stranger," he said in an almost whisper, his breath catching in his throat.

"Am I guaranteed no harm will come to me, good sir dwarf?"

"I never make such guarantees, lass," Teeand said, "so if you won't come to me I'll be comin' to you then..." He halted in the doorway leading from the spa room to the grand hall.

"Hiya Tee," Gin said. "It's been a long time."

The dwarf's face was ashen as he rubbed frantically at his eyes with stubby fists. "This be a trick!" he thundered.

"No. No trick. I've...come home," Gin said, her voice barely concealing her fear. Teeand most likely hated her for leaving Sath and staying behind with Dorlagar back in Bellesea Keep, and she was sure he had never fully accepted her decision to go off with Taeben and leave the Fabled Ones. Teeand and Sath were as close as brothers, and his stubborn nature had made it nearly impossible to forgive her for the pain she'd caused the Qatu.

"More trouble yet to cause?" the dwarf sneered. Gin shook her head. There it was. "Why are you hiding in the shadows there, then, our Gin?" he asked. "Something you're ashamed of maybe? Not wanting to show your face around here after..." Teeand's words died in his throat as Gin stepped closer to him.

Her appearance was haggard at best. Her dirty auburn hair, normally tied back in a neat ponytail at the nape of her neck, was loose and flowing in tangled waves over her shoulders. She wore a faded leather tunic that had no arms, stained an odd bluish color, and leather trousers. Her boots, like the rest of her clothes, were leather but the soles seemed to be barely hanging on to the rest of the boot. As she pushed a stray lock of hair behind one of her delicately pointed ears, Teeand could see dirt caked under her nails and scars all over her exposed arms, neck, and face.

"I know that my appearance is not what is normally proper for a great hall, Tee," she said quietly. "I only ask that I might wash up in the healing pool and clean my clothes, and then I will collect the things I left here and be on my way. I have come to let you know that I make no further claims on any of the Fabled Ones." She dropped her pack on the floor, its straps worn thin with use, and then carefully laid her staff, which seemed to seethe and glow with magical thorny vines carved all along its length, at the surprised dwarf's feet. "That is the only weapon I possess, but please feel free to search my bags and belongings while I bathe if you feel the need." She walked past him toward the room where the healing pool and fireplace awaited.

"Gin," Teeand said quietly. "Wait."

She stopped, the hair on the back of her neck standing on end. "Yes?"

"Did **he** come back with you?"

"He who, Tee? *Sath*?" she asked, the Qatu name sounding so foreign on her tongue even though she had been living so close by to his kind for so long.

"No, not our Sath…the wizard," he said.

"Oh. No, **he** did not." She continued toward the spa room when she felt a hand on her arm, squeezing tightly. She stopped, fearing that she had outstayed her welcome and readied herself for the blow that would surely come to the back of her head.

"Did he do this to you?" Tee asked, his voice sounding strangely small. "The wizard, did he do this?" He held onto her arm with one hand while pointing at the scars with the other. Gin looked down at the floor, still waiting for the other shoe to drop.

"No." Gin lied, as she held her breath. She was too weary to know if Taeben was listening in, and she wasn't ready for him to know where she was just yet.

Instead of releasing his grip, Teeand turned Gin around and caught her up in his arms. "Good," he murmured as he hugged her. "I'd hate to have to take him off Hackort's list of people not to kill…"

The weight and worry of her journey, coupled with relief that Teeand had not split her skull in half with his oversized axe, suddenly hit Gin's soul like a thunderbolt. She fell into Teeand's embrace and wept, her body convulsing with sobs. The dwarf held on to the crying wood elf tightly, cooing at her as though she were one of his many children.

"There, there," he said, stroking her hair. "You go get yourself cleaned up, lassie, and we'll go and see someone that can make you feel better when you've had your rest." Gin nodded and untangled herself from the dwarf's grip before disappearing into the back room. Teeand again took up his stein and absently fingered the corona design on its side before taking a swig of the ale therein. "Aye lassie, someone that will make you feel better…and will do a world a' good for him as well I think."

Gin felt as though she had lost the weight of the world from her shoulders. A good long soak in the healing waters had continued what forgiveness from Teeand had started. The events of the recent past - though still present in her mind - washed away and she felt more like herself than she had in ages. Her traveling clothes - hung by the fireplace - were drying quickly, so she padded over to her haversack to look for something suitable to wear in the meantime. Though she was still planning to leave the Fabled Ones, she could spend one night, safe and warm, in the Grand Hall as a farewell.

She rummaged through her things but could only find clothing that was rough and road-weary. Smiling suddenly, she crept over to the drawers, hollowed out of the marble that made up the walls of the Fabled One's Great Hall. There were eight of them, in a rectangular pattern, and each had a special design that denoted the owner of the contents. These were installed after their former guild leader, Ailreden, left, and they held treasures and supplies alike for the six original members of the guild: Gin, Teeand, Elysiam, Hackort, Tairneanach, and Sath. Gin ran a hand lovingly over the thorny vine that decorated the second one from the right, the one that had been hers in the time that seemed a million years prior. She let her gaze linger for a moment on Sath's drawer which was right next to hers, the indentation of a swipe of his claws marking the wood, and reached out a hand to touch it, but her fingers hung in the air just shy of contact.

She pulled open her drawer and inside she found what she was looking for: a clean tunic made of cream-colored linen, embroidered at the sleeves and neck with a knot work pattern in dark forest green. Under the tunic, she found a pair of trousers made of the hides of the stag that made the Great Forest their home, and her favorite pair of boots that had been a gift from Teeand upon her joining the Fabled Ones. They were soft hide like the trousers, but lined with fur and studded with emeralds across the toes and up the sides. Pulling on her old clothes felt like again shedding the past few months of her life, but as she passed by the large mirror that hung on the wall, she paused.

Her eyes were sunken in dark circles, and her normally oaken-tinged skin retained its sickly pallor from months of no access to the outdoors while living in the embassy with Taeben. As soon as his name entered her mind, she thought that she could feel him waking up in the dark recesses of her mind, and could almost imagine him standing behind her in her reflection, arms folded across his chest as he looked disapprovingly down his nose at her. Gin shuddered and quickly tried to force him from her mind, for fear that he would be able to find her just that easily. After all, he had said that, hadn't he? That no matter where she tried to run, he would find her…

Shaking that off, she retrieved a brush from her drawer and began brushing her hair, having worked out most of the tangles while in the healing pool. It was nearly dry, and soon she pulled it back into the tidy ponytail that she always wore at the nape of her neck. Gin smiled. She was starting to look like herself again. Instead of replacing the brush in the drawer, she put it in her haversack and then did the same with the rest of the contents of the drawer: the spell book that had belonged to her mother, maps of the Forest and the lands to the south, and her father's ring that her older brother Cursik had given her. That ring was the beginning, the catalyst that launched her out of her safe and warm home and into…what? She slid it onto her thumb and studied it a moment, noting the condition of her hands.

Her nails were clean, but she noticed as she extended her fingers that her hands shook with a barely noticeable tremor. Hunger? Fear? Dehydration? It could be any of those reasons. Gin looked at herself again and frowned before returning to the drawer to leave the ring behind and retrieve her armor. Ben…HE had required that she leave it there when they had last left the Outpost, promising to have more for her at their new home. All he had prepared for her there was pain and suffering and obedience. There was no protection without obedience. No love without obedience. Familiarity breeds suffering and death. How many times had she heard him repeating that when he thought he had knocked her unconscious? How many times had he forced her to repeat the words to him before she could eat or drink or given respite from…from what? Why were there **still** holes in her memory?

Gin tried to shake off the tide of memories assaulting her senses. They were coming fast and furious now, and she was not ready to deal with them all at once. "Going somewhere?" came Teeand's voice from the doorway, thankfully breaking through her nostalgia and bringing her back to the present.

"I told you, Tee, I just needed to get cleaned up and then I would be on my way. I know there was someone you thought I needed to see, a healer perhaps, but I am fine now, I promise," she said.

"And I told you," he said, coming closer and taking her slender fingers in his stubby ones, "that there is somewhere we need to go."

"Where?"

"Always with the questions!" Teeand chuckled. "Can't you trust me, Gin?" She narrowed her eyes at him, no longer worried about the threat of his axe, and he chuckled. "There's our Gin! No, I suppose you can't, considering, but you need to try this time. It will be a good thing, I promise you."

"Who are we going to see?" she asked, softening her tone a bit. "You can't expect me to trust you if you don't tell me anything, Tee."

"Oh, aye, I can lass, and I will," he replied, a twinkle in his eye. "You'll be wanting to get some sleep, I'd think. I've...well, I tried to put a pallet up there on the balcony where your desk used to be, thought you might like to be somewhere familiar."

"Used to be?"

"Aye." Teeand chuckled. "When Sath...well, the last time he and ...He was here for a visit, and, well, he was a bit too big for your desk, and..." Gin's hands flew to her mouth to hide her smile and hold in laughter at the thought of the desk splintering under the giant Qatu's frame.

"Oh, he sat on it didn't he?" she said through a fit of giggles. Teeand nodded, unable to speak for laughing. "Was there anything left?"

"You mean on the floor or in his hide?" Teeand asked, bending over double in a roaring laugh. He stood back up, wiping his eyes, and Gin's laughter abruptly ceased.

"You were going to say that Anni was with him that time, wasn't she? How many times did he and Anni hunt with you after I left with…the wizard?" she asked quietly.

"He didn't," Teeand replied. His countenance, once buoyant and light, fell. "He…had a new life and…anyway, you need some rest, our girl," he said, clapping her on the back with a bit too much exuberance and nearly sending her sprawling. "We will leave at first light…oh, Ginny!"

Gin pushed his hand away. "Don't call me that," she said as she got to her feet under her own power and took a very visible step away from him. "Don't ever call me that again, please." She moved past him and positively scampered up the stairs, pleased that he did not try to follow her. The name rang in her ears as she spread out the bedroll Teeand had left for her and crawled inside. Gin lay there for a long time, staring up at the stained glass and letting silent tears flow as she longed for sleep.

Ginny. His voice was as clear as though he was curled around her in the bedroll. She closed her eyes tightly, knowing that there was no way that anything could hurt her here. Teeand was just at the bottom of the staircase.

Leave me alone, wizard.

Ginny, I miss you, please come home.

No.

Please. I need you; you know how much I need you, Ginny.

Gin shut her eyes tightly and balled up her fists, hoping that he could not see exactly where she was. *Stop it.*

Ginny. You know I will find you if you do not come home.

I am home. Go away.

Ginny, my love, you know that you do not want me to be angry when I find you – and I WILL find you.

"STOP IT!" she called out, unaware that she had spoken aloud until she heard the sound of Teeand's boots on the stairs.

"Gin? You all right?"

"Yes, I'm sorry, I was…just having a bad dream, Tee," she called out, holding her breath until she heard him go back down the stairs. "A nightmare," she whispered, "that I hope soon will be at its end." She pulled the bedroll up around her ears and began naming the stars that she knew in the stained glass repeatedly until she finally fell asleep.

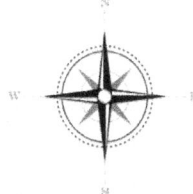

EIGHTEEN

The knock on the marble door leading to the royal bedchamber rang in Sath's head. He struggled to sit up, weighed down by layers of fine bedclothes and pillows. The servants that were never more than a tail's length away sprang to their feet, fussing over him, but he shoved them away.

"*Your Majesty, forgive the intrusion,*" called out one of the *Sahi Kalah* from the hallway outside his bedchamber. "*There is the rudest little man demanding audience with you, he says it's very important that he see you right away, my Lord.*"

Sath growled as he pulled on a thick wooly robe. The emblem of the Royal House of Qatu'anari was embroidered on a pocket on the chest, and the red wool was edged in black satin. "*This had better be very important, Kinjab,*" Sath responded

"*I was firm with the dwarf, Your Majesty,*" Kinjab answered, "*but he was quite insistent. Threatened to wake the lot of Qatu'anari if he didn't get to see you.*"

"Dwarf?" Sath opened the door and sighed loudly as Kinjab immediately went to one knee as was customary. "*Kinny, stand up, it's just the two of us here.*" The guard rose slowly and flashed an impish smile at Sath.

"*Just keeping you on your toes, Sath,*" he said. "*Where shall I tell the dwarf that you will see him? He says he brings a present for you but we've searched him and all we found was a beer stein.*" Kinjab wrinkled his nose. "*He claims the gift waits outside the city walls, but we sent him to fetch it lest he waste Your Majesty's valuable time.*"

"Good," Sath said. "*I'll receive him in the throne room. All this hubbub hasn't awakened my son, has it?*"

"*No Your Maj...Sath,*" Kinjab said, again grinning. "*I checked on His Highness and he is soundly asleep, but I placed an extra guard there just in case our dwarf friend isn't a friend at all.*"

"*Excellent work, Kinny. Please go show him into the great hall.*" Sath smoothed out his robe and made his way to the throne room where he received petitioners twice a week. Normally the marble walls filled with teeming masses of Qatu, come to see the *Rajah* to ask for any number of trivial favors. Sath rather liked being in the room late at night, and often took his supper there with Khujann; once the teeming masses had left, the room was so silent, as it was now. Sath could feel the presence of his parents there, and he hoped that they were proud of him.

Sath lit the lanterns on the wall by the throne and then sat down, cursing inwardly as he did that he had forgotten an extra cushion. "*Apparently dear old dad had more padding on his rump than I do,*" Sath mused with a grin. The grin fell away to his stern *Rajah's* countenance as the doors to the other end of the hall swung open and a dwarf dressed in green armor strode into the room.

Another individual followed Teeand, with features obscured second by a heavy brown cloak. Sath judged the person to be Elvish from the height, but dark elf or wood elf he could not tell. He smiled as he rose from his throne and extended a hand to the dwarf. "*Tee...it's been too long my friend.*"

Teeand grinned as he grasped Sath's arm just above his massive hand and shook it heartily. "*Aye indeed Cat, it has been far too long!*" The dwarf scanned the room, his eyes settling on the guards that had advanced when he touched their king. "*Is all that brass really necessary, Sath? I promise I won't be hurting your Rajah there, boys, at least not too much!*" Teeand called out to the guards as a throaty laugh erupted from Sath.

"*Leave us,*" he said in a commanding tone. The *Sahi Kalah* slowly filed out of the room, and Sath noticed that the person behind Teeand was trembling a bit under the cloak. *"So, what's the surprise then, Tee? Who is this under the..."* Sath knocked the hood of the cloak back with one clawed finger and gasped.

Gin's eyes met his a moment but then she immediately went to her knees. *"Your Majesty,"* she said in a voice that sounded far away. *"My apologies for the dwarf feeling that we must wake you from your rest, Your Majesty,"* she mumbled, the Qatunari words sounding stiff and rehearsed. *"I did try to reason with him that tomorrow would be better, but..."*

"Bah, woman, do you ever shut up?" Sath thundered. He focused his gaze on Teeand. *"At least **your** accent has improved a bit. Where did you find her? What does she want with me this time?"* Teeand remained silent, shaking his head from side to side, his arms folded over his chest as he nudged Gin with his boot.

"He seemed to think I needed to see you, Your Majesty," Gin said quietly, returning to the common tongue for fear that her knowledge of Qatunari would desert her.

"Call me Sath, please Gin," Sath said. He knelt down and gingerly hooked one finger under her chin, raising her eyes to look up into his. "It's been a long time."

"Aye it has, Your...erm...Sath," she stammered. Gin was positive that Sath and everyone in the room could hear her heart pounding against her ribcage. "Are you sure this familiarity is proper? I mean you are..." Gin closed her eyes and wrinkled her forehead, searching her mind for the Qatu word for king. It came to her with a memory of the female Qatu guard she met, and she opened her eyes. "You are *Rajah* now, is it right for me to call you by your first name?"

"You can call me whatever you want, Little One," Sath said, struggling to keep his hands from trembling as he imagined holding her tiny face in them. "Just so there aren't any backpacks or pots or pans hurtling at my head following the name, all right?"

Gin blushed to the roots of her hair, and Sath felt tears prick his eyes. She looked at him a moment, he saw that look cross her face that was only reserved for him… but just as quickly as it had come it was gone, and then she stood up and took a step back from him. Sath turned quickly and gestured toward the large cushions that littered the floor by the throne. "Please, sit down; tell me why you're here, Gin?"

"Tee brought me, ask him," she said. Sath felt a slight pang in his gut at the sudden icy tone that crept into her voice. He noticed that she kept her eyes on the hem of her cloak, fingers busily fiddling with a loose thread.

"Bah, the druid is as malcontent and troublesome as she ever was, Sath," Teeand grumbled. "You should have seen the mess that showed up at the great hall! Why, her hair was hangin' in her eyes and her hands were just filthy, and... OW!" Gin silenced the dwarf with a hard pinch on the elbow, in the exposed part between the plates of his armor. "Honestly, woman, you do that again and you'll look worse when I'm done with ya!" Teeand rubbed his elbow, frowning and grumbling to himself.

"The dwarf exaggerates," Gin said, carefully choosing her words. "I'd just been walking and sleeping rough for some time before I arrived at the great hall and was in dire need of a bath. Nothing more," she said, glaring at Teeand. He stuck his tongue out at her in response.

Sath rubbed his eyes with one of his hands. "Regardless, what brings you to the palace in the middle of the night? Will not one of you just tell me what is going on?"

Teeand stood carefully and moved a few feet away from Gin. "I came to bring her to you, Sath. She doesn't have anywhere to be and your son needs a tutor, doesn't he?"

"Son?" Gin's eyes widened a moment, and then she assumed the icy façade she had been wearing since they arrived. "How wonderful for you, Sath, a son. I'm sure he is as handsome as his father." She swallowed hard. "Is there a... I don't know the word in Qatunari...Queen to whom I might pay my respects?" Tee covered his face with one of his hands and shook his head.

Sath sighed loudly. "Tee, I am either going to owe you or kill you. I don't know which yet." The dwarf looked up at his friend and grinned from ear to ear. "If you'd like to stay, quarters will be made ready, old friend. Try to behave around the servants, will you? One of them may use her claws if you aren't careful."

Teeand rubbed his hands together, grinning. "That's what I'm hopin' for, Sath m'boy. Feisty women are the best!" He headed back out of the throne room with Gin hot on his heels.

"Gin," Sath said, using the voice he normally reserved for belligerent petitioners. "I have not dismissed you yet."

Gin's eyes widened as she mouthed the word *dismissed*, but she recovered herself and turned around, eyes cast downward. "Was there more you needed from me, *Rajah*?" she said, gritting her teeth slightly.

Dismissed indeed! The chuckle in the back of her mind distracted her for a moment but she regained her focus. *This is how that filthy cat treats you?*

Go away, Ben.

"*Rajah*," Sath muttered to himself. He crossed the room and sat down on the floor in front of Gin, patting the ground just in front of her. Flustered, she plopped down on the floor, making sure to keep her eyes cast downward. "Gin, just call me Sath, please? We've never had this kind of formality between us before." He reached for her chin but she ducked just out of his reach. "Fine, study my carpets if you like, but please, tell me why you are here?"

"I told you, the dwarf brought me. I don't know why, I was too busy being thankful that he didn't kill me." She mindlessly twirled the fringe on the edge of one of the carpets around with her finger.

"What did he mean when he said that you were a mess when you got to the great hall?"

Gin sighed loudly. "Does NO one listen to me when I talk? I had merely traveled a long way, that's all."

Good girl, you are not spreading lies about me. There is hope for us yet, Ginny.

They would not be lies. Leave me alone, Ben.

Gin looked up at Sath when he did not answer her. "That's all! Teeand was creating drama that just isn't there." She pushed an errant lock of hair behind her ear, and Sath gently caught her tiny hand in midair. The sleeve of the cloak fell back and his brows furrowed when he saw the scars on her arm. She yanked her arm away, nearly slicing her skin open on his clawed fingers.

"Did the wizard do that to you?" Sath said quietly.

"No," she lied, though sorely tempted to tell him the truth now that she was certain that Taeben was listening. "How do you know that I was still with Ben...the wizard?" she asked, her voice growing annoyed. "I have had no contact with you since...Lairky..."

"You left from the beach with him, it was a logical assumption. Also...I know. I am *Rajah* remember? He was one of my father's ambassadors. Were you still in the embassy with him? Where did you two go when I ended that diplomatic arrangement? Answer me, Gin. **Who did that to you?**"

"It isn't important. You need to get to back to bed. This was a mistake. I will find Teeand and let him know I am leaving."

"*Gin,*" Sath said, growling in Qatunari, "*who did that to you?*"

Gin swallowed back some irrational fear as her eyes met his. He wouldn't hurt her, would he? That was just an idea Taeben put in her mind - wasn't it? "I said it is not important. I have had a long journey just to end up returning to this part of the world. It was not always a pleasant journey. There are bandits and outlaws that do not like sharing their lands. I do not know what you want me to say, Sath."

"I missed you, *darlin*," Sath said, and then was immediately sorry that he had let the words slip out. His heart was the one pounding now as he watched the reaction on her face.

"I do not wish to keep you from your family, your wife," Gin said as she stood on wobbly knees.

"I have no wife," Sath said, unable to take his eyes off her. "I have a son, but I have no wife. His mother was Anni, and she is dead, as you well know. There is no one else but...there is no one else." He studied her face, and smiled inwardly at the look of relief he saw there – though it was followed by an ashen gray that crept across her face. "Gin, are you all right?"

"I feel rather...dizzy...," she said as she collapsed into a heap. She had not eaten anything but bread and water for days before arriving at the Grand Hall, turned away wherever she stopped and asked for food or lodging. She and Teeand had shared traveling rations on the way to Qatu'anari but it was not much, and as a result, she was exhausted from her journey. Sath gathered her up in his arms after making sure she was breathing, and carried her out of the throne room into a smaller bedroom adjacent to his bedchamber.

"Tonight you will sleep like a queen, Gin," he murmured as he set her down gently on his bed and then tucked her into the luxurious bedding. Sinking into the armchair across from the huge bed, he stared at the tiny wood elf's form. The comparisons to seeing her in Bellesea Keep were impossible to avoid; though this time there were no chains. She was no prisoner, and she was safe as long as she was with him. *"Tomorrow we set about making things right."*

Soon her breathing settled into the smooth rhythm of sleep, and Sath managed to rise from his seat and stretch. Sleeping in the chair would not be comfortable in the least, but he could not risk crawling into the bed with her, even if it was only to rest. He padded over to a window across from his bed and looked out at the stars. Long forgotten memories of camping out on the plains to the north of the Grasslands and naming all the stars they could see resurfaced and made the *Rajah* smile. He looked back at Gin, now soundly asleep and wound up to her pointed ears in the thick duvet, and his smile grew wider.

Wake up, Ginny! WAKE UP!

The next morning, Gin woke with a start. Her eyes scanned the room as her fuzzy mind struggled to remember where she was.

The silk sheets and fluffy duvet covering her did not seem familiar, but they were luxurious and soft against her still bruised skin.

"*Finally,*" purred a deep voice from across the room. Gin's gaze shot to the source of the voice.

"Sath?" she said, barely believing what she was hearing. The *Rajah* of Qatu'anari strode out of the darkened corner and sat down on the edge of the bed. Gin instinctively put space between them by pressing into the pillows, and he scooted back, a hurt look crossing his face.

"*Aye, darlin,*" he said, the purr still present behind his words. "*How did you sleep?*"

"Where am I?" she demanded in the common tongue.

"You're in Qatu'anari, in the palace Gin. Don't you remember?" Sath's teal eyes overflowed with concern at the fear he smelled on her. That was new.

"No." Gin rubbed her own ice blue eyes with her fists, wincing as she did. She opened her eyes wide then, and scrambled out of the bed. "I mean…Yes, I do…are you…" A look of horror crossed her face. "Did we…"

"No." Sath stood and turned away before she saw the stricken look on his face. He busied himself with rearranging the cushion on which he had been sitting. "No, you collapsed last night, from… exhaustion I imagine, so I brought you here to get a proper night's sleep."

"Thank you," Gin said, as she gathered up her backpack and cloak. "Now, if you will be kind enough to show me to the servant's quarters, I believe I'm to be your new tutor for your son?" *Thanks to that dwarf,* she thought angrily.

You are not really going to stay there, playing house with that mangy Qatu are you? I thought you had finally seen your true worth, and how he only thinks of you as a servant, Ginny!

Perhaps I will. I would like to see you come for me here, Ben. Now leave me alone.

"These are your quarters," Sath said carefully, "and you will stay here for now. "I want you close by so that you may keep a good eye on my son. There is another bedroom off to the side there that is Khujann's when he is not in the Royal Nursery." Gin nodded, and replaced her things. She sank down onto the bed again for a moment, her body weary. Sath knelt down in front of her, slowly and carefully this time, so that he could be at eye level with her. "Who did this to you, Gin? Who left those marks?" he whispered menacingly. "I will make them pay. You are a member of the royal house of Qatu'anari now and..."

Gin felt Taeben uncoiling like a snake in the back of her mind and knew that he was still listening. She could not risk him being angry with Sath and potentially taking it out on this cub that she had yet to meet, but would be in charge of very soon. "It isn't what you think, Sath," she said, cutting him off. "I know that's what you're thinking but it wasn't Ben that was responsible for my condition upon arriving at the great hall." That was not exactly a lie. Gin scowled at the approval she felt from Taeben's presence in her mind.

Sath looked away as he stood up. "Then who?" he asked, his heart breaking at the thought of her defending the wizard. One moment she felt so familiar to him, and the next she was a complete stranger. He tensed his hands but avoided cracking his knuckles and startling her.

"There were others... I happened upon some men that had issues with a female travelling alone," she said finally. Her eyes blazed for a moment at the memory, and then settled into the safety of a vacant stare. "That's all there is. Poor choices, bad luck, and rough living. Now, where is your son?"

Sath sighed. He recognized the tone in her voice and knew that the discussion was over. "Get yourself cleaned up," he said, using the tone he used with other servants. "I will return with my son in an hour's time. You will speak common with him because your Qatunari isn't as good as it was...before...and he does not know Elvish." He stood and left the room but hovered outside the door after it closed behind him. The silence from within her room puzzled him. Such a tone from him in the past would have reduced her to sobs.

After walking into the side bedroom to look around, Gin sat on the huge bed and sighed. She had no tears left to cry, so instead she rose after a few long minutes and went to the washbasin to clean herself up. She had to be presentable to meet the *Rajah's* son. The wood elf stared at her reflection in the mirror. The black circles under her eyes were starting to fade and turn a greenish yellow, the indication that they were healing. She hoped her magic was replenished enough to heal them so that she did not frighten the Prince.

She gingerly touched the cut just under her bangs, the one she got during the altercation with Taeben that she had not been able to heal with her magic, but found it, to her surprise, almost healed. How long had she been asleep? "Sath..." she sighed. He had probably called in healers while she was unconscious...the shamans of Qatu'anari were known across all the kingdoms for their healing prowess. She lifted her bangs and inspected the cut, remembering the night that it happened and scowling. She could still hear Ben's screams in her memories and knew that he was lurking in the back of her mind like a snake, coiled and ready to strike. She would never be free of him. "You will never have me, Ben," she hissed at her reflection.

Care to wager on that?

Gin scowled at her reflection, hoping that he could see her, and then recited some words of a magical healing spell that brightened her appearance.

Wiping away all traces of you, Ben. Now leave me alone.
Never, Ginny.

Gin was barely ready when Sath returned, holding Prince Khujann in his arms. "What is she, Papa?" the cub asked as he stared at Gin, saucer-eyed.

"She is a wood elf, Khuj, and her name is Ginolwenye. Can you say that?"

"Gino...Ginnel...nope, I can't Papa. Can I call her Ginny?" Gin thought her heart would break at the young one's question. She pushed the echoing laughter out of her mind and focused on the young cub Sath was struggling to hold. "Papa, is this the wood elf you told me to find if I was ever in trouble? The one that will help me?" He wriggled out of his father's arms and trotted over to her as Sath struggled to find anything else to look at but Gin's face. She smiled, wondering how long it would be until the cub would be as tall as she was.

"You may call me whatever you like, Your Highness," she said, kneeling down so that they were eye to eye. "My friend Hack used to call me Ginny, but I think he wouldn't mind that much if you did as well." Sath took a deep breath at the mention of Hackort. He had tried to put all those memories away for their appearance let loose a longing in his heart to be just Sathlir again, leader of the Fabled Ones and Gin's... No. Those memories would do him no good now.

"Okay, Ginny, let's play!" Khujann said, grabbing her hand and nearly pulling her off her feet. She planted them firmly but kept a good grip on his tiny hand.

"A moment, Your Highness," she said, barely able to contain her grin. Sath smiled down at them. His son had won over the heart of his "little dru" just as he'd known would happen. "Majesty, if I may?"

"One thing first, Gin," Sath said, locking his teal gaze onto hers. She swallowed hard, recognizing the seriousness of the look and fighting the alarm rising in her, and then recovered herself. "Please call me Sath? I will expect weekly reports on the little beastie's progress on my desk."

"Of course, your...Sath," she said as she followed the cub out the door. Sath smiled. Perhaps there was a chance after all?

Nancy E. Dunne

ONE MONTH LATER

My Lord Sathlir,

I am writing you to update you formally on the progress of your son in my care, weekly as you commanded. I know that you have been called away on matters of state recently and I wanted to make sure that you have the most current information where he is concerned.

Your son is quite intelligent. He is more well-read and more talented in the language arts than he pretends. The tutors in the royal nursery are to be commended.

In fact, I am helping him to hone his literary talent by making him rewrite the death threats on my life and ransom notes concerning bits of my things that have gone missing until they are well written and easy to read. His imagination knows no bounds, as evidenced by the myriad of objects, herbs, and even occasional critters that I have found in my tea, my food, and most recently under my pillow.

To this day, I am sure that your son and the snake that he wrapped around the handle of my backpack are becoming fast friends as he cares for it as a pet. He has also come up with a variety of colorful names for me, some of which actually relate to my status as his tutor, or my own heritage.

He is also quite manipulative. On many occasions I have caught him with a lute or a pipe, and while I do not completely understand your reasoning it is not my place to question why you do not wish him to have musical instruments. He has tried to con me into letting him keep them, *and seems frustrated that the strings of my heart are not so easily tugged as those of the lute and no doubt those of nannies before me.*

He was quite surprised, I think, to discover my proficiency in your native tongue. While I did not let on to him that I was not aware that those particular adjectives could be joined together in reference to my posterior, I did make sure that he could properly conjugate the verb he used in both Qatunari and the common tongue. I had hoped to teach him Elvish but I think we should take our insults one language at a time, don't you agree?

In short, your son has done everything except set off some sort of trap under my bed (and I sleep with one eye open for I expect nothing less from that brilliant cub) in order to rid himself of my presence, but to no avail. I see now why you picked one with my...tenacity, shall we say... to work with your stubborn, ill tempered, malicious, manipulative, conniving, precious and amazing son.

He is the mirror image of his father. Every so often he looks up at me and those teal colored eyes burn me to my very soul, reminding me of a time when I was much younger... But that time is past, and I have a job to do. Now if I can only convince him that wood elves are not as gullible as he thinks we are, we will be making progress.

Your faithful servant, G.

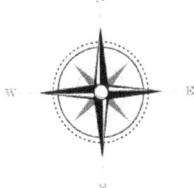

NINETEEN

The moon was shining brightly through the window in Gin's quarters, making it hard for her to sleep. She plagued by nightmares about her time spent with Ben and tonight was no exception. In her dreams, the memories that would not surface in her waking hours came to the forefront, replaying in a constant loop. Tonight's selection took her back to her imprisonment in Bellesea Keep, when she was chained to the bed and Ben simply stood across the room, arms folded, and watched her. Her dream-self pleaded with him to help her, to release her, but he just stood there and stared at her, arms folded. "Please, Ben, please? You can help me, I know you can, please? I will do whatever you ask," she watched herself say. However, the dream was different this time because Ben answered her – with Sath's voice.

"You beg for him in your sleep. What are you up to, Gin? What can I do to rid you of him?"

"Rid me of who? What are you talking about? Just let me out of here and I will…" Gin sat up in her dream and opened her eyes to find herself sitting up in her bed in the Qatu palace. She rubbed her eyes and then jumped to see a figure across the room, standing in the same position Ben had struck in her dream. "No, no, no, no!" she cried out as she scrambled out of the bed. Moving quickly, she retrieved the dagger from her boots that stood by the bed and brandished it at the intruder, waving it wildly. "You need to go, I told you that you will not have me again! How did you get in here, past the *Sahi Kalah?*"

"It isn't hard. They answer to me." Gin stood rooted to the spot as the figure moved away from the window, advancing on her.

"Don't you come an inch closer," she said as threateningly as she could.

"Gin, it's me, Sath…" Sath said as he took another step toward her with his hands raised to show her he meant her no harm.

"Sath?" Gin looked around wildly, realizing that the wizard had been a part of her dream. Sath was real. Sath was here. Sath was here? "Why are you here, in my room? Is something wrong?"

The *Rajah* of the Qatu blushed to the roots of his fur as his hands fell to his sides. "I am here because this is where I am most nights," he said.

"What do you mean, most nights?"

Sath hung his head. "Now, Gin, I don't want you to get mad, but I am in here most nights because I watch you sleep. I…worry that once Khujann is asleep and I am asleep that you…well, at first I worried that the wizard would come for you and I wanted to be ready and now…well, now I worry that you want the wizard to come for you because you call his name out in your sleep."

Gin stood, dumbfounded, for a few minutes as she tried to work out what he was saying to her. "What?"

Sath moved closer to her and carefully wrapped his fingers around hers to remove the dagger. "Let's start by putting this away, shall we? Unless you want to add an attack on the *Rajah* to your list of accomplishments, that is." Gin looked down at their hands and gasped, and then released the dagger. It slid out of her hand and into Sath's grasp and he quickly replaced it in her boot. "That's better."

"Sath, I – I was sleeping, I didn't know who you were, and in my dream…"

"In your dream you were back with Ben. I heard you."

"Did you say you watch me most nights?" she asked, finally awake enough to put together the pieces of what he was telling her.

"Changing the subject?"

"Answer me."

Sath growled low in his chest, and Gin's eyes widened but she stood her ground, hoping he could not hear her heart pounding against her ribcage. "Yes, most nights I sit in here in the corner and watch you sleep.

Gin fought the smile that tugged at the corners of her mouth. "That's why in my dream tonight when the wizard spoke it was with your voice, I suppose."

Sath did not share her amusement. "I heard you calling for him, begging him to free you." He leaned in closer to her. "This was not the first time, either. As soon as your breath falls into the rhythm of sleep, his name is on your lips. I suppose part of the reason I watch is so that when he comes for you I will be here, waiting." The smile fell away from Gin's face. "And there it is. You don't want me here when he comes, Gin, I can promise you that. Not for either of you." He turned away from her but stopped when he felt her hand on his arm.

"I was dreaming about the time that Dorlagar was holding me in Bellesea, Sath," she said quietly. "Taanyth sent Ben in to guard me because he had magic. Once I figured out who he was – well, you're right, I did beg him to help me to escape but he wouldn't."

"You did not trust that I would come for you?"

"Not then! I did not trust YOU back then, Bane of the Forest," she snapped. "But Sath, you need to believe me – I do not want Ben to come here and take me away." The buzzing in the back of her mind grew louder. She had hoped he was listening. "I do not want to leave here and go to him. Sath, I am done with him. I am here and I am your – Khujann's tutor, and…" Sath held up his hands to stop her from talking.

"I will stop watching you sleep," he said, knowing that it was a lie.

"No you won't. It's all right though," she said softly. "In truth I make sure that the *Sahi Kalah* are right outside the door at all times when I'm alone here." Gin focused for a moment on the buzzing, which had increased. She thought of the guard outside her door and Sath sitting in the room with her and enjoyed the pain she felt from Ben.

That will do you no good, Ginny. Soon enough you will be out, on your own, away from that beast, and then I will have you back where you belong.

Would YOU care to wager on that?

"Are you all right?" Sath asked, bringing her back out of her mind. "Gin, your knuckles are turning white." She had wound her fingers into his fur and tightened them as she focused on pushing Ben out of her mind.

"Yes, I'm sorry," she said as she released him. "I'm just tired, I suppose."

"Go back to sleep for a while," Sath said. "I can spend a morning with my son." Gin nodded and padded back over to the bed. She climbed in and pulled the covers up.

"Sath?"

"Hmm?"

"Thank you."

"For?"

"Just thank you." She snuggled down into the bed. Sath smiled as he left her room and headed for his son's quarters.

Gin sighed as she relaxed into the bed. The idea taking shape in her mind just might work. But would it be safe? Taeben's words echoed in her mind as his buzz grew louder. Sath only had to approve her request to take Khujann traveling. The prince needed time away from all the chaos and intrigue of palace life so that he could turn out to be a *Rajah* like his father one day. She didn't dwell on that thought, though, because that would mean Sath was gone if Khujann took the throne – and she had just gotten him back.

Just gotten him back? You are his slave, Ginny, no better than his other servants.

You know nothing about this, Ben.

Oh, you think I don't know that beast? You think I didn't watch him through Annilanshi's eyes all those years? You underestimate me yet again, Ginny. I know what is best for you, and it is not the Rajah.

Go away, Ben.

She filled her mind with images of Sath smiling at her in the throne room or playing games in the courtyard with her and Khujann and felt the rage come again. This time, however, she was ready. In her mind's eye, she laughed as hard as she could – and the rage subsided. It was a precarious game played with a treacherous wizard, but she felt stronger than she had in ages.

Nancy E. Dunne

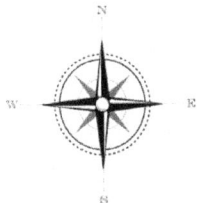

TWENTY

My Lord Qa, (I do hope that is your title and your son hasn't fooled me again.)

Now that I have worked with your son for the better part of a year, I would like permission to take your son with me on a journey for a few months. While I believe that the palace is, of course, an excellent place to raise a young one and I know that he wants for nothing here, I believe that his environment is spoiling him. One thing that I firmly believe makes you the Rajah that you are is that you are well grounded. The Qatu trust you because you are one of them. Therefore, I believe it would help His Young Highness to learn about the world outside of his pampered playpen.

When I mentioned this idea to the other servants they laughed at me and said that a member of the Royal House of Qatu'anari would travel in such a manner that would take the sumptuousness of their palace with them wherever they go. I cannot imagine you traveling with such a circus in tow unless you have changed greatly in the time we have been apart. I can still imagine you sleeping rough with the stars as a backdrop, not huddled in a velvet tent with cushions and servants. They also told me that you would never allow your son to be taken from the safety of Qatu'anari due to the potential of threats against his life.

I am asking you to trust me, something which I know I have no right to expect, and I ask that you know that I would give my own life protecting your son's. I know that I have done much to drive doubt into your mind, and I would like the chance to correct that. On a selfish note, I admit that being here on Qatu'anari is painful to me, and I long to see my home again, if only from a safe distance.

I await your decision and will abide by whatever you deem fair.

Your Faithful Servant, G.

Gin chewed her fingernail as she waited in the throne room. She knew that her summons had to do with her request to take the prince on a trip, just the two of them. Further, she knew that the answer would likely be no because Sath did not trust her with his son. He didn't trust anyone with Khujann, to be fair – even the females that worked in the Royal Nursery said that they felt that way about Sath. She could understand it, absolutely; after all, he had been through Anni giving his son away.

You always give that monster the benefit of the doubt, Ginny. Why is that?
Go away, Ben. Leave me alone.
Answer my question.
No. I said leave me alone.
Ginny, if you would just come back home you wouldn't have to bow and scrape like Sath makes you do. You could come and go as you please, no royal permission required.
Go away, Ben. Leave me alone.

She could feel him growing angrier, and took the time while still waiting for Sath's arrival to focus on pushing him out of her mind. Ben fought her with every trick he had, including giving her a blinding headache. When Sath finally entered the room, Gin was sitting on the floor on a cushion with her fingers pressed firmly against her temples.

"Are you well, Gin?" he asked, kneeling down and, against his better judgement, placing a hand gently on her shoulder. She looked up at him, her eyes wide and wild for a long moment, before she realized who he was.

"Sath! Majesty! Oh – I'm sorry, just another one of my headaches," she said as she scrambled to her feet and away from being so close to him. The pain subsided, she realized, as the wizard settled in to listen. Smiling, she spoke to Sath in his language. *"I got your summons. How many I serve?"*

"Honestly, Gin, if you do not stop acting like one of the palace servants...!" Sath exclaimed. *"I called you here to discuss your request to take my son away from the palace. I would like to know why."*

Gin's face screwed up in confusion and, honestly, a little bit of frustration. *"I told you why in my request, Sath. I think that Khujann could benefit from some time away from the pampered life he lives here."*

"The pampered life that you also enjoy as his tutor?"

"Fair enough." Gin rubbed her temples again. Trying to keep Ben from rummaging about in her memories was causing her headache to get worse. *"I too would like to sleep out under the stars again, and to go on adventures to parts of the continent I have yet to explore."*

Sath considered her for a moment. *"There are just so many dangers that you don't understand, Gin. He is the only heir to the throne. If I had more than one son, or a brother, it would be different, but he has a target on his head and –"*

"And you don't think I can protect him. I understand."

Sath paused and cracked his knuckles before answering her in the common tongue. "It isn't that. Of course I trust that you would try to protect him."

"Try?"

You see, Ginny? He doubted you could do anything but heal before, and he doubts you still.

Shut up, wizard.

"Yes, try. Gin, this isn't like taking down Dorlagar with the Fabled Ones. This is espionage; this is military level forces that could come after Khujann if he is away from Qatu'anari." Sath ran a hand over the top of his head as he did often when he was frustrated.

Gin walked over to him and placed a hand on his arm. "Sath, you must believe that I would give my own life to save your son. He is a precocious little monster, and don't you dare tell him, but I adore him. He just has some rough edges that need smoothing, and I am certain that you know as well as I do that will not happen here. Who would you be today if you had not left the palace?" She immediately regretted that example as his eyes darkened.

"I would still be the Crown Prince, Mama and Papa would be alive, your sister would be alive, and you would never have had to live under the threat of the Bane of the Forest. I can see how you think that would be better," he snapped.

"Sath, that's not what I meant –"

"Enough!" he roared, looking down at her as he would another house servant. Gin pressed her fingers to her temples as Ben's laughter threatened to drive her mad.

"You are a better father and ruler because of your experiences. You are smarter, faster, and fairer than you would have been otherwise, and you know it, so don't pull that *Rajah* Almighty act with me," she said. Sath stared at her. "I have known you too long to be afraid of a little bluster."

Sath felt his mouth tug upward at the corner. She was right, he could smell no fear on her as she stood there staring at him, her arms folded across her chest. Maybe a trip to the tree city wouldn't be the worst thing – he knew that Gin would give her life to protect his son, if for no other reason than she knew what would happen to HER if anything happened to Khujann. "You will be as inconspicuous as you can be, and do not tell anyone who my son really is or I will send a quad along behind you to protect you...and him. I will expect the same reports from him, perhaps not as frequent, but as often as you can send them."

Gin did not try to hide the grin that burst across her face. "Of course, as detailed as I can make them."

"And I will expect him to be learning what he would learn here from his tutors. The history of Orana. Languages. Can you do that?"

"*Of course I can,*" she replied in the language of the dwarves. Sath smiled. "But I won't teach him the swear words that Tee taught me, I promise."

"I'm going to regret this, I just know it. That boy will come back here smarter than his Papa and then what will I do?"

"Be proud of him," Gin said, smiling. "Thank you, Sath. This means so much to me and I know that it will be an amazing experience for Khuj…and me." Before she thought about it, she threw her arms around him and hugged him. Sath's eyes bugged out a bit, but he patted her on the back. She realized what she had done and slowly released him before backing up. "Oh, my goodness, I forgot myself there, I am so –"

"Gin, if you take a knee right now, so help me I will pick you up and throw you to Aynamaede," he snarled. She met his gaze and he chuckled, making her laugh. "Go, go before I change my mind."

Nancy E. Dunne

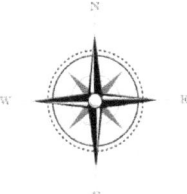

TWENTY-ONE

Sath,

Before I give you my monthly report on your son, thank you for allowing me to take your son on this adventure. He has proven to be quite the resourceful traveler once out of his indulged environment. He has learned to follow my rules, which were reinforced by someone laughing at him when he said he was the son of the Rajah. I'm not sure that he understood what the person THOUGHT he was the son of, and I have not covered that part of Qatu reproduction in his studies just yet.

In the past three months, we have traveled south to the Grasslands, and are currently staying in some rented accommodation outside of Calder's Port. Luckily for me, it has been long enough since I was here before that no one remembers me or the band of misfits with which I travelled. Your son's use of the common tongue improves daily, and he and I regularly have spirited conversations in a mix of languages over topics such as why he has to go to bed and how I am the only one allowed to light the cook fire (or be anywhere near it, for that matter). He has learned to speak Elvish well enough to remind me of a time so long ago when I was in charge of taking care of my sister, but he speaks it more colorfully, like my older brother, so that is a bit confusing in and of itself.

We avoided the Forest on our way down, but I have recently heard from my cousins there who tell me that I am no longer exiled. It seems that my former companions, by whose association I was deemed guilty, have been pardoned, but in truth I feel that I have simply been gone for such a long time that no one cares anymore. My plan is to take His Highness to stay with my family for a short time before we return to Qatu'anari for the winter. I have instructed him that while we are among my kind he is not to tell anyone who he is for fear of someone putting two and two together and coming up with the Bane of the Forest. You have come so far from those days, but I fear there are some that are not as forgiving as others.

This is a far more personal letter than I'm sure is appropriate from one of your staff, so I will leave you with a short story of your son's kindness, something that I am more than certain he has inherited from you. We were walking along the road back to our hut last evening and His Highness spotted a little girl coming toward us. His eyesight is remarkable, as she was still so far out that even I hadn't noticed her. He sped up to a trot and I had to run to keep up with him – I think he grows in height and strength nightly. The little girl was human, and was crying as we approached her. I told your son to pull up his hood for fear that she was afraid of him, but he said that was not what was wrong and then called me a few names in a mix of Qatunari and Gnomish. Hack would have been proud.

She was lost, and your son was insistent that we would walk with her back to the port city as that's where she said her home was. I have heard many stories of children being used as bait in these situations, to lure unsuspecting travelers into dangerous situations, but your son would have none of my protestations and walked alongside her, holding her hand, all the way back to her door. The only time that he was willing to do as I say was when she stepped up to knock on the door. I think that he might have been crying a little himself on the way back to our hut, for missing her.

This is another reason I want to take him to the Forest on our way back north to Qatu'anari. He misses the other cubs in the Royal Nursery, I think, and will only benefit from a visit with the young ones in the school in Aynamaede. I appreciate so much your trust in me to care for and protect the heir to the throne of Qatu'anari, but understand that to me, he *is the son of my oldest friend, for whom I would give my life, and to whom I owe more than I can ever repay.*

Your faithful servant, G.

Nancy E. Dunne

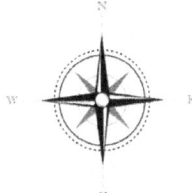

TWENTY-TWO

Gin took a moment to steady herself as she opened her eyes to see her treetop home. She approached the lift on the northernmost end of the city, and paused when she saw one of the guards headed in her direction.

"Mistress Ginolwenye," he said, causing her to wince at the formality of the title. "The Forest Guard would have a word with you, if you don't mind?"

"What is this regarding, Edhelthi... Sergeant?" she asked. The soldier and Gin had grown up together and it was difficult for her to remember to address him using his title and not his first name.

"You will come with me, please?" the sergeant gestured toward the lift and Gin made her way there without hesitation.

"I assume this is about the young Qatu that was taken from the lift earlier?" she said, searching her old friend's face. He betrayed no emotion, and when the lift jerked to a stop she nearly fell face-first into him as she was still peering up at him.

"You will follow me, please?" he said, walking briskly toward the druid guild hall.

"Wait," she said, grasping his arm. He stopped and took a deep breath before he spoke, still avoiding her gaze as she removed her hand.

"I'll ask you not to do that again, Mistress," he said, his voice quivering a bit. "You'll do as you're told and follow me. There are questions to be answered." Gin bit her lip and nodded, following him in silence the rest of the way up to the chambers of the council that ruled Aynamaede.

"How is it, Ginolwenye, daughter of the Forest, you came to have the son of Sathlir Clawsharp, *The Bane of The Forest*, as your companion?" Dhel Sarborn, one of the oldest wood elves in the Forest, was widely considered the wisest counsel in Aynamaede in the ongoing absence of the *Nature Walker*. He sat, hunched over with age, in the middle of a long table with other druids and rangers flanking him on each side. All of them were familiar to Gin save one, and only then because he kept his hood raised at an angle that prevented her from seeing his face. "We are aware of the time you spent...um.... traveling with him..."

"I do not deny it. You may say that in front of these, my assembled kin. I was the *Rajah*'s companion at one time, before he took the throne. We were both members of the Fabled Ones." Gin held her head high, hoping that she was the only one that could hear the pounding of her heart in her chest.

"*Rajah?*" Dhel had stopped his pacing and turned to face her. His pointed eyebrows knitted in confusion, making his normally stern appearance seem rather comical. Gin's memory flitted back for a second to a late-night conversation with Taeben deep in the snowy lands of the Volcanic Mountains, and his imitation of the male wood elves he had met. She swallowed a giggle, and then fought a wave of revulsion at Taeben's memory as she felt him stir in the back of her mind. "You will answer me, Ginolwenye!" Dhel's bellowing voice sliced through her memory and brought her back to the present. "How is it that you called the Bane of the Forest *Rajah?*"

"That is his title, M'lord. Upon the death of his father, Sathlir Clawsharp became the same *Rajah* of Qatu'anari with whom I think the Forest folk still maintain diplomatic relations, do we not?" She braced herself for a fierce retort, but none came. "Wasn't Taeben of Alynatalos appointed as ambassador several seasons ago under Sathlir's father, *Qa Kahzlir*? How is it that he did not report to you that the old Rajah was murdered and his son took the throne?"

"Bring the cub to me," Dhel barked as he completely ignored Gin's question. The sergeant jumped at the chance to leave the room. Gin noted with a smile that as he passed her, she saw only concern on his handsome face for her, just as he had when they were children. Some things never changed. "You surely have a very good reason for kidnapping the *Rajah*'s son, Ginolwenye? Perhaps as revenge for the crimes that he has committed against our kind. I cannot say that I approve of the methods, but..."

His voice trailed off as the sergeant returned, shoving Khujann along in front of him. The young cat's hands were shackled in front of him, and heavy chains kept his feet close enough together to prevent him from running away. Khujann's teal eyes, rimmed with red and swollen, no doubt from crying, scanned the room frantically. Gin's heart sank when she noticed cuts on his face and hands. She ran to him before the guards could stop her, and placed her hands over the cuts to heal them. Khujann rubbed his face against her palms, purring through huge tears that ran down his furry face.

"What have you done to him?" Gin said angrily, her voice barely a whisper. "He is only a child!" She looked up at the sergeant, eyes blazing. "Is this your doing, Edhelthi? You, my protector when I was a child, my friend, did you do this to *this* child, Khujann?"

"It has a name then?" Edhelthi asked sarcastically. Gin nearly jumped to her feet to attack him, but held her ground.

"*Ginny!!*" Khujann wailed. "*I wanna go home, Ginny!! I'm sorry, I'm sorry, I won't ever do nothing to you again I swear, Ginny! No more froggies in your bed, I swear!!*" He took halting breaths, sobbing as he spoke. "*Please please please Ginny can we go home now please?*" Gin threw her arms around him and held him close, the chains on his hands digging into her skin. She looked up to see the sergeant and the others looking at her, horrified.

"Do you mind taking these things off him please, Edhelthi? Dear spirits, he's no threat!!" she snapped. Edhelthi moved as though to comply, then stopped, his gaze shifting to Dhel Sarborn. The elder wood elf nodded, and Edhelthi quickly knelt behind Khujann.

"Turn around, Qatu," he said, trying not to sound too gruff. "Let's get those things off your...hands..." He shook his head and hastily unlocked the shackles. Once his hands were free, Khujann threw his arms and legs around Gin and clung to her, sobbing. She smoothed the fur on his head, whispering to him in Qatunari that it would be all right.

"*Just hang on tight, Little One,*" she said softly in the purring language of the giant cats. "*I will get you out of here, I promise. Do you trust me?*" Khujann nodded, not taking his face out of her collarbone. She turned to face Dhel Sarborn, her eyes blazing. "This," she said, again speaking her native Elvish, "is a child, an innocent. What you have done to him makes me ashamed that we are kin. When the *Rajah* comes to take his revenge on those who have harmed his son, I can only hope that he will not confuse me with you, for as of this day I am no longer one of your kind, no longer a druid of the Forest." She quickly cast a transport spell and faded away along with Khujann, who was clinging tightly to her neck.

Dhel Sarborn slammed his fist onto the desk in front of him, swearing in Elvish. "That was our leverage to get Sathlir Clawsharp here to answer for his crimes! That cub was our protection against the coming war between the Qatu and the Elves!"

The sergeant smiled at Dhel Sarborn. "On the contrary, M'lord. Ginolwenye will lead the *Rajah* here to us, but this time we will be ready." He closed a hand over his sword hilt. "I will give him scars to match the ones I gave his son for crossing me." He pulled open his tunic to reveal huge scratches on his chest. "That **innocent**, as Gin kept calling him, left these wounds on me but I made him pay. Now we, brothers, will make all three of them pay! Sathlir for his crimes against the Forest, Khujann for crimes against me, and Ginolwenye for her betrayal. The Bane of the Forest will be laid to rest at last!"

Dhel Sarborn looked to the back corner of the room, where the hooded figure now stood in a shadow. "Your advice, good sir ambassador? Did Ginolwenye speak the truth? Is the Qatu cub truly the Crown Prince of Qatu'anari? It was on your suggestion that we questioned the young Qatu and learned of his identity. Shall we strike out at Clawsharp or wait for him to come to us? We fear the warning that you brought us as ambassador that a second Forest War may indeed come to pass."

Taeben removed his hood, an icy smile crossing his lips. "Wait for now, my dear cousin. The *Rajah* Sathlir Clawsharp will come, and when he does, I will help you reduce him to a pile of singed fur. I have waited a long time for this...a very long time. Once the Qatu see the power that we have, they will bend to our will and the Forest will reclaim the beasts stolen from us by the dragons." He stood and replaced the hood over his snow-white hair. "There will be no war. I will return with your "leverage," and reclaim my Ginolwenye, as is our deal, yes? The *Rajah* will come to rescue one and avenge the other, mark my words. Then we shall all have that which we most desire." Speaking ancient words, the wizard smiled as a familiar ring of fire formed around him, then disappeared with a slight popping sound.

"Be very quiet," Gin said to Khujann, who nodded into her shoulder as she ran through the maze of platforms that made up Aynamaede. *"If I can get us to the lift, I can...OOF!"* She fell, sprawling, after almost running into one of the guards near the northernmost lift. Gin froze, still sitting on the platform, relieved that the fall had not knocked Khujann from her arms or the both of them off the edge. She moved quickly to the side of a hut by the lift, hoping the guard would not see her.

"Who's there?" he called out, spinning around and trying to locate whatever it was that had just run past him.

"Sssh," she said to Khujann, whose teal eyes, so much like his father's, were welling up with tears. He had taken the brunt of the blow and Gin was holding him tightly, one hand over his mouth

to keep him from crying out. She quietly cast a spell that would camouflage both of them from the guard's eyes.

"May I be of assistance?" said a familiar voice, speaking to the guard. Gin felt her stomach jump up into her heart. Taeben. That's why his voice had been so loud in her mind earlier. The closer he was, the stronger his magic was that let him exist in her mind. What was he doing in Aynamaede? How had he found her? She had not heard him in her mind since...Qatu'anari.

"I'm...not sure, good sir," the guard replied. "I thought I...but I don't see anything..."

"Magic," Taeben said, scoffing with mocking indignation. "So unfair that those that possess the power use it to make a mockery of those of you brave enough to stand guard and keep the rest of us safe." He clucked his tongue as he scanned the ground. Gin did not take her eyes off him, and swallowed hard when his eyes locked on hers. "Seems safe enough now, though," he said. Gin stayed still, clearly not wishing to reveal herself.

"Aye, it does, and I feel a bit the fool," the guard said.

"Not at all!" Taeben replied, grinning. His grin did not reach his eyes. "Is this your post or are you on your way elsewhere?"

"I am due at my check in, if you will excuse me? In addition, thank you, sir, for not...mentioning this. We are all on edge, as you know. If your plan works, the Bane of the Forest will come to answer for his crimes and the Forest will again be safe. We can avoid the war with the Qatu by showing them that we are stronger than they are." The guard saluted Taeben and then hurried on his way. Gin gasped, an almost inaudible sound, as the wizard again locked eyes with her and moved swiftly toward her.

"Stop!" she called out, hoping that none of the merchants nearby would hear. "Please. I want no trouble with you, Ben."

"You will call me Taeben, Ginny - or maybe ambassador, I haven't decided yet."

"Whatever. The Prince and I are leaving; do you hear me?" She tried to sound braver than she was, but even Khujann noticed she was trembling.

"What's wrong, Ginny?" he whispered. "Who's the white haired man in the dress?"

"Sssh." Gin stood up to her full height. "Let us pass, Taeben."

Taeben smiled sadly at her. "Oh, **Ginny**, I can't do that," he said. "You know I can't. It wasn't just you wood elves that lived in fear of the Bane of the Forest, you know? And now, with the Qatu threatening war...I am doing this for my people as well."

"No you aren't!" she bit back. "No one is threatening war. You are doing this to hurt ME because you can't control me anymore."

"Think that highly of yourself, do you?" the wizard replied, chuckling. "My, my, at least you've learned a bit of self-esteem since you ran away from me, from the only male that understands you and loves you. I choose to let you think you are **free**, never forget that, **Ginny**." He emphasized the nickname as he took a step closer and Gin automatically stepped back and away from him, wobbling as her heel grazed the edge of the platform. "You don't want to do that now, do you? You would be fine if you fell, though I would hate to see it, but think of that mangy cub in your arms. Just a child, I believe I heard you tell the council?"

"That's what the guard meant!" Gin exclaimed as all the pieces fell into place. "You have been behind it all! You admitted that you knew that bard charmed Sath, which was just part of your plan, but this?" She stared at him, saucer-eyed with shock. "All of this for me?"

Taeben saw his chance and once again tried to push into her mind. *Give me the cub, Ginny,* he pleaded with her consciousness. The pushback he felt was not as strong as he had expected, but it was still there.

Give me the cub and I will take you to a place where you are safe. No one will get hurt; you have my word.

He frowned, unable to tell if he had made complete contact with her mind or not. Slowly, Gin put Khujann down. The cub clung to her legs, peeking out from behind her to glare at Taeben. She slowly rolled up her sleeves and held her arms out to him.

"No one will get hurt? You want me to go with you so you can do THIS to me again?" she hissed, the scars on her arms forming a crisscross pattern that covered her skin from wrist to elbow. "I'm going to have to pass on that, I think. **Nowhere** that you are is SAFE."

Rage consumed Taeben and he grabbed her arms, pulling her into him. "I have the druid and the cub!" he shouted. "They're here!" Gin struggled against him but he used his slight height advantage against her. As she thrashed, he managed to get a hand around her face to stop her screaming just as the guard that had just left him ran back. Gin's eyes widened as she saw her cousin, Iseabel, running along behind him.

"Take the beast," the guard shouted at Iseabel, who snatched Khujann up and carried him off as the tiny Qatu wailed and hissed.

"NO!" Gin screamed from behind Taeben's hand. The guard ripped her from the wizard's arms, secured her hands behind her, and gagged her to keep her from casting any spells.

"Our humblest thanks, good sir," the guard said, "but we will take it from here."

"But the female is MINE," Taeben barked back as he smoothed his hair and robes. "That was our deal."

"Aye, she will be once she has answered for her crimes against her own kind. I am sure the penalty will be exile, at which case she is yours to do with as you please." The guard turned on his heel and dragged Gin along behind him. She did not break eye contact with Taeben until they disappeared down one of the many ramps that connected the platforms, and her furious gaze remained emblazoned on his mind for a time even after that.

The Council was waiting for her, full of faces that Gin had known since her childhood. She did not know for sure who was on the Council because the membership constantly changed. Gin managed a smile at the elves that had raised her, taught her, sheltered her for so many seasons, but met her now with stony silence. Kae, a young elf seated at the end of the Council's table, rose and faced Gin. Gin drew in a sharp breath. Kae was Iseabel's sister and the daughter of Gin's maternal aunt, and had grown up to be the spitting image of Gin's own dead sister, Lairceach.

"Mistress Ginolwenye, the Council wishes to hear your testimony concerning the Qatu Sathlir Clawsharp. It is their understanding that you lived with him for many seasons and you know his comings, goings, and whereabouts. The Council wishes to thank you, in advance, for assisting in our efforts to bring The Bane to us to answer for his crimes against our kind and hopefully head off the threat of war between our people and the Qatu." The young female paused for a moment before continuing. "You will provide all details of the *Rajah*'s life to us, including all entrances and exits from the city of Qatu'anari that are known to you in case we are required to take Clawsharp by force or retaliate in time of war. You will relate to us, to the best of your recollection, the *Rajah*'s prowess with different weapons and combat styles, as well as his magic abilities such as healing and combat magic. Have you any questions before you begin your testimony?"

Gin looked Kae in the eye, and then looked at each member of The Council in turn. She nodded her head. "I do have one question for the Council," she said.

"Then proceed," Kae said.

Gin took a deep breath and then said in Qatunari, "*Have you all lost your minds to think that I would turn in Sath to you for slaughter? Do you truly believe that I would provide information that would allow you to harm one hair on his head?*" She grinned for a moment in the stunned and somewhat confused looks on the faces of the Council, then said, "I am ready to make my testimony," this time speaking in Elvish. She looked to Kae, who nodded. "You want me to tell you what I know of the Qatu Sathlir Clawsharp, yes?" Again, Kae nodded, joined by several members of The Council. Gin looked at each one in turn, took a deep breath, and said, "Nothing."

Kae's eyes widened. "What did you say, Ginny...err...Ginolwenye? Are you refusing to cooperate with The Council?"

Gin grinned. *"That is exactly what I am doing,"* she said, again speaking Qatunari. A ripple of questions and a flurry of terse conversation flew around the Council chambers. Gin took a step back, wondering for a moment if she should make a break for the door. One member of the Council stood and turned to face her. His name was Aiidan, and he was a half elf who had chosen to make his home in the Great Forest with his mother rather than in Calder's Port with his human father.

Aiidan cleared his throat and then addressed Gin, to her surprise speaking Qatunari. *"We have not lost our minds, as you accused, Mistress Ginolwenye."* He grinned at her. *"I bet you are wondering how I have learned the cat language. I learned it while traveling to the Western Tower to explore with his sister, Kazhmere, and the female that charmed Sathlir; the same female that bore him the cub that we now have in custody."* Gin's eyes widened. *"Ambassador Taeben was kind enough to convince her to charm him for us. I suppose we owe Clawsharp a debt, albeit a small one, for saving us from the task of disposing of her."* He spat, wiped his mouth on his oaken tinged hand, and then continued, returning to speaking Elvish. "Further, we are not interested in your assessment of our plan or in your desire to defend the Bane of the Forest. If you will not help us, then we have no use for you. I ask you one last time, will you give your testimony and share with us your knowledge of Sathlir Clawsharp?"

Gin looked Aiidan squarely in the eyes. "I know nothing," she said. The half elf snapped his fingers at the guards standing behind her who moved swiftly to her sides and lifted her off the ground.

"You have outlived your usefulness," Aiidan said. "Dispose of her, she is no longer welcome here," he said to the guards. Gin heard Kae catch her breath as the guards carried her out the door and over to the edge of the platform.

"What of the Prince?" she asked. The guards did not answer. "What of the Qatu Prince?" she demanded, her voice bordering on a scream.

"He is no longer your concern, Mistress Ginolwenye," one of the guards said.

"No, no please no...!" Gin felt the grip on her arms loosen and then found herself falling. The Council room must have been on the top level of Aynamaede. A healing spell and a scream escaped her throat, cutting the night as she fell, before she finally connected with the soft mossy forest floor with a sickening thud. She looked up at the stars, tears rolling down her cheeks as she closed her eyes to let the magic work.

Taeben was positively vibrating with rage as he stood in the corner of the Council chambers. "With permission, my **cousins**," he said, barely able to keep his voice even, "this was not part of our deal. Where is Ginolwenye?" He had followed them when they brought her from the platform but refused entry to the private proceedings. It was not until he sensed, through his bond with her, that she was thrown out of the city, that he barged through the doors and addressed the Council.

"Were you not listening, Ambassador?" Kae asked, her voice tight with emotion. "She has been exiled, the same way that Elysiam was exiled after **your** involvement with her training at Alynatalos. Do you not remember the punishment for a sentence of exile?" Tears formed in the corners of her eyes and she discarded all the decorum of a member of the council. "They threw her off the platform, Ambassador! The highest platform in Aynamaede! If the All Mother is merciful, Gin is dead."

Taeben turned his attention around to the rest of the Council. "You have broken our agreement," he thundered. "I brought you the information of the Qatu plans to take the Forest by force. I did everything I could to work for peace between our two lands and all I asked in return was that you give me the treasonous wood elf. I will not forget the selfishness of you, my tree dwelling cousins, when the Qatu come to take you away to serve them. May **your** All

Mother have mercy on your souls." He clapped his hands together over his head and a ring of fire formed around him, swirling and growing until he winked out of existence with a slight popping sound.

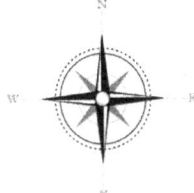

TWENTY-THREE

Gin awoke many hours later to horrible pain, as though her body was on fire. She spoke halting words of magical healing, and then lay still in the grass as she felt her body mending itself. Finally, she could sit up, and then soon after, stand. She looked upward at the platforms, ramps, and swinging bridges that made up what was long ago her home city, and sighed deeply. "Not my home anymore," she whispered. She came back to the present with a jolt. Khujann. Gin closed her eyes a moment, and then opened them again, knowing that she would need help to rescue him. "I need his father's help," she whispered, "but first I need his father's forgiveness or Khujann and I are both dead." She stood slowly and brushed herself off before heading toward the path that would start her on the journey back to Qatu'anari, with a stop by the Outpost.

She walked for several days, barely stopping to sleep or eat, but she was not yet strong enough to travel by magic or use magic to increase her speed. The Outpost was only two days journey from the tree city, and she soon refilled her supplies and was again on the move toward Qatu'anari. She kept her staff at the ready, expecting to see an angry *Rajah* around every bend and behind every tree. It had been far too long since her last report, and she was certain that Sath knew something was wrong. When she could walk no more, she sat down on the side of the path and opened her spell book. There were pages missing that Taeben had ripped out to keep her from using the spells therein against him. She kept turning the pages, searching for something that would help her get to Qatu'anari before the *Rajah* got to her.

Gin paused as she got to the last few pages of the book. She recognized Taeben's handwriting and her eyes widened as she realized these were his personal notes. Unfortunately, a lot of it was written in his own shorthand, and she could not understand it. She skimmed the pages with her finger, hoping for something that would be helpful and written in a language she could read, stopping abruptly when she came upon her name. He had concocted a spell that would immediately return her to the embassy where they lived on Qatu'anari, presumably if she ever found a way to escape. However, would it work if she read the words? Did she have the magical energy to cast such a spell, or any spell for that matter?

There was only one way to find out. Gin smiled sadly as she thought of Elysiam and Hackort calling out that very phrase as they ran into dangerous situations. She took a deep breath and stood up, spell book in one hand and her staff in the other, and read the spell off the page as written. "*You cannot hide from me, Ginolwenye. Come home NOW.*" Nothing happened at first, but then the hair on the back of her neck stood on end as a fiery circle appeared around her, expanding to a sphere that surrounded her. She felt the familiar inside out pull that accompanied transportation magic and closed her eyes.

The heat dissipated and she opened her eyes to find that she was back in the embassy, but was destroyed. There were remnants of charred curtains and rugs and streaks of black across the marble floors. It looked as though there had been a struggle there…or an angry wizard. Gin sighed loudly. She had no time to look around and was soon on her way up the beach, headed for the city of Qatu'anari.

She pushed her way through the thicket of brush at the edge of the beach and ran up the winding path through the forest. She could see the arch that separated the outer edge of the city from the forest, and picked up the pace. The walls of Qatu'anari rose in the distance and she was soon close to the city gate. Gin paused a moment and cast a camouflage spell before slipping past the *Sahi Kalah* posted there.

She wound her way through the streets, following paths that she and Khujann had walked so often before she had taken him from his home. Gin paused a moment, both to make sure she was headed the right way and to banish the guilt that would distract her from her mission. She had to get to Sath, to warn him, to offer her help and to go with him to get his son back from the elves. As she ran, she noticed an increased *Sahi* presence in the streets and her heart sank. This was not going to be an easy meeting with Sath.

The doors to Sath's chambers flew open as Gin scrambled through them, only a few steps ahead of his guards. She had tried to explain to them why she needed to see the *Rajah*, but in her halting Qatunari, they misunderstood her and tried to take her into custody. "*Sath!*" Her cry was a cross between a shout and a wail, and it raised the hairs on the scruff of Sath's neck. "*Sath! Your son! I didn't...*" His personal guards tackled the tiny wood elf and pinned her to the ground as Sath approached.

"*Let her up!*" he bellowed at them, anger blazing in his teal eyes as they ignored him.

"*Rajah forgive us, we cannot,*" one of them mumbled as he averted his feline eyes from those of his *Rajah*. "*She has done something with your son, Rajah, and...*"

"*No!*" Gin wailed from under a pile of guards. "*I didn't, he was taken, I didn't hurt him, I swear it Sath!*" She struggled to free herself but she was outnumbered. Being the personal bodyguards of the *Rajah*, these Qatu were trained to subdue enemies capable of magic and they held Gin to the ground with her arms spread so that she could not get to her feet or cast any spells.

"*I said let her up, and leave us,*" Sath repeated. His voice was no longer booming, but held the faint trace of a growl behind his words. "*NOW.*" The guards looked at each other and slowly removed their hands from Gin's arms and back. She scrambled to her feet and toward Sath, causing the guards instinctively to move toward her again. In one quick motion, Sath grabbed Gin by her throat and lifted her off the ground. His eyes locked on hers. "*Be still*," he said in a quiet, yet commanding tone. Gin did as he asked. "*You see?*" he said to the guards. "*She is hardly a threat. Leave us.*" The guards went to a knee, and then quickly rose and retreated from his chambers, slamming the large marble doors behind them. Sath dropped Gin on the ground where she landed with a thud and glared down at her with a mixture of fear and anger.

"You have to know that I would never harm your son, Sath," she whispered, rubbing her throat. She looked up at Sath, wincing at the anger in his eyes.

"*Rajah*," he corrected her firmly. "You said he was taken. By whom? Where is my son, Druid?"

Gin's face fell at his tone and the use of her title, but she immediately steeled her own resolve, her face becoming as void of emotion as her voice. She took a knee as she had seen the *Sahi* do earlier. "He has been taken, Sa...Majesty, but he lives."

"Explain." Sath's voice - along with his countenance - quivered on the knifepoint of becoming a bellowing rage.

"He was running about Aynamaede alone," Gin said, her voice as flat and smooth as a stone in a brook. "I had warned him against it, forbidden him to do it, but as you know, Majesty, your son is nothing if not stubborn, just like his...." A growl from Sath made her wince, so she continued her story. "The guards found him examining one of the lifts down to the forest floor, and when he told them who his father was, they took him into custody."

"Why would the wood elves be concerned over the presence of the heir to the Royal House of Qatu'anari?" Sath said, leaning in a bit closer to Gin. He scowled as he inhaled deeply...and only detected sunflowers but no fear.

Gin frowned. "If you will remember, I told him not to tell anyone that his father was the *Rajah*. In fact, I instructed him that while he was with me, he was to act as my apprentice and not as a member of the royal family. I thought it would teach him humility and the value of serving others, your Majesty." She paused a moment to bite the inside of her cheek in an effort to stop the falling of the tears welling in her eyes. "I thought that it would make him more like you."

"What did he tell the guards, Gin?" His voice a mere whisper, fear rose in Sath's throat. He already knew the answer.

Gin's gaze dropped to the floor. "That he was the son of Sathlir Clawsharp," she said. Sath roared with rage and Gin instinctively lowered her forehead to the floor as she had seen countless Qatu do as they trembled before Sath. "I am sorry, Majesty, I did not think that the guards would remember your name."

A stirring in the back of her mind that Gin had not felt in the many long months that she had been away with Khujann drew her attention away from the raging Qatu above her for a moment.

You will never bow like that before anyone again, Ginny. I will see to that if you will just COME HOME. Do not make me come get you. You will not like it if I have to come get you.

She ignored the voice and focused her attention on Sath. "You FOOL!" he spat as he paced back and forth in front of her, his giant hands balled into fists. "Of COURSE they remember my name. You knew it, you were taught it at your mother's knee! The Bane of the Forest! Get up off the floor." A rumble started in his chest, low and menacing, then built up to a roar as he lashed out. Gin ducked out of the way, but as he was not aiming for her, he instead connected with one of the marble doors that had slammed behind the guards only moments before. Screaming with pain and rage, Sath pounded his fist into the door again. Gin felt the tide of anger rising in the back of her mind, and it mirrored the wave that crashed in front of and around her in Sath. "You will not leave this room until I return for you," he said in a low and menacing tone and then stormed past her as he bellowed for his guard to assemble in the throne room. Gin cast invisibility magic and slipped through the door just before he slammed it shut, and then followed him down the hall. She waited just outside the throne room, gathering her courage.

Within moments, Sath was pacing back and forth in the throne room, his generals and *Sahi* foot soldiers assembled and going over their plan to attack Aynamaede in the forest. Gin slipped in, still under the cover of her magical camouflage and crept as close to the *Rajah* as she could without risking him bumping into her.

"Here, Majesty, is where we will make our attack. The former ambassador from the Forest assures us that his kind will remain within their city walls, and we hope that the dark elves will not dare to emerge from their burrows to disturb our progress. He tells us that he has a contact within their number as well, but I do not know that I believe him on that issue, for we know the distrust among the elves following the Forest Wars."

Gin put her knuckle in her mouth to keep from shouting out at them. Had they not told Sath the name of this ambassador? Was it not Taeben? Surely, Sath would not willingly be working with Taeben, not after all this time.

"Who is this ambassador?" Sath asked, but then held up his hand as one of the generals moved closer to answer him. "It does not matter. Whoever he is, thank him for his information but I have no interest in this war that the elves threaten to bring upon us." Gin cocked her head to the side. Had Taeben not told the elves in Aynamaede that the Qatu were bringing war upon them? Understanding dawned on her and she decided that she had to act. She crept as close to Sath as she could and reached out to touch his arm.

Sath cracked his knuckles, ready to send his soldiers out, when the smell of sunflowers hit his nose in force, causing him to take a step back. He felt something on his arm and grabbed it, pulling the body attached to the hand up into the air in front of him and shaking it. The magical camouflage fell away, and he found that he was holding a struggling Gin just off the ground. Moving as one, the *Sahi* turned their weapons toward her, but Sath raised his other arm aloft. "LEAVE US," he bellowed.

"*Shall we set out for the Forest, Majesty?*" one of the generals said. Sath shook his head.

"*OUT!*" he roared in response. The general nodded and followed his men out of the throne room, leaving Sath alone with a still wiggling Gin.

"*Put me down, Sath!*" she cried, but instead he lifted her up to the level of his eyes.

"*What in the name of all of Orana made you think it was a good or safe idea for you to come here, wood elf?*" he roared at her. Gin couldn't control her trembling.

"*I came to help you get Khujann back and avoid a war,*" she said. Sath released his hold on her and she fell quickly, barely able to rearrange her body to avoid landing head first on the marble floor. She looked up at him to find him laughing.

"*You? By yourself? Bah!*" He pushed past her toward the door.

"*I can at least tell you what you are up against there, and where your son is,*" she replied. Sath stopped and turned back to her, closing the distance between them with a few broad strides until he was nearly on top of her.

"*Speak,*" he barked. Gin quickly explained her exile and that Khujann was most likely held in the cells at the top of Aynamaede. She told him about the wizard that had planted the idea in their heads about a war, but hesitated before telling Sath that it was Taeben.

Sath listened, barely able to contain his rage, as Gin spoke. "*And that, Sath...*"

He glared at her. "*Rajah,*" he said sternly, determined not to allow her that much familiarity.

Gin' face flushed an oaken-tinged angry red. "*Yes, whatever, my apologies, Rajah; that is how I came to return here to Qatu'anari to let you know of your son's fate.*"

"*His...FATE? You left my son in the hands of those elves.*" Sath's voice was menacingly quiet. "*You left my son...alone...*" The giant cat balled up his fist and his knuckles cracked. Gin glared at him.

"*To be fair, Majesty, I didn't **leave** anyone, I was **thrown** out of Aynamaede.*" Sath moved his own face close to hers, his giant teeth gleaming in the torchlight. Gin took a deep breath and said, "*What shall we do now?*"

Sath scowled her. "*We? What shall WE do?*" He fumed for a moment, and then a sad look of understanding came into his eyes. "*They sent you back to lure me there, didn't they? You can speak my language, I trusted you, and they knew you would come straight to me. You've lead them right to me, you daft elf.*" He roared in frustration. "*I just hope that when they have me they will let my son go, as you said.*" The giant cat paced over to his throne and sat, staring at the wood elf before him. His mind reeled as he tried to understand how she had managed to put his son in so much danger and then left him behind. His stomach churned as he thought of the faces of those elves so close to his precious son… of their hands touching his son's fur or causing him pain. He roared again, half in frustration and half in anguish.

Gin rose from her kneeling position on the floor in front of the throne and, squaring her shoulders, strode directly up to where Sath sat. He rested his forehead in his palms, his elbows digging into his knees. Gin moved closer and placed one tiny hand on the back of one of his hands. A low growl of warning rumbled from the *Rajah* of Qatu'anari, but she ignored it.

"*Sath,*" she began, but his head snapping up, teeth gleaming, stopped her.

"*Rajah!*" he spat at her. "*You will address me as…Rajah.*"

"With all due respect," she said, drawing in a deep breath, "*I will do no such thing.*" Sath moved faster than Gin had expected and caught her up by her face. His massive hand encircled her jaw as her body twitched slightly, reacting to the sensation of hanging in midair. He drew her face close to his, blocking out the smell of sunflowers that always seemed to radiate from her skin, and turned her face away from his so that she could not look him in the eye.

"*Why have you never healed that scar?*" he hissed, annoyed that she showed no fear whatsoever at being so close to him. With a shaky hand, Gin slowly touched the side of her face, avoiding the claws so close to her skin. A long scar still appeared there from their first meeting in the tunnels. Gin had not had the healing ability she did now and the injury sustained as she fought Sath off to keep her belongings had healed on its own. Once her abilities improved, she was tempted to heal it completely, but resisted and left it alone.

"*You always ask me that. It is so that I never forget,*" she said quietly. Her voice wavered a bit but she never took her eyes off his.

"*Forget what, that I am a monster?*" he bellowed.

"No," she said. "*So that I never forget **you**, Sath.*" Sath opened the hand that held her and Gin gasped as she hit the floor with a thud. She knew he would never understand that the scar was a reminder to her of who he had been and how far he had come to change his life. Removing it from her face, to her, was akin to removing her memories of their time together from her heart. "Now," she said, drawing in a deep breath, "*what are we going to do about getting your son back?*"

"*I will surrender myself, you fool.*" Sath said, keeping his back to her so that she could not see the pain that danced around the edges of his teal blue eyes. "*You and your kind have left me no choice. Hulan will become Kazhmere's consort and they will rule as regent for Khujann until he is old enough to...*"

"Stupid proud Cat," she said in Elvish, forgetting that as she learned Qatu, Sath had learned her language.

"WHAT *did you just call me?*" he said, spinning around on his heel to glare at her. Gin grinned at him.

"*Clever Qatu,*" she said, taking a step back, "*but still stubborn and proud. Do you really think that I will allow you to just walk into the trees, hands in the air, and give yourself up?*" Her forehead creased with worry. "*Sath, they intend to have you stand trial for your past. They will kill you.*"

Sath's mirthless laughter rumbled from his chest and reverberated throughout the throne room. "*Kill me? The wood elves?*" he said, pausing to wipe a tear from his eye. Let Gin think it was from the laughter, served his purpose better that way. "*Ginolwenye, you know me better than that.*" He sat back down on the throne so that he was eye level with her, and then lightly ran a clawed finger down the side of her face, tracing her scar. "*You of all know me better than that."* Sath was disturbed, slightly, that the shiver he saw move from Gin's head to her tiny feet provoked no feeling in him whatsoever. He was already thinking of battle. The bloodlust was taking control. *"One wood elf or one hundred...still no match for me and my Sahi Kalah,"* he scoffed.

Gin took another step back. She knew that the Bane of the Forest persona was triggered by his anger and was not really who he was, but it was hard to see the Sath she knew when he was shrouded in all that anger and bloodlust. Pushing her fear and sadness down into a ball and replacing it with her own anger, she looked him dead in the eye. *"It's more than just one wood elf, more than one hundred wood elves Sath...oh, I'm sorry. Rajah."* She made a much-exaggerated bow, then turned on her heel and stomped toward the door.

"I have not dismissed you, Ginolwenye!" Sath bellowed.

Gin stopped and looked over her shoulder at him. Her eyes seared into his soul. *"Yes, you have,"* she snapped, and then stormed out of the throne room. She felt the wizard laughing in her mind, but it only spurred her on to move faster.

"Do not let her leave," Sath hissed at his guards as he burst out the front gates of the Qatu royal palace in a near blind panic. Several *Sahi Kalah* scurried along behind him, and he paid them no attention as he ran. *"Gin!"* he screamed as he ran toward the entrance to the dense forest that surrounded Qatu'anari and separated it from the beach. His mind raced in pace with his feet. Of course, Gin was trying to get to the Great Forest; she was going to save Khujann on her own. Sath growled low in his chest. How would he get there, or even close to there, without her? He was known everywhere in the Forest for his crimes against druids and rangers.

Still, he had to get there to save his son. His son, who had done nothing wrong, who was now paying for crimes his father had committed, and whom he hoped was still alive. *"Those wood elves will pay,"* Sath grumbled, *"if one hair on his precious head is out of place."* Sath searched his memory, trying to recall how he and Raedea had handled coming too close to the Forest. A disguise had worked then, but the wood elves were not on the lookout for him, either.

Gin ran faster than she had ever run before through the palace of the Qatu'anari and toward the great gates that separated the royal household from the rest of the Qatu. In her panic to get out, she forgot about the magical protectors that guarded the palace gates – two magical marble cats that could come to life at the command of a member of the royal household. Sath's command to his *Sahi* had been enough, and the two beasts were waiting for her. Gin skidded to a stop as one of them swung a giant paw toward her, knocking her backward so that the other one could pounce and pin her to the ground. Gin struggled to get away but soon the one that had caught her clapped her on the top of her head with its forehead, and everything went dark.

When she opened her eyes, all she could see was a dark stone wall. Gin blinked a few times and when her eyes adjusted to the darkness she recognized that she was in one of the cells in the dungeon under Qatu'anari.

Oh, my sweet Ginny, you're all right. How many times must that beast hurt you before you see?

The relief that she felt wedged in the back of her mind turned her stomach. "*Sath!*" she screamed in frustration as she tried to stand and found herself sore to her very bones and nearly unable to stand. Heavy chains hung off her wrists and ankles, bound to each other by a longer chain that attached to the wall by the door. Gin's heart dropped into her stomach. If she couldn't cast spells to free herself and fight back, she was caught. "*SATH!*" A growl came from outside the door.

"*Shut it, druid,*" the guard hissed in Qatunari. Gin thought quickly.

"*Who's there?*" she said, trying to keep her voice calm. She knew that several of the young cats that had been playmates of Sath's when he was a cub had been placed on his special guard, and it wasn't a stretch to think that one of those young Qatu had been sent to guard her. "*Keegan? Nomlah? Tonagh?*" The snort that followed frustrated her.

"Nice try, Ginolwenye," Sath said in Elvish. Gin's blood chilled. Had he been there the whole time she was unconscious? "*Comfortable?*"

"*Perfectly, though I've got an itch on the side of my nose, so if you'd just unlock these chains I'd be even better,*" she said in Qatunari, sarcasm dripping from her voice.

"*Oh, come on, you're better than that,*" the *Rajah* purred in her direction. "*No begging to be released? No schemes to sneak in and out of your home, to betray your people? 'Oh, Rajah, I promise I won't run away to my wizard…'*" Gin glared up at him as the door to her cell opened. Sath's huge frame filled it as he entered and crouched down in front of her. "*Not even going to try to kick me with those tiny little feet?*"

"Get on with it, Sath," she said. "*It isn't like you to gloat.*"

"You're right," he said as he leaned in toward her, "it isn't." "*Who has my son? Which one of the elves is holding Khujann?*" Gin merely stared back at him. "*Tell me, Ginolwenye.* **You will tell me!**" he bellowed. Gin didn't move, only flinched a bit at his tone. Sath decided to change tactics. "*Gin, please, it's my son we're talking about,*" he said. "*You love him as much as I do. Help me save him.*" Gin lowered her eyes.

"*You know I love him,*" she whispered, "*and that is why I won't let **you** do anything to put him in danger.*" The rumbling growl vibrating through the floor warned her to tread lightly, but her desire to protect the cub outweighed her desire for self-protection. "*Let's work together, Sa…Rajah,*" she said, realizing that her Sath was gone. Only the bloodthirsty and revenge-hungry *Rajah* remained. "*Take me back as a prisoner, a peace offering. Exchange me for your son. If Ben - Taeben sees that you have me and will hurt me…I'm what he wants, not your son, just let me talk to him…*"

"TAEBEN?" Sath said through his horrifying toothy grin. "*That wizard is working with your kin? He has my son?*"

All the color drained from Gin's face as she heard Taeben's laugh echoing through her skull. *"Sath, please, let me help,"* she said even though she knew it was too late.

"GUARDS!" Sath bellowed. *"Prepare our prisoner for travel. Make sure she has a comfortable seat for the journey,"* he said to the two young Qatu warriors that appeared in the doorway. *"She is very dangerous,"* he said, *"and will try to convince you to let her have her hands free and remove the gag from her mouth. She uses magic and will not only hurt you but escape if you allow that to happen."* The two nodded and entered the cell as Sath strode out to put on his armor. The clanging of the metal of his breastplate as he buckled it in place drowned out Gin's pleas for him to reconsider.

If he harms one hair on your head, my Ginny, I will skin that beast. You are safer with me, but you are determined to make me work for it. Challenge accepted.

Nancy E. Dunne

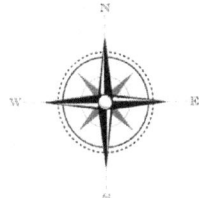

TWENTY-FOUR

The small group moved through the spreading light of dawn in near silence, bearing the *Rajah* of Qatu'anari, his quad of personal guards, and their tightly bound prisoner north toward the entrance to the caverns that tunneled under the Forbidden Sea and into the Volcanic Mountains. Known only to the Qatu, they gave the feline race a way to reach the mainland without having to worry about the Razors, a narrow strait between Qatu'anari and the mainland. The Razors was so narrow that the underside of boats were often scraped and sometimes breached as they tried to navigate through. Once on the other side, they would travel south through the foothills to the Forest. Sath's plan was to find a place for the night in the foothills and continue to the Forest in the morning. From there he would take Aynamaede.

The wood elves had an advantage, being in their tree top fortress, but a quick stop in one of the markets in the Outlands would grant him potions that could make the three Qatu guards appear as allies to the wood elves. Once they were in the trees, he would find his son and force the druid to port them to safety before he released her…or killed her, he hadn't decided yet.

The druid…Gin…Sath gritted his teeth, forcing himself not to even think of her name. She'd not made a peep since they left the city, nor had she tried to escape. The warrior side of him struggled to understand why she wasn't fighting back. The *Rajah* side warned him to take care not to sacrifice her in vain. And at the very heart of him, the him that was Sath, that had slept rough and hunted with the Fabled Ones…a small but steady voice tried to remind him how important she was to him. That voice was most concerned that he not go too far and shatter what was left of her after everything that had happened to her. He put that voice to rest, however, with just one thought of Khujann. A procession was not going to work here. They needed to have a change of plan, and he smiled as it became clear in his mind.

The cavern entrance came into view. Sath slowed to a halt, and the soldiers followed suit. "*Here is where we part company, friends,*" he said to the *Sahi*. Gin's eyes were wide above the gag in her mouth that kept her quiet. The guards began to protest but immediately fell silent as Sath raised one of his massive hands. "*You will double back toward the beach,*" he instructed them. "*Take boats to the continent and then continue south to the Forest.*"

"*They will no doubt be waiting for us. Once you are there, go at once to the druid circle just to the north of the tree city.*" The young Qatu nodded. "*Take care not to linger in the Forest or take any wrong turns. The dark elves keep creatures in their realm the likes of which we have never seen, and without an elf to guide you through it could be dangerous.*" He slid from his saddle and then lifted Gin from hers, throwing her over his shoulder before he waved the worried looking guards away. "*We will be fine in the caverns. Go.*"

Once the guards were out of sight, Sath put Gin down on the ground and made sure she could stand before he released her. Against his better judgment he removed the gag from her mouth and braced himself for the verbal onslaught that he was sure would follow. To his surprise, she said nothing.

"Shall we?" he said, grinning at her. Her face was stony as she turned to walk into the cavern, hands still chained to her sides. After a few minutes of walking, the end of the chain that was attached to her wrists held lightly in one of his hands, Sath asked Gin to cast an invisibility spell over both of them so that they wouldn't have to waste time with the less friendly inhabitants of the cavern, and she begrudgingly obeyed. Her silence was unnerving; it chipped away at his battle-ready façade. "Do you need any food or water?" he asked. "Are the manacles too tight?"

"No," she said quietly. "My wrists are calloused from being held in similar fashion by Dorlagar, don't you remember?" Sath frowned, the memory of how he found her in Bellesea Keep now flashing before his eyes. He saw again her bloody wrists and unkempt hair, and worst of all he remembered the hollow look in her eyes.

"Fine." Long pause – no response from Gin. "Tell me if you need anything," he snapped, increasing the width of his step and therefore putting a bit of distance between them, but all the while taking care not to pull too hard on her chain. She was trying to get to him, he reckoned, and he was not going to let her see that she'd succeeded. The different parts of him simultaneously whispered to stop giving her those chances and sulked.

As they rounded the western side of the first lake in the caverns, Sath slowed his pace a bit. Weary of having to stop and wait for her, he handed a potion to Gin that magically increased her speed so that she could keep up with him, and then quickly stepped back into the shadows. He wasn't fast enough, though, and one of the lizard-like creatures that lived in the cavern advanced on him, snarling, with claws bared. Smaller than the dragonkind, these creatures were the dragons that did not make it out through surface of Orana when the others emerged. They possessed more magic than the dragons because they were still so close to the source. They hollowed out the caverns, according to legend, ever digging in an effort to follow the Mother Dragon.

Sath grinned, remembering many seasons ago when one of these creatures had proved a threat. Not so anymore. The Fabled Ones had honed his baser instincts and taught him how to protect himself – and the rest of them. As the creature advanced, waving it's dirty claws about as it tried to sink them into his face. Sath deftly dodged the blow as he drew the creature to the side and away from Gin. He was not sure if it could see through the invisibility spell he had allowed her to cast on them as they entered the caverns, but he did not want to find out. It let out a bloodcurdling howl and ran at Sath repeatedly, gnashing horrible teeth and swiping at him with those claws, but he was able to dodge the blows while delivering solid hits to the creature's back and legs. Finally, it lost its balance and Sath raised his staff to deliver a solid finishing blow to the creature's head. It shuddered and lay still in the damp of the cavern floor.

"Show off," Gin muttered. She flexed her hands, wishing that they were free so that she could magically transport herself out of here.

Sath laughed. "Just keeping you safe back there, *darlin'*," he said, immediately regretting the use of the old nickname; it was sure to wound her as much as it did him. He kept his eyes forward as he moved on along the muddy path.

The sound of her snickering stopped him in his tracks. "*Darlin!*" she said through giggles.

"What's so funny?" he demanded.

"I don't know!" Gin said, her giggles giving way to almost hysterical laughter. "Something about the almighty *Rajah* calling someone *darlin'* just struck me as funny!" She doubled over laughing and lost her balance. Without her hands to stop her, she fell face-first into the damp muck that surrounded the lake, striking her forehead soundly on a small rock.

The damage broke her concentration and therefore cancelled the camouflage magic, and suddenly she was visible. "Dear spirits!" she hissed. "Sath, they can...oof!" Another of the lizard creatures had advanced, smelling the blood trickling from the tiny cut on her forehead and landed a solid blow against her back, knocking the wind out of her lungs. From a short distance, a second creature was waving its arms in the air and chanting in a strange, guttural language. Suddenly Gin felt queasy, as the spell it had cast landed. She heard the sounds of battle above her but without her hands free she couldn't roll over to see what was going on.

"Stay down!" Sath called from behind and above her left shoulder.

"Get me out of these things so I can HELP!" Gin shouted back, her anger mounting and blocking out the sick feeling from the creature's disease magic as well as the ringing in her ears from the blow to her head.

"I'm a little busy right now," Sath yelled back. He swung his staff around as though it was a part of his own body. It connected with the creature's midsection and threw it backward into its comrade, who was focused on casting the same sickness on the giant Qatu. With a few ancient words, Sath summoned his magical tiger and sent it into the fray to finish the two monsters off as he went back to Gin's side.

"Get me out of this mud!" she hissed at him. Sath sat back for a moment, listening contentedly as the gurgling noises of the creatures came to a halt and the cavern was again silent, save the dripping of water from the ceilings. "Sath!"

"I'm sorry? What did you call me?" he said, grinning at her as he spoke.

"Please!" she said, as her scream faded into a sound like a sob. "Sath, *Rajah*, Bane of the Bloody Forest, please, at least pick me up…this mud smells really bad!"

Roaring with laughter, Sath plucked her off the ground. He put her on her feet and pulled a cloth from his pack to wipe the mud off her face. She scowled as he gently moved the cloth over her face, being extra careful to keep the foul muck out of her eyes. "Better?" he said softly. She nodded as she kept her gaze on the cavern floor at his feet.

"If you let me out of these I can help you the next time," she said.

"If I let you out of those you will be **gone**, Gin, I'm not an idiot," he said, genuine sadness in his voice. "I'm sorry *darlin*, I truly am, but I need you if I'm going to get my son out of Aynamaede." He turned away from her to check his map. It had been a long time since they…since he had been on a journey through the caverns and it was too easy to get lost. "Besides, you know that I can handle anything in here on my own. Just try to stay on your feet, will you please *darlin'*?" he said, turning around to grin at her. Though she was still solidly studying the ground, he could see the corners of her mouth turn up slightly. "Let's get moving or we won't be there to meet my guard in the morning at the druid ring."

They walked all night, Sath leading the way with Gin following silently behind him. In the early hours of the morning, the entrance to the caverns from the foothills of the Volcanic Mountains came into view and Sath slowed down a bit. "No heroics," he whispered to Gin. "Straight through the tunnel that leads to the foothills," he said. She nodded. They followed the path along the top of the ravine that surrounded the lake, finally arriving at the bandit camp by the entrance. Sath checked the camouflage spell to make sure it was still holding, and then took the chain leading from Gin's manacles in one hand.

"What am I," she scowled, "your pet?" Sath chuckled in response.

"No," he whispered. "This way I can keep you from falling over and blowing our cover again." He could imagine the snarl on her lips without even having to turn around as they moved quickly through the camp. He felt some wobbles from the chain and realized she was having trouble managing the rocky climb without her hands free so he swept her up in his arms, holding her in one giant arm as he used the other to quickly scale the rocks and get them both safely into the tunnel. "Better?" he whispered.

"No, you're still here," she mumbled. He could feel her tiny fingers winding into his fur as they had in the past and he took a deep breath, pushing the memories away.

"*I need to tell you something, Sath…*" Gin quickly switched from the common tongue to Qatunari, making Sath react. She felt him tense under her fingers, still wound into his fur. "*I discovered information about Taeben before I was thrown out of the tree city,*" she said, forcing her voice to remain steady as the rumbling buzz started up in the back of her mind. Sath did not respond, fearing she would stop talking if he interrupted her. "*I don't suppose it makes a difference at this point, but I need you to believe that I would have helped you in any way I could to get your son back. I have no loyalty to the wood elves anymore, and my only desire is to see the Prince restored to his father and his home.*"

"*Just words,*" Sath said, again fighting the scent of sunflowers that filled his nose. "*Your words don't mean anything to me anymore.*"

"*He...I mean...Taeben sent her, Sath!*" Gin's patience had run out. She no longer cared if he left her in the tunnel, hands chained, defenseless; this was something that he needed to know. "*Taeben convinced Annilanshi to charm you to get you away from me, but the elders of Aynamaede are working for him now. Taeben thinks that they will hand me over to him as soon as I come back with you to rescue Khujann. They will not harm the Prince if they think of him as leverage.*" Gin paused a moment, swallowing hard as Sath turned his gaze to her. His teal eyes burned into her skin. "*Khuj has been part of Ben's plan since the day he was born. If you just let Ben take me...you can save your son. It's me he wants, just me.*" Her eyes filled with angry tears. She stared at him, daring him to respond. "*Now... will you please let me help you? I understand that you don't want me anymore, but I've got no one else but you, you and the Prince, so there is no one to miss me if you just let Ben take me.*" Sath looked down at her hands to see them balled up into tiny fists. "*I won't let you make Khujann an orphan,*" she sniffled. Silently he reached into his backpack and removed the key to her chains. Her breath caught in her throat as he released her before sitting down on a rock nearby.

"*Okay, dru – Ginolwenye, if I agree to your plan, what would you suggest?*" No way would he let that wizard take her. She was the key to getting Khujann from the wood elves and...he forced the other reasons back down behind his bloodlust as he stared at her.

"*I think your plan to use the potions to get into the city is a wise one. I think, though, we may need a potion for me as well. It does not really matter what race I become, but I cannot go walking into Aynamaede looking like me, they'll throw me off the edge again. What?*" she asked, as Sath screwed up his face into a grimace.

"*They really throw your people off the edge?*" he asked. He had not wanted to believe her when she had told him the story initially, there in the throne room on Qatu'anari. He had convinced himself she was lying, exaggerating to try to earn sympathy, but now, mentioning it again, there was such truth in her voice. Elysiam had experienced the same thing when she was exiled. And Gin had called the Qatu beasts? They were nothing compared to her people, clearly. "Can you cast anything on the way down?"

"Not from the lower levels, but sometimes from the higher ones I can." Gin looked down at the mossy tunnel floor where she sat, and mindlessly picked at the lichen that covered the floor. "I've had lots of practice at falling from great heights, though, so even falling from the tallest platform where the council meets didn't kill me. I cast what I can on the way down. Once I regain consciousness enough to stand, I just cast a healing spell and – now what?" Gin noticed the horrified look on his face.

"How do you practice falling out of the top of a tree?" Sath asked, his eyes wide. He shuddered a bit at the smile that spread over her face. Not the innocent grin that used to look up at him; it was hardened, older. "I mean we Qatu can do it because it's part of who we are, you know? We don't have to practice falling without dying."

"Well, I've never been really graceful," she said, forcing a laugh. "So I've fallen off a few platforms in my day. In fact, there were times that I sought to jump off a high place for a more permanent solution to a problem. But to build up my resistance, I..." she paused a moment, looking back at the ground, "After I...left Taeben, I made camp for about a week at the Outpost, before I was brave enough to go into the Great Hall and face Tee. To learn to withstand a fall, I jumped off the guard tower at the northern entrance to the Outpost." Sath stared at her. "After enough practice I knew how to land to minimize damage, and how to cast a healing spell on my way down so it's timed to start healing me as I hit the ground. However, if I am not expecting the fall, the surprise and shock of it might ruin my concentration so I cannot cast a spell. Anyway, back to the plan?"

"Right, so my guards will come in disguised as wood elves, as will I. What will we do with you?" Sath asked, choking down the image of Gin plummeting off the guard tower.

"I can pop over to the merchants and get a potion to change my appearance, but I won't know what is on offer until I get there," Gin said, switching back to the common tongue. Her Qatunari was getting better, but it took a lot for her to express herself in that language. Sath shook his head. "What's wrong now?"

"You're not going anywhere alone, Gin," he said. He got to his feet and held out his hand to help her up from the ground. She ignored it and stood up, keeping a slight distance between herself and Sath. He laughed as he turned on his heel and headed for the edge of the tunnel, a stupid grin settling on his face.

"No chains?" she said, taking a step to follow him.

"No, *darlin'*, there's no need," Sath said, not looking back at her. "I...am trusting you." The *Rajah* of Qatu'anari pulled his cloak hood up over his head and began hunting through his pockets for money. He soon located a small bag of platinum pieces that he tossed over his shoulder, grinning. "Let's go get some potions, shall we?"

"Sath!" Gin swore as she stumbled, taken by surprise by the bag plummeting at her head but managing to catch it. She smiled as she tucked the bag into her cloak. "Let's go get your son."

The large stone door that led to the merchant hall in the Outpost swung closed behind them, causing Gin to jump. Sath chuckled, looking down at her as she scowled at him. "This will be much easier if we split up," she said.

"No way, Gin," Sath replied. "Don't make me chain you up again." He chuckled as he looked down at her.

Gin thought quickly. "How about this then: you go in and get a potion to disguise me? I will cast invisibility on myself and follow you. Sath, lots of my friends and kin from the Forest trade here, I can't be seen with you if this is to work."

Sath thought about what she had said, running a giant hand over the top of his head. "You're right about that, at least," he said. "I still have a wood elf potion, what if I use that and then we go in together?" he asked, hopefully.

"No, still no good. They won't know you are the Bane of the Forest until you tell them your name. Keep your hood up - the crest on your cloak is that of the Rajah. Then you can pick up a high elf illusion potion or something for me and we head into the Forest. Sound good?" Gin held her breath. This was it – if he didn't agree, she wasn't sure how she would accomplish getting to Ben and Aynamaede ahead of Sath. In truth, she could have ported away from him already as he had released her from her chains, but somehow she knew she would not be able to bear the look of betrayal on his face twice. Once in Bellesea Keep was enough.

"As long as you cast something on me so that I am able to still see you," Sath said. Gin swallowed hard as she agreed. She spoke the words and as Sath looked around, he saw many figures suddenly come into view. Human women that were following human men, presumably to catch them cheating; thieves following humans with the intention of lightening the human's load unseen; dark elves with wood elves holding their invisible hands to keep their relationship secret... He would have to get this for himself, this ability to see the invisible. He frowned as he thought of how he would need the potion after Gin had left his side. Perhaps she might stay...

"Can you see me?" she asked, breaking him out of his sad musing. He nodded. Gin knew the time was now. She had to act; Sath was not going to allow her to leave his sight; even if she cast an invisibility spell on herself, he would still be able to see her. She would make it right by reuniting him with his son and handing herself over to Taeben to ensure that he left Sath and Khujann alone – but only if she made her move now.

Yes, yes my love, I will hold to my end of the deal once you are safely back with me. Good girl, Ginny. You are a good girl.

Shaking off the voice in her mind and steeling her resolve, she looked him right in the eye. "How about now?" she said, speaking rapid ancient Elvish words of solo evacuation from danger. "Home!"

"Gin, what are you…NO!" Sath roared as Gin popped out of sight. "NO! NO!" He swiped at the air with a hand and then covered his face, howling in frustration and attracting quite a bit of attention from the other patrons of the merchant hall.

Nancy E. Dunne

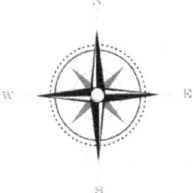

TWENTY-FIVE

"I suppose you'll want me to let you go now, won't you wood elf?" Sath said to the struggling wood elf he held by her wrists on a length of rope. In the few days since Gin had left Sath at the Outpost, he had caught up to his *Sahi Kahl*, made it to the edge of the tree city, and found an unlucky female wood elf out hunting. She knew Gin, and Sath had allowed her to trade her tracking skill for her life. With his guard unhappily but dutifully camped and waiting at the edge of the Great Forest, Sath took the wood elf to find Gin for him. He had stopped her tracking when they caught up to Gin, and kept her from crying out by wrapping a huge hand around her mouth. Removing his hand now, he frowned at the look of fear on the young ranger's face. Clearly, no one in the Great Forest had forgotten who he used to be. No one.

"Yes please," she whispered. "I found Gin for you. Please?" Her large blue eyes and brown hair were so similar to Gin's, and Sath felt his resolve waver a bit. With one deadly claw, he broke the shackles he had used to keep her from casting any spells or using any potions while tracking for him.

"Be off with you and speak of this to no one," he said. Looking down at her, teeth bared, he said in Elvish, "*I will know if you betray me, ranger.*" The tiny wood elf ranger let out a strangled gasp and scampered off into the forest. Sath grimaced, and then turned his attention back to Gin only to find that she was rapidly moving out of sight and did not seem to be alone. The *Rajah* of Qatu'anari popped the cork on a potion and downed it in one gulp, causing his image to blur and shift, and then silently ran through the forest after her.

Gin had arrived at Aynamaede and snuck in, using a rope ladder that she and her brother made when they were children that led up to the lowest platform. As she cleaned out the things she needed from her hut, Kae - Gin's cousin and member of the council - found her there. Gin had feared the worst when she saw Kae's form fill the small doorway, but then her cousin had burst into happy tears and run into Gin's waiting arms. Swearing her allegiance only to her blood family, Kae had insisted on coming with Gin to rescue Khujann who was being held at the druid circle closest to the tree city. The two wood elves had almost reached the edge of the Forest, headed west toward the Outpost, when they heard footsteps behind them. Kae palmed her dagger and Gin's tiny hand closed around her staff as they turned simultaneously to see what was coming.

"Mistress Ginolwenye?" A male wood elf approached at a dead run. His armor revealed him to be a warrior, though he had no weapon raised. "I know it is you, please, I have important information!"

"Why should we listen to anything you say?" Gin snapped. "You are one of those who pitched me out of my own home and are now making deals with..." She paused before she spoke Taeben's name, for fear that he would awaken in the back of her mind. He had been blessedly absent since she left Sath in the market, and she found that she felt more clear-headed than she had in an age. "Make it quick, my good sir warrior, for we have better things to do with our time."

"I can help you on your quest," said the elf. His shock of unruly blonde hair, most uncharacteristic of her kind, stood out against the muted greens and browns of the forest, and his oversized armor looked as though he'd already seen battle and was covered in blood. Extra lacings held each piece in place, and he fiddled with it constantly as though trying to make sure that vulnerable bits were covered, as they should be. "You need someone to fight with you. Let me help you bring my...let me help you recover the Qatu cub." Gin remained silent but considered him. Something was not right with this male but she could not put her finger on what it was.

"Why would you want to do that?" Kae asked. "You know there is a price on the head of the cub as well as on his father, the Bane of the Forest."

The young male elf laughed. "Bane of the Forest? I have not heard those words in many seasons. I doubt he is anything to fear, at least not now."

Gin's eyes narrowed. "Are you not familiar with this scourge against our kind?"

The young male stared at her. "Scourge? Now you are just being ridiculous. He is no threat to any of us, not anymore. The *Rajah* is merely a concerned father protecting his young. Any of us would do the same. Is it not in the very fiber of being of the compassionate races such as ourselves to help if at all possible?"

Gin looked him in the eye for a moment, and then started to laugh. "Seriously?" she said, doubling over with giggles. Kae stared at her.

"Are you all right, Gin?" she asked.

"I'm sorry," Gin said, wiping her eyes. "It's just clear that this warrior doesn't know **the Rajah** at all. The *Rajah*!"

The male elf narrowed his eyes. "That's his name, isn't it? Qa Sathlir Clawsharp, *Rajah* of Qatu'anari?" At this, Gin nearly lost her balance laughing. "Why is that so funny?" She looked up at him, meeting his gaze, and his teal eyes bored into her, causing her to catch her breath a moment. In the back of her mind, the wizard stirred. "What now? Are you looking me in the...why are you looking me in the eye like that?"

"*You're clever, but not that clever,*" she said in Qatunari. The male's eyes widened, and then narrowed again. Kae looked back and forth between them, clearly confused.

"What is going on here?" she demanded, still looking back and forth from Gin to the strange male elf.

"I'm not sure," he replied. "I'm also not sure what your friend here just said, but it sounded like Qatunari. All grumbly growly." He cleared his throat. "Practicing for when you get your charge back and return to serve in the royal palace?" He immediately turned his gaze away from Gin's and busied himself in his backpack.

"What is he talking about, Gin?" Kae was starting to look angry. "And you," she said, poking the warrior in the back and making him turn to face her a moment, "how did you know that Gin was looking for Khujann?"

"Prince Khujann," the male elf corrected her, and then returned his focus to his bag.

Gin stared at the back of his head, eyes blazing. "*Turn around and face me, Sath, before I root you to the spot and singe you a bit, now that you are without your protective fur.*" The male turned slowly around as Kae stared angrily at them both.

"Seriously, Gin, cut that out, you sound like a rumbly thunderstorm when you speak like that!" Kae whined.

The male looked Ginolwenye in the eye, a slight twinkle in his own teal ones. "*You would still fit right inside my pocket,*" he said, to Kae's consternation. Gin took a step back and glared at him. "I'm sorry, my dear," he said, switching back to Elvish and extending a hand. "My name is Sathlir Clawsharp, and I am in fact the *Rajah* of Qatu'anari." When she did not take his hand, he shook himself all over once to rid himself of the wood elf illusion potion that he had taken earlier. Again, he extended a hand to Kae who shrunk back behind Gin, whimpering slightly.

"Not the best idea, Sath," Gin said, her own voice quivering slightly. "This is my cousin, Kae. She knew Lairky, as did all my kin." Though the wounded look that crossed Sath's now furry face pained her, she continued her icy stare. "Now, what exactly do you want? To go with us to look for your son? Like you would not be a beacon to those holding him. You must be insane if you think I will allow it. Why do you think I left you in the merchant hall?"

"You'll ALLOW it? You have no say in the…"

"For heaven's sake, Sath, you're not in the palace now. I am not one of your subjects. Stop being so bossy and shut it for a second." Her hands on her hips, Gin stared up at the Qatu that was easily twice her height, channeling all of her unease into her worry over Khujann. Sath noticed, with a slight grin on his furry face, that she still did not seem the least bit afraid of him, so the fear he smelled must be coming from the other elf. "Kae and I are going to follow the trail and bring Khujann back to you. You are going to go back to your kind, and let us get started. The end." She wrapped one arm around her back and Kae, and recited the one-word spell that transported her quickly away and out of danger, "safety." Sath cursed loudly and swiped at the air with a deadly claw where Gin had been only seconds before.

"Difficult, she has never ceased to be DIFFICULT!" Sath roared. He ran northwest for the edge of the Forest, in the hopes that he could again catch up to his quad.

Gin and Kae hit the ground running near a clearing between the tree city and the druid circle and kept moving. Finally, they reached the safety of the deep forest and slowed to a walk, not wishing to alert to their presence any of the guards that they saw near the circle. Once they got to the other side of the ring of stones, Gin stopped a moment to sink to the ground to rest.

"How did you know?" Kae asked her cousin, eyes wild with fear. "How did you know it was the Cat? And you were with him before…you left him the merchant halls…what is going on? How were you so sure it was him?"

"His eyes," Gin replied. She swallowed and took a few deep breaths to compose herself before continuing to speak. "The potion can't change his eyes, just like it couldn't change Lairky's at first. The merchant he bought it from isn't as talented with potion making as she was, clearly." Running a hand over her fringe and then tightening her ponytail, she stared up at the sky for a moment. "When I was…removed from Aynamaede, the first place I went was back to Qatu'anari to try and get Sath's help. He…agreed and we started out on the trail but I soon came to realize that I couldn't let him just walk into the Council chambers to demand his son and be heading straight to his death. That's when I tricked him and left him in the merchant halls. We've got to find Khujann, Kae. I have to bring him back to his father and put all this right."

"You still love him, don't you?" Kae said, mild revulsion in her tone. "How I don't know, considering what he did to Lairky…and to you!" She touched a finger to the scar on her cousin's face. "How you can care about that beast is something that I will never understand."

"Doesn't matter," Gin said. "Where is Khujann? We can camp here for a few days as long as no one notices us, but we can't leave him too long in the druid circle for fear that…"

"He's not there anymore, Gin," Kae said, hanging her head in shame.

"What do you mean, he's not there?" Gin reached over and lifted her cousin's chin until they were looking into each other's eyes. She clenched her jaw to keep from demanding answers from her cousin.

"I mean he isn't there. Gin, the reason I left and the reason I went looking for you…well, it isn't right, he may be a little beast but he is still little…what they were planning for him…I just couldn't allow…"

How much like Lairky she was. Gin's heart squeezed in her chest. "Kae, focus," she said, struggling to keep her impatience and worry for Khujann under control. "Where is the Prince?"

"Prince," Kae said, scowling. She met Gin's gaze and the scowl faded. "I'm sorry. The cub was to be given to the wizard, who gave orders that…Oh, Gin, I'm so sorry. Lord Taeben…the wizard, sorry, he commanded that the cub be given to the dragon in Bellesea Keep."

The color drained out of Gin's face as she stared at her cousin. "When?" she managed to croak out. Her head spun and mouth went dry. "When was he sent?"

"A fortnight ago, but remember that he was not using magic to travel because Master…the wizard didn't take him personally." Again, Kae hung her head. "It was right after you were exiled. The wizard was furious that things had not gone the way he wanted, and he changed the plan we had agreed upon." Gin felt the stirring in the back of her mind again. Was that...amusement? She clenched her fists and tried to push him back as far as she could.

They denied me my prize, so I will deny you the prince. Fair trade, no?

You said if I came, you would give the cub back. More lies. I must have been out of my mind.

"Go on, Kae," Gin said when she realized that her cousin was again staring at her.

"They put him in a cage on a litter and took him like a beast going to a menagerie." Gin clamped her hand over her mouth as an image of the tiny prince in a cage, whimpering and afraid and cold, filled her mind and heart. Kae reached out for her but Gin pulled away. "He won't have arrived yet, I shouldn't think."

"You and your Council should hope that he hasn't," Gin hissed. "And you should BEG the All Mother for Her forgiveness. He is just a baby, Kae, and you've delivered him to that monster in the Keep." Gin's mind was reeling. "And all because of me," she whispered. "All of this because Ben wants me..."

"Not exactly."

Gin's head popped back up as she looked at her cousin. "What does that mean?"

"Well, Lord Taeben was angry when you were thrown out of the city because it was part of his bargain that he would help us bring justice to the Bane of the Forest if he could take you away from here to keep you safe from retaliation," Kae explained. "Before you say anything, I know now that isn't exactly what he wanted, Gin, but at the time..." The younger wood elf paused a moment and took a few deep breaths before continuing to speak. "Anyway, when he did not get what he was promised, he told the Council that without you, the Bane of the Forest would not rest until he had destroyed all of our city and potentially the Forest itself to find his son. He claimed that the Bane was in love with you and that if you were not here when the Qatu forces arrived there would be no mercy for any of us. He chastised the foolishness of the Council's decision to banish you, claiming that only you could tame the Bane to the point that..."

Gin held her hand up. "Sath. His name is Sath, Kae."

"Right. Only you could tame the...Sath so that he would do us no harm and simply turn himself in. He brought up the war again that the Qatu threaten against us and..."

"What war?" A memory of Sath's discussion in the palace with his generals came to Gin's mind but with the wizard now awake and attentive, she was having a hard time remembering exactly what was said.

"The war, Gin, that the Qatu will bring upon the Elves in order to capture all of us for slaves and take over our Forest, surely you heard rumblings while you were caring for the prince?" Kae furrowed her brow. "They are in league with the dragonkind. It is the Forest War begun again in the hopes that the Mother Dragon will finally return and release the dragons in Bellesea Keep and the Tower. Lord Taeben seemed quite certain."

"You still call him Lord Taeben...why?"

"He commanded us to refer to him as such since he was an ambassador and would save us from the Qatu," the younger wood elf replied. "It is what I am used to calling him, Gin."

"I cannot bear it. At least call him Taeben," Gin pleaded. "And there is no war, at least not started by the Qatu, as far as I know. I do remember hearing that Ben warned the Qatu of retaliation from the Elves for Sath's time as the Bane of the Forest, but I thought that was just Ben trying to further an agenda." She rubbed her forehead for a moment as she thought. "I guess he was," she said finally, "and the agenda is to get me as far away from anyone I love as he possibly can so that I will be his."

"Taeben must really love you, Gin," Kae said, a dreamy look in her eyes.

"He doesn't know how to love," Gin spit back. "He only knows how to take. Now, we need to have a plan to get Khujann back from that dragon...and I know just the dwarf to help us."

Barely controlled rage simmered in the back of her mind as the wizard reacted to her words, and Gin smiled.

Challenge accepted indeed, Ginny. You are only making things worse for yourself and for that mangy cub you love so much.

Nancy E. Dunne

TWENTY-SIX

The wizard drummed his long white fingers on the arm of the chair as he waited for Lord Taanyth to grant him audience. His plan was going well, save the need to move the little beast to Bellesea Keep to draw Gin back to him. However, she knew now, and would be on her way there soon if she wasn't already. Taeben licked his lips and smiled. Very soon, he would have all that he desired - the spell, the throne of Qatu'anari, and Gin, and that filthy Qatu would bear witness to it all…and then die.

The wyvern watching the room breathed its foul breath heavily on the top of Taeben's head, causing waves of nausea to churn through the high elf's stomach. How much longer would he be kept waiting? Just as he was plotting a series of spells that would first turn the wyvern to ice and then blast it into shards, the door to the ancient dragon's inner chamber opened.

"Wizard," called Lord Taanyth, "enter." Steeling his resolve, Taeben stood and strode into the room, wincing only slightly as the heavy stone doors slammed behind him. He was thankful for the improved vision that his race possessed as he scanned the room through the darkness. Lush velvet cushions lined the room's walls, and there were various bowls of food and cups of wine on a wide wooden table to one side. In the corner, chained to the wall with heavy iron chains was a tiny Qatu cub.

"M'lord, you have the Prince already I see?" Taeben cursed inwardly. How had the wood elves beat him here, and with the Prince Khujann in tow? "I thought that…"

"Silence, Wizard," hissed Lord Taanyth. "The orcs have done as they were bidden. We would not want this Qatu running loose and back to his father now, would we? Worse, to that damnable druid, Ginolwenye. She and I have issues to discuss." Always levitating, he floated over toward Khujann who shrank back, wiping tears on the back of one of his shackled hands. "The small beast misses her you know. Cries out her name in its sleep." He turned back toward Taeben. "Is there a problem, wizard?"

"Of course not, M'lord," Taeben said, his steady voice hiding the rage that boiled within him. "Shall I take the beast for you now so that you can get back to the business at hand? I assume that my former accommodation is still…available."

"No." Lord Taanyth looked back at the Prince. "I think I will keep it here, in the hopes that our dear Ginolwenye will come to me for him. She has always had a soft spot for pitiful creatures." He beamed a fangy grin at Taeben that set the high elf's skin crawling. "But you know that, don't you, Taeben?"

"Of course, you are right. Now, if there is nothing more, M'lord, I will take my leave. It is a day's journey at least back to the Outpost to search for that druid." Taeben turned on his heel but halted, realizing he had not been formally dismissed from Lord Taanyth's chambers. If there was one thing the antediluvian dragon fixated on, it was making sure that everyone knew he was the superior and was owed their respect. "Apologies, M'lord," he stammered, feeling the dragon's hot breath on the back of his neck. Taeben turned slowly and knelt in front of Lord Taanyth. "I will take my leave if it pleases you," he said, his voice finally giving way to a slight waver.

"You know what will please me, Wizard?" Lord Taanyth hissed angrily. "That druid chained to the FLOOR in my arena. The Qatu and its offspring here chained to a wall, watching as I destroy her. My spell, finally tested and ready to unleash. Can you manage any of that, Taeben?"

"As you require, M'lord," Taeben said, choking back revulsion at the closeness of the dragon's treacherous claws to his face. He swallowed hard as the claws waved him away as though finished with him. As Lord Taanyth moved silently back to the window across from Prince Khujann, Taeben moved quickly out the door and did not slow down until he had reached the drawbridge over the moat that surrounded the castle. He walked past the wyvern guards and immediately spoke the words that made him invisible to most eyes, and then headed back to his former quarters. He would not let anyone destroy his plan, not even a dragon.

"How are we going to do this, Gin?" Kae said as she peeked around the corner of the passage that lead into Bellesea Keep and stared at the wyverns guarding the front gate. "There must be five of them just at the front gate! And what about the dwarf that you said would help us?" She shivered suddenly as what felt like a cold breeze swept past her, then turned her attention back to the task at hand. "I've never been here before."

Gin smiled sadly. "Oh, I've been here plenty of times, Kae," she said. "Every time I do I seem to forget that I've already taken out my revenge on the inhabitants, and every time it's more satisfying than the last." Kae drew her dagger but Gin put her hand over her cousin's. "Put that away. Until we get well deep into the Keep I need to know you're invisible and out of harm's way, got it?" Kae looked ready to object but a look from Gin silenced her and she nodded. "It certainly looks like they have upped their security, so I'm going to assume that the prince is already here." Thinking back to her botched rescue from Dorlagar and the look on Sath's face when she did not port out with the rest of her party, Gin swallowed hard. Her betrayal of Sath had started then, and because of that, their relationship would never be as casual as it had been; though it had not been easy before that, really. The days of traveling through Orana's expanse just exploring, the nights of sleeping out under the stars gazing up at the moon's gentle glow, learning about each other, learning to trust each other…those were but memories now, thanks to her. This was the only way to make things right, and Gin was determined not to fail, even if it meant offering her freedom in return for Khujann's release. "Ready, cousin?" she asked as she cast an invisibility spell on Kae.

"Ready as I'll ever be," the younger wood elf said as the two set off for the drawbridge.

"Well then," Gin said, thinking of Elysiam and grinning like a madwoman, "Stand back a minute, I'm gonna try something." Those words, spoken by Elysiam on so many occasions, had led to equal parts success in battle and suddenly having to run for their lives, but it gave Gin a burst of courage and she cast a fast snare spell on the two closest wyverns. The spell would cause the ground beneath them to sprout magical tangling vines that would slow their ability to run. They ran at her as fast as they could, which wasn't very fast at all, and she countered by rooting both to the spot with magical roots that, similar to the snare magic, rose up from the ground to trap their feet; and then dropping a load of magical bees and other stinging insects on them. Within moments, they fell to the ground, immobilized by the stings and the twin bolts of lightning that Gin directed from the sky to their heads with a clap of her hands.

"Wow..." said the still-invisible wood elf behind her. Kae had taken a different path, and her discipline had not included magical instruction.

"Child's play," Gin said. "These are the young and less experienced. They get tougher as you move inside, because the best guard Lord Taanyth, the dragon that controls the Keep. Come on."

On the barren plains outside of the Keep, the royal guard of Qatu'anari stood watch over their ruler. "*What is your command, Rajah? The elves have entered the Keep,*" the scout asked as Sath paced back and forth across their temporary camp in the woods in the eastern Outlands. "*Shall we follow and apprehend them?*" After Gin and Kae had left Sath in the Forest, he had managed to catch up to his quad and ordered them to hunt the two wood elves; once they were found, the *Sahi Kalah* were to return to him. Scouts had informed him of a band of orcs taking his son, and the same scouts had followed the orcs and the two wood elves to Bellesea Keep.

Sath and his *Sahi* had been camping in the forest that surrounded the desert close to Bellesea Keep. If that dragon harmed his son... "No," Sath replied. "*No, if we follow too closely we will tip off Lord Taanyth to our presence and Khujann may suffer for it.*" His eyes blazed. "*I would like to know how that old lizard even knew I had a son, but I bet that it was that wizard's doing, as it always seems to be.*" He was tracing a path with a claw down the bark of a tree when one of his personal guards moved closer to him, drawing a weapon. "*What is it, Hinja?*" he asked, straining his eyes to see what had startled the guard.

"*Elves,*" Hinja said gruffly. "*I saw a high elf enter that I think is the former Ambassador.*"

Sath snatched the telescope from his guard's hand and squinted in the direction the guard had been watching. He balled up his fists in frustration. "*I was right. That is how Lord Taanyth knew about Khujann. Taeben. He is the ambassador that passed on the information about the war plans. I should have known! Apparently his infiltration and exploitation of the wood elves wasn't enough.*" His guards quickly surrounded him and drew weapons. "*No, put those down, it will do us no good to engage with the wizard now.*" He cracked his giant knuckles and then ran a hand over his head in frustration. "*When I have my son back,*" he said, "*I will deal with Taeben. And if I find out that the druid is helping him...*" The thought stopped him dead. He knew a little of what Gin had been through with Taeben but he also knew what a soft heart she had. It was something that drew him to her in the first place...her amazing capacity for forgiveness. "*If she is helping him then I will deal with her as well,*" he said, barely aloud. "*But Khujann is all that matters now.*"

Gin crept across the drawbridge, her eyes peeled for more wyvern guards. There were none to be seen, which she took to be a bad sign. "*What's wrong, Gin?*" asked Kae, who remained invisible as she was told but stuck to Gin's back like glue.

"No guards," Gin said. "Something is wrong." A commotion ahead of them stopped them in their tracks. "What the…"

"I've had it with the lot of you!" bellowed a voice that Gin knew very well. She grinned, recognizing the speaker. "Now come on over here and let's dance, ye great smelly beasts!" There was a clashing of weapons, howling from wyverns, and then a deep throaty laugh that Gin hadn't heard in ages. She rushed forward, happy and thankful tears wetting her cheeks, and left Kae standing invisibly still.

"Teeand!" she yelled as she rounded the corner. The dwarf warrior stood stock-still, his green armor tinted brown and red with wyvern gore. He squinted at her a moment, then a smile spread across his bearded face.

"Why you are a sight for sore eyes, my lass!" he said, opening his arms. "Gin! Come and give us a hug…oh, well maybe not," he said, noticing the grimace on her face and then the wyvern bits on his chest. "How are ya? How's your Qatu? Are you Ginolwenye Clawsharp, Queen of the Qatu, at last?"

Gin smiled sadly at him. "I'm as well as can be, Tee," she said, "but you know that I am no such thing. I am just Gin these days. Sath is the only Clawsharp save his son, Khujann and his sister Kazhmere."

"I've not seen the Princess in an age, but that Khujann's a fine lad," Teeand said. "Just like his father and twice as stubborn. Is he with you, our lass? You're his tutor I believe - thanks to old Tee - aren't ya?"

"I was, yes." Gin's face clouded a bit. "It's a very long story, Tee, but Khujann is in great danger. Lord Taanyth is holding him here, in the Keep, and I'm on my way to rescue him. That's why I'm so pleased I've found you, Tee, I need your skill in planning an attack. I asked after you in the Outpost and was told you might be hunting in these parts."

Teeand studied her for a moment, and then burst out laughing. "You have always thought yourself to be a battle druid when it comes to this cursed place and the Qatu you love, Gin my girl," he said, grinning. "Come to take on that overgrown saddle bag of a dragon on your own, have you?" His laughter subdued, he reached up suddenly and took her hands in his. "I'm not going to let you do that, you know? You remember what happened the last time you charged in here alone, yeah?"

A sad smile spread over Gin's face. "Aye, I remember, Tee. Dorlagar died at my hand." A shocked gasp that seemed to come from nowhere jolted Gin back to the present. "OH! Tee, I haven't introduced you to my cousin, Kae." She spoke some long-forgotten words and Kae came into view. Teeand took a step backward.

"Blimey, she looks like…"

"I know, Tee. She and Lairky could have been twins. Kae, this is one of my oldest and dearest friends, Teeand. You can't ask for a better ally if you find yourself in trouble. Tee is the best warrior I know," Gin said, grinning at the now blushing dwarf.

"Pleased to meet you, sir," Kae said. Teeand's face exploded into laughter. "Did I say something funny?"

Gin smirked. "Our little green friend here isn't used to being called 'sir' I think," she said, smiling affectionately at Teeand. "Why are you here, anyway, Tee? This place and its inhabitants are well below your skill level as a warrior."

Teeand shrugged. "I need money. The wife's about to have another little one and we will have another mouth to feed," he said. "These oversized bats are easy kills and they sometimes have a lot of money on them, running errands for their master, Lord Saddlebag. It's a win-win I think." He stared up at her intently. "But while I'm here I might as well lend a hand to help my oldest and dearest friend's son out of a jam." Gin opened her mouth to respond and Teeand stopped her cold with a look. "I know that you can do this alone, blah, blah, blah Gin. But I'm itching for a fight, I am, and a good one too. These wyverns are too easy to kill." Gin shook her head, defeated.

"Come on, then. I'm betting that Khujann is in the dragon's private quarters and not in the prison cells," she said. Pulling a map from one of her bags, she indicated the area where she thought Lord Taanyth's private quarters were. "I think this is where I was taken before…when Ben was…well, he's going to want to keep this hush-hush, so he won't be keeping the Prince here," she indicated a block of cells on the map, "because it's too close to where people are, they'd hear him. See that room there? That's where I was held by Dor and I could hear every conversation that went on in those jail cells."

Teeand winced at the memory of Gin being held captive in the Keep, and then shook it off. "So, we skip those cells and head down this way instead?" he asked, indicating a path that led directly to Lord Taanyth's chambers. She did not answer him. "Gin? *What's wrong with yeh, pet?*" he said in his native tongue as he glanced up at her stricken expression.

Gin had been staring off into space, caught up in a memory of the past, when she was held in the Keep. She was taken down to Lord Taanyth's arena, and the dragon was testing Taeben's spell on her. It was a blurry memory at best, but she remembered being alternately very cold, and then very, very hot, and constantly in excruciating pain. Taeben was there; she remembered his voice being in the background and not being able to make out what he said above the roaring sound in her ears, and she could still see the look in his eyes in her mind. She closed her eyes tight and pressed the heels of her hands into her eyes, trying to calm herself. Taeben's face swam before her eyes and his presence stirred in the back of her mind.

"Just give it up, Gin," the phantom Taeben said. "If you give up, the pain will stop. It will all stop and I will be able to get you away from here. Stop fighting him! Just stay down." Another flash of heat seared her back and Gin screamed…

...as Teeand yanked her hands away from her face and Kae put one tiny hand on either side of her cousin's head, turning Gin's face around to meet her gaze. "What is it, Gin? Tell us, please?" Kae's brow furrowed deeply with worry.

"I remembered...when I was here before," Gin stammered. She thought she could feel Taeben in the back of her mind, like a snake uncoiling in the sun. "Lord Taanyth was working on a spell with Ben...Taeben." At the sound of the wizard's name, Teeand swore under his breath. "The spell was designed for mass mind control, and it was not working on druids and rangers, so he was testing it on... on..." She paused, a sob stuck in her throat. After composing herself, she said, "he was testing it on me." Teeand muttered something under his breath about wizards but Gin turned to face him. "Lord Taanyth was testing it, Tee. Ben was trying to help me escape...well, maybe not at first, but he has a good heart and he wanted to help me...He used to have a good heart..." Unwelcome happiness filled her mind and she tried even harder to block it.

"He wanted to help you so badly that he stood and watched you get hurt? He had such a good heart that he hurt you even worse by leaving you to his enemies?" Teeand spat into the dirt. Gin felt the snake in her mind recoil to strike, and shuddered. "We need to stop talking about this, Gin, and be findin' that cub for Sath," he said, turning away from her and lowering his voice as he spoke, this time in Qatunari, *"who, by the way, never lifted a finger against you in anger."*

"Except for that one time in the tunnels, Tee?" Gin replied, turning her face toward his so that he could see the scar on her cheek.

"That was a long time ago, Ginny," Teeand replied. *"He didn't know you then. He was different then. You made the change in him."*

"Could you two please stop that?" Kae was just about to lose patience with not being able to understand them. Gin smiled and touched her cousin's cheek.

"Of course, Kae, I'm sorry. Now, let's go get the Prince back and I can promise you, no Qatunari will ever cross my lips again."

Sath took one last look over his shoulder at the tree line and then turned to his *Sahi Kahl*. *"You are dismissed,"* he said, raising a giant hand in response to the arguments that arose among the Qatu guards that surrounded him. *"That is an order from your Rajah,"* he said.

"My Lord Rajah," said Hulan, a heavily armed Qatu with deep gray fur and black spots, *"we would never disobey your command, save when it means the future of the throne of Qatu'anari. You and the Prince are all that exists of your line. We cannot allow you to..."*

"Ah, but I am not, Hulan." Sath smiled sadly. *"Remember? She had spots like mine? The most irritating cub in our nursery?"*

"Aye, of course I know the Qatu of whom you speak, my Lord Rajah," said Hulan. He and Sath had both played in the royal nursery as cubs, and had grown up together. Hulan was the only one that knew Kazhmere's identity. *"The Princess Royal, Qa Kazhmere."* Sath chuckled sadly as he nodded. He saw true affection in Hulan's gaze when the *Sahi* had mentioned Kazhmere's name, and he smiled. Hulan smiled back at him, knowingly.

"Enough. She is your top priority now. Tell the others and go. You have my orders, Hulan. Leave me here to rescue my son, and return to Qatu'anari. You will find the Princess in the palace, and you will keep close to her. I fear that I have enemies within our own city that would see themselves on the throne via my sister." Sath's eyes blazed. *"There will not be a hair harmed on her head."*

"And what of the druid, my Lord?" asked another guard. *"If she returns to Qatu'anari, she will be recognized, and is an enemy of many for her compliance in the abduction of the Prince by the Ambassador."* Sath turned his teal eyes toward the guard and the tiger-striped male seemed to shrink a few inches. *"I only ask for your guidance in handling matters should the people become... uncooperative."*

"*If Ginolwenye sets foot in Qatu'anari, she is to be brought to the palace and kept in the cells until I return. I will deal with her, no one else, understood? If I or my son...or both should not return, she is to be taken secretly to the Forest and released.*" Sath raised a hand again to silence the murmurs over the suggestion that he would not return. "*It is highly likely that I will return, and when I do, I will sort out what to do with the druid myself. Any companions with whom she is traveling are to be dispatched safely to their homelands. It is Ginolwenye alone with whom I take issue.*" The guards nodded and after kneeling in turn in front of Sath, they left one by one, taking different routes back to their home on island of Qatu'anari, as instructed by their *Rajah*.

Sath stood, alone finally, and took out a potion bottle from his pack. "I apologize for this, Gin, but it is the only way that I can get in and out of the Keep with my son." He uncorked the bottle and sniffed the contents. Making a face, he set it carefully down on a smooth rock next to his backpack. Next, from the pack he took a long blue robe that he quickly exchanged for the red and black plate armor he usually wore to battle. It was tight over his bulging frame, so he took it back off for the moment, thankful that he was alone and concealed by the outcrop of rocks. Once the armor was hidden away in a magical bag that was much larger on the inside than the outside, he returned to the potion. "This had better work, Ja'ming," he muttered. Ja'ming, the royal potion master, had made this concoction to very exact standards. Sadly, those did not include a palatable taste, and Sath nearly gagged as he downed the bottle.

His image began to shift and blur, and he felt the familiar sensation of fur replaced with smooth pale skin. The fur on his head shifted to white hair that he quickly pulled back into a ponytail at the nape of his neck. Once his hair was tied back, he took a moment to look at his arms and hands. He grimaced slightly at the long, ivory fingers that seemed so fragile, the hands that were smooth on the palms as though they'd never done a day's work.

Sath growled, thinking of hands and fingers like those touching Gin and hurting her. He pulled the robe on and tied the belt around his waist, and then took a few halting steps, trying to become accustomed to the long and willowy legs his borrowed high elf body now had. It had been much easier to adjust to the wood elf body, as their race was more compact and well proportioned. Sath pushed images of Gin's small body curled up in his arms from his mind and headed for the Keep.

Just before he stumbled out into the open desert from the tree line, he found a small pond where he could fill up his water skin. The face that greeted him as he leaned over the water caused his stomach to turn with nausea. "Hail and well met," he said to his reflection. "My name is Taeben, and I serve Lord Taanyth." Water skin in hand, he spoke ancient words that made him blend in with his surroundings and then took off at a dead run for the fortress walls that surrounded the Keep.

"Are you sure that's the right way?" Kae asked as she studied the map over Teeand's shoulder. "It looks like we should head east when we get there and not bother with the guards there on the parapets."

"Oi, lass, just because you're taller than I am doesn't mean you can read over my shoulder," the dwarf snapped. He was still reeling from the revelation that Lord Taanyth had been testing his spells on Gin when she was held captive in the Keep all those many seasons ago, and his unease coupled with his barely contained anger was starting to become obvious. The fact that it had been many hours since his last pint of ale wasn't helping either, truth be told.

"I just think you're taking the long way around so that you can kill a few extra guards if we have the time," Kae said, her dark eyes narrowed. "We need to get in there, get the Prince, and get back out. You and Gin can come back for some kind of revenge on the Keep and Lord Taanyth later." She rubbed her arms vigorously. "This place gives me the creeps."

"There's no revenge," Gin said matter-of-factly. "But Kae is absolutely right, Khujann is the most important thing here, and I've got to deliver him to his father safe and sound."

"You mean WE have to, lass," said Teeand. "I never miss a chance to visit my old pal Sath." He smiled, lost in nostalgia for a moment. "Now then, which way are we going in?"

"I think the best way," Gin said as she turned the map around to face her and indicated their position, "is to go down to the arena just outside of Lord Taanyth's chambers here. Unless the old dragon is working on a new spell, I don't think anyone will be in there. We climb down here and then make our way along the side until we get to the private chambers in the back…here. I'd bet my life he's keeping Khujann there because most that enter here are too afraid of the arena to make it past the front doors."

"I think I can understand why," Kae said. "Gin, considering all the memories this place holds for you, maybe you should keep watch while Tee and I go in and get the Prince?"

"How exactly will you heal yourselves without me?" Gin asked. Her voice shook with anger. "And which of you, pray tell, will the Prince trust enough to follow? You, Tee, that he's not seen since he was a wee cub? Or you, Kae, one of the wood elves that got him here in the first place?"

"Fair enough, our Gin, fair enough," Teeand said, sensing the rising temper in both of the wood elves. "We all go together, and we get the Prince to safety. But I will lead the way, with the wee Kae at my back." Kae bristled but kept her mouth shut. "Gin, you follow at a slight distance but keep that healing magic ready if things go wrong. Is everyone ready?"

"As ready as I'll ever be." Gin smiled sadly. "I guess there's only one way to find out, huh? Lead on, Tee…lead on." As she followed the dwarf and her cousin into the arena, she lifted her eyes upward. "Thank you, Great Mother, for sending Tee to help us. I know that he will not only keep Khujann safe but will protect my sweet cousin as well. Just give me the strength to do what I must to protect all of them when the time comes."

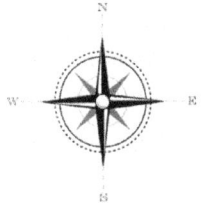

TWENTY-SEVEN

Upon reaching the front gates of Bellesea Keep, Sath decided to test his guise on the wyvern guards at the door. Palming the potion that would magically transport him out of the Keep and back to Qatu'anari, Sath shook off the spell that kept him invisible and strode up to the guards. They nodded their heads in his direction and then switched their attention back to the desert across which he had just come. *First test passed*, Sath thought.

Adjusting to the increased visual field and acuity that the elves possessed took Sath a moment or two. He could see for miles, and the normally dark passages of the Keep were as bright as day. Resisting the urge to explore more and see what he'd been missing, he hurried along toward the arena. It made sense that Lord Taanyth would be holding his son in his private chambers, as that was the most well-defended part of the Keep. It stood at the dead center of the structure, and was at one end of the arena that opened up to the roof of the Keep.

Voices and memories competed for his attention as he passed the cells where he and Teeand had met as well as the room where Gin was held. He could still see the chains on her arms that had kept her from casting spells properly, the dark circles under her eyes from many sleepless nights, and the hollow, hopeless look she gave him as he entered, disguised as a guard. The dank smell of the cells assaulted his nose, and he could swear that there were eyes on him as he passed, staring out from the despondent darkness.

Rubbing his eyes for a moment, Sath pushed the images from his mind, especially the one of Gin stepping out of the transport spell she had been casting with Elysiam...the spell that took all of them to safety save Gin herself. He focused on where he was going and on his son's furry face, and his mind cleared. There would be time to deal with Gin after Khujann was home safely.

More wyvern guards appeared in the hallway as Sath drew closer to the arena. He decided to duck into one of the empty rooms and change tactics; if there were this many guards around, one of them was bound to smell the fact that he was really a cat in a high elf suit. From one of the pockets within the robe's sleeve he withdrew a small metal object. Turning it over repeatedly, he finally found the switch that made it work and flipped it. The object fell from his hand and as it rolled out the door, Sath had the strangest feeling of vertigo. With a smile, he realized that he was seeing not what was in front of him but what the object saw as it lingered just outside the doorway. He could hear what was going on around him, but his vision was somehow tied to the miraculous device that Hackort's brother had made for him on his last trip to see the gnomes.

"You just flip the switch and go," Hackort said, impatiently tapping his foot as gnomes are want to do. *"Where are you taking this? Can I go too, Sath? Really, now that you don't have Tee with you all the time you need a warrior. You know I'm the best, right Sath? Don't you?"*

"Hack!" Sath exclaimed, in an effort to get the gnome warrior to pause for a breath. He knelt down so that he could be eye to eye with his old friend. *"It's just a scouting mission, nothing exciting. Besides, when Gin left I think she took your leash,"* he had said, grinning madly at Hackort.

"Funny Cat, you are," Hackort said, grinning back at Sath. *"Good luck old friend. If you need me or Elys you know where to find us."*

The eye sailed down passageways, so fast and small that the giant wyverns didn't notice it on the floor. Sath knew that it would only work for a short time, so he directed it toward the back of the arena. It was then he saw the two wood elves and...was that a dwarf? Teeand? Sath cried out softly with joy at the sight of his dear friend Teeand. Now he knew both Khujann and Gin had a chance to make it out alive. He gasped a bit when Kae turned and looked right at the device. She looked so much like Gin's sister Lairceach that it turned his stomach a bit. Sadly, when the spell cast by the bard that caused him to kill Lairceach had worn off, it had not taken his memory of the act with it. Nor had it erased the fact that Lairceach had been wearing an illusion that made her appear as Gin, so it was truly Gin he'd thought he was killing. He shook that off just in time to see Kae bending down to pick up the device and he immediately broke the connection with it. There was no time to waste if he was going to get to his son before Gin did.

"What is this thing?" Kae asked, thrusting the tiny metal object at Gin. "Looks like a ball but it sounds like clockwork stuff in there."

Gin took the object in her palm. The three of them were crouching on the bottom level of the arena up against the wall. "It looks like...oh, oh no, no, no, it's a clockwork eye." She threw the eye like it was on fire, and it smashed into a nearby wall.

Teeand spun around. "Kae, lass, this is important, was that thing coming toward us or passing us by?"

"What do you mean? It did spin around when I got closer, just before I picked it up."

Teeand cursed in his native language. "That means whomever was on the other end of that thing saw us, pet," he said. "Who has those things anyway, besides the gnomes that make them?"

Gin's face fell. "Wizards and other magic users," she said. "You don't think that…that he is already here…oh, Great Mother, tell me I'm wrong…" Teeand frowned and patted Gin on the arm.

"Doesn't matter, lass. We are here for the Prince, and anyone in our way is in our way, yeah?" Gin sniffed a bit and nodded. "I've wanted a crack at that wizard's noggin for some time now anyway. This will be fun," he said, grinning and cracking his knuckles. "Let's go get us a cub, shall we?" Gin followed along, steeling her resolve to follow through with her plan. If Taeben had come for her, he would have her. Khujann's safety was the only thing that mattered.

Sath practically flew the rest of the distance to the arena. He could not let the others get to his son first. It would be so much easier on everyone if he could get Khujann safely out of harm's way and then reveal to them who he really was, rather than have to fight with them to get to his son at all. He tried to think back to the days when he ran with Teeand and Gin…to remember Teeand's strategies and plans of attack. He grinned for a moment thinking of Gin's plan of attack…hide behind the Qatu and hope for the best.

Sath felt certain that Teeand would leave Gin in a safe place and head in to engage the ancient lizard alone, leaving Kae to sneak in and around to get in a few good backstabs, just enough to keep the dragon distracted. Gin would heal him and Kae, as well as cast some damaging spells to speed up the process a bit. Well, he thought she would if she could face Lord Taanyth without losing her nerve. Sath grimaced, remembering the little bit she had told him about the spell work the dragon had done with her as his target, while Taeben watched from the sidelines.

Taeben...Sath skidded to a halt. His plan was not going to work if Gin caught sight of him. They knew as well as he did that the wizard was directly involved in Khujann's kidnapping and in his removal from Aynamaede, and if she spotted him things would most likely get very ugly very fast. At best they would turn on him, at worst, it could completely incapacitate Gin if she saw him as the wizard.

Invisibility? Sath frowned. No, Gin had progressed far enough as a druid that she could see right through most of Sath's invisibility spells. Distraction? What kind? Did he dare pull out his magical tiger, and if he did, would the tiger respond to him in this getup? Would he even be able to summon the creature at all? Sath cursed in Qatunari. Time was running out, and the other three were surely advancing on Khujann and Lord Taanyth now. He had to make a move, to let them know who he was at the same time that he kept up his disguise in front of Taeben's master. What would tip Gin off without setting her off? Sath smiled as an idea came to him and dashed toward the arena.

Teeand crouched behind the wall where Gin and Kae were hiding. "Now, listen up, you two," he said quietly. "Here's the plan. I'm going to run in and create a distraction. Gin, you're on healing magic, my girl. None finer. Keep the healing coming to keep me propped up so that I can keep your cousin here alive. Kae, have your blade at the ready and I'll try to turn that overgrown pair of boots around and give you a smart target for a good backstab or two. Your part of our plan is distraction, yes?" Kae frowned, but nodded agreement. "You two keep up your side and I'll handle the pointy bits. Gin," he said, looking up at her, "if you wouldn't mind, do you have a spell that works to protect against damaging magic?"

Gin smiled. "Indeed I do," she said. Moving her hands in the ritual way, she spoke ancient words that wove a bright spell around all three of them, the light of which would repel all dangerous magic that intended to do them harm. "Take off, Tee.

Kill that bastard," she hissed, sensing the antediluvian dragon's presence.

"Oh, I will, don't you worry, flower," Teeand said, grinning at Gin. "Kae, my lass, are you ready?" Kae nodded at him, her expression a mixture of fear and exhilaration. "Aye then, let's have at him!" Teeand burst out from behind the wall where they were hiding, bellowing obscenities at Lord Taanyth. The dragon turned around, a grin spreading across his awful face as his gaze landed on the tiny green warrior running at him. Gin raised her hands, ready to send healing magic toward Teeand, when something darting across the opposite wall caught her attention. Her eyes widened and her face contorted in a silent scream as she recognized the familiar blue robes and white ponytail.

"YOU!" she hissed, taking her attention off Teeand as he managed to lead the giant dragon away from her and turn its back on the now advancing Kae. "Ben!"

Sath was ready for her, and he tossed a potion vial to the ground, casting a quick spell that would port him mere feet across the room, but would land him right behind Gin. "Careful, *darlin'*," he whispered in her ear. "We don't want Tee to get hurt now, do we?" Gin's entire body tensed, her hands still hanging in the air, ready to send the healing that Teeand was beginning to desperately need. This wasn't working. She was frozen in place, her terror getting the best of her. "Once I grab my son, you just grab onto my tail and hang on for dear life, and we'll all get out safely."

Gin's head spun around suddenly so that she was looking at him. "Let me see your eyes, wizard," she said.

"Heal the dwarf first," Sath said, careful not to get too close while she was casting her spell. He had forgotten to check the effect of the potion on his eye color and if they weren't his own teal rather than the icy white of the wizard, Gin would never believe it was him. Gin turned her attention back to Teeand, thankfully, and when the color had returned to Teeand's cheeks and Kae had resumed plunging her dagger into any soft spot she could find on the giant dragon, Sath moved back to Gin and looked her in the eyes. *"You know who I am, darlin. Let me rescue my son the Prince,"* he murmured in Qatunari.

"Not on my watch, Taeben," she hissed. "You may have thought learning some basic Qatunari would convince me to let you back into my mind but you are WRONG." Back into her mind? What was she talking about, in her mind? Before Sath knew what was happening, Gin had brought up her giant staff and clocked him in the head with it. Stars swam before his eyes and he staggered back a step or two. He regained his footing in time to see the druid darting across the room toward his son.

"NO!" he bellowed, temporarily distracted by the fact that he even sounded like the high elf. No wonder Gin did not believe who he was. Ja'ming had outdone herself with this potion. *"Na'hina!"* Sath swore in crude Qatunari as he crossed the room behind her. Gin stopped just in front of Khujann, who was huddled in a corner with his hands and arms covering his head. Sath growled at the sight of the heavy chains binding his son's arms and legs. He looked for a second over his shoulder at the melee going on between Teeand and Lord Taanyth and had to marvel at his dear friend's prowess as a warrior. "None finer," he murmured as he closed in on Gin.

She whirled around to face him. "Don't make me kill you, Ben, please," she said. "I don't want to, but I will if you try to stop us from taking the Prince out of here and away from your...master," she said, nearly spitting the last word. Sath smiled at her, proud of the bravado in her voice and her ability to stand up to him, knowing how much she loathed and feared Taeben. She was not the trembling little druid she had been before.

Khujann peeked through his hands at the sound of her voice. *"Ginny!"* he mewled at her, clearly more the terrified cub than heir to the throne of Qatu'anari. He reached out his tiny arms to her and winced as the chains held them fast. Again, Sath growled low in his throat.

Teeand felt that he was losing ground. "Kae!" he bellowed. "Give that oversized saddlebag another one to the kidney...if you can find his kidney that is!" He continued swinging his sword at Lord Taanyth, but the retaliatory fiery blasts from the dragon were clearly affecting his balance and sense of direction. He looked down for a moment as he took a step closer, and that moment was all Lord Taanyth needed. With one giant claw and no magic at all, he swatted Teeand out of the way like he was a bug and then turned on Gin and Khujann and Sath.

"So you have returned to us, Ginolwenye?" Lord Taanyth said as he floated across the room toward Gin and Sath. "Wizard, you have outdone yourself, bringing her here with a tiny warrior and irritating elf for my playthings." A swipe of his tail sent Kae crashing into the wall behind her with a sickening thud.

"Let them all go, my Lord Taanyth," said Sath, nearly choking on the word. "Your issue is with the druid, with Ginolwenye, not this insignificant cub." His eyes darted toward his son who, to Sath's horror, was sniffing the air madly. His scent! The illusion would change his voice and appearance, but not his scent. He had been so worried about tipping off the wyverns that he had forgotten about Khujann. Of course, his son would recognize him, no matter his outward appearance. Sath looked at Khujann just as the Prince lifted his tiny hands toward him, shaking his head at the cub.

"Papa!" he cried out, pointing at Sath. "*I didn't recognize you, Papa!*"

"What is this?" asked Lord Taanyth, as he turned his full attention to Sath. "Wizard, does the cub hallucinate? Or..." He floated very close to Sath and looked him up and down, red beady eyes glowing as he drew in a deep breath through his nose. "Am I the one that hallucinates?" The ancient dragon waved one hand as he spoke in *Eldyr*, and Sath's illusion fell away. Gin gasped, her hands flying to her mouth in surprise.

"*Papa!*" Khujann bawled. Sath moved toward his son, knocking Gin to the floor to get her out of the line of fire. The giant dragon was already moving on to more spell casting. Working quickly, Sath pulled the chains free from the wall, and then retrieved a potion from a hidden pocket in his other sleeve. Speaking the words that the vendor taught him in the merchant halls, he grabbed his son with one hand and threw the potion to the ground with the other. A circle of fire erupted around the two Qatu, and in a moment, they were gone from sight.

"Of no matter," Lord Taanyth hissed. "It was you that I needed all along, Ginolwenye of the Trees...the *Nature Walker*." Behind the dragon, Teeand was sitting up and rubbing his head. Gin backed into a corner, her eyes darting from Lord Taanyth to Teeand's and Kae's crumpled forms across the room.

"*Papa?*" Khujann said, tapping the side of his father's face with one of his tiny hands. "*Wake up, Papa, we're safe but we forgot Ginny!*"

Sath opened his eyes slowly. Everything was a bit blurry. The circle of fire had been a trick of the potion maker to make him appear as though he had transported himself and his son out of the Keep when all it had really done was render them invisible. Sath had grabbed his son, and then run as fast as he could, tracing his path back out of the Keep. Once outside the boundary of the curse that prevented transport magic, Sath had used the last potion in his sleeve and port himself and his son to safety. He was not accustomed to magical transportation in that manner, and it had taken a second for him to realize where he was. They had landed in a heap on the marble floor of the throne room of Qatu'anari. The plan had worked.

Sath grabbed his son by the scruff and headed for the royal apartments. The great stone door slammed behind him as he ran, carrying a squirming Khujann, up to the surprised looking *Sahi*

Kalah that were on guard there. Sath breathed in deeply, his lungs filling with the soft night air of the palace...of the salt and sea...of home.

Murmuring in Qatunari, he studied his son a moment before gathering the cub in his arms. Tears flowed down his furry face, tears of joy for being reunited with Khujann; tears of anger and fear over leaving Gin, Teeand, and Kae at the mercy of Lord Taanyth. "*May her All Mother forgive me,*" said the normally atheist *Rajah* of Qatu'anari, "*for forsaking her child, Gin, and her companions. Help them understand why. Help ME understand why.*" He squeezed the Prince until the tiny cat growled, then put him down and ran a giant hand across his head. "*Now what do I do?*"

"*You go back and get Ginny, Papa,*" said Khujann, as though it were the simplest question ever asked. "*Aunt Kazhi and I can help you!*" The Prince struggled to free himself from the grip of the *Sahi* who had stepped in as Sath had released his son.

"*You are right son, I do need to go get your Auntie Kazhi,*" Sath said, chuckling at his son's use of the nickname that used to infuriate Gin when anyone but Hackort used it. "*But you will stay here, please. I need to know that you are...*" Sath paused a moment, interrupted by the look of outrage on his son's face as well as his own restraint in not laughing at the cub, and changed his approach. "*I need to know that Qatu'anari is safe, and I can only do that if you stay here and look after your Auntie for me. Can you do that, son?*"

Khujann scowled. "*Yes, Papa. But does that mean I can go hunt with Aunt Kazhi?*"

"*NO, son, you may not. You are protecting her as well as Qatu'anari, so both of you must stay within the city and with our personal guard at all times. Do you understand me? No running away, no tricks, you stay with Hulan and Kazhi, do you hear me?*" Sath's stare halted the Prince in his tracks, and the young Qatu nodded.

"*Aye Papa, I understand. Please bring Ginny back. It's not her fault that those mean elves took me to that big mean lizard thing.*" Khujann looked around as if he was about to share top-secret information. Sath smiled down at his son as the young Qatu leaned in close before speaking. "*It was that white-haired elf. The mean one Ginny is afraid of; you know the one? The one you were pretending to be?*"

Sath growled low and loud. "*Aye, my son, I do, and I will make sure to discuss that with him should he cross me. Now, off with you, you've studies to make up and an Aunt to torment.*" He kissed the cub on the top of his tiny head and sent him off giggling with a swat to the backside. Checking his haversack, he noted that he had two bottles left: one potion that would transport him to the outskirts of the Keep as well as another dose of the Taeben-illusion potion. Sath wrapped one hand around the neck of the transport potion bottle and hurled it to the ground at his feet. "*I'm coming, Gin,*" he said as he disappeared in a whirl of fire and smoke.

Lord Taanyth advanced toward Gin. His eyes glowed crimson with rage. "So, which shall I kill first, Ginolwenye? The dwarf or the wood elf? What do you say, *Nature Walker*?" he snarled at her as he blocked her access to Teeand, Kae and in truth, the exit by his sheer size. Puffs of smoke unfurled from his nostrils, signaling fire not far behind. Gin swallowed hard and took a deep breath before she answered him.

"Is 'none of the above' an option?" Gin shouted at him as she hurled magical fireballs in his direction. Most of them bounced off him without incident but one or two stung a bit...enough to make him swat at them like flies. Flies. Flies! Gin smiled as she called up the biggest magical swarm she could muster and sent its buzzing mass straight at the ancient dragon's face. He roared in anger and frustration, swatting at the supernatural stinging swarm and temporarily taking his gaze off the druid.

Gin darted between his massive feet, grabbing Teeand by the arm as she passed him and dragging him onto her still unconscious cousin. Acting as much out of habit and instinct as any amount of training, Gin knew that she had to get Teeand and

Kae out of the Keep. A strange feeling of calm filled Gin as she focused on the Outpost and cast her spell - she looked at Teeand and Kae and used her need to protect them to boost her magic....only to be hit in the head by Lord Taanyth's tail and knocked across the room as the spell ignited. Teeand was still mostly on top of Kae and both of them disappeared from sight. Gin sat up, rubbing the top of her head, and scanned the room for her companions, smiling when she realized they were both safe. The room spun and she struggled to stand, leaning against the wall to keep herself upright.

"While I admire your courage, that's the second time you have interrupted my fun, druid," said Lord Taanyth. "Though you have proved to me who you are, *Nature Walker*, you will not be allowed to cross me again." As if on cue, two wyverns entered his chamber.

"Master, we heard noises; is all well?" one of them asked, sneering down at Gin as he knelt before the antediluvian dragon.

"No, no it is not." The wyvern head jerked up to gape at Lord Taanyth. "You will take the druid to her cell. I will not risk losing her again before she can free me from this prison. The *Nature Walker* is the only one that has enough magic to break the curse that holds me here." The wyverns looked at him apprehensively. "Ah yes, I'd almost forgotten, it's been so long since we've seen you, Gin," said Lord Taanyth. He spoke ancient words in the *Eldyr*, and phantom chains appeared around her hands, binding them together. Another few words that sounded more like hissing than language to Gin's ears, and she felt as though she'd been stunned. She could no more cast magic to escape than she could create a tiny fireball, and her knees soon gave way. "Ah, she kneels! Very nice my girl, but not necessary this time. There will be plenty of time for kneeling in the future. For now, though, I believe there is a guest waiting for you." He waved a scaled and clawed hand at the wyverns to dismiss them, and one of them hoisted Gin over his shoulder to carry her out.

As she bounced along like a sack of potatoes over the wyvern's shoulder, in her mind she screamed for Sath's help. It had worked in the past…the strange mental connection they seemed to have had gotten her out of tight spots before. But was it fair to do that now that he had his son back, and might be on the path to forgiving her for all the pain she had caused him? The wyvern interrupted her thoughts by slamming her down in the bed. No, it was not fair. This was her fate, and her choice, and as long as everyone she loved was safe and away from here, it was definitely worth whatever would come. Gin put Sath out of her mind as her heart sank.

A robed figure stood in the corner of the room, half hidden in the shadows. The wyverns bowed, and a slender white hand emerged from a sleeve to wave them away. They scampered out of the room as though burned. The figure approached Gin, whose head was still a bit swimmy from the blow to the head while she cast her evacuation spell earlier.

"Who are you?" she demanded, trying to sound more together and coherent than she really was. She had an idea, but after Sath had turned up under an illusion earlier, she was not sure. "What do you want with me?" The silence in the back of her mind was throwing her off as well.

The figure moved even closer to the bed, the hood still obscuring any features that might have provided identification. The head tilted to the side, as though sizing Gin up, and she found herself infuriated by just that gesture. "Who ARE you?" she bellowed, causing the hooded figure to snicker. "I demand that you tell me!"

"You demand, do you?" At the sound of the voice, Gin's heart sank. "You are not in much of a position to demand anything, my dear." Taeben's face emerged as the hood slid back, his features twisted into a grin. "Now, shall we see about what to do with you, or shall I leave you here to the wyverns?" He darted across the room and checked to make sure the door was locked.

"Ben...what are you doing still working for that tyrant? Why are you doing this? Why are you helping him?" Gin locked her eyes on his. "Don't you remember what happened before? Don't you remember what he did to you...and made you do to others...?"

The high elf laughed, but the sound was hollow. "Of course I do. If you had only stayed down, you would have fared far better from my understanding. That seems to be your downfall."

Anger swelled in Gin's gut. "Stayed...down?" She glared at him. "He was blasting me with so much magic it lifted me off the bloody ground and you think I should have STAYED DOWN??" His continued chuckling only made her more and more angry.

"Well, if you'd hung on to my tail like you were supposed to do, you never, ever would have stayed behind in the first place, now would you?" he said, moving closer so that she could see his teal eyes twinkling. Gin looked astonished. It was the wizard's face, but the eyes were all Sath.

"Sath?" she whispered, still not daring to believe her eyes.

"Did you think I'd come in here with only one of those potions, *darlin'*?" he said, grinning through Taeben's face. "Please...give me a little credit. I got home with Khujann, put him safely in the care of my sister and my guard, and then came back for you. Easy."

"But how...you don't have those kinds of spells..." She was looking at him with wonder, but when he moved closer to touch the side of her face she flinched as though she expected a slap. He moved back, frowning. "I'm sorry," she said, "it's just that, well, except for the eye color, you look so much like Ben..."

Sath snorted. "I'd better look EXACTLY like Taeben or I paid far too much for these potions!" he said, chuckling. "I was hoping to get some more information from the wyverns, like why the bastard was working with Lord Taanyth at all, and what that oversized pair of boots was plotting that involved my son, but no luck. Then you needed me," he paused for a moment, and Gin saw a nostalgic look in his eyes that transcended the face he was currently wearing, "so how could I refuse that? Remember? I told you I would always come for you when you needed me."

"Of course I remember, but you have to get out of here," Gin said quietly. "I didn't help you get your son back so that you could…"

"I'm sorry, what?" Sath shot her a toothy grin. "You helped me get my son back?"

"Yes, and I could have helped more if you hadn't shoved me out of the way," Gin snapped back.

"That was to get you out of the line of fire, *darlin*," Sath said, his voice gentle. "I knew that when the old oversized haversack noticed that I wasn't who I said I was, and he'd throw a bunch of awful my way." After removing the cuffs from her wrists, he moved closer and reached for the old scar that ran down the side of Gin's face. "I was not going to let you get hurt if I could help it."

Gin looked up at him and shuddered a little bit. "Sorry," she murmured, "but you just still look too much like him." Sath hung his head a moment, then looked up and caught her gaze and smiled.

"Shall we get the heck outta here?" he asked, making himself busy with the chains that bound her feet. "*Na'hina*! They're magic!" he swore.

"Aye, now stop swearing, get yourself to safety and don't worry about me, please?" Gin glared at him, but felt herself settling and feeling safe in Sath's presence. He had that effect, so calming, so strong and so very nurturing that he could lull anyone into a false sense of security by just slowing them down…Wait a tic. "Qatu, I KNOW you're not using magical calm or anything of that ilk on me right now."

"Guilty." Sath raised his hands in defeat. "But you're not exactly coming quietly, now are you? Not that you ever did. I swear, Gin, no one talks as much as…"

"Seriously, Sath? How would you like it if I hit you with the same magic?" Gin's eyes were blazing now. "Don't you get it? I traded myself for your son, whether to Ben or to Lord Taanyth himself. It is done."

Sath chuckled. "Nothing is done, *darlin.* You know that I'm not going anywhere without you, Gin. I did not ask you to exchange yourself for Khuj, nor would I ever." He considered her as she met his gaze. "You know what he will do to you if you stay."

"I know."

"Then you know why I'm not leaving you here."

"It isn't up to you," she said quietly. "I have nothing left out there, Sath, and less than that if I do not know that you are safe and free, you and Khuj and Tee and Kae. Just go. It is done."

"I can get you out of here, you daft elf," Sath hissed. "We are at a standstill. If you really want me to be safe, you have to come with me. This potion won't last forever, ya know."

Gin closed her eyes for a moment, her hands balled into fists at her sides. There was no other way to get him out of the Keep, but once they were clear, she would make sure she was as far away from Sath and all of those she loved as possible. "Fine." She glared up at him. "Your illusion still holds; you can just walk out the front door, so go! OUT. I will work on the chains. You've freed my hands; maybe I can cast another transport spell now." Still not sure how or why it had worked earlier, she stood up on the bed and began speaking ancient words of transportation. As she finished the spell, Sath charged at her, wrapping his hands around her waist and hanging on as the familiar rush of air that accompanied this form of travel surrounded them both.

As Gin and Sath made their escape, in the prison area of Bellesea Keep, a lone wyvern patrolled the long hall. A hooded figure appeared and gave him a sign, and the large winged creature shuffled off for a rest break. The figure walked down the row of cells, inspecting the contents of each. Most were empty or contained skeletons of long since departed prisoners.

The last cell on the row, however, still contained a living occupant. A high elf female was huddled in the back, her red hair wild and long. She had once worn an opulent forest green robe, but now the faded fabric hung in tatters off her gaunt body. Deep cuts glared from the skin near her wrists and ankles, left by the chains used to restrain her in the arena. Her sky blue eyes, once twinkling with intelligence and flashing with wit, were empty and dull. The figure in the hood approached the door to her cell and she slowly lifted her head but remained silent as she looked up with a hollow gaze.

Taeben removed his hood and heard her gasp. "Do you remember me, my dear?" he said, wincing as the female recoiled further into the dark corner. "I see you do. I am not here to hurt you. I am here to take you out of here and return you home to Alynatalos, if you wish."

"You…lie," she hissed at him. "You…work for…him." She wrapped her long ivory arms around her knees and pulled them up under her chin.

"Tis true, I did serve Lord Taanyth," Taeben said. "But like those of us who have served him well, you are to be released as a reward." He tried to sound as sincere as he could, since her compliance would assure that he could get her out of the Keep without a scene.

"What does your master want in return for my release?" she asked, looking him in the eye and causing him to flinch. She had been a truly beautiful woman, but now was a skeleton with skin. Her own family would not recognize her, in truth he barely did himself, but he felt sure that the druid would.

"Nothing," Taeben lied. "Will you come with me and go home, or do you prefer to stay here and continue to serve Lord Taanyth? I am sure that your family has missed you. Do you remember them? Do you remember who you are?"

She thought for a moment or two and then sad understanding seemed to seep into her expression.. "Tairneanach," she whispered. "My name is Tairneanach, sister of Nelenie, daughter of Alynatalos." Her voice grew stronger as she spoke. Standing, she moved to the door of the cell. "I will go with you, Taeben, if you will take us back to our home in the Forest. But I will do nothing more for Lord Taanyth, and if that is the game you are playing, just leave me here to die."

Taeben held up his palm to the lock on her cell and it glowed red and then melted away. He flung open the door and moved inside of her cell making her gasp and stumble backward. "Our master wants nothing more from either of us, Tairn, because, in truth, he knows nothing of your release. I am granting us freedom, I am rescuing the both of us, but in return you will do something for me," he said, grasping her by her thin neck and slamming her back against the wall of the cell. She tried to fight him, but had no strength. It had been ages since she'd had a proper meal, and was weak as a kitten against his force.

"What…what is it?" she gasped, struggling to take a deep breath.

"You will return to Ginny, your dear friend. Do you remember her? You will stay close to her, and you will watch her for me. I want to know where she is and that she is safe. When I need more from you, I will contact you." He looked deeply into her eyes, treading the waters of her mind. "You will say nothing of this to her, you will never even mention my name. Do you understand?"

"Why Ginny?" she stammered. Taeben tightened his grip on her windpipe and pushed his way into her mind. It was almost sad how easy it was for him. He strengthened his grip on her soul and repeated his question as her eyes, turned on his, grew vacant.

"Yes or no? Do you understand?"

"Yes," Tairn said, and Taeben dropped her to the floor. He focused his magic on her, and cast a spell that would render her invisible so that he could get her out of the Keep. Once that was done, he would transport her alone to just outside of Alynatalos. Tairn faded from view and Taeben yanked her to her feet before dragging her out of the cell and down the hall. After flying through the maze of hallways and staircases, they reached the drawbridge and he shoved her across it.

"Keep moving!" he ordered and she obeyed. His gaze focused on her, he called up his strongest magic and hurled it her way. With his magical ability to see through an invisibility spell, Taeben watched until Tairn's image flickered and winked out of existence, and then sank to his knees, exhausted from the energy used for the spell as well as the overwhelming guilt that he couldn't seem to shake lately.

"I will have you again, my little druid, my love, my Queen. We have been apart too long," he said, clenching a fist. "You have a destiny to fulfill, and when you do, we will make that Qatu our house pet. You will forgive me for…for everything, and then we will live happily ever after." Smiling maliciously, he rose and cast another spell, this time transporting himself to the inside of the high elf citadel. Once the woozy feeling that often accompanied transport spells had left him, he headed up the hill toward the Grand Library. There was much research to do.

Nancy E. Dunne

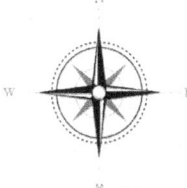

TWENTY-EIGHT

Tairn kept her eyes closed tightly until she was certain the transport was finished. Was that moss under her hands? What was that smell? The Great Forest? It seemed too good to be true. While remaining on her hands and knees, Tairn opened her eyes slowly, squinting into the sunlight that fell on the ground through the strong, tall trees of her home. She pressed her face to the ground, inhaling the soft scent of the mossy grass, and laughed until she cried. How long had it been since she'd been here? How long since she'd been free?

Lifting her face a bit she winced as she looked at the open wounds on her wrists. She needed a cleric and needed one now, or she'd bleed to death. Slowly she rose to her feet and found that she had just enough energy to cast a spell to increase her mental clarity so that she would be able to find help in the Citadel. Feeling the familiar rush of that spell, she took a deep breath and looked around to gain her bearings. She was next to the great spires that marked the entrance to the Citadel.

Tairn smiled as she remembered playing outside of the city gates, unbeknownst to her family...her family! She started walking toward the spires and her steps turned into a jog, then to a stumbling run. By the time she reached the massive gate that served as an entrance to the city, she was completely out of breath and seeing stars around the corners of her vision, but she was

HOME. She ran for the entrance, only to have the guards that stood just inside appear and block her path.

"Hail and well met," she stammered. "Is something wrong, that a child of Alynatalos may not enter her home?"

The guard looked her up and down. "I admit, the disguise is...appealing, but you are no child of Alynatalos," he said. "Be gone, beggar, we have no need of you here."

Tairn opened her mouth to protest, and then remembered her appearance. She stood up as tall as she could and looked the guard in the eye, summoning a charm spell silently as she did. "You know that I am not a beggar," she said softly, smiling as his eyes dilated and his mouth curved up into a smile to match her own.

"You are not a beggar," he repeated, looking at her with abject adoration.

"Hey now, what's this?" asked the other guard, muscling his way in between Tairn and his compatriot. As soon as he caught her eye, his grim expression softened. "You're not a beggar at all, m'lady."

"Exactly. It was a misunderstanding, wasn't it?" she murmured, and the guards nodded in unison. Tairn adjusted what was left of her sleeves and smoothed the tragically destroyed front of her robe, her movements as natural as they had been when she had left home so long ago. "Now, will you let me pass and then forget that I was here, please, my good sirs?" Again, the guards nodded in unison and moved back to their positions on either side of the entrance.

Tairn moved away from them and quickly cast a spell that would render her invisible. She looked back at the guards who were shaking their heads and wondering what had happened, and grinned. "Time to go home," she whispered, and crossed the drawbridge into the Citadel, her home. Once over the moat, she scampered through the secret passage in the hedge and reappeared by the lake that surrounded the magic user's guild. Only visible to those with the sight, it seemed to float in midair. "My, that's lovely," said a familiar male voice behind her. Tairn froze in her tracks.

"Ben… Apologies," she said, hanging her head. Tangled ruddy mats of hair hung into her eyes. "M'lord?" she whispered, afraid to turn around. Taeben moved close behind her, so close that she could feel his breath on her neck.

"Is there somewhere we can talk, my Pet?" he whispered, and she nodded, shaking visibly. She darted past him back into the hedge and he followed, smiling. "Ah, yes, the holes in the hedge, we used to hide here when I was a young wizard," he said.

"What do you want…I mean…what may I do for you, Ben…sorry, Lord Taeben?" Tairn asked, cringing inwardly.

"Your first task in repayment for your freedom, my pet, is to kill Sathlir Clawsharp, the *Rajah* of Qatu'anari," Taeben replied, his countenance as cool as if he'd just asked her to make him a cup of afternoon tea.

Tairn gaped at him. "Forgive me, M'lord, but I am quite positive that I am not capable of doing that on my own," she stammered. Taeben chuckled.

"Well of course you're not. Imagine, one of you against the whole of the Qatu. Ridiculous. No, there is a better way, my pet. You were once friends with the Qatu female called Kazhmere, were you not?"

"Aye, M'lord, I know her. She is Sath's sister, is she not?"

"Very good, pet," Taeben said. "You will charm her and bend her to your will. When she is your willing servant, as you are mine," he winked at her, causing her to shudder, "you will instruct her to kill the *Rajah*. She will not stop until she has done what her mistress commands and she will have no trouble getting that mangy cat alone and separate from his personal guards."

Tears filled Tairn's eyes. "Yes, M'lord," she said, still quaking in fear.

"Oh, poor sentimental pet, are you sad at the idea of the death of the *Rajah*?" Taeben asked, touching the side of her face. She flinched.

"Sath has never done wrong to me," she said.

"Has he not?" Taeben responded, tilting his head to one side. "Are you not aware that he rescued your mentor, Gin, from the same dire straits where I found you, but he did not free you? Do you not remember seeing him running past the cells with the druid, leaving you there to rot, not once but twice?"

Tairn sniffed loudly, a tear escaping her eye. "He didn't know I was still alive, M'lord," she whispered. "He didn't know it was me. I barely knew it was still me." Taeben grabbed her shoulders and shook her hard.

"That hardly matters now. He did not even check, nor did Ginny for that matter. They have all forgotten you. Once you assist the Princess Royal to kill the *Rajah*, our Ginny will be free of him and you will be free of me. Easy as that. You have your orders, pet," he hissed at her. "Do you understand what you are to do?" Tairn nodded silently. "Well done," he said, dropping her back into the hedge. "Quickly as you can, **Red**. Quickly as you can." He stepped out of the hedge and faded from her view. Tairn sank back into the leafy hedge and sobbed, Taeben's use of the old nickname from when they were children breaking her heart.

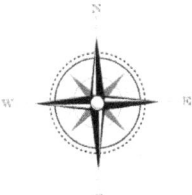

TWENTY-NINE

The transport spell had not worked quite the way Gin had intended. She looked around, expecting to find herself back in the Forest alone, but instead was in the Fabled Ones' grand hall and Sath was sprawled on the floor a few feet away. Gin muttered in Elvish under her breath. His illusion had fallen with the transport magic, and the robe he'd been wearing as Taeben had split in places to accommodate his large frame.

"I see your porting hasn't gotten any better," Sath said, grinning at her.

"Neither has your fashion sense," she snapped back. "I thought I told you to get out of there, not drag me down and cause my magic to…misfire."

Sath roared with laughter. "Misfire?" He sat up and wiped tears from his eyes. "I didn't know that your magic worked any other way, *darlin'*," he said.

Gin returned his gaze with a sneer. "Stop calling me that," she said. "I saved your hide plenty." She turned away so that he wouldn't see her grin as she dusted herself off. "I think you're confusing me with the other druid you used to run around with, Sath." She turned around to face him.

"Y'all stand back, I'm gonna try something!" they said simultaneously, just before dissolving into fits of laughter. Sath studied her for a moment. "Those were good times, weren't they *darlin'*?" he said, smiling at Gin, who quickly looked away.

"Good times, yes. But they're over now," Gin said, swallowing hard. "Too much has happened, Sath. Too much." Sath reached for her hand but she jerked it away.

"Don't say that," Sath said. "We were good, Gin, we can be again." Gin shook her head and stood up, walking over to the staircases that lead to the balcony that surrounded the hall's great room. Sath darted into the room with the healing pool for a moment to grab his spare armor out of the drawers there. He was pleased to see that there was an entire set, and that it was not the blood stained black armor. He had left that in the desert outside of the Keep. This armor was silver, given to him before he left with Anni. Sath looked at his reflection in the breastplate and frowned. "We just need time, and we can..."

"No, we can't." Sath scrambled to his feet and followed her, and she stopped two steps up so that she could look him in the eye. "Too much has changed, Sath. We just aren't the same." She touched the side of his face, resisting the urge to bury her face in his soft fur and cry. "You're the *Rajah*. I'm...well, I'm not the same as I was before either."

"Is it because...when you were a prisoner in Qatu'anari...I..." Sath hung his head, unable to continue. Memories of Gin cowering in the back of one of the cells, of him bellowing at her, of how unhinged and focused on revenge he had become...all those unwelcome and unpleasant thoughts now flooded his mind. Gin shook her head.

"You were doing what you had to do for your son, Sath," she said, looking into his eyes. "I understand that. You couldn't know how it would affect me. It's just that..."

"How could I not have known? I put that fear in you in the first place. I was the Bane of the Forest. You learned to fear me well before you learned to love...to care for me," he said sadly. "I could have easily killed you that first day that I met you, Gin."

"But you didn't, Sath," she said quietly.

"No. I continued on that path with Rae and then with...and without you, learning about myself but also learning about the world. In fact, I should probably give you something that I took from you the first day I met you," he said, digging around in his bags and finally producing a weather-beaten leather journal. He handed it to Gin who gasped as she recognized it. "I've read it probably a hundred times or more. You may have an incredible heart, *darlin'*, but you are unique in this world. Most are out for themselves and will take down anyone in their way. You know what happened when that cursed wizard sent *Annilanshi* to me," he said, wincing at the sadness he saw creep into her eyes.

"Aye." She held the book to her chest, as though it would keep her heart from bursting forth for a moment, then handed it back to Sath. "You should keep this." She had no use for those memories anymore. He studied her a moment, then tucked the journal back into his pack. "I know how Taeben used her, Sath."

"Do you know why he chose her?" he asked. Gin shook her head. "You remember, of course, that Anni was another of my playmates in the palace nursery, Gin. When her talent for music was discovered, she was sent to train as a bard. She completed her training and I believe was in the service of my half-sister, Maesha." His eyes narrowed. "After the experience in the tower, Taeben wanted you for himself. All the way back then, he was determined to take you for his own. He reached out with his mind and...well, Anni was here in the guild hall with me and...she opened her mind to him and he convinced her to..." A low growl escaped his chest, sending a shiver down Gin's spine. He inhaled, and marveled yet again at the lack of fear from the druid. "Maesha had sent Anni with Kazhmere to die in that tower in order to ensure that when my Papa died there would be no heir, male or female, to the throne of Qatu'anari other than herself. I feel that Maesha knew who Kazhmere was all along."

He paused a moment, making sure that she was still with him. "In fact, just before she died, my half-sister confessed to one of my guard that she and Taeben had plotted to take the throne of Qatu'anari and put him, that damnable high elf, as *Rajah*, and you as his...one of his wives." He hissed as the rumbling growl became continuous behind his words. "I doubt that the wizard intended to keep Maesha as his queen, though. I think he had other plans." He took a step back from her, his fists balled and his gaze distant and angry.

"How did you become *Rajah*, Sath?" Gin asked, fearing the answer. "How did your father die?"

"As you know, Anni and I were living in one of the embassy buildings when...when Lairky came." Gin turned away around, her back to Sath. "Gin don't..." He reached out for her back, but stopped, his hand hovering in midair. "Khuj was in the nursery as I had been... Anni thought it would be safer since Maesha had made Taeben the ambassador from the Great Forest to Qatu'anari. She had me convinced that you and that wizard would seek revenge on me, and Khuj as well, if he knew of my son's existence, so she sent Khuj to the nursery with my Mama while I was away. When I returned, I kept to the shadows."

"I guess I gave you every reason to think I was a threat that day on the beach, didn't I?"

Sath sighed. "I need to tell you, Gin...after the wizard took you, that awful day when I brought you Lairky's body...I took her back to the Fabled Ones, Gin. Elys made sure that Lairky went to face your All Mother with all the respect due a warrior." Gin blinked back tears as she listened, but did not respond. "I have done some pretty awful things in my time, but I was not going to let that one go unanswered. After that, I came back to Qatu'anari to find my son because I was still concerned for him."

Gin frowned, knowing how it felt to fear for Khujann's life. She turned back around to see Sath leaning against one of the pillars by the bottom of the staircase, his expression hollow and vacant. "Who killed your father, Sath?" she asked, her voice barely a whisper.

"Maesha did," Sath said, his own voice flat. "At least I think she did." He sighed, avoiding eye contact with Gin. "Either way, it wasn't me that did the deed. I am told that Maesha had attacked my father and mother and was subdued by his guards. When I arrived, Papa was dead and Mama was close. I removed the dagger from her back and she saw me just before she died." He paused a moment and Gin choked back a sob. "Kazhi brought Khuj into the Throne Room followed by the *Sahi Kalah* who were ready to arrest me because I was still disguised. Once I lowered my hood, they knew who I was, they took a knee, and they called me *Rajah*. If I had only been there earlier, I might have saved my parents. Apparently, my father claimed Kazhi, out loud, because he loved my mother so and wanted her last moments to be happy...but I couldn't save her."

"None of that was your fault, Sath," Gin whispered. He moved back to her at the staircase, one hand gently cupping the side of her face. She pulled back from him, causing him to frown. "But it's all just too much...we're so different now... And Sath, you know as well as I do that I am not welcome in Qatu'anari because it is known that I was with Ben when he was the ambassador. Why, even now I am waiting for you to remember that fact and sentence me back to the cells below the palace, which is what I deserve..."

"I get it," he said, quietly, as he stepped away from the staircase and moved away, his hands raised in surrender. Gin pressed her hands to her eyes a moment, and then lowered them to find the room before her empty. Before Gin realized he was gone, he had crossed the room to the enormous door, tripped all of the locks, and left. She turned and sprinted up the stairs to the balcony.

Expecting to burst into a flood of tears, Gin sat down under the giant stained glass window in the balcony. None came. She sat for a long time, feeling the sadness build in her chest like an unchecked pressure valve that would not release. "I'm absolutely out of tears," she said to no one in particular.

Chuckling sadly, she got to her feet and studied the colors in the stained glass. The cobalt blue brought to mind Taeben's robe, and the numerous conversations they'd had in this very spot. Gin ran her fingers along the stone window sill and then gripped it for a moment. "What went so wrong for you, Ben?" she murmured. "I don't even know who you are anymore, and I used to know you better than anyone...or was that just what you wanted me to think?" Halfway expecting an answer, she searched the depths of her own mind and was surprised to find no trace of him there this time.

Her fingers moved across to a white star, as her mind moved on to jarring memories of nights sleeping rough while still with the Fabled Ones. Sath, Teeand, Hackort, and Elysiam had been her family when her own kind had turned their backs on her due to her actions and ill-fated relationships. How many dark corners of Orana had they explored? How many pints of ale had Teeand bought while trying to correct her pronunciation of words in his language in front of a roaring fire in a pub? How many times had Elysiam stood by her side, both of them speaking the same words in the ancient language of the wood elf druids, watching enemies fall at their feet?

Clutching her fist to her mouth, Gin turned around and looked down into the now empty hall. It was over, all of it, and she was left with nothing but memories and pain. There was no more Fabled Ones, not as they had been anyway. Hardly seemed fair, considering all she'd put into their lives together. "MY boys," she whispered, smiling through her tears as Teeand and Hackort's grinning faces floated before her eyes. "Mama Gin's boys. And Elys...oh, and Sath..." The pressure ramped up in her chest as his face lingered a moment in her mind.

No stranger to self-indulgent pity, Gin leaned over the balcony rail and looked down at the giant circle carved into the stone floor on the first level, tears starting to slide past her eyelashes to wet her cheeks. She wiped them away, feeling the sting of the saline in the corners of her eyes, as she thought of the other Fabled that had frequented this grand hall.

Gin smiled as she recalled young bards running in circles, practicing their arts while on the run. She thought of the rangers, stringing their bows and fletching arrows as they sat by the roaring fireplace near the healing pool. Over by the Fabled Ones' bank, she imagined Tairn, one of her oldest friends, speaking in hushed tones to the banker… Wait a tic. Gin gasped and again wiped the tears from her eyes, not daring to trust what she was seeing. It was simply not possible; Taeben had told her that Lord Taanyth had killed Tairn in the spell experiments…

At the sound of a gasp, Tairn whirled around. "Who's there? Show yourself!" she demanded, her voice shaking.

"Tairneanach?" Gin whispered, barely able to believe her eyes.

Tairn's heart simultaneously leapt and broke at the sound of her old friend's voice. She felt the wizard sit up to attention in the back of her mind. "Gin? Where are you?" she whispered, as though Taeben would not be able to hear her and know she was with Gin if she could speak softly enough.

"TAIRN!" Gin quickly cast a spell that gave her the ability to levitate and then leapt over the balcony rail. She floated slowly down in front of Tairn like a leaf on the wind, and simply stood for a few minutes staring at the high elf female. "Is it really you? Oh, you've lost so much weight, are you all right?" She moved slowly over to her friend, extending a hand and lightly touching Tairn's cheek. "When Ben told me you'd died…that horrible place…how are you here? How are you alive?" Tears fell down both elves' faces.

"I am here because I had a good teacher when I was younger that taught me to believe and trust in myself: you, Gin," Tairn said, hating already the lies that she would be forced to tell in order to keep her deal with Taeben. "It was Taeben who freed me, in the end," she said, as it took all she had to keep her voice steady.

Tell her I've changed. Tell her how much I love her.

"I know you must hate him Gin, but he's changed. I did too, after all, it was Taeben that delivered me to Master Taanyth in the first place." As soon as the name left her lips, Tairn realized she'd made a mistake. Throbbing pain at her temples told her that Taeben agreed with her assessment.

"Master...Taanyth?" Gin took a step back from her friend and took a deep breath. "Let me be clear, Tairn, I am thrilled beyond words that you are alive, but if you are working for either of those monsters you may remove yourself from my sight at once." She kept Tairn's gaze, her eyes steely and cold.

"The dragon made me call him that Gin, I swear, it was an accident that I said it now." Tairn thought fast, trying to find reasons that would come faster than the shocks of pain coming from the wizard. "He was harder on me if I didn't call him Master; surely he did the same to you?"

Gin laughed sadly. "No. He never cared what I said, only that I screamed and fought back." Tairn shuddered and Gin took her friend's hands in her own tiny ones. "I am sorry for overreacting, Tairn," she said, looking up at the taller female. Tairn's heart squeezed at the lack of pain in Gin's face. She had been broken, but by who? Taanyth? Taeben?

FOCUS.

"Please, my sweet friend, tell me how Ben helped you escape. I should like to hear that my...old friend has rediscovered his heart, found compassion... Though I fear that sort of change is a leap into the absurd."

Tairn took a deep breath, and repeated word for word the story that Taeben had given her and made her memorize, hating every sentence. "He came to me in my cell, Gin. He told me that he was sorry for all he had done and that he was making amends as he could, beginning with freeing the prisoners he'd delivered to the Keep while in the service of Ma…Lord Taanyth." She swallowed hard and continued, knowing that Taeben was attending to her, hearing every word she spoke. "He made sure that I could stand and walk, and then transported me to the Forest with money for clothes, food, and shelter. I owe him my very existence, Gin!" Sobs overcame her words and she was grateful for the interruption as she felt bile rising in her throat. Images flooded her consciousness suddenly, of Taeben holding Gin by the throat, and she knew without a doubt he knew everything she said and did. "He…he wants to make amends with you as well, Gin, because he loves you so very much, but he fears it is too late."

"He is correct," Gin said sadly. "There is nothing left between us, Tairn. He was…well, I was…I mean…things went too badly wrong to be made right." Tairn's heart fluttered; Taeben was not happy with that response in the slightest.

Convince her. You aren't even trying, **RED.**

The nickname ricocheted around her mind like an angry hornet and Tairn felt new tears prick at the backs of her eyelids. "Oh, Gin, you just need to see him and you will understand the change."

Gin shook her head, smiling sadly. "No more talk of my past mistakes, please? Now," she said, "shall we go for a wander, get some fresh air to improve our moods? "

"Aye, Gin, let's," Tairn said, forcing a smile and hoping that Gin would not notice the pain in her eyes. The more Gin said no, the more she felt the wizard bearing down on her to change the wood elf's mind. "I'd say some revenge on the jailers in the Keep would make us both feel better, but I never want to see that place again. What about…" she winced as she spoke the words that she knew would please Taeben, "the Volcanic Mountains? Or the beach and forest around Qatu'anari?"

Gin's smile turned into a smirk. "I think a visit to the Forbidden Sea might be just what I need to unwind," she said. "It has been an absolute age since I've fought my way through the jungles on the southern side of Qatu'anari. I think the last time was when I was going up there with Sath and..." Her voice faded away to nothing. "Better idea, let's hit the Outlands and the foothills of the Volcanic Mountains. I could use some wolf pelts for the winter," she said, smiling as broadly as she could.

"After you, Mama Gin," Tairn said, her smile genuine as she looked down at her old friend and mentor.

"Ah, Tairn, I do need to make one stop, if that's all right with you?" Tairn nodded and Gin continued. "I do need to go to Qatu'anari and visit the Prince. He needs to hear from me why I won't be his tutor anymore."

YES. Encourage this. Finally, someone is listening to me!

"Okay, that works for me," Tairn said brightly. "I'm sure the Prince will be pleased to see you. Won't he?" Tairn was taken aback by the look on her mentor's face. "Gin? What's wrong now?"

"Blast," the diminutive elf replied. "I can't just go walking into the palace in Qatu'anari, pretty as you please, I'll be arrested as an accomplice to Ben in Khujann's kidnapping. They...don't like me so much anymore there."

"Gee, where DO they like you, Gin?" Tairn teased, only causing Gin's frown to deepen. "I'm sorry. How can I help?"

A smile spread over Gin's features. "You can cast illusion spells, yes? Have you learned a spell that causes someone to appear as a Qatu?" Tairn nodded, grinning madly. "Then what are we waiting for? Let's head to the Qatu'anari beach and then we'll get me into my cat suit." The elves giggled and then beat feet for the guild hall door.

After buying Tairn a horse and summoning Beau for the first time in an absolute age, they were ready to ride toward the north, to Qatu'anari. As they trotted out of the Outpost, Gin paused a moment. Could it be true that Taeben was trying to make amends? She'd fallen for his apologies before only to end up on the bad end of his wizard's staff, what made this time any different? And why couldn't she feel him in her mind any longer? That last query should have been a happy one, but Gin knew the wizard better than to think he would just give up.

Gin pushed the thoughts out of her mind as she placed her hand on the saddle horn and settled into her seat for a long ride. Tairn rode only steps ahead of Gin, and she was already looking for the spell, her massive spell book - retrieved from Alynatalos - out in front of her. Flipping through the pages, she finally found what she wanted. The wizard's presence was merely a low hum in the back of her mind, so Tairn thought that he must be pleased as well.

It was nightfall by the time they had reached the coastline and had missed the gnome that arranged passage across the forbidden sea. "I guess it's bedrolls for us under the stars," Tairn said as she slid from her saddle.

"Nope, I have a secret," Gin said conspiratorially. "Call it a gift from Ben. I just hope it will work for both of us." Tairn cocked her head to one side as Taeben's presence came sharply into focus in her mind. "Back when I was… well, being forced to live with him in the embassy on Qatu'anari," she said as she thumbed through her spell book, "he came up with a spell that would instantly transport me back to the building if I…got lost."

"You mean if you tried to escape?" Tairn said, and then immediately wished she had not.

BAD PET!

Taeben raged in the back of her mind. She rubbed her temple. "How do you have access to it, though, if it is a spell that he would use to bring you back?"

"He thought he was so clever," Gin said, smirking. "He wrote it down in the back of my spell book, see?" She turned the page around for Tairn to look at, and as she struggled to read his handwriting it felt as though he was burning holes in her eye sockets from the inside. "I suppose that he thought either I would be too worn out to understand it or that I would never be out from under his control enough to use it. But I have, I used it once before, when I was going to tell Sath that…well that Ben had convinced my people to kidnap Khujann. It should still work. Tie up your horse here, Tairn, we will be back for him before he knows we have been gone."

Tairn closed her eyes a moment and rubbed her forehead before complying. Why was the wizard so furious? If the spell worked then it would take them directly to Qatu'anari and she could get this whole unpleasant task over with and be done with him.

Never, Pet, you'll never be free of me.

"Okay, now, come over here, close to me," Gin said and Tairn did as she was told. "Hang onto my arm, just in case." Gin began reciting the words from the spell book as Taeben echoed them in Tairn's mind and soon a ring of magical fire formed around them. Tairn closed her eyes as the inside-out feeling hit her, and when it ceased she opened them again to find herself in the ruined embassy.

"Is this…where you lived? What happened here, Gin?" she asked, her voice barely a whisper.

"My guess is a wizard who didn't get his way happened here," Gin said with a chuckle. A sharp pain shot through Tairn's neck and back but she bore it without making a sound, further angering her unseen watcher. "I'm sure that when I left him, he ripped this place to shreds. He remained in the back of my mind for a long time, like a nightmare that just can't be shaken, you know? And even now, now that I can't sense him at all, sometimes I wonder if he can still hear me." Tairn grimaced. "Ben? Are you listening? I am done with you!" she shouted as she spun in a circle, hands outstretched as she laughed.

She will pay for that one herself.

Tairn winced. "Let's get out of here," she suggested. "This place gives me the creeps and you have to… change clothes into your Qatu suit!" Gin giggled and nodded, leading the way out of the crumbling building. Once they were on the beach, Tairn stopped and considered her friend for a moment. There was no turning back after the illusion was cast. "Come close, Gin," she said. "You have to be in range for this to work." Gin moved closer to her, smiling up at her. Reciting the ancient words, Tairn focused her magical will on her friend, and then watched with a pleased expression as Gin's oaken tinged skin rippled and transformed into creamy smooth fur. She laughed as the wood elf grew by several feet, and then held out her now fuzzy arms to inspect Tairn's handiwork.

"Well done, Tairn," Gin said, grinning at Tairn's own smirking reaction to her Qatu body. "Oh, my goodness, listen to my voice! You've progressed so far since the last time I saw you."

"You are ever kind, Gin," Tairn said, blushing. Gin turned to face her, ice-blue eyes flashing out from behind the dark fur mask on her face. "Um, one problem, your clothes didn't exactly last through the transition." Horrified, Gin looked down at herself to see the leather armor she had been wearing hanging in shreds on her new and very tall body. "Gimme a sec," Tairn said, returning to her spell book. "Nope, I've got nothing for clothes, really. OH! Wait, I'm almost your height." She reached into her backpack and retrieved an extra shirt and some silk trousers. "Not the height of Qatu fashion, but it will do in a pinch I think and it should fit." She grinned as Gin pulled on the clothes and then turned around to model them for Tairn, a grin to match Tairn's own splitting her features. "Much better. Now, we have a Prince to see," she said just before they dashed up the beach toward the entrance to the walled city of Qatu'anari. Gin slowed their pace as they arrived at the archway that denoted the entrance to the city, and tried to walk slowly and carefully. She was clearly having trouble moving in her much taller Qatu body.

Just before they arrived at the entrance to the palace, a stinging pain tore through Tairn's mind. *Do not lose sight of your goal*, a voice shouted in her ears. *You will find the Princess and you will charm her to kill the Rajah and his son. Do not disappoint me, Tairn.*

"Yes, M'lord," Tairn whispered.

"Did you say something to me?" Gin called back at her. Tairn marveled at the change in her friend, and how at the same time her voice, underpinned with the purr of the Qatu race, was still Gin's.

"Nope, nothing," Tairn lied. "Which way to the palace?" Gin took off again, and as she gained more control over her new longer legs, Tairn could barely keep up with her. She almost ran over the wood elf-turned-Qatu when Gin skidded to a stop at the palace entrance. She had been so accustomed to entering the palace as she pleased that she almost ran right up the steps and through the door.

"Let's try that a bit more slowly," Gin said in Qatunari. Her eyes widened suddenly. "I'm sorry, Tairn," she said, switching back to Elvish, "do you speak Qatunari?"

Tairn smiled. *"I speak most of the languages of Orana, Gin, part of my research training,"* she said in flawless Qatunari.

"Show off," Gin growled playfully, her Qatunari halting compared to Tairn's dulcet purring. She turned and headed up to the stairs, pausing at the guards and kneeling. *"I wish an audience with his Royal Highness, the Prince Khujann,"* she said, her voice as steady as could be.

"And you are?" the guard on the left said, turning his attention to Tairn and speaking in Elvish.

"I am with the female," she responded, her perfect Qatunari a shock to both the guards.

"We mean the Prince no harm," said Gin, silently casting a spell that would produce feelings of harmony among the guards. "Only to tell him in person how happy we are he is returned here to his people."

"Aye, it is a happy day in Qatu'anari, sister," said the other guard. "No offense miss," he said to Tairn, "but those elves were begging for a war had they kept the Prince for a moment longer." He stepped aside and motioned them through the doors and into the palace.

"None taken," Tairn said as she passed him. "After all, it was the wood elves that were responsible, not high elves like myself. Nasty tree dwellers." Gin turned and glared at the younger female, who replied with shrugged shoulders, mouthing the word "What?"

As they moved down the long corridors, Gin found that she could have found Khujann's quarters with her eyes closed. She peeked in the door and nearly cried with joy when she saw him sitting at his little desk, head bent over his studies. Before he raised his head, the little Qatu drew in a deep breath. "*Ginny?*" he whispered, as though he didn't want to believe it was true. She held up one clawed finger to her lips, and then she and Tairn stepped inside and shut the door as she smiled down at him.

"Aye, Khuj, it's me," she said, shaking off the spell that Tairn had cast on her. She squatted down just in time for the Prince to run into her arms and almost knock her over.

"*Interesting, I didn't think we'd see you again,*" purred a female Qatu voice from the corner. Gin looked up, worried, but her face melted into a smile.

"*Kazhmere!*" she said, delighted to see Sath's sister again. "Or should I say, Highness...How are you? Don't tell me you've been given the task of looking after this monster?" She ruffled the fur on Khujann's head affectionately as he clung to her.

"It is not a task, but a duty, druid," Kazhmere responded, her eyes as cold as her voice. Gin frowned, but she understood why Kazhmere felt the way she did. There would never be a day when

Kazhmere would put their friendship above the love and loyalty she bore her brother, Sath. "*I should alert the Rajah that you've come under false pretenses but to be honest that is the happiest I've seen my nephew since…well, since all of this unpleasantness began.*" Her gaze shifted to Tairn and softened somewhat. "*Tairn, how good to see you, it has been ages since we shared a meal in the halls of the Fabled Ones.*" Tairn chuckled, desperate not to change her mind about what she must do.

"*Kazhi, why don't you and I give the Prince and Gin a moment alone to talk, and then I promise she won't bother you or him again. We need to catch up!*" Strolling over to the Princess Royal, Tairn linked her elbow in Kazhmere's and dragged her toward the door before the Qatu had a chance to object. Kazhmere paused a moment and looked sternly at Gin, one clawed finger pointed at the wood elf's face.

"*One hair on his head is out of place, druid…*" she said, and Gin shook her head.

"*We'll be fine, I promise. No harm will come to the Prince, I swear it on my life,*" she said. Once the door shut behind them, Gin sat down on the floor so that she could see Khujann eye to eye. "Now then, Your Highness, what are you working on there?" she asked in the common tongue, fighting back tears at how big he had gotten in the short time that had passed.

"It's stupid," Khujann said, his language skills clearly improving. "Just history stuff, like why the Qatu came to this island, blah, blah, blah. Are you coming back to be my tutor again? I love my Auntie Kazhi but she is strict! And she won't let me hunt with her."

"I wouldn't let you either, you know," Gin said, grinning at him. "But no, I can't be your tutor anymore, Khujann. You're too big to have me as a tutor."

"Try telling Papa that. After the white haired wizard was in the trees and made the elves mad at me, Papa won't let me do anything by myself. If he knew Auntie Kazhi had gone outside with your friend, he would be so angry!" Khujann's eyes welled up with tears. "He's so mad at you, Ginny, what did you do? I begged him to go to the trees again to see you but he just says no. Doesn't play with me anymore, just sits on his stupid throne reading some stupid old leather-bound book."

Her heart firmly lodged in her throat, Gin gathered the cub into her arms and held him tightly as he cried, taking the opportunity to swallow her own sadness. The "stupid leather-bound book" had to be her journal. Sath was still reading her journal. She wasn't sure if that made her happy or sad.

"Now, don't you worry about that, Khujann," she said. What goes on between me and your Papa has nothing to do with you, understand? I made a mistake that hurt your Papa's feelings very much, and I have to make it right. I'm still working on how to do that." She paused and wiped a tear from her own eye. Maybe she should give Sath a chance. Maybe they could find some common ground. "Until then, Khuj, you just keep studying hard and making your Papa proud. You may not see it, but he loves you more than anything and wants to you to be *Rajah* when you're older like he is."

"So, Kazhi, *what have you been up to?*" Tairn asked, narrowing her eyes and focusing her will on the Princess Royal. She could feel Taeben in the back of her mind – she was revolted at his pride that she had correctly performed the spell he had taught her. Kazhmere started to respond, then blinked a few times and stood still, her eyes vacant. "*You will do as I wish, will you not?*"

"*Yes, Mistress, of course I will.*"

"*And once you have done as I wish, you will not remember that I willed you to do anything, will you?*" Tairn looked closely at Kazhmere's face, pleased at the lack of recognition there. "*You will not remember who I am, will you?*"

"*No, Mistress.*"

"Do you even know who I am? Do you know my name?"

Kazhmere blinked again. "No, Mistress, I do not. I am sorry, I should know your name but I do not."

"Sssh. That is good," Tairn whispered, stroking the side of Kazhmere's furry face. "Now, here is what I wish. You will leave at once and find your brother, the Rajah. When you find him, you will set your magical tiger upon his to distract him, and then you will kill the Rajah using any method required," Tairn said, lowering her voice to a mere whisper. "Do you understand me?"

"Yes, Mistress, I will kill the Rajah as you wish."

"Well done. Hurry along now, you must do this for me as soon as you can." Kazhmere dashed off toward the throne room leaving Tairn in the shadows. "THERE!" she yelled at no one and anyone.

I have done as you asked, Lord Taeben. Now please, leave me and Gin alone. The answer thundered in her ears, though she was the only one to hear it.

Oh, my pretty little Tairn, you know it is not that simple. I will leave you alone when I am finished with you! And as for Ginny, she will be mine very soon. Now leave that cat city, NOW.

Backing into a shadow, Tairn spoke the words that would magically transport her back to safety. "I'm sorry, Gin, you're going to have to get out of here on your own," she whispered as she faded from sight under a magical camouflage.

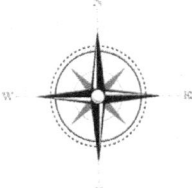

THIRTY

Sath sat alone in the throne room, waiting for the afternoon petitioners to arrive. While it took a lot of his time, he truly enjoyed this part of being *Rajah*. He usually granted the wishes of his citizens as long as they were genuine needs, and his citizens responded in kind by not bringing frivolous requests before him. The sound of the throne room door closing caught his attention and he looked up from his desk and smiled. *"Well then, who is first...Kazhmere? What brings you here, Sister?"*

Kazhmere didn't answer him, but summoned her supernatural tiger instead. Sensing a threat to its master, Sath's own tiger came forth from under the desk and growled loudly. Sath stood up and came around to the front of his desk, his expression one of puzzlement. *"Kazhmere, what is the meaning of this? Is something wrong?"* Kazhmere sent her tiger with a hand signal toward Sath's, and the two tigers began circling and snarling. *"Kazhmere! Stop this!"* Sath bellowed.

*"I fear I cannot, **Rajah**,"* she said. Her staff spun up into her hand, just as he and Hulan had taught her, and she took on an offensive stance. Sath spoke a word that would send his tiger away, and the creature disappeared...but not before looking over its shoulder at his master in confusion. Immediately Kazhmere's

tiger returned to her side, but then turned and charged at Sath. His razor sharp claws glistening, Sath faced the tiger head on.

Lightning spilled from above their heads and struck Sath. Most of the electricity bounced off of him and one stray bolt even struck Kazhmere in the chest, knocking her back a few feet. He brought his staff down hard on the tiger, delivering a fatal blow. The magical creature fell to its side and faded from view. Roaring with anger and bloodlust, Kazhmere ran at her brother, her staff raised above her head. Sath spoke ancient words in Qatunari that slowed her attack; the fact that she suddenly felt as though she was moving in neck deep water enraged her even more. She paused, her eyes blazing with the savagery that Sath knew all too well. Had she not been acting so erratically, he would have been fiercely proud of her and her abilities. His baby sister was a formidable fighter in her own right.

"Why are you doing this?" he shouted at her. She did not reply, only attacked, and Sath blocked her every strike. He had taught her to fight, so he anticipated her movements. Over the sound of his staff connecting with hers and her clawed weapon whistling through the air, he could hear the low roar of his personal guards trying to get through the door that, he now noticed, Kazhmere had locked from the inside. *"Guards! Stand down! Stand down!"* he called out. Sath looked his sister in the eye as they circled each other, their shared ancestry apparent as they squared off like lions on the plains of the Grasslands. *"I can handle this. Go to the Prince and see that he is safe!"* Sath raised his staff, using it to keep her at arm's length. *"Now, sister,"* he whispered, *"tell me how I have offended you so?"* Kazhmere only stared at him, her eyes still blazing. Because he recognized the same look that his own eyes took on, Sath knew that there was no way to snap her out of it but to fight, but at the same time, he could see the hollow look in their depths of one charmed by magic. With a yelp, he ran at her and swept his staff behind her knees, knocking her off her feet. Kazhmere's staff went flying but she quickly recovered by pulling a spiked mace from her belt.

Sath saw stars as the mace connected with the side of his head. He staggered backward a moment and tightened the grip on his staff. Shaking his head to clear it, he turned around just in time to see Kazhmere lunging for him, so he did the last thing he would ever want to do to his own sister. His staff whistled through the air, and the crack that sounded when the tip of it slammed into her chest hurt him to his core. She fell backwards awkwardly and hit her head against the corner of Sath's desk. She slumped to the ground, motionless.

Sath threw his staff away, sickened, and ran to his sister's side. As gently as if he was cradling a newborn, he turned Kazhmere over and was relieved to see that she was still breathing. He carefully placed her on the ground and ran for the doors, nearly pulling them off their hinges and breaking the lock to splinters. "GUARDS!" he roared. "*Bring a healer! Sound the alarm!*" He could not take the chance that whomever had charmed his sister would try to flee the city. "*Lock down the gates!*" He ran back to his sister's prone form and carefully stroked the fur on the side of her face. "*Kazhi, I don't know who did this to you, but I will find out. Please come back to me, you're the only family I have.*" He continued stroking the side of her face, and suddenly her eyes fluttered open. Sath cried out in joy, pulling his sister to him in a powerful hug.

Kazhmere blinked a few times, shook her head, and looked around. Near her on the ground was the letter opener that had fallen from Sath's desk when she ran into it. Inching her fingers ever closer, she finally felt them close around the jeweled handle.

"My...mistress...commands...it..." she gasped, then sunk the letter opener up to its ruby hilt in Sath's back. Sath screamed in pain and dropped Kazhmere on the ground. Her skull hit the marble floor with a sickening crack. "My...mistress..." she murmured, eyebrows furrowed in confusion, and then her head lolled to the side, eyes staring blankly in death.

On the other side of the Royal compound, the *Sahi Kalah* burst through the door suddenly and then swarmed into Khujann's nursery. Gin had heard shouts followed by running footsteps that could only be them coming down the hall, and holding a finger to her mouth to bid Khujann not to tell on her, she faded away into the background. Just as she disappeared, the door to the chamber nearly came off its hinges. The guards swept in and grabbed the prince all in one motion before he even had a chance to mention that Gin was there.

She followed them, still carefully camouflaged with magic. They seemed to be running toward the safe room deep within the palace with the Prince. Sath had shown her where it was once when she was still new to working for him, and she felt certain that he would be safe there. Gin scanned the corridors as they passed them – where had Tairn and Kazhmere gone? A roar cut through the night, stopping the *Sahi* for a moment, but they soon carried on their frenetic pace through the hallways.

Gin, however, could not move a muscle as a searing pain tore across her back and ending up in her heart. She knew that sound. **Sath**...she thought, she felt, she was certain it was him, and she changed course for the throne room. There was no other thought in her mind, nothing clearer than the knowledge that she had to get to Sath and she had to do it NOW.

Gin ran down the hallway that lead to the throne room and flung her hands out in front of her to open the massive marble doors but they would not open. Were they locked from the inside or just stuck? With no time to think, she threw her deadliest magic at the doors as she ran at them, and this time they swung open, almost causing Gin to fall face first into the throne room.

Once through the doors, she skidded to a stop, her hands over her mouth. Sath was slumped over Kazhmere's body, the letter opener still sticking out of his shoulder between the shoulder blade and his broad neck. Neither of the Qatu moved as they lay in a pool of blood.

"Sath?"

ABOUT THE AUTHOR

Nancy E. Dunne is the alter ego of Ginolwenye, and is an avid gamer, adventurer, reader, language nerd and all around geek girl. The Nature Walker Trilogy is a love letter of sorts to the various worlds in which she has found herself immersed over the years, and the lifelong friends, memories, and wild tales that have come along with them. When not writing, Nancy is an American Sign Language/English interpreter and spends her free time drawing inspiration from her dogs and her husband as well as dreaming of visiting her second home, the United Kingdom.

BOOKS IN THE NATURE WALKER SERIES

Wanderer: Origin of the Nature Walker
Tempest: Fall of the Nature Walker
Guardian: Rise of the Nature Walker (coming in 2018)

Made in the USA
Columbia, SC
25 August 2020